EDITED BY DEBORAH TREISMAN

FARRAR, STRAUS AND GIROUX
NEW YORK

20

UNDER

40

STORIES FROM

THE NEW YORKER

Farrar, Straus and Giroux
18 West 18th Street, New York 10011

All the pieces in this collection were originally published in *The New Yorker*.

Grateful acknowledgment is made for permission to reprint the following material:

Excerpt from *The Newlyweds* by Nell Freudenberger, copyright © 2011 by Nell Freuden-berger. Used by permission of Alfred A. Knopf, a division of Random House, Inc.

Excerpt from *Great House: A Novel* by Nicole Krauss, copyright © 2010 by Nicole Krauss. Used by permission of W. W. Norton & Company, Inc.

Excerpt from *How to Read the Air* by Dinaw Mengestu, copyright © 2010 by Dinaw Mengestu. Used by permission of Riverhead Books, an imprint of Penguin Group (USA) Inc.

Excerpt from *Swamplandia!* by Karen Russell, copyright © 2011 by Karen Russell. Used by permission of Alfred A. Knopf, a division of Random House, Inc.

Excerpt from *Super Sad True Love Story* by Gary Shteyngart, copyright © 2010 by Gary Shteyngart. Used by permission of Random House, Inc.

Library of Congress Cataloging-in-Publication Data
20 under 40 : stories from The new yorker / edited by Deborah Treisman. — 1st ed.
    p.   cm.
  ISBN: 978-0-374-53287-1 (alk. paper)
  1. Short stories, American.   2. American fiction—21st century.   I. Treisman, Deborah, 1970–   II. Title: Twenty under forty.   III. Title: Stories from The new yorker.

PS648.S5A1466 2010
813'.010806—dc22

                                                                    2010032677

Designed by Jonathan D. Lippincott

www.fsgbooks.com

7   9   10   8   6

CONTENTS

CONTENTS

INTRODUCTION

In June, 2010, for its annual summer fiction issue, *The New Yorker* took on the task of naming twenty North American writers under the age of forty who we felt were, or soon would be, standouts in the diverse and expansive panorama of contemporary fiction. Beginning in that issue, and continuing in the following twelve issues, we published stories and excerpts of novels-in-progress by those writers.

The magazine had put together a similar list once before, in 1999. That issue, titled "The Future of American Fiction," featured several writers who were already well on their way, such as Michael Chabon, whose first novel, "The Mysteries of Pittsburgh," had been a bestseller eleven years earlier (he went on to win a Pulitzer Prize for his novel "The Amazing Adventures of Kavalier & Clay," which was excerpted in that issue), and David Foster Wallace, whose magnum opus, "Infinite Jest," had appeared in 1996. But it also included writers whose most ambitious work was still ahead of them. Junot Díaz was the author of a story collection, "Drown," but "The Brief Wondrous Life of Oscar Wao," his Pulitzer Prize–winning novel, was still eight years away. Jonathan Franzen had published two novels—"The Twenty-Seventh City" and "Strong Motion"—but "The Corrections," his hugely successful, National Book Award–winning work (which was excerpted in that issue), did not appear until 2001. Jhumpa Lahiri's first book, the story collection "Interpreter of Maladies," came out the same month as the fiction issue and went on to sell millions of copies worldwide. The 1999 issue, with its linguistic verve, its narrative vitality, and its sprawling range—it included writers as unalike as Sherman Alexie, Edwidge Danticat, and George Saunders—became something of a handbook for young writers trying to locate their own voices.

This time around, the fiction editors—Cressida Leyshon, Willing Davidson, Roger Angell, and I—again selected writers who were at different stages in their careers. The youngest, Téa Obreht, was twenty-four, and her first book was still almost a year away from publication. The oldest, Chris Adrian, was thirty-nine, and was finishing up his fourth book. Without making it a specific goal, we ended up with a surprisingly diverse list—diverse in many ways. Although all the non-native writers on the list had made a home for themselves in the United States (or, in one case, in Canada), the range of origins was striking: Nigeria, Peru, Latvia, China, Yugoslavia, Ethiopia, and Russia were all represented. Many of the writers on our list also had vocations outside the literary world. David Bezmozgis had directed a feature film. Chris Adrian was completing his training as a pediatric oncologist and, like C. E. Morgan, had studied at Harvard Divinity School. Rivka Galchen had completed medical school at Mount Sinai. Yiyun Li had moved to the United States to pursue a Ph.D. in immunology. Philipp Meyer, before starting his novel, had worked as a derivatives trader and driven an ambulance. Joshua Ferris wrote advertising copy. Salvatore Scibona, at one point, worked for a bricklayer.

So how did these twenty writers end up here? We were able to read at least one complete book or manuscript by each of them, and at least a portion of whatever work was coming next. In some cases, we saw an explosion of talent from the first chapter or story: a freshness of perspective, observation, humor, or feeling. In others, there was a stealthier buildup of thought and innovation. Some were brilliant at doing one thing. Others made radical shifts of focus and style from one piece to the next. But what was notable in all the writing, above and beyond a capacity for language and for storytelling, was a clear sense of ambition. These writers are not all iconoclasts; some are purposefully working within existing traditions. But they are all aiming high. In a culture that is flooded with words, sounds, and pictures, they are fighting to get our attention, and to hold it. They are digging within themselves—and around themselves—to bring us news both of the world and of the human heart.

The habit of list-making can seem arbitrary or absurd. Good writing speaks for itself, and it speaks over time; the best writers at work today are the ones that our grandchildren and their grandchildren will read. Yet the lure of the list is deeply ingrained. The Ten Commandments, the seven deadly sins, the Fantastic Four—they have the appeal of the countable and the contained, even if we suspect that there may have been other, equally compelling commandments, sins, and superheroes. Perhaps the best reason for making such lists is to encourage that kind of second-guessing, to trigger argument and debate, a passionate public discussion about the nature of fiction writing today.

And argument and debate did follow (and precede) the publication of *The New Yorker's* "20 Under 40." Some people fumed and deplored our choices, wrote them off, picked out one writer to praise and ignored the rest. They came up with entertaining alternate lists: the small-press 20 under 40, the British 20 under 40, the 20 best writers over 80, 15 over 75, 20 between 40 and 50, 10 under 10. They took issue with the very concept of an age limit, pointing out what we already knew: that drawing a line at a writer's fortieth birthday is, to some extent, meaningless. There are people who don't start writing until they're in their forties or even later. And, as *The Guardian* noted, age limits such as these have historically discriminated against women who were forced to postpone their writing careers until after they had raised children. (We were happy to note, while working on this issue, that that particular lag seems to come into play less these days, perhaps because women are now more likely to postpone the children until their careers are launched. Our 1999 issue included fifteen men and five women; this time around, without making any particular effort to balance the sexes, we ended up with a ten-ten gender breakdown.)

But you can't look at a generation without, in some way, defining the boundaries of that generation. We could have made the age limit forty and under (as we did in the 1999 issue, which included a couple of forty-year-olds), or thirty-five, as *Granta* did for its last "Best of Young American Novelists" issue. What we noticed while reading the works of close to a hundred and fifty novelists and short-story writers in this age group, however, was that, for many of them, there had come a point where things seemed to fall into place: the voice was suddenly distinct; the influences less blatant, more absorbed; the plotting more skillful; the emotional thrust stronger; the humor sharper. For some people, this happened in a second book, for some in a third, for some lucky writers earlier. But, in most cases, it happened when the writer was somewhere in his or her mid-thirties. Forty just seemed to make sense as a cut-off point for this generation of writers.

Some critics took aim at what they saw as a kind of élitism in our choices, suggesting that these twenty writers had made it in because of their "power agents" or mainstream publishers. This seemed to us an odd argument. No writer begins his or her artistic life with an agent or a publisher in hand: these connections are made on the merit of the work that he or she produces. Talent rises, and agents, editors, publishing houses, magazines—and readers—chase after it. What we were chasing, in these twenty writers and in their twenty pieces of fiction, was this: the sharp social insights of Chimamanda Ngozi Adichie, Nell Freudenberger,

INTRODUCTION

Yiyun Li, and C. E. Morgan; Joshua Ferris's and Gary Shteyngart's wildly innovative comedies of errors; the nuanced ventriloquism of Chris Adrian, Karen Russell, and Wells Tower; Daniel Alarcón's, David Bezmozgis's, Dinaw Mengestu's, and ZZ Packer's subtly plotted narratives of cultural change; Nicole Krauss's, Philipp Meyer's, and Salvatore Scibona's memorable meditations on loss and guilt; the poignant playfulness of Jonathan Safran Foer and Rivka Galchen; and the lush, dreamlike scenarios of Sarah Shunlien Bynum and Téa Obreht.

These writers are, of course, not the only gifted storytellers of their generation. Some terrific candidates were excluded solely because they didn't have a new piece of fiction available by our deadline. Others would have been on the list had it come out a year earlier; their only mistake was to be on the wrong side of our birthday cutoff. What was especially heartening about this project was the number of writers whose work called for serious consideration. We will inevitably look back, in a decade or so, and see that we missed a writer—or even several. But for now, for us, these twenty women and men dazzlingly represent the multiple strands of inventiveness and creativity at play in the best fiction being written today.

—Deborah Treisman

BIRDSONG

CHIMAMANDA NGOZI
ADICHIE

The woman, a stranger, was looking at me. In the glare of the hot afternoon, in the swirl of motorcycles and hawkers, she was looking down at me from the back seat of her jeep. Her stare was too direct, not sufficiently vacant. She was not merely resting her eyes on the car next to hers, as people often do in Lagos traffic; she was *looking* at me. At first, I glanced away, but then I stared back, at the haughty silkiness of the weave that fell to her shoulders in loose curls, the kind of extension called Brazilian Hair and paid for in dollars at Victoria Island hair salons; at her fair skin, which had the plastic sheen that comes from expensive creams; and at her hand, forefinger bejewelled, which she raised to wave a magazine hawker away, with the ease of a person used to waving people away. She was beautiful, or perhaps she was just so unusual-looking, with wide-set eyes sunk deep in her face, that "beautiful" was the easiest way of describing her. She was the kind of woman I imagined my lover's wife was, a woman for whom things were done.

My lover. It sounds a little melodramatic, but I never knew how to refer to him. "Boyfriend" seemed wrong for an urbane man of forty-five who carefully slipped off his wedding ring before he touched me. Chikwado called him "your man," with a faintly sneering smile, as though we were both in on the joke: he was not, of course, mine. "Ah, you are always rushing to leave because of this your man," she would say, leaning back in her chair and smacking her head with her hand, over and over. Her scalp was itchy beneath her weave, and this was the only way she could

3

come close to scratching it. "Have fun oh, as long as your spirit accepts it, but as for me, I cannot spread my legs for a married man." She said this often, with a clear-eyed moral superiority, as I packed my files and shut down my computer for the day.

We were friends out of necessity, because we had both graduated from Enugu Campus and ended up working for Celnet Telecom, in Lagos, as the only females in the community-relations unit. Otherwise, we would not have been friends. I was irritated by how full of simplified certainties she was, and I knew that she thought I behaved like an irresponsible, vaguely foreign teen-ager: wearing my hair in a natural low-cut, smoking cigarettes right in front of the building, where everyone could see, and refusing to join in the prayer sessions our boss led after Monday meetings. I would not have told her about my lover—I did not tell her about my personal life—but she was there when he first walked into our office, a lean, dark man with a purple tie and a moneyed manner. He was full of the glossy self-regard of men who shrugged off their importance in a way that only emphasized it. Our boss shook his hand with both hands and said, "Welcome, sir, it is good to see you, sir, how are you doing, sir, please come and sit down, sir." Chikwado was there when he looked at me and I looked at him and then he smiled, of all things, a warm, open smile. She heard when he said to our boss, "My family lives in America," a little too loudly, for my benefit, with that generic foreign accent of the worldly Nigerian, which, I would discover later, disappeared when he became truly animated about something. She saw him walk over and give me his business card. She was there, a few days later, when his driver came to deliver a gift bag. Because she had seen, and because I was swamped with emotions that I could not name for a man I knew was wrong for me, I showed her the perfume and the card that said, "I am thinking of you."

"*Na wa!* Look at how your eyes are shining because of a married man. You need deliverance prayers," Chikwado said, half joking. She went to night-vigil services often, at different churches, but all with the theme Finding Your God-Given Mate; she would come to work the next morning sleepy, the whites of her eyes flecked with red, but already planning to attend another service. She was thirty-two and tottering under the weight of her desire: to settle down. It was all she talked about. It was all our female co-workers talked about when we had lunch at the cafeteria. *Yewande is wasting her time with that man—he is not ready to settle down. Please ask him oh, if he does not see marriage in the future then you better look elsewhere; nobody is getting any younger. Ekaete is lucky, just six months and she is already engaged.* While they talked, I would look out the window, high up above Lagos, at the acres of rusted roofs, at the rise and fall of hope in this city full of tarnished angels.

Even my lover spoke of this desire. "You'll want to settle down soon," he said. "I just want you to know I'm not going to stand in your way." We were naked in bed; it was our first time. A feather from the pillow was stuck in his hair, and I had just picked it out and showed it to him. I could not believe, in the aftermath of what had just happened, both of us still flush from each other's warmth, how easily the words rolled out of his mouth. "I'm not like other men, who think they can dominate your life and not let you move forward," he continued, propping himself up on his elbow to look at me. He was telling me that he played the game better than others, while I had not yet conceived of the game itself. From the moment I met him, I had had the sensation of possibility, but for him the path was already closed, had indeed never been open; there was no room for things to sweep in and disrupt.

"You're very thoughtful," I said, with the kind of overdone mockery that masks damage. He nodded, as though he agreed with me. I pulled the covers up to my chin. I should have got dressed, gone back to my flat in Surulere, and deleted his number from my phone. But I stayed. I stayed for thirteen months and eight days, mostly in his house in Victoria Island—a faded-white house, with its quiet grandeur and airy spaces, which was built during British colonial rule and sat in a compound full of fruit trees, the enclosing wall wreathed in creeping bougainvillea. He had told me he was taking me to a Lebanese friend's guesthouse, where he was staying while his home in Ikoyi was being refurbished. When I stepped out of the car, I felt as though I had stumbled into a secret garden. A dense mass of periwinkles, white and pink, bordered the walkway to the house. The air was clean here, even fragrant, and there was something about it all that made me think of renewal. He was watching me; I could sense how much he wanted me to like it.

"This is your house, isn't it?" I said. "It doesn't belong to your Lebanese friend."

He moved closer to me, surprised. "Please don't misunderstand. I was going to tell you. I just didn't want you to think it was some kind of . . ." He paused and took my hand. "I know what other men do, and I am not like that. I don't bring women here. I bought it last year to knock it down and build an apartment block, but it was so beautiful. My friends think I'm mad for keeping it. You know nobody respects old things in this country. I work from here most days now, instead of going to my office."

We were standing by sliding glass doors that led to a veranda, over which a large flame tree spread its branches. Wilted red flowers had fallen on the cane chairs. "I like to sit there and watch birds," he said, pointing.

He liked birds. Birds had always been just birds to me, but with him I became someone else: I became a person who liked birds. The following Sunday morning, on our first weekend together, as we passed sections of *Next* to each other in the quiet of that veranda, he looked up at the sky and said, "There's a magpie. They like shiny things." I imagined putting his wedding ring on the cane table so that the bird would swoop down and carry it away forever.

"I knew you were different!" he said, thrilled, when he noticed that I read the business and sports sections, as though my being different reflected his good taste. And so we talked eagerly about newspapers, and about the newscasts on AIT and CNN, marvelling at how similar our opinions were. We never discussed my staying. It was not safe to drive back to Surulere late, and he kept saying, "Why don't you bring your things tomorrow so you can go to work from here?" until most of my clothes were in the wardrobe and my moisturizers were on the bathroom ledge. He left me money on the table, in brown envelopes on which he wrote "For your fuel," as if I could possibly spend fifty thousand naira on petrol. Sometimes, he asked if I needed privacy to change, as if he had not seen me naked many times.

We did not talk about his wife or his children or my personal life or when I would want to settle down so that he could avoid standing in my way. Perhaps it was all the things we left unsaid that made me watch him. His skin was so dark that I teased him about being from Gambia; if he were a woman, I told him, he would never find a face powder that matched his tone. I watched as he carefully unwrapped scented moist tissues to clean his glasses, or cut the chicken on his plate, or tied his towel round his waist in a knot that seemed too elaborate for a mere towel, just below the embossed scar by his navel. I memorized him, because I did not know him. He was courtly, his life lived in well-oiled sequences, his cufflinks always tasteful.

His three cell phones rang often; I knew when it was his wife, because he would go to the toilet or out to the veranda, and I knew when it was a government official, because he would say afterward, "Why won't these governors leave somebody alone?" But it was clear that he liked the governors' calls, and the restaurant manager who came to our table to say, "We are so happy to see you, sah." He searched the Sunday-magazine pullouts for pictures of himself, and when he found one he said in a mildly complaining tone, "Look at this, why should they turn businessmen into celebrities?" Yet he would not wear the same suit to two events because of the newspaper photographers. He had a glowing ego, like a globe, round and large and in constant need of polishing. He did things for people. He gave them money, introduced them to contacts, helped their relatives get jobs, and when the gratitude and praise came—he showed me text messages thanking him; I remember one that read "History will immortalize you as a great man"—his eyes would glaze over, and I could almost hear him purr.

One day he told me, while we were watching two kingfishers do a mating dance on a guava tree, that most birds did not have penises. I had never thought about the penises of birds.

"My mother had chickens in the yard when I was growing up, and I used to watch them mating," I said.

"Of course they mate, but not with penises," he said. "Did you ever see a cock with a dick?"

I laughed, and he, only just realizing the joke, laughed, too. It became our endearment. "Cock with a dick," I would whisper, hugging him in greeting, and we would burst out laughing. He sent me texts signed "CwithaD." And each time I turned off the potholed road in Victoria Island and into that compound full of birdsong I felt as though I were home.

The woman was still looking at me. Traffic was at a standstill, unusual this early in the afternoon. A tanker must have fallen across the road—tankers were always falling across the roads—or a bus had broken down, or cars had formed a line outside a petrol station, blocking the road. My fuel gauge was close to empty. I switched off the ignition and rolled down the window, wondering if the woman would roll down hers as well and say something to me. I stared back at her, and yet she did not waver, her eyes remaining firm, until I looked away. There were many more hawkers now, holding out magazines, phone cards, plantain chips, newspapers, cans of Coke and Amstel Malta dipped in water to make them look cold. The driver in front of me was buying a phone card. The hawker, a boy in a red Arsenal shirt, scratched the card with his fingernail, and then waited for the driver to enter the numbers in his phone to make sure the card was not fake.

I turned again to look at the woman. I was reminded of what Chikwado had said about my lover the first day that he came to our office: "His face is full of overseas." The woman, too, had a face full of overseas, the face of a person whose life was a blur of comforts. There was something in the set of her lips, which were lined with cocoa lip pencil, that suggested an unsatisfying triumph, as though she had won a battle but hated having had to fight in the first place. Perhaps she was indeed my lover's wife and she had come back to Lagos and just found out about me, and then, as though in a bad farce, ended up next to me in traffic. But his wife could not possibly know; he had been so careful.

"I wish I could," he always said, when I asked him to spend Saturday afternoon with me at Jazz Hole, or when I suggested we go to a play at Terra Kulture on Sunday, or when I asked if we could try dinner at a different restaurant. We only ever went to one on a dark street off Awolowo Road, a place with expensive wines and no sign on the gate. He said "I wish I could" as though some great and ineluctable act of nature made it impossible for him to be seen publicly with me. And impossible for him to keep my text messages. I wanted to ask how he could so efficiently delete my texts as soon as he read them, why he felt no urge to keep them on his phone, even if only for a few hours, even if only for a day. There were reams of questions unasked, gathering like rough pebbles in my throat. It was a strange thing to feel so close to a man—to tell him about my resentment of my parents, to lie supine for him with an abandon that was unfamiliar to me—and yet be unable to ask him questions, bound as I was by insecurity and unnamed longings.

The first time we quarrelled, he said to me accusingly, "You don't cry." I realized that his wife cried, that he could handle tears but not my cold defiance.

The fight was about his driver, Emmanuel, an elderly man who might have looked wise if his features were not so snarled with dissatisfaction. It was a Saturday afternoon. I had been at work that morning. My boss had called an emergency meeting that I thought unnecessary: we all knew that His Royal Highness, the Oba of the town near the lagoon, was causing trouble, saying that Celnet Telecom had made him look bad in front of his people. He had sent many messages asking how we could build a big base station on his ancestral land and yet donate only a small borehole to his people. That morning, his guards had blocked off our building site, shoved some of our engineers around, and punctured the tires of their van. My boss was furious, and he slammed his hand on the table as he spoke at the meeting. I, too, slammed my hand on the cane table as I imitated him later, while my lover laughed. "That is the problem with these godless, demon-worshipping traditional rulers," my boss said. "The man is a crook. A common crook! What happened to the one million naira we gave him? Should we also bring bags of rice and beans for all his people before we put up our base station? Does he want a supply of meat pies every day? Nonsense!"

"Meat pies" had made Chikwado and me laugh, even though our boss was not being funny. "Why not something more ordinary, like bread?" Chikwado whispered to me, and then promptly raised her hand when our boss asked for volunteers to go see the Oba right away. I never volunteered. I disliked those visits—

villagers watching us with awed eyes, young men asking for free phone cards, even free phones—because it all made me feel helplessly powerful.

"Why meat pies?" my lover asked, still laughing.

"I have no idea."

"Actually, I would like to have a meat pie right now."

"Me, too."

We were laughing, and with the sun shining, the sound of birds above, the slight flutter of the curtains against the sliding door, I was already thinking of future Saturdays that we would spend together, laughing at funny stories about my boss. My lover summoned Emmanuel and asked him to take me to the supermarket to buy the meat pies. When I got into the car, Emmanuel did not greet me. He simply stared straight ahead. It was the first time that he had driven me without my lover. The silence was tense. Perhaps he was thinking that all his children were older than me.

"Well done, Emmanuel!" I said finally, greeting him with forced brightness. "Do you know the supermarket on Kofo Abayomi Street?"

He said nothing and started the car. When we arrived, he stopped at the gate. "Come out here, let me go and park," he said.

"Please drop me at the entrance," I said. Every other driver did that, before looking for a parking space.

"Come out here." He still did not look at me. Rage rose under my skin, making me feel detached and bloodless, suspended in air; I could not sense the ground under my feet as I climbed out. After I had selected some meat pies from the display case, I called my lover and told him that Emmanuel had been rude and that I would be taking a taxi back.

"Emmanuel said the road was bad," my lover said when I got back, his tone conciliatory.

"The man insulted me," I said.

"No, he's not like that. Maybe he didn't understand you."

Emmanuel had shown me the power of my lover's wife; he would not have been so rude if he feared he might be reprimanded. I wanted to fling the bag of meat pies through the window.

"Is this what you do, have your driver remind your girlfriends of their place?" I was shrill and I disliked myself for it. Worse, I was horrified to notice that my eyes were watering. My lover gently wrapped his arms around me, as though I were an irrational child, and asked whether I would give him a meat pie.

"You've brought other women here, haven't you?" I asked, not entirely sure how this had become about other women.

He shook his head. "No, I have not. No more of this talk. Let's eat the meat pies and watch a film."

I let myself be mollified, be held, be caressed. Later, he said, "You know, I have had only two affairs since I got married. I'm not like other men."

"You sound as if you think you deserve a prize," I said.

He was smiling. "Both of them were like you." He paused to search for a word, and when he found it he said it with enjoyment. "Feisty. They were feisty like you."

I looked at him. How could he not see that there were things he should not say to me, and that there were things I longed to have with him? It was a willed blindness; it had to be. He chose not to see. "You are such a bastard," I said.

"What?"

I repeated myself.

He looked as though he had just been stung by an insect. "Get out. Leave this house right now," he said, and then muttered, "This is unacceptable."

I had never before been thrown out of a house. Emmanuel sat in a chair in the shade of the garage and watched stone-faced as I hurried to my car. My lover did not call me for five days, and I did not call him. When he finally called, his first words were "There are two pigeons on the flame tree. I'd like you to see them."

"You are acting as if nothing happened."

"I called *you*," he said, as though the call itself were an apology. Later, he told me that if I had cried instead of calling him a bastard he would have behaved better. I should not have gone back—I knew that even then.

The woman, still staring at me, was talking on her cell phone. Her jeep was black and silver and miraculously free of scratches. How was that possible in this city where okada after okada sped through the narrow slices of space between cars in traffic as though motorcycles could shrink to fit any gap? Perhaps whenever her car was hit a mechanic descended from the sky and made the dent disappear. The car in front of me had a gash on its tail-light; it looked like one of the many cars that dripped oil, turning the roads into a slick sheet when the rains came. My own car was full of wounds. The biggest, a mangled bumper, was from a taxi that rammed into me at a red light on Kingsway Road a month before. The driver had jumped out with his shirt unbuttoned, all sweaty bravado, and screamed at me.

"Stupid girl! You are a common nuisance. Why did you stop like that? Nonsense!"

I stared at him, stunned, until he drove away, and then I began to think of what I could have said, what I could have shouted back.

"If you were wearing a wedding ring, he would not have shouted at you like that," Chikwado said when I told her, as she punched the redial button on her desk phone. At the cafeteria, she told our co-workers about it. *Ah, ah, stupid man! Of course he was shouting because he knew he was wrong—that is the*

Lagos way. So he thinks he can speak big English. Where did he even learn the word "nuisance"? They sucked their teeth, telling their own stories about taxi-drivers, and then their outrage fizzled and they began to talk, voices lowered and excited, about a fertility biscuit that the new pastor at Redemption Church was giving women.

"It worked for my sister oh. First she did a dry fast for two days, then the pastor did a special deliverance prayer for her before she ate the biscuit. She had to eat it at exactly midnight. The next month, the very next month, she missed her period, I'm telling you," one of them, a contract staffer who was doing a master's degree part time at Ibadan, said.

"Is it an actual biscuit?" another asked.

"Yes now. But they bless the ingredients before they make the biscuits. God can work through anything, *sha*. I heard about a pastor that uses handkerchiefs."

I looked away and wondered what my lover would make of this story. He was visiting his family in America for two weeks. That evening, he sent me a text. "At a concert with my wife. Beautiful music. Will call you in ten minutes and leave phone on so you can listen in. CwithaD." I read it twice and then, even though I had saved all his other texts, I deleted it, as though my doing so would mean that it had never been sent. When he called, I let my phone ring and ring. I imagined them at the concert, his wife reaching out to hold his hand, because I could not bear the thought that it might be he who would reach out. I knew then that he could not possibly see me, the inconvenient reality of me; instead, all he saw was himself in an exciting game.

He came back from his trip wearing shoes I did not recognize, made of rich brown leather and much more tapered than his other shoes, almost comically pointy. He was in high spirits, twirling me around when we hugged, caressing the tightly coiled hair at the nape of my neck and saying, "So soft." He wanted to go out to dinner, he said, because he had a surprise for me, and when he went into the bathroom one of his phones rang. I took it and looked at his text messages. It was something I had never thought of doing before, and yet I suddenly felt compelled to do it. Text after text in his "sent" box were to Baby. The most recent said he had arrived safely. What struck me was not how often he texted his wife, or how short the texts were—"stuck in traffic," "missing you," "almost there"—but that all of them were signed "CwithaD." Inside me, something sagged. Had he choreographed a conversation with her, nimbly made the joke about a "cock with a dick" and then found a way to turn it into a shared endearment for the two of them? I thought of the effort it would take to do that. I put the phone down and glanced at the mirror, half expecting to see myself morphing into a slack, stringless marionette.

In the car, he asked, "Is something wrong? Are you feeling well?"

"I can't believe you called me so that I could listen to the music you and your wife were listening to."

"I did that because I missed you so much," he said. "I really wanted to be there with you."

"But you *weren't* there with me."

"You're in a bad mood."

"Don't you see? You weren't there with *me*."

He reached over and took my hand, rubbing his thumb on my palm. I looked out at the dimly lit street. We were on our way to our usual hidden restaurant, where I had eaten everything on the menu a hundred times. A mosquito, now sluggish with my blood, had got in the car. I slapped myself as I tried to hit it.

"Good evening, sah," the waiter said when we were seated. "You are welcome, sah."

"Have you noticed that they never greet me?" I asked my lover.

"Well . . ." he said, and adjusted his glasses.

The waiter came back, a sober-faced man with a gentle demeanor, and I waited until he had opened the bottle of red wine before I asked, "Why don't you greet me?"

The waiter glanced at my lover, as though seeking guidance, and this infuriated me even more. "Am I invisible? I am the one who asked you a question. Why do all of you waiters and gatemen and drivers in this Lagos refuse to greet me? Do you not see me?"

"Come back in ten minutes," my lover said to the waiter in his courteous, deep-voiced way. "You need to calm down," he told me. "Do you want us to go?"

"Why don't they greet me?" I asked, and gulped down half my glass of wine.

"I have a surprise for you. I've bought you a new car."

I looked at him blankly.

"Did you hear me?" he asked.

"I heard you." I was supposed to get up and hug him and tell him that history would remember him as a great man. A new car. I drank more wine.

"Did I tell you about my first bus ride when I arrived in Lagos, six years ago?" I asked. "When I got on the bus, a boy was screaming in shock because a stranger had found his lost wallet and given it back to him. The boy looked like me, a green, eager job seeker, and he, too, must have come from his home town armed with warnings. You know all the things they tell you: don't give to street beggars because they are only pretending to be lame; look through tomato pyramids for the rotten ones the hawkers hide underneath; don't help people whose cars have broken down, because they are really armed robbers. And then somebody found his wallet and gave it back to him."

My lover looked puzzled.

"Rituals of distrust," I said. "That is how we relate to one another here, through rituals of distrust. Do you know how carefully I watch the fuel gauge when I buy petrol just to make sure the attendant hasn't tampered with it? We know the rules and we follow them, and we never make room for things we might not have imagined. We close the door too soon." I felt a little silly, saying things I knew he did not understand and did not want to understand, and also a little cowardly, saying them the way I did. He was resting his elbows on the table, watching me, and I knew that all he wanted was my excitement, my gratitude, my questions about when I could see the new car. I began to cry, and he came around and cradled me against his waist. My nose was running and my eyes itched as I dabbed them with my napkin. I never cried elegantly, and I imagined that his wife did; she was probably one of those women who could just have the tears trail down her cheeks, leaving her makeup intact, her nose dry.

The traffic had started to move a little. I saw an okada in my side mirror, coming too fast, swerving and honking, and I waited to hear the crunch as it hit my car. But it didn't. The driver was wearing a helmet, while his passenger merely held hers over her head—the smelly foam inside would have ruined her hair—close enough so that she could slip it on as soon as she saw a LASTMA official ahead. My lover once called it fatalism. He had given free helmets to all his staff, but most of them still got on an okada without one. The day before, an okada, the driver bareheaded and blindly speeding, had hit me as I turned onto Ogunlana Drive; the driver stuck his finger into his mouth and ran it over the scratch on the side of my car. "Auntie, sorry oh! Nothing happen to the car," he said, and continued his journey.

I laughed. I had not laughed in the three weeks since I had left work at lunchtime and driven to my lover's house. I had packed all my clothes, my books, and my toiletries and gone back to my flat, consumed as I went by how relentlessly unpretty Lagos was, with houses sprouting up unplanned like weeds.

During those three weeks, I had said little at work. Our office was suddenly very uncomfortable, the air-conditioning always too cold. His Royal Highness, the Oba of the town near the lagoon, was asking for more money; his town council had written a letter saying that the borehole was spewing blackish water. My boss was calling too many meetings.

"Let us give thanks," he said after one of the meetings.

"Why should we be praying in the workplace?" I asked. "Why must you assume that we are all Christians?"

He looked startled. He knew that I never joined in, never said "Amen," but I had never been vocal about it.

"It is not by force to participate in thanking the Lord," he said, and then in the same breath continued, "In Jesus' name!"

"Amen!" the others chorused.

I turned to leave the meeting room.

"Don't go," my co-worker Gerald whispered to me. "Akin brought his birthday cake."

I stood outside the meeting room until the prayer ended, and then we sang "Happy Birthday" to Akin. His cake looked like the unpretentious kind I liked, probably from Sweet Sensation, the kind that sometimes had bits of forgotten eggshells in it. Our boss asked him to give me or Chikwado the cake to serve.

"Why do we always have to serve the cake?" I asked. "Every time somebody brings in a cake, it is either Chikwado serves it or I serve it. You, Gerald, serve the cake. Or you, Emeka, since you are the most junior."

They stared at me. Chikwado got up hurriedly and began to slice the cake. "Please, don't mind her," she said to everyone, but her eyes were on our boss. "She is behaving like this because she did not take her madness medicine today."

Later, she said to me, "Why have you been behaving somehow? What's the problem? Did something happen with your man?"

For a moment, I wanted to tell her how I felt: as though bits of my skin had warped and cracked and peeled off, leaving patches of raw flesh so agonizingly painful I did not know what to do. I wanted to tell her how often I stared at my phone, even though he had sent two feeble texts saying he did not understand why I'd left and then nothing else; and how I remembered clearly, too clearly, the scent of the moist tissues he used to clean his glasses. I didn't tell her, because I was sure she would deliver one of her petty wisdoms, like "If you see fire and you put your hand in fire, then fire will burn you." Still, there was a softness in her expression, something like sympathy, when I looked up from my computer screen and saw her watching me while her hand went slap, slap, slap on her head. Her weave was a new style, too long and too wiggy, with reddish highlights that brought to mind the hair of cheap plastic dolls. Yet there was an honesty about it; Chikwado owned it in a way that the woman in the jeep did not own her Brazilian hair.

A young boy approached my car, armed with a spray bottle of soapy water and a rag. I turned on my wipers to discourage him, but he still squirted my windscreen. I increased the wiper speed. The boy glared at me and moved on to the car behind me. I was seized with a sudden urge to step out and slap him. For a moment, my vision blurred. It was really the woman I wanted to slap. I turned to her jeep and, because she had looked away, I pressed my horn. I leaned out of my window.

"What is your problem? Why have you been staring at me? Do I owe you?" I shouted.

The traffic began to move. I thought she would roll down her window, too. She made as if to lean toward it, then turned away, the slightest of smiles on her face, her head held high, and I watched the jeep pick up speed and head to the bridge.

THE WARM FUZZIES

CHRIS ADRIAN

Her parents always gave the new kids a tambourine and stuck them back with Molly, because it was easy to play the tambourine, though there were intricacies to it that nobody else understood or appreciated, and because she was nice, though she was actually only about half as nice as everyone supposed her to be. The new boy was not very different to look at than any of his predecessors, the black foster brothers and sisters who came and went and came and went, circulating one at a time through her actual family until they were inevitably ejected. She had barely learned to remember Jordan's name before he was gone, trundled off to a Job Corps assignment in Houston, and now here was Paul, at thirteen years old a little younger than his unmet foster brother once removed, and just as bad with the tambourine. Molly stepped closer to him in the garage and tried to keep the beat in a way that was more obvious and easier to copy, but he didn't catch on, and though he stayed in tune when he sang, he kept getting the words wrong. "I love you," Molly sang, coming in with the rest of the family for the chorus. "I love you a lot. I love you more than you can know, but Jesus loves you *more more more more!*" It wasn't the hardest refrain to remember, but still he kept singing "I love you so much" instead of "a lot," and "more than you can imagine" instead of "more than you can know." It boded ill when they couldn't get the refrain right on this song. It meant that nothing would be easy for them.

It was useless, though, to worry about them, even at this early stage, when you'd think something could be done to help them out, to make them fit in better, or to defuse the inevitable conflicts that would lead to their being sent back to the pound or shipped off to some other family, or a trade school, or the Marines, or to any number of pseudo-opportunities that were the consolation prize for not actually becoming a member of the musical Carter family of Virginia Beach, Virginia.

Molly smiled at Paul, and he nodded coolly at her, which was something different. Usually on the first day, they just gave her a nervous smile, but he seemed to be appraising her somehow, looking her up and down with the nod. Then he turned, swinging his hips one way and his shoulders another, and he gave the same look to her sister Mary where she stood tossing her hair back and forth at the keyboards, using one finger on each hand to play. He did one shake of the tambourine at her—it was out of time—and then at her brother Colin where he was playing the guitar, toward the front of the garage, near their parents. Colin was strumming and dipping from the waist, left and right and left, and hopping in place during the chorus. He was as pale as Molly, and looked sickly, all of a sudden, compared with the new boy. Molly held her breath and closed her eyes and with an effort—it was like squeezing something inside her head—she refrained from thinking something unpleasant about her brother.

The new boy did the same thing to Malinda, singing between their parents, to Craig, on the violin, and Clay, on the bass. He turned around to do the thing—a salute? a shake of the fist?—to Chris, on the drums, and to her parents, and then to little Melissa, a moving target since she played no instrument and did not sing but just danced around enthusiastically, and finally to the life-size picture of Jesus taped to the back side of the garage door, where a different sort of family, or a different sort of band, might have taped a picture of a stadium crowd. It was two shakes for Jesus.

He closed his eyes then, and kept dancing in place and mumble-singing the wrong words. "Jesus Loves You More" did not rock very hard. None of their songs did, though their father, who wrote them with minimal input from Mary and Craig, the two eldest, would have said otherwise. Molly did what she could to shake things up. She and Chris had a thing going, where she accented his drumming just so, jingling grace beats that brought out the rhythm underneath their father's vanilla melody, which was always one of only four melodies. You could do only so much, though. If you shook it too hard, you merely drew attention to yourself in a way that made it clear you had given up on the song or were trying to drag it someplace it just didn't belong. It was a subtle bit of tambourine lore, not something to be intuited the first time you picked one up. But the boy was stomping and shaking and spinning and clapping to a song that was the breathless, hopped-up cousin of the one they were playing. Chris and Mary and Clay frowned at him, but the others, standing in front of him with their hearts turned to Jesus, didn't notice for another minute. The song stopped, not entirely on their father's karate-chop cue, but the boy did not. His eyes were closed, his hands and his feet were flying, and he was smiling as he sang: "Jesus, he's my friend, sort of! He's my kind of sometimes friend. Jesus!" Melissa laughed, and danced along until Mary grabbed her shoulder.

"Paul," their mother said. *"Paul!"* He stopped dancing and looked at her.

"When the music stops," their father said, "the song is over."

"My name," the boy replied, "is Peabo."

There was a time when they had been just the Carters, and not the Carter Family Band, but Molly could barely remember it. There was a time when her father had been a full-time instead of a part-time dentist, and her mother had been the dental hygienist in his office, when they had all gone to regular school instead of home school, when the family car had been a Taurus instead of a short bus, and when Melissa hadn't even been born. Then her parents woke up one morning—without having seen a vision or having experienced a dark night of the soul—with a new understanding of their lives' purpose. They both took up the guitar, never having played before, and started to praise Jesus in song.

There was a time, too, before they made albums or went on tours or appeared in Handycam videos produced and directed by their Aunt Jean, which aired (rather late at night) on the community cable channel and then, eventually, on Samaritan TV, when Molly liked being in the band, and liked being in the family. She had had Melissa's job once, and had danced as enthusiastically as Melissa did now, and had felt the most extraordinary joy during every performance, whether it was a rehearsal in the garage or a school-auditorium concert in front of three hundred kids. Then one morning two months ago, she had woken up to find that the shine had gone off everything. It was a conversion as sudden as the one her parents had suffered. She had come to breakfast feeling unwell but not sick, and was puzzling over how it was different to feel like something was not right with you and yet feel sure you were in perfect health, but she didn't know what her problem could be until she noticed how unattractive her father was. It wasn't his old robe or his stained T-shirt or even how he talked with his mouth full of eggs; he wore those things every morning, and he always talked with his mouth full—it was just how he was. She kept staring at him all through breakfast, and finally he asked her if there was something on his face. "No, sir," she said, and a little voice—the sort that you hear very clearly even though it doesn't actually speak—said somewhere inside her, *He's got ugly all over his face.*

•

Peabo sat next to her at dinner that first night. Molly had just been getting used to the extra room at the table, to being able to eat with her natural right hand instead of her don't-bump-elbows-with-Mary left hand. She had said goodbye to the empty seat the night before, when their father had announced to the family that they were getting another brother.

"Already?" Chris asked, because Jordan had been gone only three months.

"Already?" their father said. "You mean finally!"

"I miss Jeffrey," said Malinda.

"His name was Jordan," said Chris.

"What's his name?' asked Melissa. "Is it Jeffrey? Is it Elmo? Is it Sarsaparilla?"

"Paul," said their father, and their mother said, "Paul Winner," and Chris said, "Yeah, I bet he's a real *winner*." Colin gave him a high-five, and they were both subsequently disfellowshipped for the course of the meal, their chairs turned away toward the wall, their faces turned to their laps, and their desserts divided between chubby Mary and fat Craig.

Chris and Colin stayed in the corner while all the others got to speak their gratitudes. Mary went first and used up the obvious one: she was grateful for their new guest; she was grateful for the totality of his life and for his spirit. She was always saying things like that. Molly could tell by the way Colin's shoulders were moving that he was poking his finger in his mouth to gag himself. Clay was grateful for the tension in his guitar strings. Craig was grateful for the color alizarin crimson. Malinda was grateful for the note of D-flat, and Melissa was grateful for fur, but, when pressed by their father to be more specific, she said, "Furry creatures." Molly had been feeling a little panicked lately when her turn approached. There was a lot to be grateful for—the whole point of uttering one's gratitudes was just that. It was meant to be easy, a nightly reminder that they lived their lives surrounded by visible and invisible bounty. But sometimes, out of sheer nervousness, Molly failed to think of anything, and sometimes the things that popped into her head were not the things she was supposed to be grateful for: the way her breasts were exactly the same size, while Mary's and Malinda's looked like they had traded four markedly different boobs between them; the way it felt when she rested all her weight on the tapering edge of her bicycle seat; the way Jordan's right eye had been ever so slightly out of synch with his left eye. And lately the voice had been speaking with her, so when she said out loud, "Dandelion fluff," or "The spots on the wings of a ladybug," the voice would say *poverty*, or *measles*. She said, "This fork," and held it tightly, as if clutching it could keep her from saying "My asshole."

Peabo was quiet during his first dinner. Colin had predicted that he would be ravenous and nose for scraps off other people's plates, but he hardly ate, tasting everything and finishing nothing but praising it all politely. Molly watched him, expecting him to pick up his plate and shake it at her, but he only cocked his head when he caught her looking. The family made the usual first-dinner conversation. On their mother's instructions, they were supposed to let lie all the presumed horrors, and not ask him anything directly about his past, and so the gist of the conversation was something like "I like potatoes, Peabo . . . Do you like potatoes?" He answered these questions the same way every time, with a solemn nod of his head and "I do." Molly thought about the presumed horrors anyway. He had a burn on his left arm that she had noticed right away, and though she didn't stare at him she wondered how he'd got it, and there was a scar on the side of his neck that had healed all bunched up and thick.

It would have been tantamount to suggesting that they cast Jesus out of the household to say that an end should be put to the endless stream of foster brothers and sisters who had been coming and going in the seat next to her for as long as she could remember. But she wondered if it reduced the sum total of any-body's suffering to keep him around for a few months in a situation that ultimately did nobody any good, that changed nothing in anybody's life, that only rearranged some things for a little while. But that was like wondering if they should stop playing and singing because their songs did not in fact enter into people's hearts and make them love themselves and each other and Jesus, who mediated all love of any kind, the love clearinghouse and the love circuit board. Looking at the new boy, she thought that it might be easier for everyone if he just went away right now, and she waited for the voice to add something snarky and cruel to that thought. She waited and waited, but nothing came, and when he glanced her way again and caught her staring she put a piece of broccoli in her mouth and looked at her lap.

W hat an unusual name," Mary said later, when the four girls were in the bathroom getting ready for bed. "Peabo. Pea . . . *bo*."

"It's a dog name," said Malinda. "Here, Peabo. Here, boy!"

"Here, kitty kitty!" said Melissa, then thought a moment and added, "It has 'pee' in it. I bet his middle name is Doody." She struck a pose in front of Mary and stuck out her hand. "Hello, my name is Pee Doody. How do you doo-doo?" Mary slapped her hand away, and Melissa laughed. It was as typical and ordinary and expected as the dinner questions, or starting the new kid off on the tambourine—it had all happened before, and it would all happen again, the touch of cattiness in the beginning, relatively innocent doo-dooisms that lacked any deep venom. These would fade away little by little, and the giggling denigrations would be replaced by goggling admirations, a slow fade-up that might not be noticed if it weren't part of the eternal foster cycle. Molly paused while brushing her teeth to sigh expansively.

"What?" Malinda asked.

"Nothing," Molly said, because Malinda had become convinced in the past few months that Molly thought she was better than the rest of them, and she had taken it upon herself to teach Molly just how un-Christian and bitchy it was to go around heaving big sighs to let everyone know you were bored by your own superiority. That wasn't it at all, of course. Molly actually felt pretty lowly, compared with the rest of them—just because she was always unwillingly coming up with insults for them all didn't mean she thought she was better than anybody else. But she didn't tell Malinda that.

"What?" Malinda said again.

"His middle name is Bo," Molly said. "I saw his papers on Dad's desk. B-O. Paul Bo. P. Bo."

"You like him," said Mary, smiling.

"You're not supposed to be looking at things on that desk," said Malinda.

"Molly and Doody," Melissa sang, "sittin' in a tree."

"He won't last a month," Molly said. She rinsed out her mouth and put her toothbrush back into her color-coded space—blue—in the holder, and went to her bedroom. It was hers that year by lottery; her sisters shared a room. Malinda said that having her own room had gone to Molly's head.

She turned out the light, neglecting both her regular and her special Bible study, neglecting to kneel at her bed to pray, and only very quickly (though not insincerely) asking a silent blessing on all the people in her family, flipping their faces through her head like a card deck, instead of turning each of them over in her mind like a little statue. She considered the new boy last, picturing him on a card all his own, in his tambourine pose, in mid-shake and mid-benediction or threat, whatever it had been, and she let her mind go quiet for a moment while she held on to that image of him, as if inviting the voice to say something cruel about him. But again nothing came. For the rest of her family, she prayed for happiness and a long life, and that they be gathered up to Heaven if they should all die that night in an earthquake or a fire (and she briefly imagined them buried under the earth, and with burning hair). For the boy, she just asked that things work out for him here after all. Then she went to sleep.

When she saw him standing at the foot of her bed, her first thought was that it was strange to be dreaming about him, since he was interesting but not fascinating, and sad but not troubling. She stared at him for a while before she realized that she was awake. She sat up. "What are you doing here?" she asked. In answer he did an explosive move, throwing his arms up and out three times, slapping his heel, and spinning in place. She flinched but didn't cry out; he did it again, and then something more complicated and harder to follow, and yet she did follow it, and preserved every move, the pointing and the spinning, the way he made double guns of his hands and fired them all around her room and then blew the imaginary smoke from the tips of his finger pistols, the splits in the air and the brief air-guitar solo and every blocky motion of the robot dance. He smiled at her when he was done. She stared back at him, not smiling, with the covers drawn up to her chin, and watched as he danced out of her room, doing a perfect curving moonwalk right out the door, which he left open. She stared at the open door for a while, considering it evidence that he had been there, since she made a point of closing it every night before she got into bed, and trying to think of what she should say to herself about what she had just seen. She didn't know what to say, so she waited, instead, for the snarky, dissatisfied voice in her to say something, fully expecting it to be something more cruel and more vile than anything it had yet dared to say. But the words, when they came, were *Nice moves*.

•

She considered those moves as she sat the next day with her mother and the other girls sewing the costumes for the new video. They were in the garage, the only place in the house with enough empty floor space to lay out the fabric, though today they were just sewing spangles on the jumpsuits, all sitting cross-legged on cushions nipped from the living-room sectional. She had wondered, until she finally fell asleep, if she should tell on him. It was probably her duty, after all, to get him whatever help he needed to keep him from entering relative strangers' rooms at night, uninvited. And maybe she ought to tell on him for her own sake, since any variety of bad behavior might be in store in him, and the little dance only a fluid, grooving prelude to a lifetime of deviance.

And yet it had only been a little dance. That was all he had done. There were Christian households where that was a crime, but this wasn't one of them. There had been some kind of infraction; she was certain of that. But what exactly it might be was not clear at all. Whatever it was, ejection from the household on only the second day of his tenure seemed too severe a punishment, and that was what would likely happen, since she knew that her father would regard the situation with considerably less sophistication than she did. She found that she cared whether or not he stuck around, because it had been nice to hear something from the voice that she could agree with. Maybe, she thought, the reign of malicious sarcasm was over and she could be a good person again.

"Pay attention, honey," her mother said, because she was about to sew a spangle fish on backward to the sea-blue one-piece, zip-up-the-back jumpsuit. The girls had lost an argument with their father about how the fishes should be placed. "The fishes all swim the same way," he said. "Up, toward Jesus." It would have been pleasing, Molly thought, to have them going every which way.

"Sorry," Molly said. Her mother handed her the seam ripper, and Molly began to undo the stitches, but she was imagining Peabo dancing in a suit of haphazardly swimming fish. Her mother was still staring at her when she handed back the seam ripper.

"Well?" her mother said.

"What?"

"You're the only one who hasn't shared yet," she said. "Cat got your tongue?"

"Huh?"

"Well, what do you think about the latest addition to our family?"

Molly shrugged. "He seems nice," she said.

"And?"

Molly shrugged again.

"And she's too fancy to share her opinions," said Malinda. Their mother shushed her with a wave of her hand. "Mary," she said. "Tell your sister what sort of family she's living in."

"A Christian Democratic Union," Mary said, not looking up from her work.

"And what does a Christian Democratic Union rely upon?" She looked at Malinda now, but it was the voice that Molly heard answering first: *Every citizen being perfectly ugly and perfectly boring.*

"The open and honest loving communication of information equally shared among all participants," Malinda said. Molly sighed, and Malinda glared at her, but she was sighing at the voice, not at her sister.

"So," their mother said to Molly. "Once more, with feelings!"

"Did something bad happen to him?" Molly asked.

"Bad things happen to all of us," her mother said.

"Something especially bad," Molly said. "Something tragic?" She hadn't read any further than the first page of the file on her father's desk, and didn't know anyway if they put that sort of thing in it, the list of his lifetime of problems: *dead mother, dead father, beaten by auntie, contracted out to a sweatshop, punished with burns.*

"Not everybody can be lucky like you," said Malinda.

"Or like *you,*" said their mother. "Or *you* or *you* or *you* or *you.*" She pointed to each of them, then to Malinda one more time, and then she suggested that they take this as an opportunity to say their love, and so Molly turned to Mary and Melissa and said it, and finally suffered Malinda's stiff hug.

"I love you," Malinda said, and leaned close to whisper, "Even though you totally suck."

"I love you, too," said Molly, and she tried hard to mean it.

L ater, during the afternoon rehearsal, she kept expecting Peabo to do the dance again. But today he was copying her exactly, doing the one-two, one-two shuffle in perfect time with her, and singing in tune on the signature piece of the new album, which was the reason they were rehearsing every day, and sewing costumes, and blocking out a video. They would start a tour in two weeks.

"The Ballad of the Warm Fuzzies" was the most complicated song her father had ever written. It didn't involve any more than the usual four chords, but it was seven minutes long, and the lyrics told an actual story. The tale of the Warm Fuzzies and their battle with the Cold Pricklies unfolded in twelve verses, with half the family squaring off against the other in song. Peabo, along with Molly, was among the Pricklies.

All day, Molly had watched him as closely as she dared to, given how closely she was being watched by Malinda for evidence of snootiness or lack of charity toward the boy. Her mother had told them that Jesus would help them along to a place where they couldn't even see that he was black, that with perfect love would come perfect color blindness, but every time Molly saw him standing next to one of her brothers or sisters it was all she noticed about him, how different he looked. *Black is beautiful*, the voice kept saying, which made her shake her head.

He talked to her in the same way he talked to all the girls, politely and never for very long. He joshed and roughhoused with the boys, and seemed to settle immediately into companionship with them in a way that belied the remote gaze he had trained on everyone during the first rehearsal and dinner. She watched him at play with her brothers. It was as if there were two boys, who didn't jibe with each other. There was the boy who had sneaked into her room to offer up the little dance for her interpretation, and then there was the boy who arm-wrestled with Craig and did algebra equations for fun with Colin. She could understand if there were two boys in him, since she had felt there were two girls in her, one for the regular voice that said regular things about people and one that spoke a language made up only of cruel insults. If she stared in the bathroom mirror long enough, she thought she could catch that other girl's features superimposed in brief flashes upon hers: her eyes were small and her nose turned up like a pig's, and her mouth was a colorless gash in her face. Malinda caught her staring at herself like that once and said, "You think you're so pretty, don't you?"

Molly tripped up on the beat, and came late to the chorus:

> *Are you a warm fuzzy?*
> *Are you a warm fuzzy?*
> *Are you gonna be a warm fuzzy?*
> *Or a cold, cold, cold, cold prickly?*

At first, it seemed no one had noticed that she'd missed a beat—Chris was the only one who usually cared, anyway—until

Peabo did the same thing, just one beat off, but didn't look at her. He did it again: another missed beat.

She missed one back, and then threw in an extra one at the end of the next verse, and then for the rest of the song they were trading omissions and additions, having a conversation above and below and around the song that no one else, not even the snarky voice in her, could understand, and it occurred to her, just before the song ended, that they were speaking tambourine.

"Off the charts!" their father said, because they all stopped playing at exactly the same time for once, and everyone had been in key and no one had forgotten any verses; even Melissa's flailing dance had been more graceful than usual. "He is risen! He is *risen!* Off the *charts!*" he said. Peabo was nodding soberly as they all put down their instruments and began to exchange hugs, something they usually did at the end of the rehearsal, though they were only half done now. It was one of those moments that Molly would really have appreciated a couple of months before. They were all hugging with breathless abandon, entirely caught up in how much they loved the music, one another, this day, and Jesus, of course. *Jesus, Jesus, Jesus*, Molly said to herself, but the voice said *Mariah Carey, Mariah Carey, Mariah Carey*, which lent a new emergent sense of alarm to her effort really to feel what they were feeling, and with her eyes shut tight she tried to feel it by sheer force of will. She strained, and there was a sensation in her like a bubble popping, and clear as day she had a picture in her head: a lizard sunning itself on a rock, staring rapt and remote into the distance.

They went to church that evening. Molly sat there, looking around without moving her head. It was worse here, surrounded not just by her family but by the whole congregation, hairy Mrs. Louque in the row in front of her and ancient Mr.

Landry behind her. The church, which was as big as a ware-house, because it had once been a warehouse, was full of good, normal people who put her to shame by their example. Up on the stage, Reverend Duff was a lightning rod for the voice. *There once was a reverend named Fudd*, it sang, and she tried to do the mental equivalent of sticking your fingers in your ears and sing-ing la la la.

It was a different sort of Jesus time than the one they had had that day at home, but Molly was failing at it just as badly. Her mother was trembling and ululating and her father was shaking and barking and her brothers were yipping and her sisters were mewling, and beyond them the whole congregation was similarly taken up, and Molly would have to listen, later, as they all talked about how wonderful it was for them when they spoke the spirit that way. She closed both eyes, then opened one to a slit to watch Peabo, who was standing quietly next to her. The limerick about Reverend Duff faltered and was silenced as she watched him. *He doesn't look stupid like the rest of them*, the voice said, at the same time that she thought, *He doesn't look stupid like me*. Molly looked ahead at the back of Mrs. Louque's head. The lady was dancing in place like a little girl.

Their hymnbooks were touching and their elbows were touch-ing and their knees were touching. But Peabo didn't look at her, and he sang the hymns without any extra notes or extra syllables that could be put together into a message. When it came time to exchange the peace, he turned to her mother, and hugged Colin and Chris and Clay and her father, and he reached past her to hug Mary, but he didn't even look at Molly. That would have been too obvious, she told herself, and she tried to think of some clever way of communicating with him. All she could think was to tear a piece of a page from one of the hymnals and fold it into the shape of a snake, which would signify something, though she wasn't sure what, exactly. Her failure to imagine what that was made everything feel useless and dumb, and she was sure, all of a sudden, that she had imagined his unique advance. She closed her eyes, and shook her head, and found herself wanting to scream.

It would have been fine to scream. You were supposed to express the spirit however it came. This usually took the foster children by surprise, even though they were briefed about it before they came to church for the first time. But he seemed to take it all in stride. Molly did her usual thing, swaying back and forth with her eyes on the ceiling and muttering times tables in pig Latin to herself. She tried to distinguish the voices of her brothers and sisters from the cacophony. She heard Malinda saying something like "Edelweiss!" She heard her father saying "Omalaya!" and her mother saying "Paw-paw!" and then, finally, she heard Peabo, right next to her, saying something that sounded like "I love you I love you I love you I love you." There was an altered, electric quality to his voice. She did not open her eyes, or look at him, but she slipped the words into her times tables. "I-ay ove-lay oooh-yay." She kept on with the oooh-yays until the very end of it all, when folks were passing out, and the last hymn was starting up slowly, rising in various places around the hall from those who had recovered enough to sing. When she opened her eyes, she saw Peabo standing straight and tall next to her, mouth agape with the hymn, shouting it as much as singing it.

She went to his room that night, after she was sure everyone else had fallen asleep. It was the little room that they put all the foster kids in, not even really a bedroom, since it didn't have a closet, just a wardrobe. There was a dresser and a small chair, but no space for anything else except the single bed. The drapes were open, and by the light of the street lamps Molly could see Peabo stretched out in bed, on top of the covers in his pajamas. She stared from the doorway for what felt like five minutes, but she couldn't tell if his eyes were open or not.

She didn't say anything, because he hadn't said anything, and it seemed like it would be cheating to use words. She didn't know what words she would have used anyway, though it was clear what she wanted to say. She did the message: reach, reach, dip, kick, leap, leap, leap, every time a little higher, though not too high, since his room was right above her parents' room. But she went high enough to kick her feet—one, two, three times—and when she landed softly she dropped into a squat and then exploded upward. This was a move from the video for "Jesus Loves You More." Her hands were supposed to stretch out, and then fall, fingers fluttering, to her sides. But the same not-part of her that spoke with the voice that was not a voice took control of them just as she was stretching, and her hands opened up at the top of her reach into two perfect "Fuck you" birdies, aimed not at Peabo but at the whole world.

He didn't stir the whole time she danced, which wasn't very long. Her dance was even shorter than his had been, and she regular-walked, not moonwalked, out the door. Back in her bed, she wondered if he had been awake at all, not sure if it would be disappointing to talk to him at length, now that they were communicating at a higher level. She imagined going on forever this way, through his successful fosterhood and eventual adoption, through weddings and family reunions and funerals, proceeding in parallel past family milestone after family milestone. She imagined them at Malinda's funeral, softly jangling their tambourines at each other, communicating shades of irony and grief not contained in the mundane verbal condolences of the others. She had nearly fallen asleep, and was sure she was about to enter a dream in which, knowing it was a dream, she could enjoy Malinda's death, and say things like "No, I don't miss her at all," when she felt a pressure on her mattress, and awoke with a start.

He was sitting on her bed. "Do you want to see my Jesus?" he asked her.

•

D arkness," said Aunt Jean. "And light! Light . . . and darkness!" She was doing Molly's makeup for the video, painting half of her face black and half of it white for the concept
portion of the shoot, which involved the family taking turns pre-
senting their black faces and their white faces to the camera as
they sang in a black-and-white checkered "dreamspace." That
was a sheet that Jean had colored herself with a reeking marker.
Melissa, who had insisted on having her face done first, kept
sniffing at it curiously. Jean had paused in front of Peabo, a tub
of makeup in either hand, and said, "Why, the dark is built right
in, isn't it?"

"Uh-huh," he said, and gave her a neutral stare. In the end,
she painted him just like the rest of them, but his black side was
darker, and his white side more startling, than everyone else's.

"Cold," Jean said, throwing her head back and raising her
hand to make mouthy little singing motions with it as she showed
them her black profile. "Warm!" She pivoted sharply on her heel
to show them her white face. Molly felt sure that the total effect,
with the checkered background and their swiveling Kabuki faces,
would make people dizzy, or possibly give them a seizure, but she
didn't say so. And the voice didn't say so, either. It had been quiet
all day. She didn't really care anyway if someone had a seizure.
She didn't really care if she was playing well, during the fish-
spangled band-shot portions of the video, when Jean roller-skated
around the garage with the video camera to her eye. She didn't
care if she kept the beat or not, and she didn't care if Peabo did,
either. If he was throwing her grace beats, she ignored them.

"Everything will be different, after you see Him," he had said,
and that was true. As Molly had tried unsuccessfully to sleep,
with the Jesus swinging languidly in her mind in a five-second arc
that measured the minutes until dawn, she tried to see how she

could not have understood what he actually meant, and she pictured herself on trial before her family, with Malinda seated as judge and the others in the jury box, listening with impassive faces as she attempted to explain. "I thought he meant he was going to share his Jesus with me. His own, personal Jesus. His *experience* of Jesus." And it had been true that part of her thought that that was going to be the case, and that same part had wondered what it would be like to show him hers. She could only imagine the obvious thing, opening her chest to show him the very shape of her heart.

Everything looked the same. Her father looked the same, singing with his eyes closed and strumming those same four chords on his guitar. Her mother looked the same, shimmying in place. Chris and Craig and Colin looked the same, and Clay looked the same, thrusting his chin out like a lizard while he played the bass. Mary was stabbing, the same as she always did, at the keyboards, and Malinda was managing to open her pinched-up little mouth just enough for her weak voice to slip out. Melissa was dancing around like a fool who didn't have a clue what was in store for her, and Peabo . . . it didn't even matter what Peabo was doing. They were all hideous, and she knew without a mirror to tell her so that she was uglier than any of them. As soon as the video shoot was over, she found her father in his study and told him.

They started their tour in the auditorium of the New Calvary School, which was where they started all their tours, because it was down the street from their house, and because it could be relied upon to provide a crowd that was both sympathetic and constructively critical. Though the family had technically abandoned the institution, the principal was still a good friend of their father's and a member of their church, and he passed out evaluation forms, dutifully completed by all the students, which scored their performance from one to ten in areas like musicality and spirit and goodness of news. More than a week after Peabo's departure, there was still a shadow on the performance, though Melissa was the only one who said that she missed him, or that they had played better with him around, or that the music sounded different without him. "Don't be stupid," Malinda said. "He only played the *tambourine*."

All their parents would say was that he had done something that demonstrated that it wasn't in God's plan for him to live with them, which was what they said about everyone who got sent back or sent away, but the children suspected that it must have been something horrible, because no one before had ever been sent away after only a week. "I guess you were right about him," Malinda said to Molly. "He didn't last a month." She gave Molly a hard stare.

"I guess so," Molly said, finding it easy to stare back blankly at her sister as if she'd had nothing at all to do with Peabo's ejection. It was exactly as easy as it was to stare blankly at her parents, together and separately, when they asked if anything else had happened besides just a *viewing*. Aunt Jean took her shopping, though she wouldn't buy any of the things Molly picked out for herself. The special attention almost gave away that something had happened to her, and Molly hid the condolence barrette that Jean had given her, after a weepy interrogation in the car. "It must have been so horrible for you!" she said, and Molly said, with perfect calmness, that it was.

They opened with "Sycamore Trees" and then played "Jesus Loves You More" before their father talked a bit to the audience. He wasn't a preacher, but he liked to give sermons, and he told stories meant to throw the message of the song into starker relief. He was saying something about choices, which led into "The Ballad of the Warm Fuzzies," and Molly had a moment in which she thought that she could hear the silence into which the voice should be speaking an insult to him. But it had been silent since Peabo left, as if it were sulking. She didn't miss it, but she didn't feel any better now that it had shut up. She wondered where Peabo was. She had been succeeding fantastically at not thinking about him, though not about his Jesus, which accompanied her everywhere. It was not exactly that she could not stop thinking about it, or even that she saw it in cucumbers or carrots or bunches of bananas. It was with her in a way that was hard to describe, because nothing had ever stayed with her this way before, a permanent afterimage not perceived with the eyes.

The music started without her; she had missed her father's cue. She came in late, and settled down into an unthinking rhythm. She looked around at the audience, and found herself searching for Peabo, but there were only three black kids in the whole student body, and they were all girls. "Don't you miss him?" Melissa kept asking. Molly could swear that she did not, but now she thought she might cry. That was O.K. Her father approved of tears, though not sobs, during a performance. She missed the chorus the first time around, waiting for the tears to come, but not a single one fell, even though everywhere she looked she saw the shimmer and the blur of them. Her family were moving all around her, and she didn't know why, until they squared off into their fuzzy and prickly sides. They sang at her, cocking their heads as they asked if she was going to be a warm fuzzy, but it was clear from their faces that they were asking what was wrong with her.

I don't know, she tried to say, right into her microphone, but something else came out, not even a word but just a noise made in a voice that did not sound like her own voice, though it was very familiar. It was lost in the singing. The family stepped expertly back to their original positions and started the second verse. Melissa picked up a bag and started to throw Warm Fuzzies—really just plush kittens with their hair teased up and their legs cut off, bought in bulk from the five-and-dime—into the crowd. Molly spoke again, louder this time and clearer, so it might have been heard over the music if it hadn't been lost under the noise of the crowd. "Bitch!"

Malinda turned around to glower at her, and raise her hand to her lips in a gesture denoting not "Shush" but "Shut up and sing." Molly shook her tambourine at her, two shakes off the beat. Malinda furrowed her brow and stamped her foot, which warranted another shake of the tambourine and a spoken response: "Bitch! Bastard! Bitch!" Then her mother turned around. She got a shake as well, and then Molly gave one to everyone in the family, one here and two there, and then a scattering of them to the audience. She imagined her family in the audience, and imagined herself in the audience, and imagined Peabo in the audience, and imagined his Jesus in the audience, and now she was singing to all of them. It was a whole audience of delicately curving, uncircumcised Jesuses, and each of them was asking her a question. "Fuck!" she answered. A twisted moan, it hardly sounded like the word, but it was the answer, as she shouted it, to every question she could ask. Where did he come from? Where did he go? Where had the shine gone when it disappeared off everything? What was wrong with her? The noise she was making—"Fargh! Foo-ack!"—was the answer, and then it was the question, too. She stood up straight and tall, shaking her tambourine and singing for a long time after the music had stopped.

SECOND LIVES

DANIEL ALARCÓN

My parents, with admirable foresight, had their first child while they were on fellowships in the United States. My mother was in public health, and my father in a library-science program. Having an American baby was, my mother once said, like putting money in the bank. They lived near downtown Baltimore, by the hospital where my mother was studying, in a neighborhood of dilapidated row houses. Baltimore was abject, ugly, my mother said. Cold in winter, a sauna in summer, a violently segregated city, full of fearful whites and angry blacks. America, in those days, had all its dirty laundry available for inspection—the world's most powerful nation making war with itself in the streets, in universities, in the South, in Vietnam, in the capital just down the road. And yet my parents set about trying to make babies: on spring nights, when they made the room smell of earth, summer nights, when the city felt like a swamp, autumn nights, falling asleep on top of the covers, winter nights, when the room boiled with sex. They were not newlyweds, strictly speaking, but Baltimore reënergized them, made of their pairing something indispensable, something chemical.

For their efforts, they were rewarded with a son, whom they named Francisco. The district they lived in was one of the poorest in the country at the time, and once the birth was registered my parents were entitled to free baby formula, delivered to their doorstep every Monday morning. They found this astonishing, and later learned that many of the foreign doctors at the hospital were receiving this benefit, too, even a few who didn't yet have children. It was a gigantic bribe, my father said, the government pleading with its poverty-stricken residents: Please, please don't riot! Baltimore was adorned with reminders of the last civil disturbance: a burned-out block of storefronts, a boarded-up and untended house whose roof had collapsed after a snowstorm. Every morning, the sidewalks were littered with shattered car windows, tiny bits of glass glinting like diamonds in the limpid sun. No one used money in the neighborhood stores, only coupons; and, in lieu of birds, the skies featured plastic bags held aloft on a breeze. But none of this mattered, because my parents were happy. They were in love and they had a beautiful boy, his photo affixed to a blue First World passport.

Their American moment didn't last long. They would have had another child—they would have had me—if their visas hadn't run out. By the time my mother was done nursing Francisco, a coup had taken place back home, and the military junta that came to power was not entirely friendly with the Johnson Administration. My parents were required to renew their papers every eighteen months, and that year, to their great surprise, they were denied. Appeals, they were told, could be filed only from the home country. The university hospital wrote a letter on my mother's behalf, but this well-meaning document vanished into some bureaucrat's file cabinet in suburban Virginia, and it soon became clear that there was nothing to be done. Rather than be deported—how undignified!—my parents left of their own accord.

And then their gaze turned, back to their families, their friends, the places they had known, and those they had forgotten they knew. They bought a house in a suburb of the capital, where I was raised, an out-of-the-way place that has since been swallowed entirely by the city's growth. I guess they lost that old Baltimore feeling, because I wasn't born for another seven years, a crying, red-faced bit of flesh, a runt, undersized even then. No blue passport for me, but they consoled themselves by giving me an Anglo name, Nelson, which was the fashion at the time. Eventually, I got my Third World passport, the color of spilled red wine, but it was just for show. I still haven't had a chance to use it.

Francisco, of course, fled at the first opportunity. It was January, 1987, the situation was bleak, and leaving was the most logical thing to do. I was ten years old; the idea was that he'd get me a visa and I'd join him as soon as I finished school. We went as a family to see him off at the airport, took the obligatory photographs in front of the departures board, and waved as he passed through security. He promised to write. He promised to call. He disappeared into the terminal, and then we climbed the stairs to the greasy restaurant above the baggage claim, where we sat by the wall of windows, waiting for a plane that looked like it might be my brother's to take off. My father drank coffee, fogged his glasses with his breath and polished the lenses between the folds of his dress shirt. My mother drew a palm tree on a paper napkin, frowning. I fell asleep with my head on the table, and when I woke up the janitor was mopping the floor beside us, wondering, perhaps, if we ever intended to leave.

My brother went to live with the Villanuevas, old friends of my parents from their Baltimore days, who'd settled in Birmingham, Alabama. His first letter was three handwritten pages and began with a description of winter in the Southern United States. That year, the Alabama rains fell almost without pause until the middle of March, a soggy prelude to an even wetter spring. For Francisco, unaccustomed to this weather, the thunderstorms were impressive. Occasionally, there'd be a downed power line, and sometimes the lights would go out as a result. It was in this familiar darkness, Francisco wrote, that he'd first felt homesick.

The second half of the letter dealt more specifically with the routines of family life at the Villanuevas. Where they lived wasn't a neighborhood so much as a collection of houses that happened to face the same street. Kids were permitted to play in the back yard or in the driveway, but never in the front yard. No one could explain why, but it simply wasn't done. People moved about only in cars; walking was frowned upon, socially acceptable for children, perhaps, if they happened to be accompanied by a dog. The Villanuevas did not have pets. Nor was there anywhere to walk to, really. A two-pump gas station sat about a mile away on Highway 31; its attractions included a pay phone and a magazine rack.

The Villanueva children, Marisa and Jack, ages fifteen and ten, respectively, made it clear from the outset that they spoke no Spanish. The language didn't interest them much, and their father, who insisted that my brother call him Julio and not Mr. Villanueva, considered this his greatest failing as a parent. It was his fault, he confessed to Francisco, for marrying an American woman. In general terms, though, things were good. Speaking English with the Villanueva kids, while challenging at first, helped my brother learn the language faster. At school, not a soul spoke Spanish, not even Señora Rickerts, the friendly, well-intentioned Spanish teacher. Francisco was not enrolled with Marisa, as had originally been planned. She went to an expensive private school, which would not permit Francisco to audit classes, so instead the Villanuevas sent him to Berry, the local public high school, with the hicks. This last word, Francisco explained, was the rough English equivalent of *campesino* or *cholo*, only it referred to rural white people. He'd learned it from Marisa, and had been advised by Mr. Villanueva never to use it if he wished to make friends. My father found this part of the letter very amusing. How remarkable, he said, that Villanueva's daughter spoke no Spanish but had somehow imported her father's classism to North America! How ironic, my father noted, that his own son should learn proletarian solidarity in the belly of the empire!

My parents read and reread the letter at the dinner table, alternately laughing and falling into worried silence. In the early months, I recall them wondering aloud if they'd made a mistake by sending him away like this. Whose idea had it been? And where was Birmingham, anyway? Was it a city or a town? What kind of school was this place called Berry?

They wrote back, urging Francisco to send photos. A month passed, and the next letter arrived with a single picture. We saw Francisco with an umbrella and a yellow raincoat, standing next to the mailbox in front of the Villanuevas' house, a dense knot of purple clouds above. The front yard sloped dramatically, and Francisco stood at an odd slant. He'd put on a little weight—you could see it in his cheeks—and his hair had grown out. His face was changing, my mother said. He was growing up.

By his third letter, the winter rains had become spring rains, which were the same, only warmer. Storms spread like inkblots across the sky. On sunny days after a rain, the woods behind the Villanuevas' subdivision looked as if they'd been dipped in light. Everyone said that it was an unusually wet year. Francisco didn't mind—he was fascinated by the weather. It was everything else that bored him. His great disappointment that spring was that he'd tried out for the Berry High soccer team, and spent three games on the bench, watching the action unfold without him. He'd quit in protest, and, to his surprise, no one had begged him to come back. They hadn't even noticed. Americans, he wrote, have no understanding of the game. The issue was not mentioned again.

By the fourth letter, the weather had turned; breezy, pleasant stretches were punctuated now and then by days of blasting heat. School would be over soon. He no longer complained about Berry or his classmates, whose dialect he could barely understand. Instead, he seemed to have settled in. Each week, Francisco went to the Spanish class and led conversation exercises with his American peers, and several of them had sought him out for further instruction. An exchange student from Mexico City had spent time at Berry the previous year, seducing Alabama girls and confounding deeply held stereotypes—he didn't wear a poncho, for instance, and was apparently sincere in his love of punk music. He'd also left behind a folkloric legacy of curse words: *panocha*, *no manches*, and *pinche guey*. Francisco wrote that he considered it his responsibility to teach these poor gringos to curse with dignity, and this was, as far as he could tell, the only linguistic knowledge they truly thirsted for. He introduced them to important words, words like *mierda*, *culo*, and *pendejo*, while offering the more advanced students a primer on the nearly infinite uses of *huevo* (*huevón*, *hasta las huevas*, *hueveo*, *huevear*, *se hueveó la huevada*). My parents were proud: "Our son the educator," they said. Photos included with this letter were of nearby Lake Logan Martin, where the Villanuevas had a weekend house. Sun glinting off the water, bathing suits hanging on a line, barefoot games of Frisbee in the freshly mowed grass. In summer, Francisco might learn to water-ski.

This was the first letter in which he forgot to ask us how we were.

That year—the only year he consistently wrote to us—the photos were mostly of Francisco by himself. Occasionally, he'd pose with the Villanuevas: Julio, his wife, Heather, and their two dark-haired, olive-skinned children, who really looked as though they should speak some Spanish. Once, Francisco sent a photo of the Berry High gymnasium, which was notable only for its size. The entire high school, he wrote, would soon be razed and replaced by an even bigger complex farther out in the suburbs. Everyone was excited about this, but he wouldn't be around to see it. He didn't intend to stay in Alabama; on this point he was very clear.

We did eventually get a photo of the few American friends Francisco acquired in those first months, and perhaps this could have clued us in about his eagerness to move on. At home, Francisco had always been part of the popular crowd, the center of a fitful, manic group of friends who loved trouble and music and girls. At Berry, he was on the margins of it all, one of a bunch of skinny outcasts, happy to have found one another in the crowded, cliquish hallways of this immense public school. In these photos: a Korean named Jai, a red-haired boy called Anders, who wore a neck brace, and a frail black kid named Leon, carrying a stack of books and looking utterly lost.

It was just as well that Francisco didn't ask us how we were. My parents might not have been able to explain. Or they might not have wanted to. Nineteen eighty-seven was the year of the state-employee strike, which was particularly troubling for us, since my father worked at the National Library and my mother at the Ministry of Health. It started in May, around the time that Francisco was learning to water-ski. There was also dismaying talk of a new currency to replace the one that was soon to be destroyed by rising inflation. Together these horrors would wipe out our already diminished savings. War pressed down on the country in all its fury. Adults spoke of politics as if referring to a long and debilitating illness that no medicine could cure. Presidential elections were on the horizon; no one knew who would win, but none of the options were good. My father was shedding weight and hair at a frightening pace, the stress carving him to pieces.

Our letters to the U.S. did not include photographs, a small concession to my father's vanity in those taxing months. Nor did they mention the fact that Francisco was attending the public school because the tuition at Marisa's school was simply out of the question for us. Or that my parents had already written a letter to Mr. Villanueva postponing the monthly payment for his room and board. Certainly, my parents didn't tell Francisco how much shame they felt at having to do this. I doubt they even told him that they were afraid they'd lose their jobs, and were speaking with a lawyer about getting citizenship for all of us and coming as a family to join him. These were the issues my parents talked about at home, in front of me (as if I weren't there) but not with my brother. Why worry the boy? The calls were too expensive to waste time on unpleasant things, and wasn't he busy enough, learning English and spending his afternoons jumping from the Villanuevas' pier into the cool, refreshing waters of Lake Logan Martin?

For most of my childhood, our neighbors across the street were a friendly couple named Alejandro and Luz. They were a little older than my parents, the rare neighborhood couple with no kids, possessing no concept of the kinds of things children might like. They visited from time to time, usually bringing some sort of gift for my brother and me—a jump rope, a pinwheel, that sort of thing.

Alejandro had big ears and a quirky grin. He wore dark suits and liked to talk politics until late in the evening. He was a good man, my father told me once, and decency was not something to be taken lightly, but when it came to world view—he said this quite sternly—"we simply do not agree with him." Even now I'm not sure if this meant that Alejandro was a reactionary or a radical. Those were confusing times. Alejandro worked long hours, and months might pass between his visits, whereas Luz often came by to chat with my mother or to play with us. And when both my parents were working late Francisco and I sometimes spent a few hours at her house, deeply involved in card games whose rules the three of us invented as we went along, or listening to the dark, suspenseful stories Luz loved to tell. Ostensibly about her family, these tales of adventure and daring seemed to draw more from Hollywood Westerns, featuring spectacular kidnappings, gambling debts settled with knife fights, or long, dismal marches through unforgiving mountain terrain. Luz's manner of speaking made it clear that she had no idea what she might say next. It wasn't that she made things up, strictly speaking—only that facts were merely a point of departure for her.

Luz modified whatever game we played, never apologizing, and we rarely minded letting her win, whether at cards or dominoes or hide-and-seek; in fact, it didn't feel like a concession at all. My brother, who usually kept a studied distance from me and all things preadolescent, regressed in her company, becoming, as if by magic, a gentler, more innocent version of himself.

Often Luz would let us watch an hour of cartoons while she rested on the couch with an arm draped over her face. We thought she was asleep, exhausted from so much winning, but every time a news break came on Luz would sit up in a flash, cover our eyes, and make us press our hands over our ears. The news in those days was not for children, she always said, and I took her word for it. But afterward, when I had opened my eyes and was blinking hopefully at the television, waiting for the cartoons to come back on, Francisco would say, "Did you see that, little brother? That's why I'm leaving."

Soon after Francisco had gone, Alejandro moved out. It happened almost without anyone realizing it, though the dearth of concrete details was soon overwhelmed by the neighborhood's combined speculative power: Alejandro had run off with his secretary, with the maid, with the daughter of one of his business associates. The mistress, whoever she might be, was pregnant, or maybe she already had children of her own, whom Alejandro had agreed to take care of. It seemed likely that she was much younger than Luz, that he wanted, after all these years, to be a father. There were a few who thought that his sudden disappearance had more to do with politics, but my father rejected that theory out of hand.

A few weeks had passed when Alejandro came by late one night. He wanted to speak to my father, alone. They shut themselves in the kitchen with a bottle of pisco, and when they emerged, a few hours later, it was clear that Alejandro had been crying. His eyes were swollen and his arms hung limply by his sides. My mother and I were in the living room. I was supposedly doing homework, but really I was waiting to see what would happen. Nothing did. Alejandro gave us a sheepish nod, while my father stood next to him, pisco bottle in hand. They hadn't even uncorked it.

The following day, my mother clarified things a bit. Or tried to. "An affair," she said, "is when a man takes up with a woman who is not his wife. Do you understand that, Nelson?"

Sure I did, or at least I thought I did. "And what if a woman takes up with a man who is not her husband?"

My mother nodded. "That, too."

I had other questions as well. "Takes up with"? Something about the way my mother said this phrase alerted me to the fact that it was a metaphor.

And she sighed, closing her eyes for a moment. She seemed to be thinking rather carefully about what she might say, and I waited, tensely, perhaps even holding my breath. My mother patted me on the head. It was complicated, she said finally, but there was one thing I should be aware of, one thing I should think about and learn now, even if I was too young to understand. Did I want to know? "It has to do with a woman's pride," she said, and waited for these puzzling words to take hold. They didn't. It was all opaque, delightfully mysterious. Alejandro's affair was different from others, she said. Yes, he had left Luz, and, yes, this was bad enough. Plenty bad. But a woman is proud, and at a certain age this pride is tinged with self-doubt. "We grow old," my mother told me, "and we suspect we are no longer beautiful." Alejandro's new mistress was ten years older than Luz. This was what he'd confessed to my father the night before. A younger woman would have been understandable, expected even, but this—it wasn't the sort of insult that Luz would easily recover from.

I knew it was serious by the way my mother's eyes narrowed.

"If your father ever does something like this to me, you'd better call the police, because someone's going to get hurt. Do you understand?"

I told her I did, and her face eased into a smile.

"O.K., then, go on," my mother said. "Go play or something."

In those days after Francisco left, "go play" came to mean something very specific: go sit in your room and draw and create stories. I could spend hours this way, and often did. My scripts were elaborate, mostly nonviolent revenge fantasies, in which I (or the character I played) would end up in the unlikely position of having to spare the life of a kid who had routinely bullied me. The bully's gratitude was colored with shame, naturally, and my (character's) mercy was devastating to the bully's self-image. I returned to this theme time and again, never tiring of it, deriving great pleasure from the construction of these improbable reversals.

With my brother gone, the room we had shared seemed larger, more spacious and luxurious than before. I'd lived my entire life there, deferring without complaint to my brother's wishes on all matters of decoration, layout, music, and lighting. He'd made it clear that I was a squatter in his room, an assertion I'd never thought to question. Just before he left, he'd warned me with bared teeth, frightening as only older brothers can be, not to touch a thing. In case he came back. If I were to change anything, Francisco said, he'd know.

"How?" I asked. "How will you know?"

He threw an arm around me then, flexing it tight around my neck with the kind of casual brutality he often directed at me. I felt my face turning red; I was helpless. At ten and eighteen, we were essentially two different species. I wouldn't see him again until we were both adults, fully grown men capable of real violence. I suppose if I'd known this, I might have tried to appreciate the moment, but instead I remained defiant, gasping for breath and managing to ask one more time, "Yeah, but how will you know?"

Francisco, or versions of him, appeared in many of my early works.

I took note of what my mother had said about a woman's pride, and when I was alone with my father I decided to ask him about it. I wasn't sure if I'd got the full nuance, but I relayed the conversation with my mother as well as I could, concluding with the last bit about the police.

"She said that?" he asked.

I nodded, and my father, instead of shedding any light on the situation, just laughed. It was a hearty, surprising laugh, with tears pressing from the corners of his eyes.

"What?" I asked. "What did I say?" But he wouldn't answer me, and, finally, when he'd regained his composure, he gave me a big hug.

"Your mother is a dangerous woman," he said, and I knew enough to understand that when he said "dangerous" he meant it as a compliment.

Meanwhile, Luz drew her curtains and rarely left the house. Alejandro never came back.

A few months later, we learned that Luz was planning to travel to the United States, to visit a cousin of hers in Florida. This was in June, when the strike was under way, and my parents were beginning to feel the stress most acutely. We'd seen little of

Luz in the weeks since Alejandro's visit, but she was often mentioned, always in the same pitying tone. Inevitably, the conversation veered back to my mother's comment about the police, and
my father would tease her about it, until they laughed together.
I'd chuckle, too, so as not to be left out.

Luz's trip couldn't have been more perfectly timed. It was
scheduled for July, three or four weeks before Francisco's birthday, the first he would be spending abroad. My mother wanted to
send Francisco a gift, just a token, so that he'd know we were
thinking of him. After some deliberation, she bought him a dark-
blue necktie embroidered with the logo of the National Library.
My father approved, said it would help him get a good job. It was
a joke, really; we knew that Francisco wasn't interested in the
sort of job where he might need a necktie. The three of us signed
a card; separately, my father wrote a long letter, and the whole
thing was wrapped and sealed and ready to go. Naturally, there
was no talk of trusting our local postal service for this, or for
anything, really. We would ask Luz to take it for us and drop it in
an American mailbox. Perhaps, my mother said, Luz could even
hand-deliver it, should her itinerary include a jaunt through Alabama, and, upon her return, report back—tell us how she'd found
Francisco, what she thought of his prospects in the U.S.

One Sunday afternoon, my mother and I crossed the street
and knocked on Luz's door. She seemed surprised to see us, a
little embarrassed, but beckoned us into the house all the same.
Immediately, we encountered a problem: there wasn't anywhere
to sit. Sometime in the previous months, much of the furniture
had been moved out, and the rooms, half empty now, seemed
lonely and sad. Of the chairs that remained, no two faced each
other. We strolled through to the living room, where a small television set rested awkwardly on a wooden chair. Luz was thinner
than I remembered her, subdued; she seemed to have staggered
recklessly toward old age, as if trying to make up in a matter of

weeks the ten years that separated her from Alejandro's new lover. Her hair had faded to a stringy yellowing gray—she'd stopped dyeing it, my mother explained later—and her skin had taken on a similarly unhealthy pallor. Her eyes, even in the dim light, were glassy and unfocussed. Luz asked me to put the television on the floor.

"Where?" I asked.

"Oh, Nelson," she said. "Anywhere."

I placed it next to the chair, and Luz indicated that I should sit on it. I looked at my mother for reassurance. She nodded, and so the three of us sat, forming a not quite intimate circle.

Luz and my mother went through the protocols of a civilized visit: inoffensive questions, anodyne chitchat, the usual phrases and gestures intended to fill up space rather than convey meaning. It occurred to me as I listened that my mother and Luz were not close. They spoke without much fluency about a minor universe of events that affected neither of them: the vagaries of neighborhood life, people they both knew but didn't much care about. My mother seemed determined not to speak of our family, of my father, my brother, or even me. It was excessive decorum, as if the very mention of family might be insulting to our grieving hostess. The strain to keep the words coming was noticeable, and I wondered how long it would be necessary to maintain this charade before coming to the point of the visit, Francisco's gift. Ten minutes? Twenty? An entire hour?

Luz, as she spoke, as she listened, scanned the room as if looking for someone who was not there. The easy assumption would have been that the someone was Alejandro, but I understood instinctively that this wasn't the case. There were many people in the room with us, it seemed, a wide variety of people my mother and I could not see: principally, the players in Luz's life, those who'd known her at various stages of childhood, adolescence, and adulthood, at moments of joy, of whimsy, of expectation. Of anxiety and fear. It seemed to me that Luz was wondering, How did I get to this place? How did this happen? Or perhaps, What are all these people doing in my house, and what must they think of me now? And it was all she could do not to ask these questions aloud. She was gritting her teeth, forcing her way through a conversation with my mother, an artificial exchange about nothing at all, hoping soon to return to her more important, unfinished dialogue with this other, floating gallery of observers. This was my theory, of course. Luz's eyes drifted to the near distance, to the seemingly empty space just behind us and around us. To the window, to the floor, to the ceiling.

At a certain point, my mother took Francisco's festively wrapped package from her purse. She passed it to Luz, who accepted it without saying much. I'd lost track of the words being exchanged, was focussing instead on the minute shifts in Luz's facial expressions: a sharpening of the creases at the edges of her mouth, or her eyes fluttering closed. My mother explained that the gift was for Francisco, that it was his birthday, that we hated to ask the favor but we hoped it wouldn't be a problem. Could she take it with her?

Luz sat, shoulders slouched, neck curling downward. The gift was in her lap, and by the tired look in her eyes you might have thought that it weighed a great deal.

I'm not sure how I knew, but I did: she was going to say no.

"What is it?" Luz said.

My mother smiled innocently; she didn't yet understand what was happening.

"A necktie."

Luz's eyes were wandering again, following a dust mote, or the disappearing image of an old friend. She was ashamed to be seen this way, and she was going to take it out on us.

"Are you well?" Luz asked.

"We are," my mother said. "We miss Francisco, of course, but we're well."

"And the strike?"

At the mention of it, my mother's expression darkened. She and my father were walking the picket line five days a week, exhausting in and of itself, and, of course, there was the constant threat of violence, from the police, from the more radical elements within their own syndicate. My parents talked about it every night, oblique references at the dinner table, and later, as I fell asleep, I heard the worried hum of voices drifting from their bedroom.

"We're getting by," my mother answered. "God willing, it'll be over soon."

Luz nodded, and reached over to the coffee table. She pulled open a drawer and took out a letter opener. We watched, not knowing exactly what she was after, but she spoke the whole time, carrying on a sort of conversation with herself, a monologue about the declining state of morals in the nation, about a new, aimless generation, and its startling lack of respect for the rules of society as they'd been handed down since the time when we were a colony of the Spanish Empire. A colony? The Empire? I looked toward my mother for help, but she was no less confused than me. There was sadness in Luz's tone, a defeated breathiness, as if the words themselves were part of a whispered prayer or lament she would've preferred not to share with us. At the same time, her hands moved with an efficiency completely at odds with her speech: she held the package now, and, without pausing in her discourse, used the letter opener to cut the red bow my mother had tied. It fell unceremoniously to the dusty floor.

"Oh!" my mother said.

It was as if Luz had cut her.

Then, with the edge of the opener, she peeled back the clear tape my mother had stuck to the wrapping. The paper slipped to the floor, landing at Luz's feet. She pushed it away with the edge of her shoe. Her hands kept moving.

"People these days can't be trusted. So much has changed from when I was a girl. We knew our neighbors—our town was small. When a boy came around, my father would ask who his parents were, and this was all he and my mother needed to know. If they didn't approve of his lineage, they'd send the servant out to have a talk with him. To shoo him away, you understand. I watched everything from my window. I was very pretty then."

"I'm sure you were," my mother said, her voice breaking, unable to hide the concern she felt for Francisco's gift. The box was open now, the white tissue paper was out, ripped in places, and the tie dangled from Luz's knee, its tip just grazing the floor. Luz opened the card we'd all signed, and spread my father's letter on her lap, squinting at the handwriting as if decoding a secret message.

"Is there something wrong?" my mother asked.

Luz didn't answer. Instead, she held the necktie up with one hand, and ran her thumb and forefinger carefully along the seam, lightly palpating the length of the fabric. She'd already checked the box and its lining. What was she looking for?

My mother watched in horror. "What are you doing? Is there a problem?"

"Where are your people from?" Luz asked.

"I'm sorry?"

"The north, the south, the center? The mountains, the jungle? How well do we know each other, really, Monica? Do I know what you do? What your family does? What about that union you belong to, the one making trouble downtown? Did you expect me to get on a flight to America with a package I hadn't bothered to check? What if there were drugs inside? What if there was *cocaine*?"

My mother was stunned. Absolutely immobilized.

"Am I supposed to rot in an American prison because your impoverished family is willing to gamble with my life?"

Luz's eyes were open wide, and she held them that way, staring at us.

My mother stood abruptly, snatching the necktie and my father's letter from Luz's hands. I ducked to grab the box, the wrapping paper, and the bow, but my mother took me by the arm. Her face was a bright and unnatural shade of red.

"Leave it."

Luz reverted now, drawn back into that lonely place she'd been trapped in for months. "Did I say something wrong?" she asked, but the question wasn't addressed to us.

The empty rooms were a blur as we raced toward the street. On our way out, I managed to kick over a chair, and I knew by my mother's expression that she didn't mind at all.

The day passed and my mother was in a foul, toxic mood. The neighborhood, always so eager to gossip, was now gossiping about us. We'd tried to send contraband to America, people were saying. Drugs. Tried to take advantage of an unsuspecting elderly woman with a broken heart.

These were the kinds of humiliations we put up with for Francisco's sake. There were others. Francisco left Birmingham that October, and only later did we find out why: one afternoon Marisa skipped her S.A.T. prep class, and Mrs. Villanueva came home early to find them groping in the downstairs television room. For me, the most astonishing aspect of the story was undoubtedly the idea that the Villanuevas had a downstairs television room. The rest of the anecdote—even the titillating hint of sex—hardly registered next to this remarkable detail. Mrs. Villanueva gave my brother an hour to pack his things. By the time her husband got home, Francisco had already been dropped off at his friend Jai's house, forever banished from the Villanuevas' ordered American lives.

For months after he'd moved on, we continued to wire money to the Villanuevas to pay off our debt. My father sent several long letters to his old friend Julio, apologizing for his son's behavior, but these went unanswered, and, eventually, he gave up trying to make things right. The friendship was never repaired, of course, but, then, how could it be? The two men had met in the nineteen-seventies and had seen each other only twice in the intervening years. The mutual affection they felt was an almost entirely theoretical construct, based on memories of long-ago shared experiences—not unlike what I felt toward my brother by then, I suppose. Part fading recollections, part faith.

Francisco never got around to applying to college, as my parents had hoped he would. He moved briefly to Knoxville, where his friend Leon had enrolled at the University of Tennessee. But soon after that we got a letter from St. Louis (along with a photo of the Arch), and then one from Kansas City (with a picture taken in the parking lot of a rustic barbecue joint). Francisco's constant movement made it difficult for my parents to get their citizenship paperwork going, though at some point, I imagine, they must have told him what their plan was and how desperate our situation was becoming. Maybe he didn't understand. Or maybe it was inconvenient for him to think about. Maybe what he wanted most of all was to forget where he'd come from, to leave those troubles and stunted dreams behind and become what his passport had always said he was: an American.

People talk a lot these days about virtual reality, second lives, digital avatars. It's a concept I'm fully conversant with, of course. Even with no technical expertise or much interest in computers, I understand it all perfectly; if not the engineering, then the emotional content behind these so-called advances seems absolutely intuitive to me. I'll say it plainly: I spent my adolescence preparing for and eventually giving myself over to an imagined life. While my parents waited in line at the American Embassy, learning all the relevant statutes and regulations to insure my passage, I placed myself beside my brother in each of his pictures. I followed him on his journey across America, trying always to forget where I really was.

He repaired bicycles in suburban Detroit; worked as a greeter at a Wal-Mart in Dubuque, Iowa; moved furniture in Galveston, Texas; mowed lawns at a golf course outside Santa Fe. At home, I read Kerouac and Faulkner, listened to Michael Jackson and the Beastie Boys, studied curious American customs like Halloween, Thanksgiving, and the Super Bowl. I formulated opinions on America's multiple national dilemmas, which seemed thrillingly, beautifully frivolous: gays in the military, a President in trouble for a blow job.

My brother turned twenty-one in Reno, Nevada, gambling away a meagre paycheck he'd earned busing tables at a chain Italian restaurant. It could be said that he was happy. This was 1989. He was going by Frank now, and had shed whatever Southern accent he might have picked up in those first few months as a putative member of the Villanueva household.

Six months passed, and we learned that he had abandoned water-skiing for snow skiing; he was working at a ski resort in the Rockies, and sent photos, panoramic shots of the light mirroring brilliantly off the white snowpack. It was intriguing and absolutely foreign territory. He spent a page describing the snow—dry snow, wet snow, artificial snow, powder—and I learned that people can get sunburned in winter from all the reflected light. I never would have guessed this to be true, though in hindsight it seemed fairly obvious, and this alone was enough to depress me. What else was obvious to everyone but me? What other lessons, I wondered, was I being deprived of even now?

In school, my favorite subject was geography. Not just mine, it should be said. I doubt any generation of young people has ever looked at a world map with such a powerful mixture of longing and anxiety; we were like inmates being tempted with potential escape routes. Even our teacher must have felt it: when he took the map from the supply closet and tacked it to the blackboard, there was an audible sigh from the class. We were mesmerized by the possibilities; we assumed every country was more prosperous than ours, safer than ours, and at this scale they all seemed tantalizingly near. The atlas was passed around like pornography, and if you had the chance to sit alone with it for a few moments you counted yourself lucky. When confronted with a map of the United States, in my mind I placed dots across the continent, points to mark where my brother had lived and the various towns he'd passed through on his way to other places.

Of course, I wasn't the only one with family abroad; these were the days when everyone was trying to leave. Our older brothers applied for scholarships in fields they didn't even like, just for the chance to overstay their visas in cold and isolated northern cities. Our sisters were married off to tourists or were shipped to Europe to work as nannies. We were a nation busy inventing French great-grandparents, falsifying Spanish paperwork, bribing notaries for counterfeit birth certificates from Slavic countries that were hardly better off than we were. Genealogies were examined in great detail—was there an ancestor to exploit, anyone with an odd, foreign-sounding last name? A Nazi war criminal in your family's dark past? What luck! Pack your bags, kids—we're going to Germany! This was simply the spirit of the times. The Japanese kids headed back to Tokyo, the Jewish kids to Israel. A senile Portuguese shut-in who hadn't spoken a coherent sentence in fifteen years was dusted off and taken to petition the Embassy; suddenly all his grandchildren were moving to Lisbon.

The state-employee strike didn't last forever. It ended, as everything did in those days, with an uneasy and temporary resolution: across-the-board pay cuts but no immediate layoffs, a surfeit of mistrust and rancor on all sides. My father was there at the climactic march, when a bank in the old center was burned by government infiltrators and dozens of protesters were beaten and jailed. He was gassed and shot at with rubber bullets, and he, like tens of thousands of others, fled the violence like a madman, running at full speed through the chaotic streets of the capital, a wet rag tied across his nose and mouth. It was, he told me later, the moment he realized he wasn't young anymore.

The dreaded election came and went; the crisis deepened. The new President privatized everything, selling the state off piece by piece and dividing the profits among his friends. The truce that had been reached at the end of the strike was broken, and the next year thousands of workers, including my mother, were suddenly laid off. She was unemployed for months. Prices shot up, the currency crashed, the violence spread, and our world became very small and very precarious. We waited in breadlines, carrying impossibly large stacks of banknotes, which had become a requirement for even the tiniest transaction. People spoke less; strangers distrusted one another. The streets, even during morning rush, had a perverse emptiness to them. We listened to the radio in the dark and emerged each morning fearful to discover what tragedy had befallen us in the night.

These emotions are quite beside the point now, like an artifact looted from an ancient grave, an oddly shaped tool whose utility no one can quite decipher. But back then, walking through the gray, shuddering city, I thought about my brother all the time. I was ten, I was eleven, unfree but hopeful; I was thirteen, I was fourteen, and my brother had escaped. Fifteen, sixteen: waiting for something to happen, reading obsessively about a place I would never see for myself, in a language I would never actually need. Twenty, twenty-one: small failures, each humiliation a revelation, further proof that my real life was elsewhere. Twenty-five, twenty-six: a dawning awareness that my condition as a citizen of the Third World was terminal.

And Francisco lived through none of this. As punishment, I set about trying to forget him: the sound of his laughter, his height relative to mine, the content of the conversations we'd had after the lights went out but before we fell asleep.

I never managed it, of course.

THE TRAIN
OF THEIR DEPARTURE

DAVID BEZMOZGIS

In the spring of 1976, before the start of their affair, before he became her husband, before she knew anything about him, Polina had noticed Alec in one or another of the V.E.F. buildings, always looking vaguely, childishly amused.

"If my Papatchka ran the factory, maybe I'd also go around grinning like a defective," Marina Kirilovna had said to Polina when Alec appeared in the technology department.

Marina Kirilovna occupied the desk beside Polina's at the radio factory. In her mid-forties and a widow twice over, Marina Kirilovna treated men only with varying degrees of contempt. They were sluggards, buffoons, dimwits, liars, brutes, and—without exception—drunks. The tragedy was that women were saddled with them and, for the most part, accepted this state of affairs. It was as though they had ingested the Russian saying "If he doesn't beat you, he doesn't love you" with their mothers' milk. As for her own departed husbands, Marina Kirilovna liked to say that the only joy she'd got out of living with them had been outliving them.

Later, when Marina Kirilovna began to suspect Polina's involvement with Alec, she admonished her.

"Not that it's my business, but even if your husband is no prize at least he's a man."

"It isn't your business," Polina said.

"Just know that no good can come of it. Believe me, I'm not blind. I see him skipping around like a boy with a butterfly net. And if you think that this business will lead to a promotion, then half the women at the factory are eligible for it."

At the word "promotion," Polina almost laughed. The suggestion of some ulterior motive for the affair, particularly ambition, was risible in a way that the widow could not have imagined. First, the mere idea of ambition in the factory was ludicrous. Thousands of people worked there, and—with the exception of the Party members—none of them had a salary worth envying. But, beyond that, if anything had led her to consider Alec's overtures it was her husband's ambition—insistent, petty, and bureaucratic. In the evenings she was oppressed by his plots and machinations for advancement, and on the weekends she was bored and embarrassed by his behavior at dinners with those whom he described as "men of influence." By comparison, Alec was the least ambitious man she had ever met.

Much later, when Polina looked back on her younger self, the girl who at twenty-one had allowed Maxim to dictate the terms of her life, she understood that she had made a mistake. But she also understood that, at the time, she had been incapable of acting differently. In her life she had never had a great love. Her friends had descended into infatuations; she never did. Some people's conceptions of what was available to them coincided with what was actually available to them; other people's conceptions did not. There were men whom she found more engaging than Maxim, but they tended not to pursue her. They found her too serious. She knew that she was pretty enough to attract them, but she also knew that there were many pretty girls who fawned and laughed more easily. What put those men off drew Maxim to her.

They met at a party in her friend's dormitory room. Polina was sitting and talking to one of her friend's roommates when she turned her head and saw Maxim standing beside her. Maybe she smiled at him; maybe she didn't. As if reading from the pages of a courtship manual, Maxim asked if she would care for a drink of any kind. Polina couldn't think of a reason to decline, so he returned with a glass of lemon soda and installed himself at her side for the rest of the evening. He inquired after her name, where she lived, what she was studying, her opinion of her program, her career aspirations. Having established these fundamentals, he proceeded to cultural and recreational interests: movies, books, ballet, music, figure skating, volleyball, rhythmic gymnastics. To be polite, Polina answered his questions. She had no interest in him but did wonder if his robotic approach was a consequence of nervousness or if it was simply the way he was. She was still unsure when Maxim asked to see her again. Because she didn't want to say no, she said yes. She then forgot all about him until he appeared one evening at her door. Her mother told her that she had a gentleman caller, and she couldn't imagine who it might be until she saw him waiting there. Worse still, she felt panicked because she couldn't remember his name. But she experienced her first affectionate feeling for him when he rescued her by reintroducing himself. He appeared to do this not because he inferred that she had forgotten his name but because he believed that a person was well advised to repeat his name upon meeting someone for only the second time.

That night, he took her to see a figure-skating competition at the Palace of Sports. He recalled, he said, that she had expressed an interest in figure skating. She recalled having expressed only the same generic interest in figure skating as in volleyball and rhythmic gymnastics. But she was aware that tickets to the figure-skating competition were scarce, and even though the seats Maxim had got were among the worst in the building, she suspected that he had paid for them dearly in one way or another. After the competition, he took her to a café. He opened the door for her and held her chair. He did everything with precision and earnestness. At some point in his life, someone had taken him aside and informed him that, in the civilized precincts of planet Earth, there existed certain protocols. At some point in life, everyone heard a variation of this speech, but not everyone took it to heart. Maxim had. In Polina he seemed to recognize that he had found someone with an equal respect for protocols.

Polina didn't encourage him but he didn't require encouragement. He courted her with the measured discipline of a person climbing a long flight of stairs. There was something endearing about Maxim's doggedness, as, step by step, he insinuated himself into her life. He asked to be introduced to her parents. He brought flowers and a bottle of cognac. He also brought a gift for her younger sister, Nadja, and subsequently invited her along on outings. She was then only twelve or thirteen. They went to the zoo. He hired a boat and rowed them on the Lielupe River. Nadja teased him in a playful way. In the boat, she hopped up and down in the bow, leaned over the edge and made a theatrical speech about the cruel, cruel world and the weedy river's irresistible call.

"I'm going to do it, Maxim," she said. "Are you going to jump in and save me?"

"Don't be silly," Maxim said.

"I'm going to do it," Nadja said.

"Polina," Maxim appealed.

"Nadja," Polina cautioned.

"Oh, it's all just too much for a delicate girl to bear," Nadja said, and flopped over the side.

The green water closed over her like a curtain. Polina looked back at Maxim with apology and exasperation. They watched the water and waited for Nadja to part the curtain again. Polina stole glimpses at Maxim. Just when he seemed on the brink of plunging in, Nadja thrashed to the surface, gasped for help, and then disappeared again. Maxim waited a few moments longer and then, stalwartly, as if complying with an order, removed his shoes and jumped in after her. A lesser man, Polina thought, would have let Nadja flounder until she grew bored. Another kind of man, however, would have embraced the game.

After some requisite diving and searching, Maxim found Nadja peeking out from under the keel. When they floated back into view, Nadja had her head tipped back and one arm around Maxim's neck. Her free arm swayed dramatically above her. "My hero," she said, sighing, her eyes half closed. Maxim endured the performance with the consummate face of the adult: distaste subjugated to obligation.

Reason, or its pale ambassador convention, ruled Polina and Maxim's time together. It extended to everything, including sex. Before Maxim, Polina had had three encounters that had approached but not crossed the line. On two of those occasions she had halted things before they went too far. The other time, at a Komsomol retreat, she had been willing but, at the critical moment, another couple had entered the barn and started climbing to the hayloft.

Polina couldn't say that she was eager to take this next and inevitable step with Maxim, but she did wonder when he would grant himself the license to do it. During their gropings and fumblings she felt like a spectator, watching Maxim as he denied himself for the sake of her honor. These preliminary bouts always ended with Maxim apologizing for the liberties he had taken. Polina either pardoned his liberties or said nothing at all. Afterward they would sit or lie together on a bench in the public gardens, or on the embankment of the river in Riga's industrial quarter, or in the cold, shadowy entrances to public buildings, and share momentous and ostensibly soulful silences. Eventually, Maxim interrupted a bout of groping to ask Polina for her opinion and her permission. She consented with a simple "All right," and waited as Maxim scrupulously tore the edge from the yellow paper wrapper she had heard about but never actually seen. Inexpertly, he put the rubber on himself and then spat on his hand and pawed Polina clumsily in preparation. Polina shifted her weight from one hip to the other so as to help him and then put her hands on his chest to resist his weight. She said, "Careful," because she wasn't quite ready and she didn't know how to explain that to him. It was the only word that passed between them. When it was over, Maxim acted as if something significant had transpired, and Polina didn't contradict him.

From then on, they repeated the act with some regularity. Polina saw that Maxim liked it and wanted it, so she obliged him. What they did they did with no variation. For Polina, intercourse began when Maxim tore the edge from the yellow paper wrapper. She assumed that it was the same for everyone until she overheard other girls speaking about their experiences with their mainly drunken boyfriends. That was when she learned that most men went to great lengths to avoid having to deal with the contents of the yellow wrapper, and that, despite the risks, most women relented. They rationalized their actions by maligning the quality of Soviet condoms, which were known to rupture or slide off. It made little sense, they said, to put your faith in something so unreliable. In Polina's experience, the condoms had never ruptured or slid off. She also thought that the alternative measures the women cited—hot water, wine vinegar, urine—sounded dubious, but several weeks later, when Polina and Maxim were alone in Polina's apartment, her parents having gone with Nadja to attend a choral recital, and Maxim found that he did not have any condoms, Polina insisted that they do it anyway.

It was not something she had planned in advance, but neither was it entirely spontaneous. It was the first time she had ever challenged Maxim's authority, and she was as aroused by the prospect of luring him into temptation as by the recklessness of what they were doing. Maxim was sitting up on his knees when she told him what she wanted, and he wavered for a few seconds, a look of fear and doubt on his face, before Polina reached out and took him into her. After that, the fear and doubt were replaced by something insular and fierce. Shortly before it ended, Polina hissed in Maxim's ear that she wanted him to do it inside her. It was a sentence that had been circling malevolently in her head from the moment she had insisted that they have sex. As she said it, she knew it couldn't have had less to do with a desire for children. And as soon as Maxim finished, Polina slid out from under him and went to the kitchen for a basin and a purple, thin-necked vase. She returned to the bedroom, set the basin in the middle of the floor, and urinated. Carefully, under Maxim's silent gaze, she transferred the urine from the basin into the vase, spilling several drops onto the floorboards. She then lay down, arched her pelvis, and instructed Maxim to pour the urine into her. What they were doing was disgusting and sordid, and Maxim avoided Polina's eyes as he carried out her instructions. He was pliable then in a way that he had never been before and would never be again. She had made him complicit in something depraved, and she expected, in some inchoate way, that she would eventually be punished for this. Later, when her punishment was meted out, Maxim never once blamed her for what she knew was entirely her fault.

The punishment was administered by a taciturn doctor in a green-walled hospital clinic. The doctor, a woman, walked into the surgery and parted Polina's knees without quite looking at her. She offered no explanation of what she intended to do or when she intended to do it. She said nothing at all until a nurse came in, at which point she berated her for not having already prepared and sterilized the patient.

Like a magician's assistant, Polina felt as if she had been split in two. The doctor and the nurse pretended that her top half didn't exist and dealt only with her bottom half. Polina relinquished it to them. She concentrated on her top half, and tried to retain this focus in spite of the pain, refusing to cry out, as though what was happening below were incidental and remote. She imagined that the pain was coming at her from a vast distance, from the unseen bottom of a gorge.

When they were finished, Polina was transferred onto a gurney. She was rolled out into the hallway and left there, once again, without explanation. Polina thought that she could still feel blood seeping. The loss of blood, the pain, and the cold metal of the gurney chilled her and she started to shiver. She was exhausted and drained, too weak to call out, and yet the tremors became so violent that her gurney creaked from side to side on its rubber wheels. Time and again, people rushed by and ignored her. When she saw her doctor hurrying past, she reached out and caught her by the arm. Through chattering teeth, she told her that she was cold, that she wanted a sheet for her gurney.

"How old are you?" the doctor asked.

"Twenty-one," Polina said.

"You're not a child. Pull yourself together," the doctor said.

"Please, is there a sheet?" Polina asked.

"Who are you to make demands? You don't like it here, don't fuck so much next time."

When they released her that evening, Maxim was waiting for her outside. She wasn't really in any condition to take the bus by herself, so, in a way, she was grateful to have someone to help her. She only wished it were someone else. Who, exactly, she couldn't have said, even a stranger, anyone but Maxim. She saw him through the square, wire-reinforced windows of the hospital doors. He was at the bottom of the stone steps, bent slightly at the waist, listening to another young man, who was smoking and talking. When Polina opened the door, Maxim looked up and mounted the steps as if to help her with it. But by the time he reached the top the door was already swinging shut behind her. He looked lost for a moment. Polina expected him to offer her his arm. She looked forward to refusing him. Only he didn't offer his arm. He also didn't do or say any of the unwelcome things she expected him to do or say, which, curiously, irritated her even more. She looked at him and saw penitence and relief vying for dominion in his face.

"Did you happen to see a kind of chubby girl in a blue cloud-patterned dress in there?" the young man with the cigarette asked when Polina and Maxim reached the bottom of the steps.

"I don't think so," Polina said.

"Raisa is her name. She has shortish brown hair and sort of a dimple in her chin."

"I really don't know," Polina said.

"Her girlfriend brought her in this morning. That's a long time. Let me ask you, and please be honest: What do you think, should I keep waiting?" he said.

Polina allowed Maxim to escort her home on the bus. They walked the two blocks from the bus stop to her building without speaking. It was only when he stopped to say goodbye that Maxim delivered his line. He had employed it many times in the discussions that had led to the abortion.

"It's better for our future," Maxim said.

The following day, Maxim brought her carnations and inquired after her well-being. Several days later, he brought carnations again. After a week, he returned with more carnations, this time on account of the fact that he had, before the abortion, established a habit of bringing her flowers once a week. He presented these to Polina in such a way as to communicate that he believed things had returned to normal. Though she had an indefinable urge to protest, she admitted that things had indeed returned to normal. She couldn't justify her lingering resentment. Her experience at the clinic had been horrid, but she'd had no reason to suppose that it would be otherwise. Almost everyone she knew had had at least one abortion. Some had gone to the hospital; others, hoping to conceal the pregnancy from their parents, had had their boyfriends pay twenty-five rubles and submitted to the procedure at the apartment of a nurse or a doctor. Not a few of them had ended up in the hospital anyway, with infections and complications. Compared with these, her ordeal hardly ranked.

In their own way, Polina and Maxim had kept the abortion to themselves. Maxim had given a tin of caviar to the doctor at the regional polyclinic who had referred Polina to the hospital. It was understood that the doctor wouldn't say anything to Polina's parents. Polina also didn't share the information with her sister. Which was why, since they knew nothing, both her mother and her sister made a point of commenting on Maxim's extraordinary romantic display.

"Three bouquets in one week. It's a very refined and thoughtful gesture," Polina's mother said.

"He's probably going to propose," Nadja said.

Maxim had already talked seriously about marriage. But he'd refrained from making a formal proposal, because they were at a crucial point in their lives. They would both have to pass their exams and, ideally, finish near the top of their respective classes. After that, Maxim would have to perform his military service. He would be gone for two months and would then be obliged to write another exam. If he passed the exam, he would get his shoulder bars, become a reserve lieutenant, and be free to pursue a normal civilian life. If he failed, he would be conscripted into the Army for two years. It was rare for people to fail, but to make a significant life decision with this question unresolved would be rash. Finally, neither of them yet knew where they would be posted for work. There were no guarantees that they would both secure positions in Riga or, failing Riga, that they would secure positions in close proximity to each other. So they agreed to wait.

On the day of her graduation ceremony, Polina sat with her parents and Nadja under the glass roof of the university's great hall. According to custom, her father held a bouquet of flowers—white, fragrant calla lilies. Polina's hair, freshly shampooed and styled by her mother, shone brilliantly, as if radiating intellectual light. She wore a new dress of luminous green cloth—the material purchased by her mother and then sewn by a seamstress after a French pattern. Polina was the first person in the family to receive a university degree. Anything her father had learned after eight years of primary school had come courtesy of the Soviet Navy. Her mother had grown up in a small Byelorussian town where the pursuit of higher education was rare for anyone, and particularly for women. So when Polina heard her name called, she rose from her chair and felt herself propelled to the stage as if by the cumulative force of her parents' dreams.

In the evening, Polina joined her classmates for a party at the Café Riga in the old city. All over town, graduates were dancing and toasting the end of their student days. A number of Polina's classmates had brought their instruments and played the songs of the Beatles, Raymond Pauls, and Domenico Modugno. Glasses of champagne were circulated, and they all dropped the diamond-shaped lapel pins they'd been awarded into them, then downed the contents in one swallow, leaving the shiny blue enamel glinting between their teeth. At around ten o'clock, Maxim left his class's party and joined Polina at the Café Riga. When she spotted him in the crowd, she was surprised by how glad she was to see him. A warm, proprietary feeling bloomed inside her. This man, blinking through the haze of cigarette smoke, intently searching the room for her, rubbing absently at the scar above his eyebrow where, when he was a boy, a schoolmate had hit him with a badminton racquet—this was her man. Out of the many, he was hers, and this simple recognition was enough to endear him to her. Flushed with optimism, alcohol, and affection, Polina fell into his arms and swept him onto the dance floor. Her classmates offered them a steady flow of champagne, vodka, and wine. Before long, Maxim forgot his usual reserve, loosened his tie, and danced with uninhibited, clumsy exuberance to the band's rendition of the Beatles' "Get Back."

At dawn, as they weaved together along the cobblestones of the old city, Maxim proposed and Polina accepted. Their future seemed as assured as a future could be. Like Polina, Maxim had scored well on his exams and had his choice of prestigious factories. She had a job waiting for her at V.E.F., and he would take a position at the highly regarded Popov Radiotechnika. They would marry, move in with his parents, file a request with the municipal housing authority for a separate apartment, and start a family. They would embark upon productive and satisfying adult lives.

For Alec, Polina had been like the still point at the center of a gyre. He'd seen her, day after day, at her desk in the technology department, poised and delicate as a china figurine. Beside her was a stern old matron. Every time Alec thought to approach Polina, the matron was there, discouraging him with castrating looks. For at least a month he contemplated ways to breach this system of defense. At first, he wanted only a few words with Polina, just to see if he could elicit a smile. That was all. Nothing more. Just for a start.

Finally, one afternoon, as Polina prepared to leave work, her sentinel vacated her post and Alec approached, accompanied by his brother, Karl.

"My brother and I are going out to seek adventure. We require the company of a responsible person to make sure that we do not go to excesses."

"What does that have to do with me?"

"You have a kind and responsible face."

"So does Lenin."

"True. But Lenin is unavailable. And, at the risk of sounding unpatriotic, I am sure we would prefer your company."

She said little that evening; she let him entertain her. After she finished her drink, she discreetly checked her watch and rose to say goodbye.

"You can't leave yet," Alec said.

"I can't?" Polina asked, pausing, as if allowing that there might be substance to Alec's words.

She stood a moment and regarded him, waiting for him to give birth to the reason. Alec looked up at her from his place at the round café table, hardly big enough to accommodate their glasses and ashtray.

"You see," Karl said, "my brother can't bear to have a woman leave until she's confessed that she thinks he's the sexiest, most desirable man on earth."

"Do many women say that?" Polina asked.

"Surprisingly," Karl said.

"Or not," Alec offered.

"So this is the reason I can't leave?"

"Only if you think it's a good reason," Alec said.

"Honestly speaking, I don't," Polina said.

"Then it isn't."

"So what is?"

"There are many. Very important ones. To list them all would take some time. Please sit and I'll buy you another drink."

"Your reason to stay is to hear the reasons to stay?" Polina asked.

"Not good enough?"

•

She went home that night, but Alec perceived an opening. Weathering the glares of Marina Kirilovna, he made a habit of stopping in at the technology department to say hello. And not long after the evening with Karl, on the day of the annual Readiness for Labor and Defense Exercises, Alec finagled his way into Polina's group. The testing was done according to department, but Alec, in part because of his father's position but mainly on account of his own gregariousness, moved fluidly throughout the plant. It raised no eyebrows when his name was included with those of the technology department. Broadly speaking, nobody cared about any of the official and procedural events. At meetings, people sat, stood, and spoke at the requisite times, for the requisite lengths, employing the requisite phrases. Celebrate the Workers on the anniversary of the Revolution? Why not? Honor the Red Army on Red Army Day? Who could object? Either was a good excuse to avoid work. Lenin's birthday? Stalin's first tooth? Brezhnev's colonoscopy? Each merited a drink, a few snacks, and maybe a slice of cake. So, too, the Labor and Defense Exercises—only with less drinking and without the cake.

The morning of the exercises, Alec took his place among the young workers of the technology and transistor-radio-engineering departments. Dressed in tracksuits and running shoes, they crossed the street from the plant proper to the site of the V.E.F. sports stadium and target range. At the range, .22-calibre rifles awaited them, having been retrieved from the armory. In the stadium, members of V.E.F.'s athletic department—the trainers and coaches of the factory's various sports teams—had already prepared the field for the shot put, the long jump, the high jump, and the short-distance footraces. The trainers and coaches roamed about with their stopwatches, measuring tapes, and lists of the norms that had to be met. Somewhere, presumably in the Kremlin, a physical-culture expert had determined the basal fitness level young Soviet workers needed to possess in order to establish their superiority over the Americans and the Red Chinese. Should these foes come spilling across the borders, they would encounter a daunting column, ready to repulse them with heroic displays of running, jumping, shot-putting, and small-arms fire.

Before the start of the events, Alec sought Polina out and tried to strike a bargain with her. He told her that he wanted to see her again.

"You're seeing me now," Polina said.

"One more evening," Alec said. "All I ask. In the scheme of a life, what's one evening?"

"Depends who you spend it with."

"A valid point," Alec said.

To reach the decision, Alec proposed a contest. If he scored better at the rifle range, Polina would grant him another evening; if she scored better, he would leave her in peace.

"I should warn you in advance," Alec said. "Last summer, in the officers'-training rotation, I placed eighth in marksmanship."

"Out of how many?" Polina asked.

"Sixteen," Alec said.

"That doesn't sound very good," Polina said.

"No, it doesn't," Alec said. "That's the idea."

"I don't understand," Polina said.

"Well, I was specifically trying for eighth place."

"Why is that?"

"In the Army, it's best to be somewhere in the middle. Trouble usually finds those at the bottom or at the top."

"So you mean to say that you're a good shot?"

"Eighth place," Alec said.

"In that case, I should tell you that two years ago at Readiness for Labor and Defense I finished second in my department. They awarded me a ribbon and printed my name in the factory newspaper. My husband pasted a copy of it into an album."

Alec noticed that Polina didn't brandish the word "husband" like a cudgel. She seemed to place the same emphasis on "husband" as she did on "ribbon" and "album." But Alec wasn't fool enough to believe that she'd included the word innocently. In a sense, since she hadn't unequivocally rebuffed him, anything she said about her husband bordered on betrayal. Any information Alec had about him was information that he could use against him. For instance, the fact that he was the kind of man who would save something printed in the factory's idiotic newspaper. Then again it was possible that Polina found such a gesture endearing. She might have been implying that this was precisely the kind of man she wanted. A man unlike Alec, who, in his ironical sophistication, couldn't hope to access or appreciate such pure, sentimental feeling.

But, whatever she meant, she had tacitly agreed to the contest.

Refereeing the shooting range was Volodya Zobodkin, one of the circle of young Jews with whom Alec and Karl played soccer on the beach at Majori. When Volodya distributed the rifles, Alec asked if he could have one with a reliable sight.

"Who are you? Zaitsev?" Volodya said. "This isn't the Battle of Stalingrad. Just aim in the general direction of the target."

"Do you have one with an adjusted sight or not?" Alec persisted.

"What's with you?" Volodya asked. "Have you been drinking? It's not even lunch."

Without much elaboration, Alec told Volodya what he'd arranged. Volodya glanced quickly at Polina, raised an approving eyebrow, and sorted through the stack of rifles for something suitable. He handed a rifle to Alec and then offered to find another, grossly inferior one, for Polina.

"There's one here that practically shoots sideways," Volodya said.

But that wasn't the kind of contest Alec wanted, largely because he sensed that it wasn't the kind of contest Polina would accept. She seemed like the type who respected rules, including rules that dictated the breaking of other rules.

Alec shot first. For all his pride at having placed eighth, he had to admit that he couldn't compare the effort required to achieve mediocrity with that required to achieve excellence.

Everything naturally flowed toward mediocrity; for this, the world needed little in the way of your coöperation. Whereas total incompetence or extreme proficiency demanded some application.

To his credit and mild surprise, Alec shot well. Volodya called for ceasefire and presented Alec with his perforated target—a cluster of holes grouped reasonably close together, reasonably close to the bull's-eye. Even if Polina shot better, Alec felt that he'd performed well enough to warrant the date.

"Is this how you shot in the Army?" Polina asked.

"I've never shot so well in my life," Alec said. "But then I've never had such motivation. As my teachers used to write in my school reports, 'Alec is personable and shows signs of intelligence, but is lazy, inattentive, and lacks all motivation.' "

For the sake of equity, Polina shot with the same rifle that Alec had used. Alec watched her assume the prone position and take careful aim, the rifle's stock pressed correctly against her cheek, its butt in the crook of her shoulder. As she shot, Alec stood behind and slightly to the side and used the opportunity to admire her in a way he hadn't been able to before. Unchallenged, he let his eyes linger on her small lobeless ear, the creases at the corner of her squeezed-shut eye, the strong, sculptured tendons of her neck, and the fine symmetry of her profile. He watched her shoot with steady regularity, squeezing off a shot and then sliding the bolt to chamber the next round. It looked to Alec as if she were shooting to win, which he couldn't but construe as a bad sign.

Later, when things between them were better defined, Polina explained that she had shot the way she did not because she wanted to avoid seeing him again but because she couldn't perform otherwise.

"The graveyards and songbooks are full of people like you," Alec had commented, a fact she had not disputed.

After Polina had finished shooting, Volodya collected her target and compared it with Alec's. Polina had shot well, but there was no doubt that Alec had shot better.

"Imagine that," Alec said, feigning bashfulness.

"Maybe it's not too late," Polina said. "You could still make general."

"There's a disturbing thought," Alec said.

After this, they ran, jumped, hurled the shot put, and killed time until the exercises were finished. As Alec was leaving the stadium, Volodya caught up with him and congratulated him again on his great triumph. He wanted to inform Alec that his shooting performance had earned him more than the date with Polina. It had earned him first place over all. As the top shooter, Volodya explained, Alec would be in line for a commendation as a Stakhanovite marksman, and this would include official recognition at the Young Communists meeting and special mention in the factory newspaper.

"Come on, Vovka," Alec said. "Don't spoil the day for me. Write that I came in eighth and give the honor to some other schmuck."

"Next in line is your girl," Volodya said.

"Perfect," Alec said. "Her husband likes to paste articles from the factory newspaper."

The following week, when Polina's name was printed, an acquaintance spotted it and told Maxim. As before, he asked for a copy. Polina described to Alec how she'd had to watch Maxim paste the silly article into his album. If only he weren't so foolish, Polina had said, which Alec took as no ringing endorsement of his own appeal as a lover. But Polina always spoke plainly. If only Maxim weren't so foolish, she'd said, she would have remained faithful to him, would never have taken up with Alec, and would have lived a regular, quiet life.

Through the summer and fall they carried on the affair. At times they saw each other quite regularly; other times weeks might pass between their meetings. Polina had her marriage to Maxim, and when she wasn't available Alec tried to take what life cast his way. All this time, unbeknownst to them, the train of their departure was approaching, at first distant and barely audible, but gaining momentum with every passing week.

Then, on a blustery afternoon in March, after Karl had announced his intention to seek his fortune in the West and had begun a campaign to persuade Alec to go with him, Polina came to see Alec at his tiny bachelor apartment. Cold, and drenched from the rain, she sat down at the kitchen table and let the water drip from her hair and the hem of her coat.

They exchanged all the questions and answers: Was she sure? Yes. How could she be sure? She was sure. And then the more delicate, unpleasant questions that he couldn't restrain himself from asking: And she was sure? Almost certain. But not certain? As certain as she could be. Did he want her to go into details? To provide a tally? She could do it. It wouldn't take long. No, he didn't want that. They could wait until it was born, then they could run the tests. Was that what he wanted? No, he didn't want that, either. So what did he want?

As gently as he could phrase it, he told her what he wanted.

"I did that once," she said. "I swore I'd never do it again. Not that I believed I'd ever be faced with the choice."

He was unable to think clearly. His mind raced, seeking a way out. It didn't help that in her condition, soaked and chilled, her lips nearly drained of color, Polina cast an image of injured, poignant beauty.

Afterward, he consulted with Karl and there was the agonizing enumeration of options: Did he want to marry her and raise the child? Did he not want to marry her but let her raise the child?

Alone or with her husband? Did he want to join Karl and leave Riga? And what then? Marry her? Bring a pregnant woman along? Or an infant? Emigrating was hard enough without that added burden. Karl knew of happily married women who'd aborted their pregnancies when they received their exit visas. And what were her designs? What did she want? What could be done about her?

Even if men did it all the time, Alec said, he didn't want to leave his child behind. He didn't think he could simply forget. It would always trouble him.

But what alternative did he have if she wouldn't agree to an abortion?

Three days after she'd delivered the news, Polina returned for Alec's answer. The day was cold but clear, and she arrived this time in a very different state. Instead of martyred, clinical. Under her coat she wore a heavy gray woollen turtleneck, whose collar rose to the line of her chin. She matched this with a long navy skirt and high black boots. Except for her face and hands, she was somberly, thickly covered. The clothes seemed chosen to negate her body, to discourage any sensual thoughts, in him or in anyone else. What other reason could there have been for such a shapeless outfit? Not to conceal the pregnancy. The tiny being that had latched on inside her was less than three months old. Alec imagined it having the size and vascular translucence of a gooseberry. He pictured it in the red convection of the womb, growing, thriving, and encroaching on his life. He'd tried to think of it in other, more positive terms, to envision it as a source of happiness. Why not? Many people were very glad to have children. And he wasn't categorically opposed to one day having a child. At some future time, he could see himself surrounded by children, horsing around with them, walking them to school, putting them to bed. But not like this. Like this, he foresaw only a tangle of complications.

And, of all the tangled complications, Alec's mind seized upon the most perplexing. By the third day, he'd seized upon it to the exclusion of everything else. The more he thought about the worst possible scenario—emigrating and leaving a child behind—the more imperative emigration began to feel. He pictured himself conscience-stricken somewhere in the generic West, or, conversely, stranded by his conscience in Riga, unwilling to deny his paternity.

"Screw conscience," Karl had scoffed. "Conscience is the least of your problems. You could get stuck here regardless of your conscience."

By this he meant that if Polina had the child and he was proven to be the father he'd need her written permission to leave the country. She'd have to sign an affidavit stating that she had no material claims on him.

"It goes without saying," Alec declared, "that if I left a child behind I'd send money. Polina would know that."

"She might or she might not," Karl countered.

"She's not vindictive. She'd never cause problems."

"Have you ever stiffed her with a kid before?"

"She's not the type. Of this I'm sure."

"You don't know, and you can't know. There's no telling how a person will react from one day to the next. There's only one way to avoid a problem, and that's not to create it in the first place."

"Well, the problem exists."

"It does and it doesn't," Karl said. "But wait much longer and it will be *finita la commedia*."

"She won't agree to it."

"Is this the first time you've got a woman pregnant?"

"What does that have to do with anything?"

"You charmed your way in—charm your way out."

"Charming in is a lot easier."

93

"Yeah, well, write that on your forehead so you'll remember for next time."

"Anything else?"

"What else? You have to take care of it. I can't do it for you. But, if you haven't got one yourself, I know of a good doctor. Quiet, expert, and clean."

"Rosner?"

"You've used him?"

"Never needed to. Have you?"

"I know him strictly by reputation."

Apart from recommending a doctor, Karl was no help. Alec was left to his own devices. And, with Polina sitting in his kitchen, it occurred to him that life, which he'd treated as a pastime, and which he'd thought he could yet outdistance, had finally caught up with him. And he discovered, much as he'd suspected, that once life caught up with you, you could never quite shake it again. It endeavored to hobble you with greater and greater frequency. How you managed to remain upright became your style, who you were.

Style was the difference between him and Polina. On that March afternoon, he wanted to approach the problem from the side, circle it a few times, until, sidling over with such roundabout movements, the two of them would discover themselves at the destination as though by happenstance.

Polina, meanwhile, wanted to get there directly.

"It was an accident," Alec began. "You wouldn't have planned it this way."

"How could I plan something I thought impossible?"

"But, if you could, would you have planned it like this?"

"No. But what does that matter? It happened. I'm not sorry that it happened. Even if you want me to be," Polina said with controlled defiance.

"I don't want you to be sorry," Alec said. "I want you to be happy. Will having the baby make you happy?"

She didn't answer immediately, but seemed to carefully consider.

"It might."

Gently, Alec tried to enumerate the options he'd hashed out with Karl.

"Would you be happy having the child with Maxim?"

"If this is where you begin," Polina said, "you don't need to say anything else. I have my answer."

"I think you're wrong."

"Do you want me to have the child?"

"No," Alec said.

"So I'm not wrong."

"If that's the only question, then, no, you're not wrong."

"It's the only question that matters," Polina said.

"And about what happens to the child and to you?"

"We'll find our way somehow. We won't be the first."

"Here in Riga?"

"I imagine. Where else?"

"Living with Maxim or on your own?"

"Or, in time, with someone else."

"Yes, there's that, too. Raising my child."

"Biologically."

"That isn't insignificant."

"To whom?"

"To me."

"I'm afraid you can't have it both ways."

"It may also not be insignificant to the child."

"Alec, that is also having it both ways. You can't claim to care for the feelings of the child you want to abort."

There was logic in what she'd said, but it didn't change the fact that Alec felt quite certain that he *could* care for the feelings of the child he wanted to abort. That is, once the child was born.

DAVID BEZMOZGIS

"Polina, I understand what the child means to you," he said. "I understand how you feel about giving it up. Do you believe me?"

"Does it matter?"

"It matters to me. If I could agree to having the child, I would. If I could be a father to it, I would."

"I never asked you to be a father to it."

"So what did you hope I would say?"

"I don't know. Or, rather, I do," Polina said, and laughed dryly. "It wasn't what I hoped you'd say but what I hoped you wouldn't say. That's all."

A stillness of dénouement settled upon her, or she summoned it from within. It looked to Alec as if she'd composed her parting face. Somehow the conversation he'd planned had escaped his control. It wasn't that he'd misled himself by thinking it would be easy. He'd imagined a thorny path that led, in the end, to a favorable resolution. He'd pictured Polina's happiness—gratitude, even—at his proposal. But now, in actuality, he feared that she would leave before he could even make his big redemptive offer. The offer that would recast him radically and heroically, not only in her eyes but in his own.

Sensing that his time was short, he rushed ahead and told her that he was leaving Riga.

He then unfurled his grand plan, like a carpet to a bountiful future. Polina would divorce Maxim. The two of them would marry. An expert doctor would perform the operation with incomparable care in an atmosphere of total privacy. It would be nothing at all like the savagery of the public abortion clinic. No harm would come to her. She would still be able to conceive. Once they settled somewhere, they could try again properly. This was their once-in-a-lifetime opportunity to slip the shackles of the Soviet Union.

"It's all very rosy," Polina said.

"It could be. I think we could make a good life together over there. I truly believe it."

"Don't try so hard, Alec," Polina said. "Next you'll tell me you love me."

With that warning she bracketed a great length of silence, long enough to accommodate everything that had happened or would happen: the abortion clinic, Maxim, Alec's parents, the private doctor, her parents, their spiteful co-workers, the dreadful sunny day when she would sit on a park bench waiting to say goodbye to her sister, and the gauntlet of stifling, overcrowded train compartments that would ultimately deliver them from Riga to the West.

THE ERLKING

SARAH SHUN-LIEN BYNUM

It is just as Kate hoped. The worn path, the bells tinkling on the gate. The huge fir trees dropping their needles one by one. A sweet mushroomy smell, gnomes stationed in the underbrush, the sound of a mandolin far up on the hill. "We're here, we're here," she says to her child, who isn't walking fast enough and needs to be pulled along by the hand. Through the gate they go, up the dappled path, beneath the firs, across the school parking lot and past the kettle-corn stand, into the heart of the Elves' Faire.

Her child is named Ondine but answers only to Ruthie. Ruthie's hand rests damply in hers, and together they watch two scrappy fairies race by, the swifter one waving a long string of raffle tickets. "Don't you want to wear your wings?" Kate asked that morning, but Ruthie wasn't in the mood. Sometimes they are in cahoots, sometimes not. Now they circle the great shady lawn, studying the activities. There is candlemaking, beekeeping, the weaving of God's eyes. A sign in purple calligraphy says that King Arthur will be appearing at noon. There's a tea garden, a bluegrass band, a man with a thin sandy beard and a hundred acorns pinned with bright ribbons to the folds of his tunic, boys thumping one another with jousting sticks. The ground is scattered with pine needles and hay. The lemonade cups are compostable. Everything is exactly as it should be, every small elvish detail attended to, but, as Kate's heart fills with the pleasure of it all, she is made uneasy by the realization that she could have but did not secure this for her child, and therein lies a misjudgment, a possibly grave mistake.

They had not even applied to a Waldorf school! Kate's associations at the time were vague but nervous-making: devil sticks, recorder playing, occasional illiteracy. She thought she remembered hearing about a boy who, at nine, could map the entire Mongol Empire but was still sucking his fingers. That couldn't be good. Everybody has to go into a 7-Eleven at some point in life, operate in the ordinary universe. So she didn't even sign up for a tour. But no one ever told her about the whole fairy component. And now look at what Ruthie is missing. Magic. Nature. Flower wreaths, floating playsilks, an unpolluted, media-free experience of the world. The chance to spend her days binding books and acting out stories with wonderful wooden animals made in Germany.

Ruthie wants to take one home with her, a baby giraffe. Mysteriously, they have ended up in the sole spot at the Elves' Faire where commerce occurs and credit cards are accepted. Ruthie is not even looking at the baby giraffe; with some nonchalance, she keeps it tucked under her arm as she touches all the other animals on the table.

"A macaw!" she cries softly to herself, reaching.

Kate finds a second baby giraffe, caught between a buffalo and a penguin. Although the creatures represent a wide range of the animal kingdom, they all appear to belong to the same dear, blunt-nosed family. The little giraffe is light in her hand, but when she turns it over to read the tiny price tag stuck to the bottom of its feet she puts it down immediately. Seventeen dollars! Enough to feed an entire fairy family for a month. Noah's Ark, looming in the middle of the table, now looks somewhat sinister. Two by two, two by two. It adds up.

How do the Waldorf parents manage? How do any parents manage? Kate hands over her Visa.

She says to Ruthie, "This is a very special thing. Your one special thing from the Elves' Faire, O.K.?"

"O.K.," Ruthie says, looking for the first time at the animal that is now hers. She knows that her mother likes giraffes; at the zoo, she stands for five or ten minutes at the edge of the giraffe area, talking about their beautiful large eyes and their long lovely eyelashes. She picked the baby giraffe for her mother because it's her favorite. Also because she knew that her mother would say yes, and she does not always say yes—for instance, when asked about My Little Pony. So Ruthie was being clever but also being kind. She was thinking of her mother while also thinking of herself. Besides, there are no My Little Ponies to be found at this fair—she's looked. But a baby giraffe will need a mother to go with it. There is a bigger giraffe on the table, and maybe in five minutes Ruthie will ask if she can put it on her birthday list.

"Mommy," Ruthie says, "is my birthday before Christmas or after?"

"Well, it depends what you mean by before," Kate says, unhelpfully.

Holding hands, they leave the elves' marketplace and climb up the sloping lawn to the heavy old house at the top of the hill, with its low-pitched roof and stout columns and green-painted eaves. Kate guesses that this whole place was once the fresh-air retreat of a tubercular rich person, but now it's a center of child-initiated learning.

Ruthie's own school is housed in a flat, prefab, trailer-type structure tucked behind the large parking lot of a Korean church. It's lovely in its way, with a mass of morning-glory vines softening things up, and, in lieu of actual trees, a mural of woodland scenes painted along the outside wall. And parking is never a problem, which is a plus, since at other schools that can be a real issue at dropoff and pickup. At Wishing Well, the parents take turns wearing reflective vests and carrying walkie-talkies, just to manage the morning traffic inching along the school's driveway. Or there's the grim Goodbye Door at the Jewish Montessori, beyond the threshold of which the dropping-off parent is forbidden to pass. For philosophical reasons, of course, but anyone who's seen the line of cars double-parked outside the building on a weekday morning might suppose a more practical agenda—namely, limited street parking does not allow for long farewells. To think that the Jewish Montessori was once the school Kate had set her heart on! She wouldn't have survived that awful departure, the sound of her own weeping as she turned off her emergency blinkers and made her slow way down the street.

But she had been enchanted by the Jewish Montessori, helplessly enchanted, not even minding (truth be told) the ghastly tales of the Door. Instantly she had loved the vaulted ceiling and the skylights, the Frida Kahlo prints hanging on the walls, the dainty Shabbat candlesticks, and the feeling of coolness and order that was everywhere. On the day of her visit, she'd sat on a little canvas folding stool and watched in wonder as the children silently unfurled their small rugs around the room and then settled into their private, absorbing, intricate tasks. She'd felt her heart begin to slow, felt the relief of finally pressing the mute button on a chortling TV. How clearly she saw that she needn't have been burdened for all these years with her own harried and inefficient self, that her thoughts could have been more elegant, her neural pathways less congested—if only her parents had chosen differently for her. If only they had given her this!

But the school had not made the least impression on Ondine. Every Saturday morning for ten weeks, the two of them had shuffled up the steps with eighteen other applicants and undergone a lengthy, rigorous audition process disguised as a Mommy & Me class. Kate would break out in a light sweat straightaway. Ondine would show only occasional interest in spooning lima beans from a small wooden bowl to a slightly larger one. "Remember, that's *his* job," Kate would whisper urgently as Ondine made a grab for another kid's eyedropper. The parents were supposed to preserve the integrity of each child's workspace, and all these odd little projects—the beans, the soap shavings, the tongs and the muffin tin, even the puzzles—were supposed to be referred to as jobs.

Ten weeks of curious labor, and then the rejection letter arrived, on rainbow stationery. Kate was such an idiot—she sat right down and wrote a thank-you note to the school's intimidating and faintly glamorous director in the hope of improving Ondine's chances for the following year. Maybe a few more spots for brown girls would open up? She had never been so crushed. "You're not even Jewish," her mother said, not a little uncharitably. Her friend Hilary, a Montessori Mommy & Me dropout, confessed to feeling kind of relieved on her behalf. "Didn't it seem, you know, a bit robotic? Or maybe Dickensian? Like children in a bootblacking factory." She reminded Kate about the director's car, which they had seen parked one Saturday morning in its specially reserved spot. "Aren't you glad you won't be paying for the plum-colored Porsche?"

Kate wasn't glad. And she did take it personally, despite everybody's advice not to. Week after week, she and her child had submitted themselves to the director's appraising, professional eye, and, for all their earnest effort, they had still been found wanting. What flaw or lack did she see in them that they couldn't yet see in themselves? Even though Kate spoke about the experience in a jokey, self-mocking way, she could tell that it made people uncomfortable to hear her ask this question, so she learned to do so silently, when she was driving around the city by herself or with Ondine asleep in the back of the car.

·

Can I get the mommy giraffe for Christmas?" Ruthie asks at the end of what she estimates is five minutes. She stops at the bottom of the steps leading up to the big green house and waits for an answer. She wants an answer, but she also wants to practice ballet dancing, so she takes many quick tiny steps back and forth, back and forth, like a "Nutcracker" snowflake in toe shoes.

"People are trying to come down the stairs," her mother says. "Do you have to go potty? Let's go find the potty."

"I'm just dancing!" Ruthie says. "You're hurting my feelings."

"You have to go potty," her mother says. "I can tell. And Daddy told you: no more accidents." But Ruthie sees that she is not really concentrating—she is looking at the big map of the Elves' Faire and finding something interesting—and Ruthie will hold the jiggly snowflake feeling inside her body for as long as she wants. This will mean that she wins, because when she doesn't go potty regular things like walking or standing are more exciting. She's having an adventure.

"It says there's a doll room. Does that sound fun? A special room filled with fairy dolls." Her mother leans closer to the map and then looks around at the real place, trying to make them match. "I think it's down there." She points with the hand that is not holding Ruthie's.

Ruthie wants to see what her mother is pointing at, but instead she sees a man. He is standing at the bottom of the hill and looking up at her. He is not the acorn man, and he does not have a golden crown like the kind a king wears, or the pointy hat of a wizard. She has seen Father Christmas by the raffle booth, and this is not him. This is not a father or a teacher or a neighbor. He does not smile like the brown man who sells Popsicles from a cart. This man is tall and thin, with a cape around his neck that is not black or blue but a color in between, a middle-of-the-night color, and he pushes back the hood on his head and looks at her as if he knows her.

"Do you see where I'm pointing?" Kate asks, and suddenly squats down and peers into Ruthie's face. Sometimes there's a bit of a lag, she's noticed, a disturbing faraway look. It could be lack of sleep: the consistent early bedtime that Dr. Weissbluth strongly recommends just hasn't happened for them yet. A simple enough thing when you read about it, but the reality! Every evening the clock keeps ticking—through dinner, dessert, bath, books, the last unwilling whiz of the day—and, with all the various diversions and spills and skirmishes, Kate wonders if it would be easier to disarm a bomb in the time allotted. And so Ruthie is often tired. Which could very well explain the slowness to respond, the intractability, the scary, humiliating fits. Maybe even the intensified thumb-sucking? It's equally possible that Kate is just fooling herself, and something is actually wrong.

Tonight she'll do a little research on the Internet.

Slowly, Kate stands up and tugs at Ruthie's hand. They are heading back down the hill in search of the doll room. They are having a special day, just the two of them. They both like the feeling of being attached by the hand but with their thoughts branching off in different directions. It is similar to the feeling of falling asleep side by side, which they do sometimes, in defiance of Dr. Weissbluth's guidelines, their bodies touching and their dreams going someplace separate but connected. They both like the feeling of not knowing who is leading, whether it's the grownup or the child.

But Ruthie knows that neither of them is the leader right now. The man wearing the cape is the leader, and he wants them to come to the bottom of the hill. She can tell by the way he's looking at her—kind, but also as if he could get a little angry. They have to come quickly. Spit-spot! No getting distracted. These are the rules. They walk down the big lawn, past the face-painting table and some jugglers and the honeybees dancing behind glass, and Ruthie sees on the man's face that her mother doesn't really have to come at all. Just her.

She has a sneaky feeling that the man is holding a present under his cape. It's supposed to be a surprise. A surprise that is small and very delicate, like a music box, but when you open it it just goes down and down, like a rabbit hole, and inside there is everything—everything—she has wanted: stickers, jewels, books, dolls, high heels, pets, ribbons, purses, toe shoes, makeup. You can't even begin to count! Part of the present is that she doesn't have to choose. So many special and beautiful things, and she wants all of them—she will have all of them—and gone is the crazy feeling she gets when she's in Target and needs the Barbie Island Princess Styling Head so badly that she thinks she's going to throw up. That's the sort of surprise it is. The man is holding a present for her, and when she opens it she will be the kindest, luckiest person in the world. Also the prettiest. Not for pretend— for real life. The man is a friend of her parents, and he has brought a present for her the way her parents' friends from New York or Canada sometimes do. She wants him to be like that, she wants him to be someone who looks familiar. She asks, "Mommy, do we know that man?," and her mother says, "The man with the guitar on his back?" But she's wrong, she's ruined it: he doesn't even have a guitar.

Ruthie doesn't see who her mother is talking about, or why her voice has got very quiet. "Oh, wow," her mother whispers. "That's John C. Reilly. How funny. His kids must go here." Then she sighs and says, "I bet they do." She looks at Ruthie strangely. "You know who John C. Reilly is?"

"Who's John C. Reilly?" Ruthie asks, but only a small part of her is talking to her mother; the rest of her is thinking about the surprise. The man has turned his head away, and she can see only the nighttime color of his cape. She sees that there is something moving around underneath his cape, like a little mouse crawling all over his shoulders and trying to get out. She is worried that he might not give the present to her anymore. She is sure that her mother has ruined it.

"Just a person who's in movies. Grownup movies." Kate's favorite is the one where he plays the tall, sad policeman; he was so lovable in that. Talking to himself, driving around all day in the rain. You just wanted to hand him a towel and give him a hug. And though something about that movie was off—the black woman handcuffed, obese and screaming, and how the boy had to offer up a solemn little rap—John C. Reilly was not himself at fault. He was just doing his job. Playing the part. Even those squirmy scenes were shot through with his goodness. His homely radiance! The bumpy overhang of his brow. His big head packed full of good thoughts and goofy jokes. Imagine sitting next to him on a parents' committee, or at Back-to-School Night! She'd missed her chance. Now he and his guitar are disappearing into the fir trees beyond the parking lot.

Kate sighs. "Daddy and I respect him a lot. He makes really interesting choices."

"Mommy!" Ruthie cries. "Stop talking. Stop talking!" She pulls her hand away and crosses her arms over her chest. "I'm so mad at you right now."

Because another girl, not her, is going to get the surprise. The man isn't even looking at her anymore. He liked her so much before, but he's changed his mind. Her mother didn't see him— she saw only who she wanted to see—and now everything is so damaged and ruined. It's not going to work. "You're making me really angry," Ruthie tells her. "You did it on purpose! I'm going to kick you." She shows her teeth.

"What did I do now?" her mother asks. "What just happened?" She is asking an imaginary friend who's a grownup standing next to her, not Ruthie. She has nothing to say to Ruthie; she grabs her wrist and marches fast down the hill, trying to get them away from something, from Ruthie's bad mood, probably, and Ruthie is about to cry, because she is not having a good day, her wrist is stinging very badly, nothing is going her way, but just as her mother is dragging her through the door of a small barn she sees again the man with the surprise. He has turned back to look at her, so much closer now, and when he reaches out to touch her she sees that he has long, yellowish fingernails and, under his cape, he's made out of straw. He nods at her slowly. It's going to be O.K.

Inside the barn, Kate takes a breath. It actually worked. Nothing like a little force and velocity! Ruthie has been yanked out from under whatever dark cloud she conjured up. Kate will have to try that again. The doll room, strung with Christmas lights, twinkles around her merrily. Bits of tulle and fuzzy yarn hang mistily from the rafters. As her eyes get used to the dim barn and its glimmering light, she sees that there are dolls everywhere, of all possible sizes, perched on nests of leaves and swinging from birch branches and asleep in polished walnut-shell cradles. Like the wooden animals, they seem all to be descended from the same bland and adorable ancestor, a wide-eyed, thin-lipped soul with barely any nose and a mane of bouclé hair. They are darling, irresistible; she wants to squeeze every last one of them and stroke the neat felt shoes on their feet. Little cardboard tags dangle from their wrists or ankles, bearing the names of their makers, faithful and nimble-fingered Waldorf mothers who can also, it's rumored, spin wool! On real wooden spinning wheels. What a magical, soothing, practical skill. Could that be what she lacks—a spinning wheel? She glances down at Ruthie—is she charmed? happy?—and then looks anxiously around the room at the sweet assortment of milky faces peeking out from under tiny elf caps or heaps of luxuriant hair. Please let there be some brown dolls! she thinks. And please let them be cute. Wearing gauzy, sparkly fairy outfits like the others, and not overalls or bonnets or dresses made of calico. A brown mermaid would be nice for once. A brown Ondine. She squeezes her daughter's hand in helpless apology, for even at the Elves' Faire, where all is enchanting and mindful and biodegradable, Kate is again exposing her to something toxic.

But Ruthie isn't even looking at the dolls, because now she has to pee very badly. Also, she can't find her giraffe. It isn't there under her arm, where she left it. Her baby giraffe! It must have slipped out somewhere. But where? There are many, many places it could be. Ruthie looks down at the floor of the barn, which is covered in bits of straw. Not here. She feels her stomach begin to hurt. It was her one special thing from the Elves' Faire. A present from her mother. Maybe her last present from her mother, who might say, If you can't take care of your special things, then I won't be able to get you special things anymore. But she won't need special things anymore! She is going to get a surprise, one that gets bigger and bigger the more she thinks about it, because she has a feeling that the man is able to do things her mother is not able to do, like let her live in a castle that is also a farm, where she can live in a beautiful tower and have a little kitten and build it a house and give it toys. Also, she's going to have five—no, she means ten—pet butterflies.

The man is standing outside the barn now, waiting for her, and maybe if she doesn't come out soon he'll walk right in and get her. Ruthie wants to run and scream; she can't tell if she's happy or the most scared she's ever been. "Nooooooooo!" she shrieks when her father holds her upside down and tickles her, but as soon as he stops she cries, "Again, again!" She always wants more of this, and her father and mother always stop too soon.

The man in the cape won't stop. The dolls in this room are children, children he has turned into dolls. Ruthie can help him— she'll be on his team. She'll tell the children, "I'm going to put you in jail. Lock, lock! You're in jail. And I have the key. You can never get out until I tell you." Her friends from school, her ballet teacher Miss Sara, her best friends Lark and Chloe, her gymnastics coach Tanya, her mommy and daddy, her favorite, specialest people, all sitting with their legs straight out and their eyes wide open, and no one can see them but her. She will be on the stage copying Dorothy, and they will be watching. She will do the whole "Wizard of Oz" for them from the beginning, and the man will paint her skin so it's bright, not brown, and make her hair smooth and in braids so she looks like the real Dorothy. It will be the big surprise of their life!

Kate knows there must be a brown doll somewhere in this barn, and that it's possibly perfect. If anyone can make the doll she's been looking for, these Waldorf mothers can: something touchable and dreamy, something she can give her child to cherish, something her child will love and prefer, instead of settle for. Considering that she's been searching for this doll since the moment Ondine was born, a hundred and thirty dollars is not so much to spend. For every doll in this barn can be purchased, she's just discovered; on the back of each little cardboard tag is a pencilled number, and it's become interesting to compare the numbers and wonder why this redheaded doll in a polka-dot dress is twenty-five dollars more than the one wearing a cherry-print apron. She wanders farther into the barn, glancing at the names and numbers, idly doing arithmetic in her head: how much this day has cost so far (seventeen for the giraffe, eight for the smoothies, two for raffle tickets) and how much it might end up costing in the future. Because, if she does find the doll she's looking for, it'd be wonderful to get that white shelf she's been thinking about, a white shelf that she could buy at Ikea for much less than a similar version at Pottery Barn Kids, and nearly as nice, a shelf she could hang in a cheerful spot in Ondine's yellow room from which the doll would then gaze down at her daughter with its benign embroidered eyes and cast a spell of protection. All told, with the doll and the giraffe and the smoothies and the shelf, this day could come in at close to two hundred dollars, but who would blink at that? She's thinking about her child.

"Ladies and gentlemen!" Ruthie will say. "Welcome to the show!" And the man with the cape will pull back the curtains and everybody will be so surprised by what they see that they will put their hands over their mouths and scream.

But Ruthie's own surprise is already turning into something else, not a beautiful secret anymore but just a thing that she knows will happen, whether she wants it to or not, just as she knows that she will have an accident in the barn and her giraffe will be lost and her mother will keep looking at the tags hanging from the dolls' feet, looking closely like she's reading an important announcement, looking closely and not seeing the puddle getting bigger on the floor. When it happens, her mother will be holding her hand—she is always holding and pulling and squeezing her hand—which is impossible, actually, because Ruthie, clever girl, kind girl, ballet dancer, thumb-sucker, brave and bright Dorothy, is already gone.

THE PILOT

JOSHUA FERRIS

He hadn't heard from Kate Lotvelt in two weeks. Not that he absolutely should've necessarily. He and Kate, they weren't . . . were they friends? Well, yeah, they were friends. They were acquaintances. They'd met twice, once at the producer Sydney Gleekman's yearly blowout, and then, a few months later, at the actor's dinner party.

Kate's invitation had come by e-mail. She was considerate, or she was canny, not to include the addresses of the other invitees. She'd sent the message to her husband and bcc'd everyone else.

From: Kate Lotvelt.
To: Eaton Aiken.
Subject: Death is a Wrap! "Come for the drinks & stay for the pool."

He'd R.S.V.P.'d, but not immediately. Two days after the message came in. Two days plus maybe an hour. And said something like: Just can't wait. Heading to tax-friendly Winston-Salem in a few days to shoot this godawful underarm commercial. Remember that particular station of the cross? Maybe not, probably scrubbed it from memory. But, hell, work's work. That pilot I told you about is coming along, I think. Gleekman's enthusiastic, or at least Pleble claims enthusiasm on his behalf. But the sad reality is always reality television. It's why I so admire "Death." It's a sick little fuck-you every week to the swapped wives and tarantula eaters. Congratulations, by the way. Three seasons! God damn if that's not impressive in this climate. But the show . . . well, do you ever tire of hearing how good it is? And I thought life was over after "The Wire." Listen, no need to reply to this longwinded e-mail. You're wrapping! But can't wait to see you at the party. Consider this an R.S.V.P. No way I'd miss it. Not a chance in the world. Hooray! Cheers cheers, Lx.

He didn't expect a reply. It was a mass e-mail—she couldn't reply to everyone who'd replied. She was busy, she was wrapping the third season. He would have liked a reply. After a few days went by, he'd have liked a reply a lot. Was his e-mail too effusive? Was it a mistake to use the word "sick" to describe her show? Or maybe she was just busy shooting the season finale. She was just busy shooting the season finale. He should have just written back quick-like, something like "Thanks for the invitation, Kate. See you then." Then she might have quick-like hit Reply, with a confirmation, and he'd have known that she knew he was coming. Did she even know she'd invited him? Sometimes, with e-mail, some programs, you hit All Contacts or something and invite people you don't mean to invite. Of course she'd meant to invite him. He just didn't have any confirmation that she'd received his R.S.V.P. That was kind of unnerving. But, think about it, would he then have to confirm her confirmation? That wasn't really feasible. It was just . . . Everything was fine. She was just wrapping. He was too effusive. "Sick little fuck-you": that might have been—no, it was fine—just a little insulting? No, no, it was fine, who knows, not him.

At the actor's dinner party, the night they exchanged e-mail addresses, he and Kate had been seated together. Ten minutes passed before he managed to settle his heart. Then they talked about the Guild and its troubles. When he thought she had warmed to him, he peppered her with questions about her show—how she ran a room, what her writing habits were. He tossed hints of his awe but scrupulously avoided rhapsodizing. He had rhapsodized in the past to mere cameramen, and his impulse upon returning home had always been to beat the fan-boy in him into a permanent coma. After dessert, while the other guests were drinking an expensive port—he'd been dry sixteen months now—Eaton Aiken, to everyone's delight, took off his shoes and, standing on some old newspaper, painted a mural on the far wall of the actor's dining room with some house paint and a stiff brush.

He thought about how different his anticipation about the party would be if he were Eaton Aiken. If he were Eaton Aiken, it would be *his* party. He wouldn't have to worry about anything but what he already had: a nineteen-twenties Mediterranean, with a porte cochere, at the top of Griffith Park; an infinity pool with Moroccan tile rippled with blue fins of light (he had seen photos in *People*, against his will, while waiting in line to buy gum); money for the booze and the hired hands to serve it; and a solo show at the Getty before the age of forty. Now that he remembered the Getty show, he could no longer think as Eaton Aiken; he could think only of Eaton Aiken himself. Successful, attractive, untroubled. Eaton Aiken hadn't just finished shooting a deodorant commercial in tax-friendly Winston-Salem.

Part of the problem was that two weeks had gone by and she hadn't sent a reminder to everyone saying in case you forgot about the party, looking forward to seeing you, etc. The party was tonight. Was the party still on? He couldn't be totally one-hundred-per-cent sure, and here it was the middle of the afternoon. He was in his darkened room—irrepressible L.A. sunlight battering the closed blinds, unwashed bedsheets reeking of tobacco smoke—watching DVR'd TV backlogged since W.-S. and checking-rechecking his e-mail for a reminder e-mail. Of course it was still on. If you were Kate Lotvelt, would you worry about guests coming? She had succeeded beyond the pedestrian sorrows of social anxiety. It was an awesome thing to behold, his inbox without the reminder e-mail. It was also unsettling. Wasn't it possible that now that she had wrapped she'd taken better care to select from her contacts the people she really wanted at the party and sent the reminder e-mail only to them?

Finally he got a message from Pleble: "Yo bro, how'd the shoot go? I'm in Indio. Do not fucking go to fucking Coachella. Time was there were a hundred great bands and ten people in the know. Now it's a refugee camp for neohippie fuckheads. What exactly are you asking about a reminder e-mail from Kate Lotvelt? She needs to drop that Romanian douche and sign with me. Back on Monday if you need to talk. In the meantime, why not finish that pilot? Your humble Pleeb."

No help at all. He'd hoped to hear that Pleble was going to the party so they could go together. Or, if they didn't go together, at least he'd know that he'd know someone there. But maybe Pleble hadn't been invited. But if *he'd* been invited Pleble would have been invited. Kate and Eaton knew Pleble better than they knew him. Didn't they? Now he was thinking that there really must have been a contacts mishap. It would have been nice if Pleble had confirmed or denied that he'd been invited. But Pleble was shrewd. If he hadn't been invited, he wouldn't say, "Kate's having a party? Why wasn't I invited?" He'd say just what he'd said. So maybe Pleble was invited, but he was in Indio, which sucked, because it would have been nice to go with someone or at least know someone there. Or maybe Pleble hadn't been invited, in which case there must have been a contacts mishap, and he shouldn't have been invited, either. Either way, now things were more uncertain than before Pleble's totally unhelpful and possibly calculating e-mail. Maybe he wasn't even in Indio! He was tempted to write Gleekman and ask him if he'd been invited and if he was going or at least if he'd received a reminder e-mail. But he didn't want to give Gleekman the impression that he was feeling insecure about his place at Kate's party. That would be sending the wrong signal. The pilot was but a polish away.

THE PILOT

Kate Lotvelt was the creator of and show runner for "Death in the Family," as well as its head writer and a member of the ensemble cast. The show's meandering, almost nonexistent plotlines revolved around the Michaelson family: Connor and Jean, adult son Mike and wife Sally, teen-age daughter Irene, adopted Korean child Koko, dog Revolution, and neighbors the Washingtons. In every episode, someone died. Connor murdered Jean, Jean set fire to Sally, Mike was wrongfully executed, Irene caught cold, Koko fell into the pool, Revolution was shot, the Washingtons were poisoned by Sally's casserole. Everything sacrosanct about death was lampooned: disease, hospitals, the squeamish austerity of the burn ward, funeral homes, unbearable sadness. And by the next episode everyone was alive again! Everyone was swell! No memory of last week's suffering and no suspicion of the coming doom. The question for the folks at home was: Who will get it this time? And how? The best episodes left him breathless. There was the effectiveness of the show's satire, but also the stupefying entertainment of its metaphysics. How, week after week, did Kate Lotvelt turn something so morbid and frightening into the funniest show on television?

He hoped to do the same thing with "Life of the Party," but it needed a polish. It needed a fresh set of eyes. Somebody smart. But it might be better to stay in and polish the pilot to the best of his ability, on the off chance that he had a breakthrough, and then on Monday give the pilot to Pleble, to give to Gleekman, so they could finally start seriously engaging each other. If he stayed in and polished the pilot, he could stop worrying about whether he'd been invited to Kate's party or if he'd know anyone there or why he hadn't received a reminder e-mail.

But half of this business was networking. And what was the better option—go to the party of the year, to which he'd been invited, and network with actors and executives? Or return home to Atlanta and die? Those were his choices. So what that the protocol for kissing hello kept shifting on him? So what that he'd never established an easy routine with which to confront the beautiful people? There was such a variety of behavior on display at these parties that when he came home and lay down on the bed, finally removing his sunglasses for the evening, he would soberly play back for himself his insufficiencies. Should he have been more casual? Intense? Fawning? Detached? Happy? Was happy an option?

He needed a new pair of eyes on the pilot, someone smart, like Kate Lotvelt. He also needed a new pair of sunglasses. For a long time he'd taken refuge behind that pair of sunglasses, which had been the Gangster's. But not even the head Gangster's! The head Gangster's cousin's sunglasses. They had disguised his drunkenness and, later, dimmed the unbearable brightness of the sober world. He'd left them behind at the W.-S. CountryAir Motel and hadn't found a replacement, the gangster show having concluded seasons ago, and fashion having moved on.

He was debating inviting his roommate. On the one hand, he'd have someone to go with. On the other, his roommate was a musician, and he trembled before the mystical competition of a musician's night life. His roommate had something going on every night, possibly something more vibrant and exclusive than the pale thing he generally had going on, and he felt it was better to withhold the invitation than risk suffering the indignity of rejection, even if that rejection was due to a simple conflict of interest—preëxisting plans, for example. It was hard not to take even conflicts of interest personally, for some reason—specifically, the possibility that his roommate would be grateful for having a legitimate conflict of interest, which would excuse him from entertaining another, lesser invitation, even when tonight that "lesser" invitation was to a party at Kate Lotvelt's. If that invitation still stood. If the invitation didn't stand, the last thing he wanted was to show up at Kate's with his roommate in tow and discover that Kate didn't remember meeting him at Gleekman's or at the actor's dinner party and had no idea why he'd come and brought his roommate—who, no doubt, would have preferred to do something in the subterranean world of musicians. So he decided not to invite him.

He did, however, ask to borrow his jacket.

He didn't like to borrow other people's clothing, but there was something about the thought of arriving wearing that particular jacket that made the party less intimidating. There was some relief in having lost his sunglasses, because what had started as a talisman had become a kind of crutch, and if he could go without the alcohol he could go without the glasses. The next step in his recovery, losing those glasses—that was how he looked at it. He'd admired the jacket, though, the one time he'd seen it on his roommate, almost a year ago now.

His roommate was on the sofa, curled over his guitar, shirtless, wearing white rayon gym shorts and a pair of cowboy boots. Periodically he stopped strumming to make notations on the sheet music fanned across the coffee table. Above him hung a buck's head wreathed with leis and party beads, a steel helmet from the Second World War hooked on the tip of an antler.

"Hey, so, what do you have going on tonight?"

He was still unsure—maybe he should invite him. If he wasn't invited, it might be comforting to have someone with him even less invited than he was, despite the embarrassment, and if he was invited it would be nice to have someone there to eliminate any awkward walking alone through rooms.

"Giving myself an ultimatum" was the roommate's reply, as he leaned back on the sofa. "Write three new songs by the end of the day, or shoot myself in the head."

He was not infrequently put to shame by his roommate's work ethic. He watched as he leaned forward again, picked up his little pencil, and made a few more notations on the sheet music. The example made him sure that the only thing to do now was to stay in and put a polish on the pilot. Was there really any other option? What was he thinking, going to a party, even a party like Kate Lotvelt's, when the pilot, with a little work, could be given to Pleble, and he could finally maybe say goodbye to tax-friendly backwaters and start taking real meetings with actors and executives? So that was settled. Stay in, work on the pilot. Finish the pilot, or shoot himself in the head.

"Why, what's going on with you?"

"Oh, there's this party," he said, "but I don't know. I think I'm going to stay in and work on the pilot. Do you have any interest in going to a party?"

"How's the pilot coming?"

"It's close. I'd say real close. Which is why I should stay in. But I don't know. I was going to ask if I could borrow that jacket of yours, in case I go. Would you like to go?"

"Hey, man, I'm not joking. If I don't write three new songs tonight, look for me with a bullet in the brain. I won't do it in the house, out of courtesy. Look for me in the car. What jacket?"

His roommate left and came back with the jacket he'd described. It fit! He went to the bathroom to look at himself in the mirror, and when he came back he asked his roommate how he thought it fit.

"Fits perfect," the roommate said. "You want it? It's yours."

"You don't want it?"

"I never wear it."

"Why not?"

"Not since what's-his-name started wearing it, and then everyone else starting wearing it."

"Since who started wearing it?"

"What's-his-name, the anti-terrorist cop dude. What's his name?"

"Oh," he said, as it dawned on him—the cop, the jacket, the show. "Right."

"Don't get me wrong, it's a great jacket."

He took it back to his room and set it on the bed. God damn it. It fit, too. He was determined not to go to the party now, certainly not in that jacket, which annoyed him. But he was relieved to be staying in and putting a polish on the pilot. So he sat down at his desk and called up the document. It was finish it or die. It was finish it or return to Atlanta. Finish it or live forever promoting morning-fresh roll-on with no unattractive residue.

Problem was, scrolling through it, he was looking at the same old pilot. What it needed wasn't a night's polish. It needed a fresh pair of eyes.

He was procrastinating in the parking lot when his mother called. It was curious timing and he considered not answering. The ritual of her call was now so invariably a part of the day that it had moved beyond the initial phase of support and nurture into something self-conscious, liturgical, and annoying. She'd been calling every day for nineteen months—by now their little exchange was entirely formal and meaningless. But was it meaningless *this* time, right as he was sitting in the parking lot, procrastinating? The day was almost over in Atlanta. Usually she didn't wait this long. Wasn't that a sign? He would have preferred to let her go to voice mail, but tonight he wasn't so sure. It might be wise to pick up tonight. Maybe she'd say the thing that would get him out of the parking lot and headed in the right direction.

He greeted her and then she said, to no one's surprise, "Will you do me a favor today, Lawrence?"

He abided by answering, "What's that, Mom?"

The unvarying reply was "Will you please promise me you won't take a drink today?"

"I promise you," he said, "that I won't take a drink today."

"Thank you," she said.

"Thanks for calling, Mom."

"I love you, Lawrence," she said.

"I love you, too, Mom."

"I'll talk to you tomorrow," she said.

"O.K.," he said. "Goodbye."

"Goodbye," she said.

The call ended and he got out of the car and went into the bar. He walked past an abandoned wait station with a toothpick dispenser and a bowl of peppermints into the dark and mostly empty room, where he pulled out a red vinyl stool for himself and sat down before all the labels of his misery. His eyes began to water. The bartender broke his trance by tossing a coaster down Frisbee style. He paused theatrically, as if debating, then ordered a whiskey and a chaser. A whiskey and a chaser was all he needed to make it to Kate Lotvelt's party unconcerned about his place there and at ease without his sunglasses or the jacket, and sufficiently fortified that if the opportunity presented itself he could ask Kate to have a look at his pilot. It was only twenty-four pages. It was only a whiskey and a chaser.

Waiting for his drinks to arrive, he turned his back on the few patrons to his right. Better not to be looked at. You remain there in your misery, I'll dwell invisibly here in mine. He now faced the entrance of the bar, and his eyes landed on the toothpick dispenser. Staring, he thought, Huh, that's interesting. He had this intuition. It had something to do with all the television he'd watched that day. He found himself walking over and placing his finger on top of the dispenser. He pressed down and a toothpick tumbled out. He took the toothpick between his fingers and looked at it. He placed it in his mouth and let it roll around, releasing its bland, minty flavor. Then he removed it and stabbed the air with it sharply, squinting and mouthing a few words, as if chastening someone. The gesture was filled with righteous instruction. Then he put the toothpick back in his mouth and stood there, staring hard into the imagined eyes of the recently chastened. He moved the toothpick around, still staring, transformed.

Who did that?

That was the Coach. The Coach did that.

The Coach was on every Friday night, winning games, teaching his boys how to be men.

He turned in time to catch the bartender setting his drinks down. What to do? He went back to the bar and told the bartender he could have the drinks himself—he'd been called away. He left a courteous tip. On the way out, he removed a number of toothpicks and put them in his pocket.

Now we detour away from Lawrence's mind, he thought, and enter a new space. A space of rigor and discipline, of noble spirit, few words, and the best of intentions. To find the Coach in himself—that was the best of intentions. Or not the Coach, exactly, because he wasn't the coach of anything, but the best aspects of the Coach's character—limited, yes, by the emotional restraint of athletic-minded people, their incurious and circumscribed intellects, but liberated by their expansive, inspired, and victorious hearts. The Coach was always victorious, even in defeat. But was it unsavory to channel the Coach? He stopped at a sporting-goods store to purchase a blue windbreaker to go with the toothpick, and a cap whose bill he worked hard to break in on the drive to Kate's. He could even use the Coach's circumscribed intellect. Thought was the enemy. People believed it was drink. It wasn't drink. The enemy was looping destructive gnawing thought. Drink was just a cure. A cure, in the end, worse than the disease. Wasn't it better to channel the Coach than to return to drinking? Better, maybe, but just a little creepy? Enough thinking. He gave the keys to the valet and started toward the house.

He was now there not to network with actors and executives, which would have been beneath the Coach (if, say, the Coach had been hoping to break into TV, instead of being a football coach on TV), or even to enjoy the party, but to ask Kate Lotvelt a favor. The Coach, when he had to ask a favor—which was always in the name of something more important than the Coach himself— put aside his pride and approached his task with a humble resolve you admired in a man. He walked up the drive to the courtyard, where splendid light splashed the perfectly paved cobblestones, and the leaves of the palm trees appeared golden between dark shadows, and the baroque fountain tinkled vigorously. People hung in the doorway, glamorous people, or maybe just filler people, and he greeted them with a tight little smile and a nod of the head. The same head that wore the cap with the nicely arced brim. Moving the toothpick around the mouth. That was all he had to do the entire evening: meet people's eyes, nod politely, say nothing, sip his seltzer. Shuffle around the margins with an air of generalized boredom that would convey, hopefully, preoccupation rather than rudeness, a pressing obligation kept in check by good old-fashioned manners. The pages of the pilot were folded lengthwise in his back pocket.

He began his walk-and-nod through the house, looking for Kate. Squeals issued from the pool while, inside, people stood in intimate clusters or lounged on giant leather sofas complemented by outsized ottomans. Normal furniture just wouldn't have worked in such enormous rooms, one of which was the size of his entire armpit apartment. Some of the rooms were separated by a little tap dance of stairs, some by a transition from carpet to hardwood. The walls were hung not with movie posters or buck heads but with framed canvases large and small. He was sure that, when he found her, noisy groupies would be crowded around. He'd have to bide his time. He'd have to show restraint. It might take the entire night for the right moment to announce itself. But when it did he would appear before her in windbreaker and cap, nod and smile and extend his hand, and ask if she had a moment to read his pilot. One look at him and she'd know he'd come with the purest intentions.

But he couldn't bide his time—he could never bide his time. To bide time was to think. So he went straight up to her, to the group she was in, or more like the center of, because she was Kate Lotvelt, the tallest woman in the room—which he'd forgotten, how tall she was—but, more important, *Kate Lotvelt*, which meant that everyone there was in rapture listening to her tell a story, including the man who played Connor on "Death in the Family," and the actress who played Irene, and one of the Washingtons. They were all listening to Kate's story, which he couldn't follow entirely because he'd missed the beginning, and was nervous; but it had something to do with a guy selling coat hangers on the highway, the blue plastic kind, and how Kate, finding this outrageously funny, had rolled down her window to ask how much he was charging, and the guy had said twenty-five cents a hanger, and she had to wonder, was that a reasonable price to pay for a decent-looking blue plastic hanger? It was practically new, maybe even new-new. Would the Container Store charge less per hanger, or was this just a steal?

"So this is the guy I go to now to buy hangers. He's my hanger guy."

Someone asked her how many hangers she'd bought.

"Twenty hangers, four bucks."

"Wait . . . *four* bucks?"

"He's homeless, and he's selling hangers on the highway," she said. "You're not going to haggle?"

Everyone laughed.

"Hey, I need hangers," someone said. "Which highway?"

"Excuse me," he said. "Kate?"

Everyone turned to look at him. He wasn't standing next to her, but more like three or four people away in that amorphous little circle. She turned to look, too. His hand was on his toothpick. The outer half of the toothpick, though soggy, still had its pointy tip, but the inside half had turned to mash between his teeth. He wished he could get rid of it. The whole point of having it was to gesture with it, but it wouldn't be a good idea to take it out of his mouth at this point, it being all milled and stringy. Plus bits were starting to come off and float around his mouth. The clean toothpicks were in the windbreaker, but should he switch now, with everyone looking? People were quietly looking.

"Sorry to interrupt," he said. "Kate, could I maybe have a word with you?"

He'd grown up in Atlanta, which wasn't Texas, where the Coach coached, but it was the South, so the accent wasn't totally disingenuous.

She looked a little startled. "Sure," she said. She turned and gently touched the arm of the person directly to her right. "Excuse me a second," she said.

They convened a few feet away. He took the opportunity to quickly pocket the old toothpick and replace it with a new one, which was much easier to move from one side of his mouth to the other with his flagging tongue, a soothing motion that also relieved his teeth from their chomping and gave him the appearance, he hoped, of a man in command, which he wasn't just then, because she didn't seem to recognize him.

"I'm sorry to take you away," he said.

"That's O.K.," she said. She stood a few inches taller than him, because of the heels, maybe, in part. "Is everything O.K.?"

"I just wanted to ask you a favor."

"I'm sorry," she said. "Do I know you?"

"I think so," he said. "My name's Lawrence? Lawrence Himshell?"

She removed his cap. Someone watching, he thought, might have thought that was sweet, how she just grabbed his cap like that, as if they were old friends. "Lawrence!" she said. "I didn't recognize you!"

"Yeah, it's the cap," he said.

She put the cap back on his head. "You look like what's-his-name," she said. "With that cap and the windbreaker."

"Yeah, I know."

"You know who I mean?" she said. "What's his name?" She snapped her fingers to try to jog her memory. "Ah, I can't remember. And I'm in TV! Anyway. What's your favor, stranger?"

"Did you invite me?" he asked.

"What?"

"Did you invite me here tonight?"

"Of course," she said. "What do you mean? You're here, aren't you?"

"I just wondered if you meant to."

"Of course I meant to," she said.

"I thought it could have been a contacts mishap."

"A contacts mishap?" she asked. "What's that?"

"You know, like when you press Select All and don't mean to."

"I've never heard of someone doing that," she said. "Hey, it's nice to see you. How's your pilot?"

"My pilot?" he said. He was surprised to be asked. "My pilot's close, I think. It's real close."

"That's great," she said. "Congratulations."

"I think it just needs a polish," he said.

"That's fantastic."

"Hey, and congratulations to you."

"Thank you," she said.

"On wrapping the third season."

"Thanks."

They talked about wrapping the third season, and then she was called away. She didn't leave without first touching him on the arm and promising she'd be right back. He felt enormous relief. He walked straight to the bar and asked for a whiskey. While it was being poured, he asked himself what he was doing and told himself to shut up. He had a second one in hand before finishing the first.

He moved from group to group and from room to room. He double-kissed and triple-kissed and single-kissed and sometimes only shook hands with the beautiful people. One of them, he sort of stabbed her cheek a little with the toothpick. But, for the most part, it was nice to have it to touch when he wasn't drinking. It was a relaxed and easy party. Disappointment in himself nagged at him. He ignored it. He went up to Eaton Aiken and spoke his name while staring at his back. Eaton was forced to pivot away from the conversation he was in. He was wearing a maroon velvet suit coat and a pair of strikingly red slip-on sneakers. "Yes?" he said.

Lawrence extended his hand. "Lawrence," he said. The Coach's accent was gone but another one, from a different Southern region, was emerging more with each new drink. "We met at Neil Connell's dinner party?"

"Neil who?"

"Neil Connell? He's an actor? He plays—well, he did play, until they cancelled the show, now he's just . . ."

"Neil Connell," he said. "Neil Connell. I vaguely remember a vapid little fuck by that name. A standard self-satisfied industry personage?"

"Who? Neil?" Lawrence said.

"Yes, I remember the empty night I spent in his company. And I remember you. You never removed your sunglasses. Somehow you remained sober through that entire evening. Are you an

132

alcoholic? No, you have a drink. I was a recovering alcoholic. Long before I was an alcoholic." He rattled his glass. "This just feels more like home, you know. Cheers."

"Cheers," he said.

"You can't toast with just ice. It's bad luck."

"I was just on my way to the—"

"You sat next to my wife as if she were Helen of Troy. I painted that cocksucker's wall with random splatters of house paint and then had my pant legs ejaculated on for having raised the resale value of his house a hundred thousand dollars. Is that the Neil Connell you have in mind?"

"I think maybe."

"Right," Eaton said. "And how have you been?"

He excused himself to get another drink.

He was on the sofa for a while, then he was in the bathroom looking at himself in the mirror, then he was in the kitchen doing shots. Toward the end of the evening, he followed the producer Sydney Gleekman down the hall and caught him coming out of the bathroom. Gleekman was told, without having solicited the information, that the pilot was close, the pilot was only a polish away, and that he should expect the pilot from Pleble on Monday.

"Remind me again," Gleekman asked. "Who's Pleble?"

"Mark Pleble? My agent? We met you at your big party last year?"

"Does he work for C.A.A.?"

"No."

"William Morris?"

"No."

"United Talent?"

"He works for a kind of boutique agency, I guess."

"Oh, sure," Gleekman said. "I know who you mean. Have him send it to me. Ah, there she is. Excuse me."

Gleekman left, and he headed back to the bar. Was the party winding down? He thought probably, because there were so few people around. He should probably go home, so he had a final drink with a guy who was maybe famous and then went outside to the empty patio, where he lay down on a chaise.

He took the pilot out of his back pocket and started to read by the murky blue light of the pool. He lit a cigarette, then a second. He wasn't sure he was in the right frame of mind, but as he read, and smoked, and read, and smoked, something new occurred to him. His pilot was a comedy in which the main character was a recovering alcoholic who, in every episode, found himself surrounded by drunks. In every episode—or so he envisioned it; there weren't any "episodes" yet—his character had to work hard not to drink. He was the "life of the party." The title was ironic; the life and humor came from the drunks. But could that conceit be sustained for an entire season? What if, he thought, just what if his character got on and off the wagon from episode to episode? Then the question became, every Thursday, ideally, will he or will he not take a drink? Just like "Death in the Family." Who will die this time? And who will die this time? And who will die—

He fell asleep. The embers of his half-smoked cigarette caught the pages of his pilot, which began to smolder and, in time, burn. He started coughing, which brought into his dreams the evening's first damning burning drink. He woke up with the flames alive in his lap and leaped out of the chaise. The flames didn't disperse. He panicked. He wasn't sure where the fire started and where it stopped. He was the fire. He threw himself into the pool.

He came up to the surface. He was coughing now, not from the smoke but from having taken in water. Was that dawn breaking in the sky so high up? The water was bracing. He called out for help and took in more water. Sobering infusion of chlorine. Air cut off by water in the windpipe. Desperate silent eye-popping wheezing. Could his splashing alone wake someone? Reach for the closest edge. Which way? A lot of struggle at the surface. How quickly the new dawn was disappearing! Shimmeringly at first. He was losing the surface to the depths. Happening? So much still to think about, so much to do. Of course Kate Lotvelt's party was on, had always been on, with or without a reminder e-mail. Why did he trouble himself over such trivial matters? He had received her invitation and still he doubted that he'd been invited! He was always focussed on the wrong thing at the wrong time. How easily muddled his mind could get. It spun worst-case scenarios. It second-guessed people's good intentions. He doubted his worth on so many levels and so frequently missed the point entirely. That was no way to live. He hit bottom. Launch yourself! He broke the surface again, dawn, a new day, lungs full, sank again. Soon the water turned thicker and heavier and settled around him. His eyes were open. Everything was so murky clear. This was just like the pilot. Not *his* pilot, of course. He knew how to fix his pilot. Tomorrow he was going to stay in and fix it or shoot himself in the head. He was never going to take another drink again tomorrow. At the bottom, his arms continued to make little arcs of almost peaceful effort. No more R.S.V.P. anxieties. No more fraudulent costumes. No more suppressing his natural enthusiasm. First thing tomorrow, he was going to e-mail Kate Lotvelt with an outpouring of ridiculous thanks for having invited him to the party of the year.

HERE WE AREN'T, SO QUICKLY

JONATHAN SAFRAN FOER

I was not good at drawing faces. I was just joking most of the time. I was not decisive in changing rooms or anywhere. I was so late because I was looking for flowers. I was just going through a tunnel whenever my mother called. I was not able to make toast without the radio. I was not able to tell if compliments were backhanded. I was not as tired as I said.

You were not able to ignore furniture imperfections. You were too light to arm the airbag. You were not able to open most jars. You were not sure how you should wear your hair, and so, ten minutes late and halfway down the stairs, you would examine your reflection in a framed picture of dead family. You were not angry, just protecting your dignity.

I was not able to run long distances. You were so kind to my sister when I didn't know how to be kind. I was just trying to remove a stain; I made a bigger stain. You were just asking a simple question. I was almost always at home, but I was not always at home at home. You were not able to cope with a stack of more than three books on my bedside table, or mixed currencies in the change dish, or plastic. I was not afraid of being alone; I just hated it. You were just admiring the progress of someone else's garden. I was so tired of food.

We went to the Atacama. We went to Sarajevo. We went to Tobey Pond every year until we didn't. We braved thirteen inches of snow to attend a lecture in a planetarium. We tried having dinner parties. We tried owning nothing. We left handprints in a moss garden in Kyoto, and got each other off under a towel in

Jaffa. We braved my parents' for Thanksgiving and yours for the rest, and how did it happen that we were suddenly at my father's side while he drowned in his own body? I lay beside him on the bed, observed my hand reaching for his brow, said, "Despite everything—" "What everything?" he asked, so I said, "Nothing," or nothing.

I was always destroying my passport in the wash. You were always awful at estimating. You were never willing to think of my habits as charming. I was just insisting that it was already too late to master an instrument or anything. You were never one to mention physical pain.

I couldn't explain the cycles of the moon without pen and paper, or with. You didn't know where e-mails *were*. I wouldn't congratulate a woman until she explicitly said she was pregnant. You spent a few minutes every day secretly regretting your laziness that didn't exist. I should have forgiven you for all that wasn't your fault.

You were terrible in emergencies. You were wonderful in "The Cherry Orchard." I was always never complaining, because confrontation was death to me, and because everything was pretty much always pretty much O.K. with me. You were not able to approach the ocean at night. I didn't know where my voice *was* between my phone and yours. You were never standing by the window at parties, but you were always by the window. I was so paranoid about kind words. I was just not watching the news in the basement. You were just making a heroic effort to make things look easy. I was terrible about acknowledging anyone else's efforts. You were not green-thumbed, but you were not content to be not content. I was always in need of just one good dress shirt, or just one something that I never had. You were too injured by things that happened in the distant past for anything to be effortless in the present. I was always struggling to be natural with my hands. You were never immune to unexpected gifts. I was mostly just joking.

HERE WE AREN'T, SO QUICKLY

I was not neurotic, just apocalyptic. You were always copying keys and looking up words. I was not afraid of quiet; I just hated it. So my hand was always in my pocket, around a phone I never answered. You were not cheap or handy with tools, just hurt by my distance. I was never indifferent to the children of strangers, just frustrated by my own unrelenting optimism. You were not unsurprised when, that last night in Norfolk, I drove you to Tobey Pond, led you by the hand down the slope of brambles and across the rotting planks to the constellations in the water. Sharing our happiness diminished your happiness. I was not going to dance at our wedding, and you were not going to speak. No part of me was nervous that morning.

When you screamed at no one, I sang to you. When you finally fell asleep, the nurse took him to bathe him, and, still sleeping, you reached out your arms.

He was not a terrible sleeper. I acknowledged to no one my inability to be still with him or anyone. You were not overwhelmed but overtired. I was never afraid of rolling over onto him in my sleep, but I awoke many nights sure that he was underwater on the floor. I loved collapsing things. You loved the tiny socks. You were not depressed, but you were unhappy. Your unhappiness didn't make me defensive; I just hated it. He was never happy unless held. I loved hammering things into walls. You hated having no inner life. I secretly wondered if he was deaf. I hated the gnawing longing that accompanied having everything. We were learning to see each other's blindnesses. I Googled questions that I couldn't ask our doctor or you.

They encouraged us to buy insurance. We had sex to have orgasms. You loved reupholstering. I went to the gym to go somewhere, and looked in the mirror when there was something I was hoping not to see. You hated our bed. He could stand himself up, but not get himself down. They fined us for our neighbor's garbage. We couldn't wait for the beginnings and ends of vacations. I was not able to look at a blueprint and see a renovated kitchen,

141

so I stayed out of it. They came to our door during meals, but I talked to them and gave.

I counted the seconds backward until he fell asleep, and then started counting the seconds backward until he woke up. We took the same walks again and again, and again and again ate at the same easy restaurants. They said he looked like them. I was always watching movie trailers on my computer. You were always wiping surfaces. I was always hearing my father's laugh and never remembering his face. You broke everyone's heart until you suddenly couldn't. He suddenly drew, suddenly spoke, suddenly wrote, suddenly reasoned. One night I couldn't help him with his math. He got married.

We went to London to see a play. We tried putting aside time to do nothing but read, but we did nothing but sleep. We were always never mentioning it, because we didn't know what it was. I did nothing but look for you for twenty-seven years. I didn't even know how electricity worked. We tried spending more time not together. I was not defensive about your boredom, but my happiness had nothing to do with happiness. I loved it when people who worked for me genuinely liked me. We were always moving furniture and never making eye contact. I hated my inability to visit a foreign city without fantasizing about real estate. And then your father was dead. I often wasn't reading the book that I was holding. You were never not in someone's garden. Our mothers were dying to talk about nothing.

At a certain point you became convinced that you were always reading yesterday's newspaper. At a certain point I stopped agonizing over being understood, and became over-reliant on my car's G.P.S. You couldn't tolerate trace amounts of jelly in the peanut-butter jar. I couldn't tolerate gratuitously boisterous laughter. At a certain point I could stare without pretext or apology. Isn't it funny that if God were to reveal and explain Himself, the majority of the world would necessarily be disappointed? At a certain point you stopped wearing sunscreen.

How can I explain the way I shrugged off nuclear annihilation but mortally feared a small fall? You couldn't tolerate people who couldn't tolerate babies on planes. I couldn't tolerate people who insisted that having a coffee after lunch would keep them up all night. At a certain point I could hear my knees and felt no need to correct other people's grammar. How can I explain why foreign cities came to mean so much to me? At a certain point you stopped agonizing over your ambitiousness, but at a certain point you stopped trying. I couldn't tolerate magicians who did things that someone who actually had magical powers would never do.

We were all doing well. I was still in love with the Olympics. The smaller the matter, the more I allowed your approval to mean to me. They kept producing new things that we didn't need that we needed. I needed your approval more than I needed anything. My sister died at a restaurant. My mother promised anyone who would listen that she was fine. They changed our filters. You wanted to see the northern lights. I wanted to learn a dead language. You were in the garden, not planting, but standing there. You dropped two handfuls of soil.

And here we aren't, so quickly: I'm not twenty-six and you're not sixty. I'm not forty-five or eighty-three, not being hoisted onto the shoulders of anybody wading into any sea. I'm not learning chess, and you're not losing your virginity. You're not stacking pebbles on gravestones; I'm not being stolen from my resting mother's arms. Why didn't you lose your virginity to me? Why didn't we enter the intersection one thousandth of a second sooner, and die instead of die laughing? Everything else happened—why not the things that could have?

I am not unrealistic anymore. You are not unemotional. I am not interested in the news anymore, but I was never interested in the news. What's more, I am probably ambidextrous. I was probably meant to be effortless. You look like yourself right now. I was so slow to change, but I changed. I was probably a natural tennis player, just like my father used to say over and over and over.

I changed and changed, and with more time I will change more. I'm not disappointed, just quiet. Not unthinking, just reckless. Not willfully unclear, just trying to say it as it wasn't. The more I remember, the more distant I feel. We reached the middle so quickly. After everything it's like nothing. I have always never been here. What a shame it wasn't easy. What a waste of what? What a joke. But come. No explaining or mending. Be beside me somewhere: on the split stools of this bar, by the edge of this cliff, in the seats of this borrowed car, at the prow of this ship, on the all-forgiving cushions of this threadbare sofa in this one-story copper-crying fixer-upper whose windows we once squinted through for hours before coming to our senses: "What would we even do with such a house?"

AN ARRANGED MARRIAGE

NELL FREUDENBERGER

Theirs was the second-to-last house on the road. The road ended in an asphalt circle called a cul-de-sac, and beyond the cul-de-sac was a field of corn. That field had startled Amina when she first arrived—had made her wonder, just for a moment, if she had been tricked (as everyone had predicted she would be) and ended up in a sort of American village. She'd had to remind herself of the clean and modern Rochester airport, and of the Pittsford Wegmans—a grocery store that was the first thing she described to her mother once she got her on the phone. When Amina asked about the field, George explained that there were power lines that couldn't be moved, and so no one could build a house there. After she understood its purpose, Amina liked the cornfield, which reminded her of her grandmother's village. She had been born there, back when the house was still a hut, with a thatched roof and a glazed-mud floor. Two years later, her parents had left the village to find work in Dhaka, but she had stayed with her grandmother and her Parveen Auntie until she was five years old. Her first memory was of climbing up the stone steps from the pond with her hand in Nanu's, watching a funny pattern of light and dark splotches turn into a frog hiding in the ragged shade of a coconut palm.

Nanu had had five daughters and two sons, but both of Amina's uncles had died before she was born. The elder one, Khokon, had been Mukti Bahini during the war, while the younger, Emdad, had stayed in the village so that her grandmother wouldn't worry too much. Even though he was younger, it was Emdad her grandmother had loved the best: that was why she'd kept him with her. When you tried to trick God in that way, bad things could happen. Emdad had died first, in a motorbike accident on his way to Shyamnagar, delivering prescription medicines for her grandmother's pharmacy. Two months later, Khokon had been killed by General Yahya's soldiers. Those deaths were the reason that Nanu had become the way she was now, quiet and heavy, like a stone.

Little by little, over the six months that they'd spent e-mailing each other, Amina had told George about her life. She'd said that she came from a good family, and that her parents had sacrificed to send her to an English-medium school, but she had not exaggerated her father's financial situation or the extent of her formal education. She'd explained that she'd learned to speak English at Maple Leaf International, but that she'd been forced to drop out when she was thirteen, because her father could no longer pay the fees. She'd also confessed that she was twenty-eight, rather than twenty-seven years old: her parents had waited a year to file her birth certificate so that she might one day have extra time to qualify for university or the civil-service exam. Her mother had warned her to be careful about what she revealed in her e-mails, but Amina found that once she started writing it was difficult to stop.

She told George how her father's business plans had a tendency to fail, and how each time one of those schemes foundered they had lost their apartment. She told him about the year they had spent living in Tejgaon, after having to leave the building called Moti Mahal, and how during that time her father had bought a single egg every day, which her mother had cooked for Amina because she was still growing and needed the protein. One night, when she had tried to share the egg with her parents, dividing it into three parts, her father had got so angry that he had tried to beat her (with a jump rope), and would have succeeded if her mother hadn't come after him with the broken handle of a chicken-feather broom.

Sometimes she got so involved in remembering what had happened that she forgot about the reader on the other end, and so she was surprised when George wrote back to tell her that her story had made him cry. He could not remember crying since his hamster had died, when he was in second grade, and he thought it meant that their connection was getting stronger. Amina responded immediately to apologize for making George cry, and to explain that it was not a sad story but a funny one, about her parents and the silly fights they sometimes had. Even if she and George didn't always understand each other, she never felt shy asking him questions. What level did the American second grade correspond to in the British system? What had he eaten for dinner as a child? And what, she was very curious to know, was a hamster?

It felt wonderful to have someone to confide in, someone she could trust not to gossip. (With whom could George gossip about Amina, after all?) It was a pleasure to write about difficult times in the past, now that things were better. By the time she started writing to George, Amina was supporting her parents with the money she made as a tutor for Top Talents; they were living in Mohammadpur, and of course they had plenty to eat. She still thought the proudest moment of her life had been when she was seventeen and returned home one day to surprise her parents with a television bought entirely out of her own earnings.

The other benefit of tutoring, one that she hadn't considered when she started out, was the access it afforded her to the computers that belonged to her wealthy pupils. She saw one of those students, Sharmila, three times a week; Sharmila's parents both had office jobs, and they encouraged Amina to stay as long as she wanted so that their daughter wouldn't just sit around with the servants all afternoon. Sharmila's mother confided that she thought

Amina would be a good influence on her daughter's character; Sharmila was very intelligent but easily distracted, and was not serious enough about saying her prayers. "She has been raised with everything," her mother said the first time Amina arrived, a sweep of her arm taking in the marble floors of the living room and the heavy brocade curtains on the picture windows overlooking the black surface of Gulshan Lake, which was revealed, even at this height, to be clogged with garbage, water lilies, and the shanties of migrant families. "She doesn't even know how lucky she is." Amina nodded politely, but she knew that Sharmila's mother's complaints were a performance. She would put on the same show when her daughter's marriage was being negotiated, exaggerating Sharmila's incompetence at preparing a simple dal or *kitchuri*, so that the groom's family would understand what a little princess they were about to receive.

Amina had sworn Sharmila to secrecy on the subject of AsianEuro.com, and then they'd had a lot of fun, looking through the photos in the "male gallery." Sharmila always chose the youngest and best-looking men; she would squeal and gasp when she came across one who was very old or very fat. More often than not, Amina had the same impulses, but she reminded herself that she was not a little girl playing a game. Her family's future depended on this decision, and she could not afford to base it on some kind of childish whim.

According to her mother, the man should not be divorced and he certainly shouldn't have any children. He had to have a bachelor's degree and a dependable job, and he should not drink alcohol. He should not be younger than thirty-five or older than fifty, and he had to be willing to convert to Islam. Her mother also insisted that Amina take off her glasses and wear a red sari that she had inherited from her cousin Ghaniyah for the photograph, but, once it had been taken and scanned into the computer (a great inconvenience) at the Internet café near her Auntie

No. 2's apartment in Savar, her mother would not allow her to post it online. "Why would you want a man who is interested only in your photograph?" she demanded, and nothing Amina could say about the way the site worked would change her mind.

"But the men will think you're ugly!" Sharmila exclaimed, when she heard about Amina's mother's stipulations. They were sitting on the rug in Sharmila's bedroom, with Sharmila's "Basic English Grammar" open between them. Amina's student was wearing the kameez of her International School uniform with a pair of pajama trousers decorated with frogs. She looked Amina up and down critically.

"Your hair is coarse, and you have an apple nose, but you aren't *ugly*," she concluded. "And now no one is going to write to you."

And although Amina had the very same fears, she decided to pretend to agree with her mother, for the sake of Sharmila's character.

As it happened, George did not post his picture online, either. He and Amina exchanged photos only once they had decided to become "exclusive" and take their profiles down from the site. When he saw her photograph, George wrote, he became even more convinced that she was the right person for him—not because of how pretty she was but because she hadn't used her "superficial charms" to advertise herself, the way so many American women did.

Amina hadn't believed that there was a man on earth—much less on AsianEuro.com—who would satisfy all of her mother's requirements, but George came very close. He was thirty-nine years old, and he had never been married. He had a master's degree from SUNY Buffalo and had worked as an aeronautical engineer for the I.T.T. Corporation for the past eleven years. He liked to have a Heineken beer while he was watching football—his team was the Dallas Cowboys—but he never had more than two, and he would think of converting to Islam, if that was what it would take to marry Amina.

Both of Amina's parents had hoped that she might someday go abroad, but it was her mother who had worked tirelessly with her at every step of the four-year journey that had finally led her to Rochester. If you counted their earliest efforts, it had actually been much longer than four years. When Amina was a girl, her mother had hoped to make her a famous singer, but once she discovered that Amina hadn't inherited her beautiful voice she'd switched her to the classical Bengali wooden flute. Amina had found it easy to work diligently at her studies, but could somehow never make time for the flute; she had abandoned it in favor of "The Five Positions of Ballet," and then "Ventriloquism: History and Techniques," both illustrated in manuals that she and her mother checked out from the British Council library.

Amina's parents' first really serious idea had been to apply to American universities; Amina had written to ten colleges, six of which had sent letters back. The University of Pittsburgh had encouraged her to apply for a special scholarship. Even with the scholarship, however, the tuition would have been six thousand dollars a year—that was without considering the cost of living in America. Her parents had read the letter from Pittsburgh over and over again, as if some new information might appear, and they had shown it to all the Dhaka relatives, who had, of course, begun to gossip. According to Ghaniyah, they were accusing Amina and her parents of "sleeping under a torn quilt and dreaming of gold."

A few weeks after the letter came, Amina was listening to the Voice of America. She and her mother had got into the habit of tuning in to the broadcasts in Special English, and even after those became too simple for Amina they continued to turn on "This Is

America." One day the program was dedicated to the different types of student and work visas, and the S.A.T., G.M.A.T., and TOEFL tests that foreign students might use to qualify for them. Amina was only half-listening (these were strategies that she had already considered, and all of them cost money) when the announcer said something that made her look up from her book. Her mother also paused, holding the iron above her father's best shirt and trousers, which were arranged on the ceramic tile as if there were already a man inside them.

"Of course, the easiest way to come to America is to find an American and get married!"

It wasn't as if she hadn't thought of this; ever since she was a little girl, she had loved everything foreign. When other girls traded their dresses for shalwar kameez, Amina had gone on wearing hers: she'd had to put on a white-and-gray shalwar kameez in order to go to Maple Leaf, but when she got home from school she changed back into a dress or a skirt. Her mother shook her head, but her father laughed and called her his little memsahib. Whenever he had money, he'd buy her a Fanta and a Cadbury chocolate bar.

Most of all, she had always loved fair skin. Her father was brown, and before she was born he had worried that she would be dark. But her mother was *ujjal shamla*, and Amina had come out golden, too. Once, when she was about eight or nine, she had said how much she loved fair skin in front of her father's business partner, who was as black as the fishermen who worked on the boats near her grandmother's house. Farooq Uncle had only laughed, but his wife had told Amina seriously that she had once felt the same way, and look whom she had ended up marrying. If you wanted one thing too much, she said, you sometimes wound up with the opposite.

Amina had never forgotten that advice. It was a species of Deshi wisdom that she knew from the village, and it was powerful, as long as you stayed in the village. The farther away you got, Amina believed, the less it held. It was possible to change your own destiny, but you had to be vigilant and you could never look back. That was why, when she heard the announcer's joke on Voice of America, the first thing she thought of was the Internet.

The thing that had impressed her about AsianEuro.com was the volume of both men and women looking for mates. When Amina joined, there were six hundred and forty-two men with profiles posted on the site, and, even without a photograph, Amina's profile got several responses right away. As it turned out, the problem was not making contact but staying in touch. Sometimes (as with Mike G. and Victor S.) a man would correspond for months before he suddenly stopped writing, with no explanation. Other times she would be the one to stop, because of something the man had written. In the case of Mike R., it was a request for a photo of Amina in a bathing suit; for "John H.," it was the admission, in a message sent at 3:43 a.m., that he was actually a Bengali Muslim living in Calcutta.

Her father had used these examples as ballast for his argument that the people who joined those sites could not be trusted, but her mother had weathered each disappointment along with Amina, and her resolve to help her daughter had seemed to grow stronger as the years passed and her father's situation failed to change. They had never been like an ordinary mother and daughter, partly because Amina was an only child, and partly because they'd spent so much time together after she had to leave school, studying the textbooks they borrowed from the British Council: "Functional English" and "New English First." When Amina and George began writing to each other, she and her mother had discussed the e-mails with the same seriousness they had once devoted to those textbooks. She had not hidden anything from her mother (not even the Heinekens), and eventually they had both become convinced of George's goodness. They had been a team, analyzing every new development, and so it was strange once things were finally settled, to realize that her mo~~~ not be coming with her.

Amina had been e-mailing with George for three months when he came to Dhaka to meet her family. Their courtship had more in common with her grandparents'—which had been arranged through a professional matchmaker in their village— than it did with that of her parents, who had had a love marriage and run away to Khulna when her mother was seventeen years old. Her grandparents hadn't seen each other until their wedding day, but they had examined photos. She had thought of her grandmother the day she received George's photo as an e-mail attachment. The photo wasn't what she'd been expecting, but once she'd seen it she couldn't remember the face she *had* imagined. That face had been erased by the real George: heavy-cheeked and fleshy, with half-lidded, sleepy eyes. His features were compressed into the center of his face, leaving large, uncolonized expanses of cheek and brow and chin. His skin was so light that even Amina had to admit that it was possible to be too fair.

She had put her hand over half the photo, so that only the eyes and forehead were visible. They were blue eyes, close together, with sparse blond brows and lashes. Could I love just those eyes? she asked herself, apart from anything else, and, after a certain number of minutes spent getting used to them, she decided that she could. She covered the eyes and asked the same question of the nose (more challenging because of the way it protruded, different from any nose she knew). She had slept on it, but the following day at the British Council (an agony to wait until the computer was free) she'd been pleased to discover that the photograph was better than she remembered. By the end of the day she thought that she could love even the nose.

Her father went to meet George at the airport, and her mother came to her room to tell her that he had arrived—although, of course, she had been watching from the balcony. The taxi had stopped at the beginning of the lane, which was unpaved. Her mother had worried about George walking down the dirt road to their apartment complex (what if it rained?), and they had even discussed hiring a rickshaw. But they would have had to hire two rickshaws, with the bags, and hiring two rickshaws to take two grown men less than two hundred metres would have made more of a spectacle than it was worth. Even from her hiding place on the balcony, behind her mother's hanging laundry, she could hear the landlady's sons, Hamid and Hassan, on the roof, practically falling over the edge to get a glimpse of Amina's suitor.

"What is he like?" she asked, and her mother reassured her.

"He's just like his picture. Nothing is wrong."

George said that he had known when he received her first e-mail that she was the one. When Amina asked how he had known, he was offended, and asked whether this was some kind of test. But Amina hadn't been testing him: she really wanted to know, because her own experience had been so different. With the men who had contacted her before George, she had wondered each time if this was the person she would marry. Once she and George started e-mailing each other exclusively, she had wondered the same thing about him, and she had continued wondering even after he booked the flight to Bangladesh. She wondered that first night as he ate with her family at their wobbly table, covered with a plastic map-of-the-world tablecloth, which her father discreetly steadied by placing his elbow somewhere in the neighborhood of Sudan, and during the excruciating hours they spent in the homes of her Dhaka aunts, talking to each other in English while everyone sat around them and watched. It wasn't until she was actually on the plane to Washington, D.C., wearing the gold-and-diamond ring they had bought in a hurry at Rifles Square on the last day of George's visit, that she finally became convinced it was going to happen.

Her visa required her to marry within ninety days of her arrival in the U.S. George wanted to allow her to get settled, and his mother needed time to organize the wedding party, so they waited almost two months. Amina's mother understood that it wouldn't be practical for George to pay for another place for Amina to live during that time, and she certainly didn't want her living alone in a foreign city. She agreed that Amina could stay in George's house for those months, but she made Amina promise that she and George would wait to do *that* until after the ceremony. She talked about the one thing that Amina could lose that she would never be able to get back.

In Dhaka, Amina had intended to keep her promise, although she didn't entirely agree with her mother. Especially after she got to America, and had time to think about it, it seemed to her that there were a lot of other things that could be lost in an equally permanent way. Her father had lost his business partner, for example, and he'd never found another full-time job; after that, they had lost their furniture, and then their apartments in Mirpur and Savar, and only Ghaniyah's father's intervention—securing the apartment in Mohammadpur at a special price, through a business associate—had kept them from becoming homeless altogether. These setbacks had taken their toll on her mother, who suffered from stomach ulcers and persistent rashes; Amina thought her mother was still beautiful, with her large, dark eyes and her thin, straight nose, but her mother claimed to have lost her looks for good. Worst of all, her grandmother had lost Emdad and Khokon, and nothing she could do would ever bring them back.

Compared with those losses, whatever it was that Amina lost on the third night she spent in George's house was nothing. George had agreed to her mother's conditions, and had set up a futon bed for her in the empty room upstairs. On the first two nights, they'd brushed their teeth together like a married couple, and then George had kissed her forehead before disappearing into his room. There were no curtains on the window of the room where Amina slept, and the tree outside made an unfamiliar, angled shadow on the floor. Everything was perfectly quiet. Even when she'd had her own room at home, there had always been noise from the street—horns, crying babies, the barking of dogs—not to mention the considerable sound of her father snoring on the other side of the wall.

Ordinarily she wore a long T-shirt and pajama bottoms to bed, but on the third night she experimented by going into the bathroom in only a kameez. "You look cute," George said, and that emboldened her; when he bent down to kiss her forehead, as usual, she looked up, so that they actually kissed on the mouth. (This was something that they had done downstairs on the couch during the day, but not yet at night.) Amina tried to imagine that her plain, machine-made top was a hand-embroidered wedding sari, and, when she pressed her body against her fiancé's, a strange sound escaped from him. It was as if there were another person inside him, who'd never spoken until now. That small, new voice— and the fact that she had been the cause of it—was what made her take George's hand and follow him into his bedroom.

She was surprised by how unpleasant it was, how unlike that kiss in the bathroom, which had given her the same feeling between her legs that she sometimes got when watching actors kiss on television. It didn't hurt as much as Ghaniyah had said it would, but she was too hot with George on top of her, and she didn't like the way he looked when he closed his eyes—as if he were in pain somewhere very far away. On the other hand, it was sweet the way he worried afterward, anxiously confirming that it was what she wanted. He asked her whether she minded having broken her promise to her mother, and the next morning, waking up for the first time beside someone who was not a member of her family, she was surprised to find that she had no regrets at all.

S he told George that she didn't need a wedding dress, that she was happy to get married in the clothes she already owned. She had ordered three new dresses before coming to Rochester, because tailoring was so much less expensive back at home.

"That's why I love you!" George said, slapping his hand on the kitchen table, as if he'd just won some kind of wager. "You're so much more *sensible* than other women."

Amina thought that it was settled, but later that night George talked to Ed, from his office, who reminded him that they would eventually have to show their wedding photographs to the I.N.S.

"Ed says a white dress is better for the green card," George said. "My cousin Jess'll take you shopping. Go get something you like."

Her mother wanted her to get married in a sari. Amina argued that that kind of wedding, with the gold jewelry, the red tinselled *orna*, and the hennaed hands, was really more Hindu than Muslim, and that as long as she was going to wear foreign clothes they might as well be American ones.

"No need for a red sari," her mother conceded. "How about blue? Or green?"

"It has to be a white dress," Amina said. "It has to be a real American wedding."

"Even a white sari," her mother said. "Some of the girls are doing it. I saw it on Trendz." Since she'd left, her mother had been spending hours every day in the Internet café in Savar. It was amazing to Amina that her mother could navigate even English sites like the Daily Star, where she knew how to get to the Life Style page, with its features on "hot new restaurants" and "splashy summer sandals," its recipes for French toast and beef Bourguignonne, and its decorating tips ("How about painting one wall of your living room a vibrant spring color?").

"A dress," Amina said firmly. "That's what the I.N.S. wants."

Of course her mother didn't really care about the dress, just as she would never consider visiting a restaurant (where who knew how dirty the kitchen might be) or painting one wall of the room where she brushed her teeth, chopped vegetables, and did the ironing "a vibrant spring color." The white dress was a way for her mother to talk about a concern she had had ever since the beginning—that Amina and George were not going to be properly married, by both an American civil servant and a Muslim imam.

The wedding dress was sleeveless white organdie, with white satin flowers appliquéd on the neck and the bust. She and Jessica compromised by eliminating the veil, but even without it the dress cost more than three hundred dollars, not including alterations. Amina stood on a wooden box with a clamp like a giant paper clip at her waist, and tried not to cry.

"Smile!" the saleswoman said. "A lot of girls would kill for a figure like yours."

"No kidding," Jessica said. "I wasn't that skinny when I was fourteen years old."

"Don't you like it?" the saleswoman asked.

"She's dumbstruck. Wait until George sees you in *that*."

Jessica chatted happily with the saleswoman as they paid for the dress with George's card, but once they were in the car she asked Amina whether everything was O.K.

"Everything is fine," Amina said. "Only it was so expensive."

"George doesn't mind," Jessica said. "Trust me, I could tell. Are you sure there's nothing else?"

Ordinarily when Amina felt homesickness coming on, she was able to distract herself with some kind of housework. Vacuuming, in particular, was helpful. Now, sitting in the car next to George's cousin, she was unprepared for the sudden stiffness in her chest, or the screen that dropped over everything, making Rochester's clean air and tidy green lawns, and even the inside of Jessica's very large, brand-new car, look dull and shabby. George's cousin was so kind, and still there was no way that she could explain to her what was really wrong. When they stopped at a red light, Jessica turned to Amina and put a hand on her arm.

"Because if something was wrong between you and George, I want you to know that you could tell me. I'm a good listener."

"Oh, no," Amina said, "George is no problem," and Jessica laughed, although Amina wasn't trying to be funny. She could tell that Jessica wasn't going to allow her to be silent, and so she searched for a question.

"What is the meaning of 'dumbstruck'?" she asked, feeling slightly dishonest. She had encountered that word for the first time in an exercise in a conversation primer, a dialogue between a Miss Mulligan and a Mr. Fredericks—" 'Your manners leave me dumbstruck, Mr. Fredericks,' Miss Mulligan exclaimed"— and for some reason that phrase had lodged itself in Amina's head. Often, when someone spat on the street in front of her, when a woman elbowed her out of the way at the market, or when she ran into one of her old classmates at the British Council and the girl inquired sweetly whether her father was still unemployed, she had thought of Miss Mulligan and how dumbstruck she might have been had she ever found herself in Bangladesh.

"Oh, um—surprised. It just means surprised. I bet you wondered what I was talking about!"

But it didn't just mean surprised. It meant so surprised that you could not speak. As Cousin Jessica continued to talk—about her weight and Amina's, about the foods she ate, didn't eat, or intended to eat—Amina concentrated on nodding and making noises to show that she understood. It was possible to be struck dumb by all sorts of emotion, not only surprise, and as they drove back toward Pittsford Amina thought that there ought to be a whole set of words to encompass those different varieties of silence.

At the bridal shower, Aunt Louise had wanted to know Amina's favorite flower, and had listened politely as Amina explained about the *krishnachura* and the romantic origins of its name. She felt silly when Aunt Louise showed up at city hall on the morning of the wedding, carrying a bouquet of lilacs and apologizing because there were no *krishnachura* to be found in Rochester. Then George's mother arrived with her own wedding veil, which she shyly offered to Amina for the ceremony.

"She didn't want a veil," George said, annoyed with his mother, but Amina took her mother-in-law's side, just as a bride would at home. Jessica gathered up a few of the ringlets the hairdresser had created and pinned the veil so that Amina could wear it hanging down her back. Then the small party—Jessica, George's mother, Aunt Louise and Uncle Dan, Ed from George's office and his Filipino wife, Min, and George's college friends Bill and Katie—followed them into the office, where they completed the paperwork for the marriage certificate. Amina thought that this was the wedding itself, so she was confused when the clerk ushered them into a smaller, carpeted room with a bench and asked them to wait.

"Is there some problem?" she asked George, but he was distracted by his friends, who were snapping pictures and laughing. "Is something wrong?"

"Sit down," George's mother said, but Aunt Louise grabbed her arm and jerked her upright.

"Careful!"

"What is it?" Amina said, trying to keep the panic out of her voice. For weeks she had been convinced that something would get in the way of the ceremony; this morning she had prayed—not that nothing would go wrong but that she would be prepared enough to see it coming and resourceful enough to find a way around it.

"If you sit, your dress will crease," Aunt Louise said.

"Come on," George's mother said, putting her hand on Amina's back. "It's your turn." And Amina was relieved to see that a door had opened on the opposite side of the room, and a short, bald man in a suit, a man who looked as if nothing on earth had ever disturbed his composure, was gesturing for them to enter. She understood that the wedding was continuing as planned, and she looked carefully around the room because she knew that her mother would want to hear exactly what it looked like. There were potted trees with braided trunks on either side of the window, and three rows of white plastic folding chairs, half-filled by George's family and friends. The deputy city clerk stood behind a wooden lectern underneath two certificates framed in gold. With the light from the window shining on his glasses, Amina couldn't see his eyes.

She had not expected to be nervous. George had told her what her cue would be, and Amina allowed her mind to wander while she waited for it. When she'd left Desh, there had still been the possibility that her parents would be able to come to Rochester for the wedding. Ninety days had seemed like enough time to plan, but when George went online to check the tickets they were almost fifteen hundred dollars each, even if her parents made stops in Dubai and Hamburg, Germany. George had been willing to help pay for the tickets, but she could tell that he wasn't happy about it, and so she had called her parents and given them her opinion: it would be a waste of money. The whole wedding would take maybe an hour and a half (including driving time), and Amina and her father agreed that to fly twenty hours in order to be there for something that took less than two hours didn't make a lot of sense.

In the end, as she'd expected, the problem was not her father but her mother. Her mother had agreed at first, and they'd even made another plan: as soon as Amina and George could come back to Dhaka, they would buy wedding clothes and Amina would go to the beauty salon; then they would go to a studio and take wedding photographs. Once they had the photographs, her mother could look at them all the time: it would be no different than if they'd all celebrated the wedding together for real.

Amina thought that her mother was satisfied by this, but a few nights later she got a call. Her mother was crying, and it was hard to understand her. Her father told her not to worry, but when she asked why her mother was crying he said, "She's crying because she's going to miss your wedding. She's going to miss it because I can't afford the ticket."

"No!" Amina said. "We decided—it didn't make sense. Three thousand dollars for one party!"

"Your wedding party. What kind of terrible parents don't come to their own daughter's wedding?"

She started to argue, but her father wasn't listening. Her mother was saying something in the background.

"What does she say?"

Her father paused so long that she would have thought the call had been dropped, if it weren't for the sounds in the background. It was morning in Mohammadpur, and Amina thought she could hear the venders calling outside the window: "Chilis! Eggs! Excellent-quality feather brooms!"

"She says it would have been better if you'd never been born," her father said finally.

•

D o you, Amina Mazid, take this man, George Barker, to be
your lawfully wedded husband?" the city clerk asked.

"I do," Amina said.

The question was asked of George, and then the clerk pronounced them husband and wife. "You may kiss each other," he
said.

George leaned toward her and Amina leaped back. From the
folding chairs, Cousin Jessica made a hiccupping sound. George's
face tightened like the mouth of a drawstring bag, and when
Amina glanced behind her she saw an identical contraction on
the face of her new mother-in-law. She hurriedly stepped toward
George, smiling to let him know that it had been a mistake, that
of course she wanted to kiss him in front of his family and
friends.

Many hours later, after cocktails at Aunt Louise and Uncle
Dan's, the reception dinner at Giorgio's Trattoria, and then
sweets, coffee, and the opening of gifts at the house of George's
mother (who now insisted that Amina call her "Mom"), when
they were home in bed together so much later than usual, George
asked her why she hadn't wanted to kiss him.

"You didn't tell me," she explained.

"You didn't know there was kissing at a wedding?"

Amina had to think about that for a minute, because of
course she had known. She had known since she was nine years
old and her Auntie No. 2 had bought a television. She had seen it
on "Dallas" and "L.A. Law" and "The Fall Guy," and then, more
recently, on her own television at home. There was no way to explain her ignorance to George.

"I did know. I guess I just didn't believe it would happen
to me."

"You've kissed me a hundred times," George said, in a voice
that suggested to Amina that they might be about to have their
first fight. She wanted to avoid that, especially tonight, because if

there was anything she believed about marriage it was that arguing the way her parents did was a waste of time.

"Not only kissing. The marriage in total."

"You didn't believe we were getting married? What did you think we were doing?"

"In Desh, you can make your plans, but they usually do not succeed."

"And in America?"

"In America you make your plans and then they happen."

To her relief, George finally smiled. "So you planned to kiss me, but you were surprised when it actually happened."

Amina hesitated, but her husband was patient until she found the right words.

"Not only surprised," she said. "I was dumbstruck."

THE ENTIRE NORTHERN SIDE WAS COVERED WITH FIRE

RIVKA GALCHEN

People say no one reads anymore, but I find that's not the case. Prisoners read. I guess they're not given much access to computers. A felicitous injustice for me. The nicest reader letters I've received—also the only reader letters I've received—have come from prisoners. Maybe we're all prisoners? In our lives, our habits, our relationships? That's not nice, my saying that. Maybe it's even evil, to co-opt the misery of others.

I want to mention that, when I sold the movie, my husband had just left me. I came home one day and a bunch of stuff was gone. I thought we'd been robbed. Then I found a note: "I can't live here anymore." He had taken quite a lot with him. For example, we had a particularly nice Parmesan grater and he had taken that. But he had left behind his winter coat. Also a child. We had a child together, sort of. I was carrying it—girl or boy, I hadn't wanted to find out—inside me.

I searched online for a replacement for that Parmesan grater, because I had really liked that Parmesan grater. It was the kind that works like a mill, not the kind you just scrape against; it had a handle that was fun to turn. There were a number of similar graters available, but with unappealing "comfort" grips. Finally, I found the same model. Was it premature to repurchase? Two days passed basically like that. Then, on Wednesday, my brother called. I gave him the update on my life.

"Wow, that's really something," he said.

"Yeah. It is something."

Then he said, "I thought it was a work of fantasy, Trish. I mean, I guess I should have told you about it—"

"What?"

"The blog," he said. "His blog. I-Can't-Stand-My-Wife-Dot-Blogspot-Dot-Com—"

"Are you going through one of your sleepless phases again?"

"Trish, I know it makes me sound snoopy, but Jonathan always seemed a little off to me, you know? So after he left your apartment one time, when I was alone there, I don't know, I'm sorry, I opened up his laptop, and I looked through the browser history. I was curious about his porn. I thought maybe there would be some really weird porn—"

"There was weird porn?"

"None at all, actually. Which in itself was kind of weird. No porn. Just his blog. And—"

"All right. Well. I'm thinking of buying a new Parmesan grater—"

"I thought it was satire, Trish. To be honest, it's pretty funny. Look, I knew you could never have said some of that stuff. I mean, you are kind of critical, Trish, but still. How could I have known Jonathan was serious? I thought, Maybe these things can be healthy. Funny is healthy. Maybe this is a healthy way for Jonathan to vent some anger, some hurt feelings. Healthy fantasy, you know? I didn't know what to do, Trish. I asked my shrink. He wouldn't weigh in! I decided not to interfere. Look, don't be mad at me, Trish, I'm just the traumatized bystander here—"

"You know what's weird? You keep saying 'Trish.' You do that when you're trying to avoid something. You should just come out and say whatever it is you want to say instead of saying 'Trish' all the time."

"Look, I'm going to come over and we're going to read it together. Or not. If that's what you want. Whatever you want."

I wasn't going to read the blog. So much writing out there in the world and who wants to read it? Not me.

All of this was not long after the publication of my first novel, and I had some money, even a bit of dignity, as the novel had been somewhat successful; at least, I'd been given a decent advance and money from foreign rights, too—it was a dream!—but I didn't have *lots* of dignity and I didn't have lots of money, either, just some. (The novel was a love story, between a bird and a whale.) Why was I already low on money? Partially because money just flies, as they say, or I guess it's time they say that about, the flying, but money, too—very winged. Still, one of the main reasons I didn't have much money was that I had been paying my husband's way through business school. At least, I'd thought I was doing that, but it turned out he wasn't enrolled in school—I went to look for him, of course—and he had just been making those "tuition" withdrawals for himself. He did have many nice qualities, my husband. His hair unwashed was divine. He never asked me what I'd gotten done on any particular day. We'd fallen madly in love in three weeks; that was fun. He used to call me "little chicken." I still miss him.

But back to the point. I had some money but not lots of money. Prison bars of not-money grew around me in dreams, like wild magic corn. My agent called—so nice to be called by a friend! . . . Or, no, not a friend . . . but sort of a friend—to see if I was interested in taking a meeting with some "movie people." I started crying, and then we got past that. The meeting would just be to talk over a few notions, no biggie, but maybe. They had liked the screenplay adaptation of my novel—I hadn't written a screenplay adaptation, this seemed to be a confusion—but thought it would be too expensive to have underwater filming and also flight filming. They wanted a cheaper love story. What if it was two land animals? Anyway, a meeting was proposed. My agent acted as if I might find it beneath me, like only another novel was serious work, and even though I know he didn't really think that—didn't really think that my writing was too serious to be set aside for a movie—I thought it was nice of him to pretend as if that might be the case.

"Great, great," I said, in a closing voice. "I'm, you know, all over that, totally."

"Totally?"

I coughed, as if to locate the problem in my throat.

"So you're O.K.?"

"Excited. I'll be there."

"Like even what's just happened to you—that's an idea right there."

And it struck me that maybe the meeting was the kind of thing that was going to save me, or at least that I should not entirely neglect to prepare for it, since it might kind of sort of save me a little bit. It could be a very good thing. I could watch myself put forward my best effort and then feel good about myself for having done so, for having tried. The least I could do—for me, and for my progeny, too!—was open up a Word file. Or, failing that, jot down a few notes on a legal pad. Let me just say now, because I don't believe in suspense—or at least I feel dirty when I try to engage in it, probably mostly because I'm no good at it—that I didn't prepare for the meeting at all.

My friend David came by—he needed to borrow money, he had much worse luck in life than I did, also expensive dental problems, and an addiction to acupuncture—and I told him about the leaving and also about the blog.

David already knew about the blog. He, too, had found it by going through the browser history of Jonathan's laptop. "The guy had a pretty amazing imagination," David said. "I wouldn't have guessed it. I suppose we should respect that."

"You didn't want to tell me?"

"Remember the two months you didn't speak to me when I said you were rash for getting married so fast?"

I had recently heard someone use the word "poleaxed." That word made me think back to those years in Kentucky as a child—I don't know why, that was the thought. I was a fancy citified woman now, and so my life could have properly sized disasters, ones in the comedy-of-manners way of things, rather than in the losing-a-limb-to-a-tractor-blade way of things; that was another thought. If there was no blood on the floor, then it wasn't a tragedy. That was what "urban" meant. Could mean. Poleaxed. I had also once come across a phrase about a book "lying like a poleaxed wildebeest in the middle of my life." It was my life that was lying in the middle of my life like that, like a poleaxed wildebeest.

"We were still sleeping together," I said. "People don't sleep with people they hate."

"Interesting," David said. "Verifiably false. Possibly irrelevant, regardless."

David was an aspiring screenwriter and my most reliable friend. I didn't tell him about my upcoming movie meeting. The mood of betrayal had gone general.

"Men like me," I said, hand on the belly that housed a being of unknown gender. "They really do. Just yesterday a man stopped me on the sidewalk to ask me if I was Italian."

"Who was talking about not liking you? You're just in pain."

"Maybe I'm not in pain."

"I'd put my money on pain. It's the Kantian sublime, what you're experiencing. There's your life, and then you get a glimpse of the vastness of the unknown all around that little itty-bitty island of the known."

A silence ate at the air in the room. Sublime. I thought of it as a flavor. Maybe related to Key lime. I didn't know what the Kantian sublime was. It's important to be an attentive host. And wife, for that matter. I went to the kitchen and got out some crackers and mustard and jam; it was what I had. I found some little decorative plates to make it look nicer. Suddenly I was worried that David might leave, that I'd have no friends left in the world.

"You know who I get fan letters from?" I said, as if pulling out a deck of cards to do a magic trick. "I do get fan letters. That's something, isn't it? Maybe there's a certain distance from which I am lovable. I get fan letters only from men. Only from men in prison."

I set down the confused cracker offering.

"You really haven't looked at the blog?" David let the crackers just sit there. "On the one hand, I want to congratulate you, but it might not be healthy, not looking."

I spread mustard on a cracker, and pretended not to have heard anything.

"I used to get fan letters from prisoners, too," David said. "Back when I ghostwrote that column for *Hustler*."

"You're not actually competing with me on this, are you?"

"I'm just sharing. This is intimacy, Trish."

"One of the letters—it was, like, seven pages long—was about love. Like a lengthy philosophical inquiry into the nature of love as written by a very smart fifteen-year-old. Not sex, but love. He said that, like, seven times. Maybe that means it was about sex. Anyhow. About love."

"Don't make that sex-love distinction in front of other people. It's not becoming."

Life, I was deciding, was a series of stumblings into the Kantian sublime. Not that I knew one sublime from another, as I said, but I planned on asking David about that when I was feeling less vulnerable. "Well, this kid said he wanted to confirm with me some impressions about love which he had gotten from my book. He wanted to know if I'd been honest about what love was. He said he would one day get out of jail. He said it was important that I write back to him. He said I could take as long as I wanted in getting back to him. 'As long as you need,' he said. 'You must be busy, take a year, that's fine.'"

"How gracious, for him to give you an extension at the university of him."

"I thought it was sweet. I didn't write back."

"Did I tell you that the pilot thing is finally fully dead now?"

"Gosh."

"Yeah. Well, do you miss Jonathan?"

"I wanted to tell you about this other letter. I don't know why this guy wrote to me in particular. He didn't say. He was very polite. He said simply that he had an idea for a movie, that it involved the Tunguska incident of 1908, and he wanted to know if it was a reasonable hypothesis that the explanation for the Tunguska incident could be antimatter—"

"I wonder if prison for me would be peaceful. Or intellectual—"

"I didn't know what the Tunguska incident was. I had to look it up. Turns out there was this place in Siberia where for thousands of acres the trees were suddenly laid flat. But it was the boonies, and so no scientists really bothered to check it out for years and years. There were reports of unbearably loud sounds, apocalyptic winds, strange blue lights. It must have looked and sounded like the end of the world. They think maybe it was a meteor. Some people saw a column of blue light, nearly as bright as the sun, moving north to east. Some said it moved southeast to northwest. Some said the light wasn't moving, just hovering. Windows hundreds of miles away were broken."

David was reading aloud to me from Jonathan's blog as I went and got the printouts of witness accounts I had found on that horrible thing called the Web.

"See, it's not even really *you*," he said.

"Shhh," I said. "Listen." I read out: "'The split in the sky grew larger, and the entire northern side was covered with fire.

At that moment I became so hot that I couldn't bear it, as if my shirt were on fire, I wanted to tear off my shirt and toss it down, but then the sky shut closed, and a strong thump sounded, and I was thrown several yards—' "

"God, I would have loved to be there. That really was the sublime—"

"They say that for nights the sky over Asia and Europe stayed bright enough to read the paper by."

"Did you answer the letter?"

"I did," I said. "Though who was I to answer it? I told him I couldn't think of any reason why antimatter wasn't a plausible explanation. I wished him luck with his idea. I might even have signed the note 'Love.' "

I lent David three hundred dollars, which seemed confirmation of my having taken advantage of him in some fashion.

Did I then take that movie meeting, all unprepared, after dressing in a way to accentuate my pregnancy, then to downplay it, then changing outfits again to accentuate it? Did I have no ideas? Did I start talking about the Kantian sublime, and about meteors and about love? A trans-generational love story with an old shepherd in Siberia, and a latter-day woman who knits, and a transfigurative event, and the sense that life is an enormous mystery but with secret connections that, you know, knit us all together? I did. All those things which I so studiously knew nothing about. Meteors enter the Earth's atmosphere every day. I was betraying so many, I felt so clean.

THE YOUNG PAINTERS

NICOLE KRAUSS

Four or five years after we got married, Your Honor, S. and I were invited to a dinner party at the home of a German dancer, who was then living in New York. At the time, S. worked at a theatre where the dancer was performing a solo piece. The apartment was small and filled with the dancer's unusual possessions, things he had been given or had found on the street or during his tireless travels, all arranged with the sense of space, proportion, timing, and grace that made him such a joy to watch onstage. In fact, it was strange and almost frustrating to see the dancer in street clothes and brown house slippers, moving so practically through his apartment, with little or no sign of the tremendous physical talent that lay dormant in him, and I found myself craving some break in this pragmatic façade, a leap or turn, some explosion of his true energy. All the same, once I got used to this and began examining his many little collections I had the elated, otherworldly feeling I sometimes get when entering the sphere of another's life, when for a moment changing my banal habits and living like that seems entirely possible, a feeling that always dissolves the next morning, when I wake up to the familiar, unmovable shapes of my own life.

At some point I got up from the dinner table to use the bathroom, and in the hall I passed the open door of the dancer's bedroom. The room was spare, with only a bed and a wooden chair and a little altar with candles set up in one corner. There was a large window facing south, through which lower Manhattan hung suspended in the dark. The walls were blank except for one painting that was tacked up with pins, a vibrant picture out of whose many bright, high-spirited strokes several faces emerged, as if from a bog, now and then topped with a hat. The faces on the top half of the paper were upside down, as if the painter had turned the page around or circled it on his or her knees while painting, in order to reach more easily. It was a strange piece of work, unlike the style of the other things the dancer had collected, and I studied it for a minute or two before continuing on to the bathroom.

The fire in the living room burned down; the night progressed. At the end, as we were putting on our coats, I surprised myself by asking the dancer who had made the painting. He told me that his best friend from childhood had done it when he was nine. My friend and his older sister, he said, though I think she did most of it. Afterward, they gave it to me. The dancer helped me on with my coat. You know, that painting has a sad story, he added a moment later, almost as an afterthought.

One afternoon, the mother gave the children sleeping pills in their tea. The boy was nine and his sister was eleven. Once they were asleep, she carried them to the car and drove out to the forest. By this time, it was getting dark. She poured gasoline all over the car and lit a match. All three burned to death. It's hard to explain, the dancer said, but I was always jealous of how things were at my friend's house. That year they kept their Christmas tree up until April. It turned brown and the needles were dropping off, but many times I nagged my mother about why we couldn't keep our Christmas tree up as long as they did at Jörn's.

In the silence that followed this story, which he told in the most straightforward manner, the dancer smiled. It may have been because I had my coat on, and the apartment was warm, but suddenly I began to feel lightheaded. There were many other things I would have liked to ask about the children and his friendship with them, but I was afraid I might faint, and so after another guest had made a joke about the morbid end to the night we thanked the dancer for the meal and said goodbye. As we rode down in the elevator I fought to steady myself, but S., who was humming quietly, seemed not to notice.

At that time, S. and I were thinking of having a child. But there were always things that we felt we had to work out first in our own lives, together and separately, and time simply passed without bringing any resolution, or a clearer sense of how we might go about being something more than what we were already struggling to be. And though when I was younger I believed I wanted to have a child, I was not surprised to find myself at thirty-five, and then forty, without one. Maybe this seems like ambivalence, Your Honor, and I suppose in part it was, but it was something else, too, a feeling I've always had, despite mounting evidence to the contrary, that there is—that there will always be—more time left for me. The years went by, my face changed in the mirror, my body was no longer what it had been, but I still found it difficult to believe that the possibility of having my own child could expire without my explicit agreement.

In the taxi home that night, I continued to think about that mother and her children: the wheels of the car softly rolling over the pine needles on the forest floor, the engine cut in a clearing, the pale faces of those young painters asleep in the back seat, dirt under their fingernails. How could she have done it? I said aloud to S. It was not really the question I wanted to ask, but it was as close as I could get just then. She lost her mind, he said simply, as if that were the end of it.

Not long afterward, I wrote a story about the dancer's childhood friend who had died asleep in his mother's car in the German forest. I didn't change any of the details; I only imagined more of them. The house the children had lived in, the buoyant smell of spring evenings seeping through the windows, the trees in the garden that they had planted themselves all rose up easily before me. How the children would sing together the songs that their mother had taught them, how she read the Bible to them, how they kept their collection of birds' eggs on the sill, and how the boy would climb into his sister's bed on stormy nights.

The story was accepted by a prominent magazine. I didn't call the dancer before it was published, nor did I send him a copy of the story. He lived through it, and I made use of it, embellishing it as I saw fit. Viewed in a certain light, that is the kind of work I do, Your Honor. When I received a copy of the magazine, I did wonder for a moment if the dancer would see it and how it would make him feel. But I did not spend very long on the thought, basking instead in the pride of seeing my work printed in the magazine. I didn't run into the dancer for some time after that, nor did I think about what I would say if I did. Furthermore, after the story was published I stopped thinking about the mother and her children who had burned to death in a car, as if by writing about them I had made them disappear.

I continued to write. I wrote my fourth novel, and then a fifth, which was largely based on my father, who had died the year before. It was a novel that I could not have written while he was alive. Had he been able to read it, I have little doubt that he would have felt betrayed. Toward the end of his life, he lost control of his body and was abandoned by his dignity, something he remained painfully aware of until his final days. In the novel, I chronicled these humiliations in vivid detail, even the time he defecated in his pants and I had to clean him, an incident he found so shameful that for many days afterward he was unable to look me in the eye, and which, it goes without saying, he would have pleaded with me, if he could have brought himself to speak of it, never to mention to anyone. But I did not stop at these torturous, intimate scenes, scenes that, could my father momentarily suspend his sense of shame, he might have acknowledged as reflecting less on him than on the universal plight of growing old and facing one's death—I did not stop there, but instead took his illness and his suffering, with all its pungent detail, and finally even his death, as an opportunity to write about his life and, more specifically, about his failings, as both a person and a father, failings whose precise and abundant detail could be ascribed to him alone. I paraded his faults and my misgivings, the high drama of my young life with him, thinly disguised (mostly by exaggeration) across the pages of that book. I gave unforgiving descriptions of his crimes as I saw them, and then I forgave him. And yet, even if, in the end, it was all done for the sake of hard-won compassion, even if the final notes of the book were of triumphant love and grief at the loss of him, in the weeks and months leading up to its publication a sickening feeling sometimes took hold of me and dumped its blackness before moving on. In the publicity interviews I gave, I emphasized that the book was fiction and professed my frustration with journalists and readers alike who insist on reading novels as the autobiographies of their authors, as if there were no such thing as the writer's imagination, as if the writer's work lay only in dutiful chronicling and not in fierce invention. I championed the writer's freedom—to create, to alter and amend, to collapse and expand, to ascribe meaning, to design, to perform, to affect, to choose a life, to experiment, and on and on—and quoted Henry James on the "immense increase" of that freedom, a "revelation," as he calls it, that anyone who has made a serious artistic attempt cannot help but become conscious of. Yes, with the novel based on my father if not flying then at least migrating off the shelves in bookstores across the country, I celebrated the writer's unparalleled freedom, freedom from responsibility to anything and anyone but her own instincts and vision. Perhaps I did not exactly say but certainly implied that the writer serves a higher calling, what one refers to only in art and religion as a vocation, and cannot worry too much about the feelings of those whose lives she borrows from.

Yes, I believed—perhaps even still believe—that the writer should not be cramped by the possible consequences of her work. She has no duty to earthly accuracy or verisimilitude. She is not an accountant, nor is she required to be something as ridiculous and misguided as a moral compass. In her work, the writer is free of laws. But in her life, Your Honor, she is not free.

Some months after the novel about my father was published, I was out walking and came to a bookstore near Washington Square Park. Out of habit, I slowed as I reached the window to see whether my book was on display. At that moment, I saw the dancer inside at the register, he saw me, and we locked eyes. For a second, I considered hurrying on my way, though I couldn't have said exactly what it was that made me so uneasy. But this quickly became impossible; the dancer raised his hand in greeting, and all I could do was wait for him to get his change and come out to say hello.

He wore a beautiful wool coat and a silk scarf knotted at his throat. In the sunlight I saw that he was older. Not by much, but enough that he could no longer be called young. I asked how he was, and he told me about a friend of his, who, like so many in those years, had died of AIDS. He spoke of a recent breakup with a long-term boyfriend, someone he had not yet met the last time I saw him, and then about an upcoming performance of a piece he had choreographed. Though five or six years had passed, S. and I were still married and lived in the same West Side apartment. From the outside, not very much had changed, and so when it was my turn to offer news I simply said that everything was fine and that I was still writing. The dancer nodded. It's pos-

sible that he even smiled, in a genuine way, a way that always
makes me, with my unrelenting self-consciousness, feel slightly
nervous and embarrassed when I encounter it, knowing that I
could never be so easy, open, or fluent. I know, he said. I read
everything you write. Do you? I said, surprised and suddenly agi-
tated. But he smiled again, and it seemed to me that the danger
had passed—the story would go unmentioned.

We walked a few blocks together, toward Union Square, before we had to turn off in separate directions. As we said goodbye, the dancer bent down and removed a piece of fluff from the
collar of my coat. The moment was tender and almost intimate.
I took it down off my wall, you know, he said softly. What? I said.
After I read your story, I took the painting down off my wall. I
found I couldn't bear to look at it anymore. You did? I said,
caught off guard. Why? At first I wondered myself, he said. It
had followed me from apartment to apartment, from city to city,
for almost twenty years. But after a while I understood what your
story had made so clear to me. What was that? I wanted to know,
but couldn't ask. Then the dancer, who though older was still
languid and full of grace, reached out and tapped me with two
fingers on the cheek, turned, and walked away.

As I made my way home, the dancer's gesture first baffled
and then annoyed me. On the surface, it had been easy to mistake for tenderness, but the more I thought about it the more
there seemed to be something condescending in it, even meant to
humiliate. In my mind, the dancer's smile became less and less
genuine, and it began to seem to me that he had been choreo-
graphing the gesture for years, turning it over, waiting to run into
me. And was it deserved? Hadn't he gamely told the story, not
only to me but to all of the dinner guests that night? If I had
discovered it through surreptitious means—reading his journals
or letters, which I couldn't possibly have done, knowing him as
little as I did—it would have been different. Or if he had told me

the story in confidence, filled with still painful emotion. But he had not. He had offered it with the same smile and festivity with which he had offered us a glass of grappa after dinner.

As I walked, I happened to pass a playground. It was already late in the afternoon, but the small fenced-in area was full of the children's high-pitched activity. Among the many apartments I'd lived in over the years, one was across the street from a playground and I'd always noticed that in the last half hour before dusk the children's voices seemed to get noisier. I could never tell whether it was because the city, in the failing light, had grown a decibel quieter or because the children had grown louder, knowing that their time there was almost through. Certain phrases or peals of laughter would break away from the rest, rising up, and hearing one of these I would sometimes get up from my desk to watch the children below. But I didn't stop to watch them now. Consumed by my run-in with the dancer, I barely noticed them, until a cry rang out, pained and terrified, an agonizing child's cry that tore into me, as if it were an appeal to me alone. I stopped short and jerked around, sure that I was going to find a mangled child fallen from a terrible height. But there was nothing, only the children running in and out of their circles and games, and no sign of where the cry had come from. My heart was racing, adrenaline coursing through me, my whole being poised to rush to save whoever had let loose that terrible scream. But the children continued to play, unalarmed. I scanned the buildings above, thinking that maybe the cry had come from an open window, though it was November and cold enough to need the heat. I stood gripping the fence for some time.

I didn't tell anyone what I'd heard, not even Dr. Lichtman, my therapist of many years. But the cry stayed with me. Sometimes I'd suddenly hear it again as I wrote, and would lose my train of thought or become flustered. I began to sense in it something mocking, an undertone I had not heard at first. Other times,

I'd hear the cry just as I crossed over into wakefulness or departed from sleep, and on those mornings I rose with the feeling of something wound around my neck. A hidden weight seemed to attach itself to simple objects—a teacup, a doorknob, a glass—hardly noticeable at first, beyond the sense that every move required a slightly greater exertion of energy, and by the time I negotiated among these things and arrived at my desk some reserve in me was already worn down or washed away. That cry haunted me. And slowly, Your Honor, I began to distrust myself.

THE SCIENCE OF FLIGHT

YIYUN LI

At lunch, Zichen told her two co-workers that she was considering going to a new place for her vacation. Feeling more adventurous this year? Ted said. Since Zichen had begun to work with Henry and Ted, thirteen years earlier, she had taken two weeks off every November to visit China—her hibernation retreat, as Ted called it. England, she said now when he asked, and she wondered which would be more adventurous in her colleagues' opinion, England or China.

Henry had been sent to Vietnam at eighteen, and had returned to Iowa six months later with ruptured intestines; at nineteen, barely recovered, he had married his high-school sweetheart. Every summer he and Caroline spent three weeks in a lakeside cabin in Wisconsin with their children and grandchildren. The farthest place Ted had travelled to was Chicago. A few years earlier, he had accompanied his daughter there for a high-school volleyball tournament; her team had lost in the final match, and with his daughter now a senior at the state university Ted still held Chicago responsible for the disappointment.

What's there to see in England in November? Ted asked. Zichen did not answer, because anything she said would fall short of his expectations. In previous years, he had wondered belligerently what there was to see in China, and Henry had been the one to shush Ted. Like Zichen's other acquaintances in America, they had been led to believe that in China she had a pair of parents, and that, like many, she had wedged some distance between herself and her parents, reducing her filial duty to an annual two-week visit.

What about China? Henry asked, laying out his lunch—a sandwich, a thermos of soup, and a banana—on a paper napkin. His time in the Army must have taught him to keep the contents of his life in good order. Henry was a neat man, his lab coat clean, what remained of his hair combed and parted precisely; he was quiet, but said enough not to seem sullen.

Her parents were taking a tour to Thailand with a group of retired people, Zichen said. Why couldn't she meet them in Thailand? Ted demanded, and predicted that she would see nothing in England but rain and coldness and people who were too polite to ask her to repeat her name.

There was a reason to visit a place where one's name was unpronounceable, Zichen thought, just as there was a reason that her parents continued to share a life in their daughter's mind. A month from now, rather than telling Henry and Ted about England, Zichen knew she would be relating tales of her parents' trip to Thailand: the crowded marketplace after nightfall, the cabaret show that they disliked but felt obliged to enjoy because it was said to be the highlight of their tour, the hotel bed that was too hard, or perhaps too soft. There were other moments, also imagined, though these she would keep to herself: her father's insistence on splitting a dish in a restaurant because he was unwilling to pay for two, her mother eying a grain of rice on her father's sleeve without pointing it out. They would've been one of those couples who had married young, and had, over the years, developed their separate ways to live with the mistake, he with his tyranny, she with her wordless contempt.

Henry, Ted, and Zichen worked in an animal-care center, in a two-story brick building next to a research facility that a hundred years ago had been an infirmary for tuberculosis patients. Because they were on the edge of a university town—the facility, a satellite site that housed some projects from the medical school, was in the middle of cornfields—the three of them had over the years become a more or less autonomous unit. Janice, their supervisor, a tall and angular woman who took pride in her extreme fairness and efficiency, came for a routine inspection once a week; Dr. Wilson, the attending veterinarian, a genial and absent-minded man, was about to retire any day now. The only crisis since Zichen had begun to work there—if one did not count the time the water was contaminated and fifty cages of mice contracted hepatitis, or the occasions when breeding went wrong, and the due date passed without a litter, or worse, with a disturbed mother mouse feeding on her own babies—was when a group of animal-rights activists had tried to break into the building on the eve of the new millennium. They had given up when the alarm went off, and instead liberated cages of minks from a farm thirty miles west on the country road. The farmer and his family had recovered less than a third of their loss, the local paper had reported. The rest of the minks, the farmer had told the *Gazette*, would not survive the Midwest winter and their many predators.

Zichen had been reading the newspaper in the office, pondering the fate of the homeless minks, when Henry, looking over her shoulder, said that he and the farmer had gone to the same high school. She was about to express her sympathy for his old classmate when Henry mentioned that the guy had once pursued Caroline when he was in Vietnam. She was glad that Caroline had not married the mink farmer, Zichen said, and Henry said he was, too, though come to think about it, perhaps Caroline wouldn't have minded a mink coat. Ted, entering the office with a stack of yellow death slips to file and overhearing the conversation, reminded Henry that a mink farmer's wife does not wear mink, just as cobblers' children have no shoes. What does that mean? Zichen asked. When the expression was explained to her, she thought of the way her grandmother used to clip her hair shorter than a boy's, in summer or winter, but this would not make a good office tale.

Zichen had grown up in her grandmother's hair salon—a small shack really, at the entrance of an apartment complex, with a wooden plank propped up by two stacks of bricks that served as a bench for the waiting customers, a folding chair in front of a mirror that hung from a low beam, and a makeshift washstand, next to which a kettle of water was kept warm on a coal stove. On the curtain that separated the salon from the bed shared by Zichen and her grandmother, there were prints of bunnies, white on a green-and-yellow background. There was no window in the shack, and a fluorescent light was turned on the moment her grandmother opened up the shop and continued buzzing until the end of the day, giving everything a perpetual bluish-white hue.

That her grandmother could have had an easier life in her old age was made clear to Zichen from her first years: Zichen's two uncles—her mother's elder brothers—would have dutifully taken in their mother, and between the two families they would have seen to it that she had a decent retirement. But how could you burden your own sons with a child like that? her grandmother used to ask her customers, as though the time Zichen had spent in the shop learning to sit up and then to walk, and later to assist her grandmother, handing her warm towels or cleaning the ashtrays—two blue-and-white china bowls placed at either end of the bench, the rims chipped, filled with smoldering cigarette ends and streaks of ash—had never softened the shock of the child's existence. It would have been a different story had she been an orphan, her grandmother would say; it would have been sensible for any uncle to take in an orphan, a statement her audience readily agreed with. Indeed, a woman who had run away with a man against her family's wish, who had given birth to a

baby out of wedlock, and had then been abandoned by the man—
that mother would have done her baby more of a favor had she
died during childbirth.

It hadn't taken long for Zichen to piece together her own
story from the parts alluded to by her grandmother and uncles
and customers and neighbors: that her grandmother had agreed
to raise her on the condition that her mother sever all connections with the family; that a couple had once come to the shop to
look her over, but then decided not to adopt her; that she owed
her life not only to her grandmother, who had to toil at an age
when other women could rest, but also to the patrons of the
shop, who remained loyal to her grandmother because of the responsibility they felt toward her.

Sitting on a bamboo stool in a corner and listening to her own
luck, both good and bad, discussed, Zichen would clandestinely
move her feet and make piles of hair according to a system known
only to her. Inevitably the game would be interrupted by the
strokes of her grandmother's broom, but even that did not disturb
Zichen, as the disassembling of the small hills of hair could also
be part of her scheme. Quit grinning like an idiot, her grandmother
would sometimes tell Zichen, turning from her clipping, and
Zichen would straighten her face, but when her grandmother
turned back to her customer she smiled again at the back of a
man's half-shaved head, or at the shoelaces of someone waiting on
the bench. Where on earth did the girl get that smile? her grandmother complained to the customers. One would think a child like
that should know how to make people forget her for a moment.

Hydrangea House, a sixteenth-century timber-framed house,
had served as a family home for generations before it was
turned into a B. and B.; Zichen wondered, reading the information provided on its Web site, how such a change had come

about. Perhaps the owners would tell her when she asked—if not the whole story, then bits and pieces that would nevertheless delight her.

On the Web site, there were no photographs of the kind that other places, with more business-minded management, displayed: blooming flowers in a garden or soft-colored curtains lifted by unseen wind. Instead, a small sketch of the house, made in ink or perhaps pencil, showed little except a whitewashed front wall and four rectangular windows. It was said to be "never a grand house"; two rooms, the Rose Room and the Lilac Room, were available upstairs.

The modest, almost apologetic way that Hydrangea House advertised itself made it easy for Zichen to choose it. The trip to England, despite Henry's bafflement and Ted's disapproval, was becoming a certainty in her mind. Tomorrow she would buy the plane ticket; next week she would call and reserve a room.

Contrary to Henry and Ted's beliefs, Zichen was neither an experienced nor a willing traveller. The summer she had begun to work at the animal-care center, Ted had invited her, along with Caroline and Henry, to a picnic on the Fourth of July. She had apologized and said that she needed to go to the East Coast to visit her husband, who had finished graduate school earlier that year and moved away for a job.

Before the holiday weekend, she had purchased more food than she could consume, and for four days she had hidden herself in her apartment and worked slowly through a Latin reader of Cicero's speeches. She had picked up the book from the library not for any grand ideas she might glean from the text; sometimes she forgot a sentence the moment she figured out its meaning. But the effort of making sense out of something that was at first glance indecipherable satisfied her, as did the slowness of the activity: an hour or two would pass as she made her way through one passage on a war; a day that would have otherwise been long was shortened.

Her interest in a dead language had been one of the things her husband had held against her when he asked for the divorce, which to Zichen had come neither as a surprise nor as a disappointment. There was a practical order of things for an immigrant couple like them, he had once explained to her. They would start a family when they had finally made it, he'd said comfortingly when the baby that Zichen so desired, who must have sensed itself unwanted by its father, miscarried. He'd had plans for her to go to graduate school to become a statistician, or an accountant, or a nurse, part of that order of things that would help them make it in the new country; he was finishing a Ph.D. in mathematics, and had a goal of working on Wall Street. Zichen, never arguing, for arguing was not in her nature, nevertheless dismissed his blueprint for her career with unconcealed resistance. There was no use in her copying Latin vocabulary onto flashcards, he had yelled at her—only once, as yelling was not in his nature, either—when she had outraged him by missing the G.R.E. test he had registered her to take, wasting more than a hundred dollars, half a month's rent.

The marriage had ended shortly before he moved away, but Zichen had used him to excuse herself from two years of social life. The cheek of it. When she lied to Henry and Ted, she could hear her grandmother's words, those she would say after Zichen had read her report card aloud in the shop. Unable to concentrate, the teachers commented every year; a lack of interest in both studying and participating in school activities. Her grades were meagre, barely good enough for her to proceed to the next level. What will you do with your life if you don't catch up with your schoolwork? her grandmother's customers ceaselessly asked her; not knowing the answer, she would smile as though she did not understand the question, and it was her smile more than her grades that had marked her as beyond teachable.

Zichen had given Henry and Ted a skeletal account of her divorce the third year into her work, as it had not felt right to continue to lie about a marriage that no longer existed. But an ex-husband was easy to be done with and never mentioned again, while a pair of parents, even if they lived on another continent, needed careful maintenance: an annual trip; phone calls that brought news from China; presents to take home—Wisconsin ginseng for her father, anti-aging cream for her mother.

She could easily take the usual trip back to China this year, a routine unbroken, thus causing little concern or suspense, but the truth was the shack that had housed her grandmother's shop had been demolished, her grandmother reduced to an urn of ashes. Her grandmother had lived in the shop until a month before her death, at ninety-three, and Zichen knew that for as long as her grandmother had lived there the shop door was opened every morning, the fluorescent light kept on till closing time, as it was during her annual visits.The news of the death had reached Zichen after the funeral; she had not been invited to it, as she knew her mother had not been. Together they, rather than an early widowhood, were blamed for her grandmother's harsh life; together they had been the old woman's disappointments, a daughter who had brought humiliation to the family, a granddaughter who had rashly married a man she had met twice and had then been unable to stay married for longer than three years.

The B. and B. was in a village called Neville Hill, some distance from Brighton, but to simplify the matter Zichen told Ted and Henry that Brighton was her final destination. They were eating lunch together, savoring one of the last warm autumn days before a cold front set in. She described the places she wanted to see: the promenade, the beach, the English Channel.

"Now, explain two things to me," Ted said, and for a moment Zichen thought Henry looked relieved that someone was going to confront her as he would never do. "First, why do you want to go to the beach in the winter?"

November was not winter yet, Zichen argued, and Ted merely nodded at her with a triumphant smile as though he had cornered a runaway rat that Zichen wasn't able to catch. It was rare that a mouse or a rat slipped through her grip, and when it did happen—a few times over the years—Ted would talk about it for days afterward with a childlike glee. When you touch an animal, it can tell right away if you are nervous or if you are the master, Henry had explained to Zichen when he trained her. Ted, during the first weeks, had liked to seek her out and tell her gruesome tales; his favorite one concerned a homemade rat guillotine that he and Henry had once built for a neurologist's study. But to her co-workers' surprise Zichen had never been jittery. She had applied for the opening because she had no other profitable skills, but in retrospect she wondered if she had found the right job out of blind luck. From the beginning, she had clipped a mouse's ear or prepped a rat for a skin graft as deftly as if she had always worked with animals. Even the bigger mammals had not distressed her: the monkeys that clamored in the cages and made faces at her when she came in with feed or a hose, the forlorn-looking dogs that rarely barked. After her training, Henry had told her that he and Ted would split the care of bigger mammals because they thought her too small, for instance, to dispose of a thirty-pound carcass by herself. The Rodent Queen—on her thirtieth birthday, they had left a toy crown on her desk, the words scrawled on with permanent marker.

"Now, winter or not winter," Ted said. "Why do you want to go to England all by yourself?"

People travelled alone all the time, Zichen said, and there was nothing wrong with that.

"But what are you going to do in a place where you don't know anyone?"

"How do you know I don't know anyone there?" Zichen said, but the moment the words came out she regretted them. Over the years she had become accustomed to who she was in other people's eyes: she knew she would be considered a loser by her Chinese acquaintances in America, a divorced woman toiling her life away in an animal-care facility, someone who had failed to make it; in her landlord's and neighbors' eyes she was the quiet, good-mannered foreigner who paid her rent on time, who every Halloween put out a couple of pumpkins, uncarved but with drawn-on eyes and mouths, and who had no visitors on weekends or holidays, so there was no conflict regarding the guest parking; for her grandmother and her aging customers, who spent their days in the shack for conversation and companionship more than for the care of their thinning hair or balding heads, she was—despite being a baby who should have remained unborn, a child with little merit and an unnerving manner, and a young woman who had no respect for marriage or her own future—a proof, in the end, of the ultimate mercy of life. She had been able to build a life out of her failures, to wire dollars to her grandmother, to return every year like a loyal homing pigeon and sit with the old customers, still with that unnerving smile on her face although they no longer cared; simply sitting with them and listening to them had absolved Zichen of all possible sins.

But it was who she was in the eyes of Henry and Ted that she cherished the most: sure-handed and efficient at her job, quiet yet at times chatty, uncomplicated. That she had memorized passages from "Winnie-the-Pooh," that she had read its Latin translation before reading the English text, she did not share with them, because that would make her an eccentric in their eyes. The things that gave her pleasure—the pile of wood shavings meant for the animals' bedding, which she assembled into small hills; the time she spent imagining her ex-husband in a pale-blue suburban house in New Jersey, his two sons growing up and looking more like him each year, his new wife unaging; the marriage she had given her father, whom she had never known, and her mother, whom she had met only once, in a small one-bedroom apartment in an older neighborhood in Beijing—these she did not share with Henry and Ted, because they would have made her a person with a history, in this or that time, this or that place.

"So, you are meeting someone in England?" Ted said.

"No," Zichen said. "Why should I?"

The unusual confrontational tone in her reply made Ted flinch, as though he had trespassed. He shrugged and, with a theatrical gesture, threw a half-eaten sandwich to a squirrel. Years earlier, Molly, Ted's wife, had asked Zichen if she wanted to meet someone she knew who was available; Henry's wife, Caroline, had mentioned once or twice her Chinese dentist, divorced, according to his office manager. When Zichen had not followed up on either lead, the women had not pressed her. Henry and Ted had never asked about her personal life. The ease into which the three of them had settled left her life outside work irrelevant, and she liked to imagine that for them it was as natural for her to cease to exist the moment she left work as it was natural that she could handle the animals with confidence and calm. The only time they had experienced discomfort was when Henry first trained her to breed the mice—he had asked Ted to be present when he showed her how to detect vaginal plugs, the evidence of successful copulation. Beet red, Henry had grabbed a few females to display their private parts to Zichen, then explained that sometimes the plugs did not guarantee pregnancy. Ted, rearranging the charts on the cages with a look of concentration, had remained uncharacteristically quiet on a subject that he might otherwise have joked about with Henry.

Had Ted been offended by her abruptness, Zichen wondered, but she could not find the words to soften the tension as he continued to whistle to the squirrel, which was ignoring his generosity. She had unwisely opened a door and then clumsily slammed it shut, but perhaps some harm had already been done.

"You'll do just fine," Henry said when it was apparent that Ted would not fill the rest of the lunch break with one of his favorite topics, the upcoming basketball game or a wrestling match. "When you think about it, I've seen my share of pictures of China but never any of England."

Zichen took pictures when she travelled to China, of things she imagined Henry might like to see, or of strange sights that would offer Ted an opportunity to criticize. Yes, she agreed. England would be a good change. She then dusted off the crumbs from the picnic table so that they would not find ants crawling over their space the next day. Before she had joined them, Henry and Ted used to eat in the office, the door open to the hallway with its constant odor of bleach and rodent pellets and damp bedding and dead animals; they did not seem to be bothered by this, but when Henry noticed that Zichen often sat on the steps in front of the building to eat her lunch, he had requested a picnic table as an improvement for their work environment.

Josephina, the proprietress of Hydrangea House, had been easy to talk with on the phone. If she had felt curious as to why a woman from America with an unpronounceable Chinese name would want to spend two weeks in Neville Hill she had not shown it. Zichen wondered, after the phone call, whether the thought would be shared with Josephina's husband; she wondered if they would decide that such a question did not matter in a bed-and-breakfast business.

When she got to Neville Hill, Zichen would explain to the owners that she had come in memory of an elderly woman who had befriended her when she first moved to America. Margaret was the woman's name. She had spent her childhood in Neville

Hill before marrying an American pastor, John Hubor, and had lived in the States for almost fifty years. Would the couple at Hydrangea House try to locate a girl in the village's past, one who had left, taken away by a marriage after the war? Perhaps they had heard of a girl named Margaret, or perhaps they would apologize for having no such recollection. The truth was, the name Neville Hill had never been mentioned in any of Zichen's conversations with Margaret, yet it was Neville Hill that Zichen had decided to go to, her research fitting the village to an old woman's descriptions: the school trips to Seaford taken on foot; the car rides to Brighton for special family occasions.

It was in the spring of 1994 when Zichen had met Margaret and John, in a supermarket; the autumn of 1995 when Margaret had been buried in a hillside cemetery. In the aisle between shelves of sugar, flour, and cooking utensils, Margaret had mistaken Zichen for a Chinese student she knew, who had recently graduated and moved to California; John had invited Zichen to become their friend, as the woman before her must have been invited, whose name Margaret had used for Zichen for as long as she had visited their house.

She would describe Margaret to the couple at Hydrangea House, and tell them how Margaret had tutored her in English when she first arrived in America because she had wanted Zichen, a young woman who had left her country for marriage, to have a friendship.

Growing up, Zichen had never had a close friend. A bastard was what some of the children at school had called her, the word learned from older siblings. Once, when Zichen was ten, and tired of being teased by her schoolmates, she had pointed to a neighbor who was passing by on the street and said that he was her real father. The man, overhearing Zichen's claim, had paled but said nothing—he had recently divorced, and his twin daughters had moved away with their mother.

The cheek of it; her grandmother would have been shocked by her shamelessness. The man Zichen had appointed as her father, a week later, asked her if she would like to see a butterfly exhibit that he perhaps imagined his own daughters would enjoy. Across the street from the park was the Friendship Hotel, and after the exhibit the man took her to the hotel entrance. It was one of only two hotels where foreigners were allowed to stay in Beijing, he explained; once, when he and his daughters were there, an American had given each of the girls a chocolate. It was ridiculous to stand in front of a hotel for the prospect of a chocolate; still, Zichen smiled at the two armed guards, and, later, at a pair of foreigners walking out of the hotel. The couple, both with pale skin and straw-colored hair, must have assumed that the man and Zichen were father and daughter, for they signalled and made it understood that they would take a picture of them. It was the first Polaroid Zichen had seen. The man had offered it to her, but she had refused to take it, the unspoken agreement being that their lives would go on as though the outing had never happened.

As a teen-ager she was one of the girls no one wanted to be close to; she was too strange and unpredictable to be a confidante, too inconspicuous to be a subject of any confidences. At that age, friendship had to offer drama or ease; she had been unable to provide either, and later, as a young woman, had been unable to provide either to attract a boy.

Yet it was ease she had offered in Margaret's brightly lit sunroom, giving the old woman the impression that she was tutoring Zichen, although the language they were studying was not English but Latin. Margaret's mind by then had been tangled, and Zichen, working by herself through "Wheelock's Latin," nonetheless allowed the old woman the luxury of repetitions: farmer, farmer, of the farmer, to the farmer, by the farmer, O farmer. Repeated, too, were the memories of Margaret's childhood village, which she must have known by then she would not be able to visit again: the trail that led to a secret pond, the couple in the red-roofed farmhouse giving birth to a baby who had six fingers on one hand. Every spring saw a batch of new chicks in the yard; in the summer the fluffy clouds sometimes stayed motionless for hours; any month could be called a rainy season, and the rain seemed to keep their house perpetually damp and chilly.

It was kind of Zichen to come and sit with Margaret, John had said the first time he drove her home at the end of the afternoon, apologizing for Margaret's confusions. She had come from a seaman's family, he had told Zichen on another ride home, as if that explained the fact that Margaret had picked up fourteen languages, when all of them, other than Latin and French and English, had been learned during her decades of marriage in America. Toward the summer of her last year, Margaret had shown signs of the approaching end, her words sometimes ungraspable even for John. Out of the blue one day she had produced a copy of "Winnie Ille Pu," the first edition of the Latin translation, for Zichen as a present; the translator, like Margaret and Zichen, was a man who had left home and settled in a foreign land, but that fact Zichen discovered only later.

No, she had not heard of "Winnie-the-Pooh," she had told John in the car that day. She had not had any children's books when she was growing up. It must have been the gentle sadness in John's eyes that had made her tell him other things, of being called a bastard when young, of having miscarried a baby, of not loving her husband. John, a careful driver, had removed a hand from the steering wheel and held hers for the rest of the drive. Had that been a moment of deception? Zichen wondered sometimes; had she betrayed Margaret's friendship?—not because Margaret had ever learned of the moment from Zichen or from John but because Zichen had relived it now and again, long after Margaret had been buried and John had moved away to Sioux City, to be close to his children and eventually, as he had explained to Zichen after Margaret's funeral, to be placed in a nursing home.

Once a year in December, Henry took Ted and Zichen out for a drink in a nearby village called Tiffin, since none of them liked the places in the university town, where the music was too loud, and the college students made heartless noises. The bar was on a country road and was never full. The men there were older; some of them, the more talkative ones, had once played in a paintball league with Henry; others remained reticent. The bartender, a former wrestler who had been a state champion in high school, liked to tease Ted; every year, he asked him what color underwear he had on that day, for Ted, being Ted, had once bragged that he bought only two kinds: black-and-gold for the university's colors, and red-and-white for his high school, which was also his wife's and his daughter's alma mater. The men at the bar had always been courteous toward Zichen, but as the years went by they had grown more relaxed, raising their glasses to her when she arrived, calling her the Ro-dent Queen.

A mail-order bride she was, she had told the bartender one year, when she had drunk more than she should have. It was not true, for there had not been any business transaction in her marriage: she and her ex-husband had agreed to marry after meeting twice in a teahouse near her grandmother's shop, he choosing her because she had grown up in a harsh environment, which would make her a good companion in America, she choosing him because of America.

It had made her feel happy for a moment, voicing the words "mail-order bride" and watching the bartender take in the information with an acknowledgment that felt neither aloof nor unnecessarily concerned. It would make her happy, too, she knew,

THE SCIENCE OF FLIGHT

when she told the story in Hydrangea House about Margaret and reading "Winnie-the-Pooh" in Latin, about how she herself, inexperienced with the language, had let the poor bear's head thump and thump again on the stairs.

"Your father and I did what we could for you," Zichen's mother had said, the only time they had met, perhaps the only time, too, since giving birth to Zichen that she had put herself and Zichen's father in the same sentence. Zichen did not know why her mother had agreed to see her before her departure for America, but she had recognized, at the first sight of her mother, the sternness and the stubbornness she had grown used to in her grandmother's face. One's parents could do only so much, her mother had explained, and a child was responsible for her own life. Her mother had not told her anything about her father, say-ing only that they had long since lost contact; she had not said anything about her new family, either, even though Zichen had known there was one, with a husband and two children. That Zichen's grandmother had kept her in order to spite her rebel-lious and humiliated daughter Zichen had always known; that her mother had given birth to her in order to spite her father had become evident when they met.

Every year, on the drive back from the out-of-town bar, Zichen sat in the back of the car and quietly wept. Henry drove cautiously, both hands gripping the steering wheel, as he always did after a drink, while Ted, in the passenger seat, talked with expert knowl-edge about a coming basketball game. She blamed the alcohol for her tears—that, and the cold moon in the winter sky.

One year when Ted had asked to be dropped off first, to at-tend a wrestling match, she had told Henry that she had grown up without knowing her parents' love for each other. Through the windshield she watched the frozen rain rushing toward them, and when the sound of the windshield wipers seemed too loud she said that her parents had stayed in the marriage because of her; and they had learned to tolerate each other for her sake. It was as close to the truth as she could get—she wished she could tell Henry about the man in front of the Friendship Hotel, or John's hand holding hers, but those stories would make her a different person in Henry's eyes—and afterward he patted her on the back as he walked her to her door, saying it was all right, because that was all he could say.

In Hydrangea House, perhaps she would tell the owners about her grandmother and her mother, the two women in her life whose blind passions had sustained them through the blows of fate, but even as she imagined that she knew she wouldn't. There was no way to leave herself out of their battle stories, and she knew that in all stories she must be left out—the life she had made for herself was a life of flight, of discarding the inessential and the essential alike, making use of the stolen pieces and memories, retreating to the lost moments of other people's lives.

AN HONEST EXIT

DINAW MENGESTU

Thirty-five years after my father left Ethiopia, he died in a room in a boarding house in Peoria, Illinois, that came with a partial view of the river. We had never spoken much during his lifetime, but, on a warm October morning in New York shortly after he died, I found myself having a conversation with him as I walked north on Amsterdam Avenue, toward the high school where for the past three years I had been teaching a course in Early American literature to privileged freshmen.

"That's the Academy right there," I told him. "You can see the top of the bell tower through the trees. I'm the only one who calls it the Academy. That's not its real name. I stole it from a short story by Kafka that I read in college—a monkey who's been trained to talk gives a speech to an academy. I used to wonder if that was how my students and the other teachers, even with all their liberal, cultured learning, saw me—as a monkey trying to teach their language back to them. Do you remember how you spoke? I hated it. You used those short, broken sentences that sounded as if you were spitting out the words, as if you had just learned them but already despised them, even the simplest ones. 'Take this.' 'Don't touch.' 'Leave now.'"

I arrived in my classroom ten minutes before the bell rang, just as the first of my students trickled in. They were the smartest, and took their seats near the center. The rest arrived in no discernible order, but I noticed that all of them, smart and stupid alike, seemed hardly to talk, or, if they talked, it was only in whispers. Most said hello as they entered, but their voices were more hesitant than usual, as if they weren't sure that it was really me they were addressing.

"I'm sorry for having missed class the other day," I began, and because I felt obliged to explain my absence I told them the truth. "My father passed away recently. I had to attend to his affairs."

And yet, because I had just finished talking to him, I felt that I hadn't said enough. So I continued. "He was sixty-seven years old when he died. He was born in a small village in northern Ethiopia. He was thirty-two when he left his home for a port town in Sudan in order to come here."

And while I could have ended there I had no desire to. I needed a history more complete than the strangled bits that he had owned and passed on to me—a short, brutal tale of having been trapped as a stowaway on a ship. So I continued with my father's story, knowing that I could make up the missing details as I went.

He was an engineer before he left Ethiopia, I told my students, but after spending several months in prison for attending a political rally banned by the government he was reduced to nothing. He knew that if he returned home he would eventually be arrested again, and that this time he wouldn't survive, so he took what little he had left and followed a group of men who told him that they were heading to Sudan, because it was the only way out.

For one week he walked west. He had never been in this part of the country before. Everything was flat, from the land to the horizon, one uninterrupted stream that not even a cloud dared to break. The fields were thick with wild green grass and bursts of yellow flowers. Eventually he found a ride on the back of a pickup truck already crowded with refugees heading toward the border. Every few hours, they passed a village, each one a cluster of thatch-roofed huts with a dirt road carved down the middle, where children eagerly waved as the refugees passed, as if the simple fact that they were travelling in a truck meant they were off to some-place better.

When he finally arrived at the port town in Sudan, he had already lost a dozen pounds. His slightly bulbous nose stood in stark contrast to the sunken cheeks and wide eyes that seemed to have been buried deep above them. His clothes fit him poorly. His hands looked larger; the bones were more visible. He thought his fingers were growing.

This was the farthest from home he had ever travelled, but he knew that he couldn't stay there. He wanted to leave the entire continent far behind, for Europe or America, where life was rumored to be better.

It was the oldest port in Sudan and one of the oldest cities in the country. At its peak, fifty thousand people had lived there, but now only a fraction of the population was left. Several wars had been fought nearby, the last one in 1970, between a small group of rebels and the government. There were burned-out tanks on the edge of town and dozens of half-destroyed, abandoned houses. There was sand and dust everywhere, and on most days the temperature came close to a hundred degrees. The people who lived there were desperately poor. Some worked as fishermen but most spent their days by the dock, looking for work unloading crates from the dozens of small freight ships in the harbor. My father was told that he could find a job there, and that if he was patient and earned enough money he could even buy his way out of the country on one of the boats.

The bell for the end of first period rang then. My students waited a moment before gathering their bags and leaving; they were either compelled or baffled by what I had told them. I tried to see them all in one long glance before they were gone. They had always been just bodies to me, a prescribed number that came and went each day of the semester until they were replaced by others, who would do the same. For a few seconds, though, I saw them clearly—the deliberately rumpled hair of the boys and the neat, tidy composure of the girls in opposition. They were still in the making, each and every one of them. Somehow I had missed that. None of them looked away or averted their gaze from mine, which I took as confirmation that I could continue.

As I walked home that night I was aware of a growing vortex of e-mails and text messages being passed among my students. Millions of invisible bits of data were being transmitted through underground cable wires and satellite networks, and I was their sole subject and object of concern. I don't know why I found so much comfort in that thought, but it nearly lifted me off the ground, and suddenly, everywhere, I felt embraced. As I walked down Riverside Drive, with the Hudson River and the rush of traffic pouring up and down the West Side Highway to my right, the tightly controlled neighborhood borders and divisions hardly mattered.

The next day at the Academy I told my students at the start of class that they could put their anthologies and worksheets away. "We won't be needing them for now," I said.

My father's first job at the port was bringing tea to the dockworkers, a job for which he was paid only in tips—a few cents here and there that gradually added up. On an average day, he would serve anywhere between three and five hundred cups of tea. He could carry as many as ten at a time on a large wooden platter that he learned to balance on his forearm. As a child he had been clumsy; his father would often yell at him for breaking a glass or for being unable to bring him a cup of coffee without spilling it. So as soon as he got the job he began practicing at night with a tray full of stones that were as light as the cups of tea. If the stones moved he knew he had failed and would try again, until eventually he probably could have walked several miles without spilling a drop of tea or shifting a single stone.

He hid his earnings in a pocket sewn into the inside of his pants. The one friend he had in town, a man by the name of Abrahim, had told him never to let anyone know how much money he had: "If someone sees you have two dollars, he will think you have twenty. It's always better to make people think you have nothing at all."

Abrahim was the one who found him the job carrying tea. He met my father on his third day in town and knew immediately that he was a foreigner. He went up to him and said, in perfect English, "Hello. My name is Abrahim, like the prophet. Let me help you while you're in this town."

He was several inches shorter and better dressed than most of the other men that my father had seen there. His head was bald, with the exception of two graying tufts of hair that arced behind his ears. The last two fingers on his right hand looked as if they had been crushed and then tied together. He bowed slightly when he introduced himself and walked with what might have been a small limp, which in my father's mind made trusting him easier.

At first, my father slept outside, near the harbor, where hundreds of other men also camped out, most of them refugees like him. Abrahim had told him that it was dangerous to sleep alone, but he had also said that if he slept in the town he was certain to be beaten and arrested by the police.

After a week out there, he heard footsteps near his head just as he was falling asleep. When he opened his eyes and looked up he saw three men standing nearby, their backs all slightly turned to him, so that he could see only their long white djellabahs, dirty but not nearly as filthy as some of the others that he had recently seen. As he watched, one of the men lifted his hands into the air slowly, as if he were struggling to pass something over his head. He recited a prayer that my father had heard several times on his way to Sudan and on multiple occasions in Ethiopia at the homes of Muslim friends. The man repeated the prayer a second and then a third time, and when he was finished the two other men bent down and picked up what at first appeared to be a sack of grain but which, he realized a second later, was clearly a body. The man had been lying there when my father went to sleep. There had been nothing to indicate that he was dead or even injured. When my father told Abrahim the next day, his response was simple: "Don't think about it too much. It's easy to die around here and have no one notice."

He promised to find my father a better place to sleep, and he did. Later that same day, he found my father preparing his mat near the harbor, and told him to follow him. "I have a surprise for you," he said.

The owner of the boarding house where he was going to stay from now on was a business associate of Abrahim's. "We've worked together many times over the years," Abrahim told my father, although he never explained what they did. When my father asked him how he could repay his kindness, he waved the question away. "Don't worry," Abrahim told him. "You can do something for me later."

Unlike most of what I had told my students so far, Abrahim had a real history that I could draw on. My father had mentioned him regularly, not as a part of normal conversation but as a casual aside that could come up at any time without warning. Unbidden, my father had often said that Abrahim was the only real friend he had ever had, and on several occasions he had credited him with saving his life. At other times, my father had claimed that the world was full of crooks, and that after his experiences with a man named Abrahim in Sudan he would never trust a Sudanese, Muslim, or African again.

The Abrahim who came to life in my classroom was a far nobler man than the one I had previously imagined. This Abrahim had a flair for blunt but poetic statements, like the time he told my father that even the sand in the port town was of an inferior quality to the kind he had known in his home village, hundreds of kilometres west of there.

"Everything here is shit," he said. "Even the sand."

Eventually he got my father a better-paying second job, as a porter on the docks. He told him, "You're going to be my best investment yet. Everything I give to you I will get back tenfold." Abrahim came by almost every day to share a cup of tea shortly after evening prayers, when hundreds of individual trails of smoke from the campfires wound their way up into the sky. He would pinch and pull at my father's waist as if he were a goat or a sheep and then say, "What do you expect? I have to check on the health of my investment." Afterward, as he was leaving, he always offered the same simple piece of advice:

"Stretch, Yosef!" he would yell out. "Stretch all the time, until your body becomes as loose as a monkey's."

At the docks, my father carried boxes from dawn until midday, when it got too hot to work. Before his shift at the teahouse, he would take a nap under a tree and look at the sea and think about the water in front of him. Like most of the men, he was thirsty all the time and convinced that there was something irreparably cruel about a place that put water that could not be drunk in front of you. He imagined building a boat of his own, something simple but sturdy that could at the very least make its way across the gulf to Saudi Arabia. And, if that were to fail, then he'd stuff himself into a box and drift until he reached a foreign shore or died trying.

At least once or twice a week, Abrahim would pick my father up from his room in the evening and walk him down to the docks in order to explain to him how the port town really worked. The only lights they saw came from the scattered fires around which groups of men were huddled. Despite the darkness, people moved about freely and in greater numbers than during the day. It was as if a second city were buried underneath the first, and excavated each night. Women without veils could be spotted along some of the narrow back streets, and my father could smell roasting meat and strong liquor.

"The ships that you see at the far end of the port are all government-controlled," Abrahim told my father. "They carry one of two things: food or weapons. We don't make either in Sudan. You may have noticed this. That doesn't mean we don't love them equally. Maybe the weapons more. Have you ever seen a hungry man with a gun? Of course not. Always stay away from that part of the dock. It's run by a couple of generals and a colonel who report straight to the President. They are like gods in this little town, but with better cars. If a soldier sees you there's nothing I can do to help. Not even God will save a fool.

"The food is supposed to go to the south. It comes from all over the world in great big sacks that say 'U.S.A.' Instead, it goes straight to Khartoum with the weapons. And do you know why? Because it's easier and cheaper to starve people to death than to shoot them. Bullets cost money. Soldiers cost money. Keeping all the food in a warehouse costs nothing."

In the course of several evenings, Abrahim worked his way down the line of boats docked in the harbor. His favorite ones, he said, were those near the end.

"Those ships over there—all the way at the other end. Those are the ones you need to think about. Those are the ones that go to Europe. You know how you can tell? Look at the flags. You see that one there—with the black and gold? It goes all the way to Italy or Spain. Maybe even France. Some of the men who work on it are friends of mine. Business associates. You can trust them. They're not like the rest of the people here, who will disappear with your money."

After that night, my father began to take seriously Abrahim's advice about stretching. He worked his body into various positions that he would hold for ten or fifteen minutes, and then for as long as an hour. At night before he went to bed he practiced sitting with his legs crossed, and then he stretched his back by curling himself into a ball. After four months he could hold that position for hours, which was precisely what Abrahim told him he would need to do.

"The first few hours will be the hardest," he said. "You'll have to be on the ship before it's fully loaded, and then you will have to stay completely hidden. Only once it's far out to sea will you be able to move."

My father thought about writing a letter to his family, but he didn't know what to say. No one knew for certain if he was alive, and, until he was confident that he would remain so, he preferred to keep it that way. It was better than writing home and saying, "Hello. I miss you. I'm alive and well," when only the first half of that statement was certain still to be true by the time the letter arrived.

Four months and three weeks after my father arrived in the port town, war broke out in the east. A garrison of soldiers stationed in a village five hundred miles away revolted, and with the help of the villagers began to take over vast swaths of territory in the name of forming an independent state for all the black tribes of the country. There were rumors of massacres on both sides. Who was responsible for the killing always depended on who was talking. It was said that in one village all the young boys had been forced to dig graves for their parents and siblings before watching their executions. Afterward they were forced to join the rebellion that still didn't have a name.

Factions began to erupt all over the town. Older men who remembered the last war tended to favor the government, since they had once been soldiers as well. Anyone who was born in the south of the country was ardently in favor of the rebels, and many vowed to join them if they ever came close.

Abrahim and my father stopped going to the port at night. "When the fighting breaks out here," Abrahim told him, "they'll attack the port first. They'll burn the local ships and try to take control of the government ones."

Every day more soldiers arrived. There had always been soldiers in town, but these new ones were different. They came from the opposite corner of the country and spoke none of the local languages; what Arabic they spoke was often almost impossible to understand. The senior commanders, who rode standing up in their jeeps, all wore bright-gold sunglasses that covered half their face, but it was clear regardless that they were foreigners, and had been brought here because they had no attachment to the town or to its people.

At night my father often heard gunfire mixed in with the sound of dogs howling. Every day he pleaded with Abrahim to help him find a way out.

"I have plenty of money saved now," he said, even though it was a lie. If there was an honest exit, he would find a way to pay for it. Abrahim's response was always the same: "A man who has no patience here is better off in Hell."

Two weeks after the first stories of the rebellion appeared, there was talk in the market of a mile-long convoy of jeeps heading toward the town. The foreign ships had begun to leave the port that morning. The rebels were advancing, and would be there by the end of the afternoon. Within hours the rumors had circled the town. They would spare no one. They would attack only the soldiers. They would be greeted as liberators. They were like animals and should be treated as such. My father watched as the women who lived nearby folded their belongings into bags and made for the road with their children at their side or strapped to their backs. Where are they going? he wondered. They have the sea on one side and a desert on the other.

Abrahim found him after lunch. There was no one to serve tea to that day.

"I see you're very busy," he said. "You want me to come back when it's less crowded?"

"Are you leaving?" my father asked him.

"I already have," Abrahim said. "A long time ago. My entire family is already in Khartoum. I'm just waiting for my body to join them."

By late in the afternoon they could hear distant mortar shells slamming into the desert. "They're like children with toys," Abrahim said, pointing out to the desert from the roof of the boarding house, where they were standing. "They don't even know yet how far they can shoot with their big guns. There's nothing out there— or maybe they'll get lucky and kill a camel. They'll keep doing that until eventually they run out of shells, or camels.

"It's going to be terrible what happens to them," Abrahim continued. "They think they can scare away the soldiers because they have a couple of big guns. They think it's 1898 and the Battle of Omdurman again, except now they're the British."

My father never thought that war could look simple or pathetic, but from that rooftop it did. The rebels were loudly announcing their approach, and, from what my father could see, the soldiers in the town had disappeared. He began to think that Abrahim was wrong, and that the rebels, despite their foolishness, would sweep into town with barely a struggle. He was thinking whether or not to say this to Abrahim when he heard the first distant rumbling over his head. Abrahim and my father turned and looked out toward the sea, where a plane was approaching, flying far too low. Within a minute, it was above them.

"This will be over soon," Abrahim said. They both waited to hear the sound of a bomb dropping, but nothing happened. The plane had pulled up at the last minute. Shots were harmlessly fired in its direction and the convoy kept approaching—a long, jagged line of old pickup trucks trying to escape the horizon.

When the same plane returned twenty minutes later, three slimmer and clearly foreign-made jets were flying close to it.

"The first was just a warning," Abrahim said. "To give them a chance to at least try to run away. They were too stupid to understand that. They thought they had won."

The planes passed. My father and Abrahim counted the seconds. Even from a distance they made a spectacular roar—at least seven bombs were dropped directly onto the rebels, whose convoy disappeared into a cloud of smoke and sand. From some of the neighboring rooftops there were shouts of joy. Soldiers were soon spilling back out into the street singing their victory.

"They should never have tried to take the port," Abrahim said. "They could have spent years fighting in the desert for their little villages and no one would have really bothered them. But do you think any of those big countries were going to risk losing this beautiful port? By the end of tonight all the foreign ships will be back. Their governments will tell them that it's safe. They've taken care of the problem, and soon, maybe in a day or two, you'll be able to leave."

A week later, during my father's mid-afternoon break, Abrahim found him resting in his usual spot in the shade, staring out at the water. The two of them walked to a nearby café, and for the first time since my father had come to Sudan someone brought him a cup of tea and lunch.

"This is your going-away meal. Enjoy it," Abrahim said. "You're leaving tonight."

Abrahim ordered a large plate of grilled meats—sheep intestines and what looked to be the neck of a goat—cooked in a brown stew, a feast unlike anything my father had eaten in months. When the food came, he wanted to cry and was briefly afraid to eat it. Abrahim had always told him never to trust anyone, and of course my father had extended that advice to Abrahim himself. Perhaps this was Abrahim's final trick on him: perhaps the food would disappear just as he leaned over to touch it, or perhaps it was poisoned with something that would send him off into a deep sleep from which he would awake in shackles. My father reached into his pants and untied the pouch in which he carried all his money. He placed it on the table.

"That's everything I have," he said. "I don't know if it's enough."

Abrahim ignored the money and dipped into the food with a piece of bread.

"After where your hand has just been I suggest you wash it before eating," he said. "And take your purse with you."

When they were finished, Abrahim walked my father to a part of the town he had never seen before—a wide dusty street that grew increasingly narrow, until the tin-roofed shacks that lined it were almost touching one another. Abrahim and my father stopped in front of one of the houses, and Abrahim pulled back the curtain that served as the door. Inside, a heavyset older woman, head partly veiled, sat behind a wooden counter on top of which rested a row of variously sized glass bottles. Abrahim grabbed one and told my father to take a seat in the corner of the room where a group of pillows had been laid. He negotiated and argued with the woman for several minutes until, finally, he pulled a bundle of Sudanese notes from his breast pocket. He sat down next to my father and handed the bottle to him.

"A drink for the road," he said. "Take it slow."

If Abrahim's intention was to harm him, then so be it, my father thought. A decent meal and a drink afterward were not the worst way to go. If such things had been offered to every dying man in this town, then the line of men waiting to die would have stretched for miles.

"Give me your little purse now," Abrahim said. My father handed him the pouch and Abrahim flipped through the bills. He took a few notes from his own pile and added it to the collection.

"This will buy you water, maybe a little food, and the silence of a few people on board. Don't expect anything else from them. Don't ask for food or for anything that they don't give you. Don't look them in the eyes, and don't try to talk to them. They will act as if you don't exist, which is the best thing. If you do exist then they will throw you overboard at night. Men get on board and they begin to complain. They say their backs hurt or their legs hurt. They say they're thirsty or hungry. When that happens they're gagged and thrown into the sea, where they can have all the space and water they want."

My father took a sip of the liquor, whose harsh, acrid smell had filled the air the moment Abrahim popped the lid.

"When you get to Europe, this is what you are going to do. You are going to be arrested. You will tell them that you want political asylum and they will take you to a jail that looks like Heaven. They will give you food and clothes and even a bed to sleep in. You may never want to leave—that's how good it will feel. Tell them you were fighting against the Communists and they will love you. They will give you your pick of countries, and you will tell them that you want to go to England. You will tell them that you have left behind your wife in Sudan, and that her life is now in danger and you want her to come as well. You will show them this picture."

Abrahim pulled from his wallet a photograph of a young girl, no older than fifteen or sixteen, dressed in a bizarre array of Western clothes—a pleated black-and-white polka-dot dress that was several sizes too large, a pair of high-top sneakers, and makeup that had been painted on to make her look older.

"This is my daughter. She lives in Khartoum right now with her mother and aunts. She's very bright. The best student in her class. When you get to England you're going to say that she's your wife. This is how you're going to repay me. Do you understand?"

My father nodded.

"This is proof of your marriage," Abrahim said. "I had to spend a lot of money to get that made."

Abrahim handed him a slip of paper that had been folded only twice in its life, since such paper didn't last long in environments like this. The words spelled it out clearly. My father had been married for almost two years to a person he had never met.

"You will give this to someone at the British Embassy," Abrahim said, laying his hands on top of my father's, as if the two were entering into a secret pact simply by touching the same piece of paper. "It may take some weeks, but eventually they will give her the visa. You will then call me from London, and I will take care of the rest. We have the money for the ticket, and some more for both of you when she arrives. Maybe after one or two years her mother and I will join you in London. We will buy a home. Start a business together. My daughter will continue her studies."

Even for a skeptical man like my father, who had little faith in governments, the story was seductive: a tale that began with heavenly prisons and ended with a pre-made family living in a home in London. He didn't want to see how much Abrahim believed in it himself, and so he kept his head slightly turned away. When it came to Europe or America, even people supposedly hardened by time and experience were susceptible to almost childish fantasies.

My father took the photograph from Abrahim and placed it in his pocket. He didn't say, "Of course I will do this," or even a simple "Yes," because such confirmation would have meant that there was an option to refuse, and no such thing existed between them. Abrahim told him to finish his drink. "Your ship is waiting," he said.

Soon, stories about my father were circulating freely around the Academy. I heard snippets of my own narrative played back to me in a slightly distorted form—in these versions, the story might take place in the Congo, amid famine. One version I heard said that my father had been in multiple wars across Africa. Another claimed that he had lived through a forgotten genocide, one in which tens of thousands were killed in a single day. Some wondered whether he had also been in Rwanda—or in Darfur, where such things were commonly known to occur.

Huge tides of sympathy were mounting for my dead father and me. Students I had never spoken to now said hello to me when they saw me in the hallway. There were smiles for me everywhere I went, all because I had brought directly to their door a tragedy that outstripped anything they could personally have hoped to experience.

I knew that it was only a matter of time before I was called to account for what I had been teaching my students. On a Friday, the dean caught me in the hall just as I was preparing to enter my classroom. There was nothing threatening or angry in his voice. He simply said, "Come and see me in my office when your class is over."

That day I decided to skip the story and return to my usual syllabus. I said to my students, "We have some work to catch up on today. Here are the assignments from last week. I want you to work on them quietly." If they groaned or mumbled something, I didn't hear it, and hardly cared. When class was over, I walked slowly up the three flights of stairs that led to the dean's office. He was waiting for me with the door open. His wide and slightly awkward body was pitched over the large wooden desk far enough so that it might have made it difficult for him to breathe. As soon as I sat down, he leaned back and exhaled.

"How was class today?" he asked me.

"Fine," I told him. "Nothing exceptional."

"I've heard some of the stories about your father that you've been telling your students," he said. At that point I expected him to reveal at least a hint of anger at what I had done, but there wasn't even a dramatic folding of the arms.

"It's very interesting what they're saying," he said. "Awful, of course, as well. No one should have to live through anything even remotely like that, which leads me to ask: How much of what they're saying is true?"

"Almost none of it," I told him. I was ready to admit that I had made up most of what I had told my students—the late nights at the port, the story of an invading rebel army storming across the desert. But before I could say anything further he gave me a sly, almost sarcastic smile.

"Well, regardless of that," he said, "it's good to hear them talking about important things. So much of what I hear from them is shallow, silly rumors. They can sort out what's true for themselves later."

And that was all it came down to: I had given my students something to think about, and whether what they heard from me had any relationship to reality hardly mattered; real or not, it was all imaginary for them. That death was involved only made the story more compelling.

I began my final lesson with my father and Abrahim walking down to the pier on their last morning together. They didn't say much along the way, but on occasion a few words slipped out. Abrahim had important ideas that he wanted to express, but he had never known the exact words for them in any language. If he could have, he would have grabbed my father firmly by the wrist and held him until he was certain that he understood just how much he depended on him and how much he had begun almost to hate him for that. My father, meanwhile, was desperate to get away. He was terrified of boarding the ship, but he was more frightened of Abrahim's desire.

When they reached the pier, Abrahim pointed to the last of three boats docked in the harbor. "It's that one," he said. "The one with the blue hull."

My father stared at the boat for a long time and tried to imagine what it would be like to be buried inside it, first for an hour and then for a day. He didn't have the courage to imagine anything longer. The boat was old, but almost everything in the town was old.

There was a tall, light-skinned man waiting at the end of the docks. He was from one of the Arab tribes in the north. Such men were common in town. They controlled most of its business and politics and had done so for centuries. They were traders, merchants, and sold anything or anyone. They held themselves at a slight remove from other men, gowned in spotless white or, on occasion, pastel-colored robes that somehow proved immune to the dust that covered every inch of the town.

"He's arranged everything," Abrahim said. "That man over there."

My father tried to make out his face from where they were standing, but the man seemed to understand that they were talking about him and kept his head turned slightly away. The only feature that my father could make out was an abnormally long and narrow nose, a feature that seemed almost predatory.

Abrahim handed my father a slip of yellow legal paper on which he had written something in Arabic. He would have liked Abrahim to say something kind and reassuring to him. He wanted him to say, "Have a safe journey" or "Don't worry. You're going to be fine," but he knew that he could stand there for years and no such reassurances would come.

"Don't keep him waiting," Abrahim said. "Give him the note and your money. And do whatever he tells you."

When my father was halfway between Abrahim and the man, Abrahim called out to him, "I'll be waiting to hear from you soon," and my father knew that was the last time he would ever hear Abrahim's voice.

My father handed over the slip of paper Abrahim had given him. He couldn't read what was written on it and was worried that it might say any of a thousand different things, from "Treat this man well" to "Take his money and do whatever you want with him."

The man pointed to a group of small storage slots at the stern of the boat that were used for holding the more delicate cargo. These crates were usually unloaded last, and he had often seen people waiting at the docks for hours to receive them. They always bore the stamp of a Western country and carried their instructions in a foreign language—"*Cuidado,*" "Fragile." He had unloaded several such crates himself recently, and while he had never known their actual contents he had tried to guess what was inside: cartons of powdered milk, a television or stereo, vodka, Scotch, Ethiopian coffee, soft blankets, clean water, hundreds of new shoes and shirts and underwear. Anything that he was missing or knew he would never have he imagined arriving in those boxes. There was a square hole just large enough for my father to fit into if he pulled his knees up to his chest. He understood that this was where he was supposed to go and yet naturally he hesitated, sizing up the dimensions just as he had once sized up the crates he had helped unload.

My father felt the man's hand around the back of his neck, pushing him toward the ground. He wanted to tell the man that he was prepared to enter on his own, and had in fact been preparing to do so for months now, but he wouldn't have been understood, so my father let himself be led. He crawled into the space on his knees, which was not how he would have liked to enter. Head first was the way to go, but it was too late now. In a final humiliating gesture, the man shoved him with his foot, stuffing him inside so quickly that his legs and arms collapsed around him. He had just enough time to arrange himself before the man sealed the entrance with a wooden door that was resting nearby.

Before getting on the boat, my father had made a list of things to think about in order to get through the journey. They were filed away under topic headings such as The Place Where I Was Born, Plans for the Future, and Important Words in English. He wasn't sure if he should turn to them now or wait until the boat was out of the harbor. The darkness inside the box was alarming, but it wasn't yet complete. Light still filtered in through the entrance, and continued to do so until the hull was closed and the boat began to pull away from the shore. He remembered that as a child he had often been afraid of the dark, a foolish, almost impossible thing for a country boy, but there it was. Of the vast extended family that lived around him, his mother was the only one who never mocked him for this, and even though he would have liked to save her image for later in the journey, at a point when he was far off at sea, he let himself think about her now. He saw her as she looked shortly before she died. She had been a large woman, but at that point there wasn't much left of her. Her hair hadn't gone gray yet, but it had been cut short on the advice of a cousin who had dreamed that the illness attacking her body was buried somewhere in her head and needed a way out. Desperate, she had had almost all her hair cut off, which had made her look even younger than her thirty-something years. This was the image he had, of his mother in an almost doll-like state, just two months before she died, and while he would have liked to have a better memory of her, he settled for the one he'd been given and closed his eyes to concentrate on it. It would be some minutes before he noticed the engine churning as the ship pulled up its anchors and slowly headed out to sea.

·

When I reached this point, I knew that it was the last thing I was going to say to my class. Soon, the dean would call me back to his office to tell me that, as interesting as my father's story was, it had gone on long enough, and it was time to return my class to normal, or risk my place at the Academy. The bell rang, and, as when I had begun this story, there were a good ten to fifteen seconds when no one in the classroom moved. My students, for all their considerable wealth and privilege, were still at an age where they believed that the world was a fascinating, remarkable place, worthy of curious inquiry and close scrutiny, and I'd like to think that I had reminded them of that. Soon enough they would grow out of that and concern themselves with the things that were most immediately relevant to their own lives. Eventually one bag was picked up off the floor, and then twenty-eight others joined it. Most of my students waved or nodded their heads as they left the room, and there was a part of me that wanted to call them back to their seats and tell them that the story wasn't quite finished yet. Getting out of Sudan was only the beginning; there was still much more ahead. Sometimes, in my imagination, that is exactly what I tell them. I pick up where I left off, and go on to describe to them how, despite all appearances, my father did not actually make it off that boat alive. He arrived in Europe just as Abrahim had promised he would, but an important part of him had died during the journey, somewhere in the final three days, when he was reduced to drinking his urine for water and could no longer feel his hands or feet.

He spent six months in a detention camp on an island off the coast of Italy. He was surprised to find that there were plenty of other men like him there, from every possible corner of Africa, and that many had fared worse than he had. He heard stories of men who had died trying to make a similar voyage, who had suffocated or been thrown overboard alive. My father couldn't even bring himself to pity them. Contrary to what Abrahim had told him, there was nothing even remotely heavenly about where he was held: one large whitewashed room with cots every ten inches and bars over the windows. The guards often yelled at him and the other prisoners. He learned a few words in Italian and was mocked viciously the first time he used them. He was once forced to repeat a single phrase over and over to each new guard who arrived. When he tried to refuse, his first meal of the day, a plate of cold, dry meat and stale bread, was taken away from him. "Speak," the guards commanded, and he did so dozens of times in the course of several days, even though there was no humor left in it for anyone.

"You speak Italian?" the guards asked.

"No."

Speak. Talk. Or, more rarely, Say something.

In Italy he was given asylum and set free. From there he worked his way north and then west across Europe. He met dozens of other Abrahims, men who promised him that when they made it to London the rest of their lives would finally resolve into the picture they had imagined. "It's different there," they always said. There had to be at least one place in this world where life could be lived in accordance with the plans and dreams they had concocted for themselves. For most, that place was London; for some it was Paris, and for a smaller but bolder few it was America. That faith had carried them this far, and even though it was weakening, and needed constant readjustment ("Rome is not what I thought it would be. France will surely be better"), it persisted out of sheer necessity. By the time my father finally made it to London, eighteen months later, he had begun to think of all the men he met as variations of Abrahim, all of them crippled and deformed by their dreams.

Abrahim had followed him all the way to London to test him, and my father was determined to settle that debt now that he was there. On his first day in the city he found a quiet corner of Hampstead Heath. An American guidebook that he had picked up in France had said that he would be afforded a wide, sweeping view of the city from there. At the edge of the park, with London at his feet, he set fire to all the documents that he had brought with him from Sudan. The fake marriage license turned to ashes in seconds. The picture of Abrahim's daughter melted away near a large green hedge with ripe, inedible red berries hanging from it. For many nights afterward, he refused to think about her or her father. There were no rewards in life for such stupidity, and he promised himself never to fall victim to that kind of blind, wishful thinking. Anyone who did deserved whatever suffering he was bound to meet.

WHAT YOU DO OUT HERE, WHEN YOU'RE ALONE

PHILIPP MEYER

Max had a name for what had happened to his son: the Accident, he called it. He wondered if his wife had her own name for it, though it wouldn't be the same, because she didn't think of it as an accident.

For the first few days, they had cried almost constantly. They had made love constantly as well, more than they had in the entire year previous, which seemed surprising to Max but also correct, and he had begun to wonder, guiltily, if Lilli might come back to him.

At this moment, he was lying on the floor next to the couch. Ligne Roset, picked by his wife, just like the other furniture. He was on the floor because he did not feel like taking off his shoes, though of course Lilli would not have known. She had disappeared somewhere—it was Sunday and they were both off work; Sunday and their entire future was in question; Sunday and Lilli had left without leaving a note. The previous Christmas, Max's brothers had sat him down and told him what they thought of her. An intervention, they'd said. He'd defended her, he was used to doing so, but meanwhile, at this moment, Lilli was nowhere to be found.

Before they moved to the Oaks, Lilli was the sort of person who didn't appear to care what anyone thought of her, was always joking at her own expense—about growing up in a trailer, about how you'd better not turn your back or she'd steal your TV. In Huntsville they'd made quite the couple, he the owner of the Porsche shop on the Speed Channel, she the loud, funny, slightly outrageous wife.

After they moved to the Oaks, she'd changed her hair, got a Martha Stewart wardrobe, and stopped cursing overnight. Max, meanwhile, remained himself. With the result that they were not exactly snubbed, but they were not invited to parties, either. Max did not care about this.

He knew he had to get up. It had been three weeks since the Accident, and there was a lot to be done: bills, the mortgage; it had been raining steadily and the lawn was returning to nature. The sun was coming through the big windows. He felt slightly drowsy and his back hurt, but that was just from lying on the floor. He was a small man, and fit; his body had not changed much since his youth, his hair was thick and his arms stronger than they looked, and it seemed to him that, in the past few years, other people had finally begun to see him the way he had always seen himself. The women who came to the shop would leave him presents—bottles of wine, invitations to come hunting on their husbands' ranches.

As for the shop, it was always busy. They serviced Porsches, mostly; they did frame-off restorations, setups for the track. Max was the best Porsche mechanic in Texas, the entire Southwest, if he was honest—he could sense what was wrong with a car before the factory computer did. He'd worked for a series of dealerships before opening his own shop, ten years ago, at the age of thirty-one. At thirty-three, he was making appearances on TNN and the Speed Channel. At thirty-seven, he'd been talked into buying this house.

Which was too big, for one. He had never thought he would say that about a house, but it was true—it made you feel exposed. He had got it for half the asking price, as it was widely considered the least desirable home in the community (no pool, the lot an awkward wedge shape), and, while Lilli had planned on lots of entertaining with their new neighbors, hardly anyone ever visited except their old friends from Huntsville, who drove the hour

238

to see them. So far as people in the Oaks were concerned, all Huntsville had going for it was the state prison and its death chamber.

He had been on the floor all morning—Brazilian cherry—and he knew that if he did not get up now he would end up spending the day like this. Which was fine. Something had changed since the Accident. Something was trying to communicate with him. He felt it in every molecule of air, in every sip of water, even in the sore muscles in his back: you are alive. The longing for his wife, the shock at the near loss of his son, had all been submerged under that simple, insistent fact; he might have been a man lost at sea who has woken to discover that a wind has blown him ashore, an Arctic wanderer stunned by the onset of spring.

But there was plenty to do. The lawn, for instance, which had not been mowed in three weeks; any minute now a neighbor would report them. It was not a small offense in the Oaks, and to say he hated it here . . . No, it was just that he had never wanted to buy this house. In the first place, it was too expensive; in the second, it was in a community of lawyers and oilmen. You could be sued for painting your mailbox the wrong color, for putting up the wrong fence, for installation of unapproved roofing materials. And for a three-week-old lawn—he didn't know. There was probably a firing squad, all-volunteer.

They'd heard about the Oaks from Lilli's boss at Goliad Associates, the hedge fund. Lilli ran their office. The Oaks was a new development, designed by an architect, and Max thought the houses bore a resemblance to storage buildings—flat metal roofs, cement walls. Of course, there were also floor-to-ceiling windows and various decks and balconies. Frank Lloyd Wright is what people said, and Max guessed there was some beauty in it, maybe in the way the houses contrasted with the tall pines the developer had left standing. Or maybe it was just a case of the emperor's new clothes. Meanwhile, Lilli and all the other neighbors collected *Dwell* and *Architectural Digest*, and sometimes driving along the streets at night you saw things through those tall windows that you were not supposed to see: Buck Hooper touching himself in front of the pay-per-view; Jeanne Winston throwing a Bottega goblet at her much younger husband; Clyde McCay, who owned an island off Mexico, having a long visit with the commode.

But those things were all distractions. At some point, they would bring his son home, and there were big decisions to be made, though he would have to make them on his own; he could not depend on Lilli. He stood up quickly and did a lap of the first floor—living room, den, kitchen, garden room. It was very modern; it was all the same big room, really, big and white and open, no nooks or crannies, filled with the expensive furniture they'd bought to go with the house, artsy leather couches, chairs, side tables. Everything had an intentional look. He stopped by the windows overlooking the back yard and saw a neighbor sunbathing on her deck. He wanted to linger and watch, but after a minute he made himself go back into the living room.

He considered turning on the radio; his son always left music playing, even when he wasn't home, its presence in the house like the buzzing of insects. There are parts of his mind that are dark—that was how the doctor had put it. It will take time before he recovers, he'd said. Meaning months, possibly years. Harley was in an induced coma, the bones of his skull still knitting, his brain just beginning to repair itself. In the scope of Harley's life, the doctor had told them, this will seem like a very slight interruption, and Lilli, of course, had been furious. She had wanted to sue the doctor for saying that; she wanted things to go back to the way they had been. Pure impossibility. It was only Max, in his heightened state, who understood how right the doctor was.

WHAT YOU DO OUT HERE, WHEN YOU'RE ALONE

Back in Huntsville, Harley had not exactly been popular but he'd had enough friends, he had been ensconced at the top of his class; at thirteen he was already planning to go to Rice when he graduated. Moving to Houston, to the Oaks, had thrown him off kilter. Just as it had Max. Harley had ended up with the goths, teen-agers who wore their clothing stuck with safety pins and white makeup on their faces. Most likely, that was when he'd got into drugs. Max was just speculating. Until quite recently, until the Accident, Lilli had done a good job of hiding their son's problems, taking him to a therapist that Max had known nothing about.

It didn't matter. There was work to be done. He would mow the lawn—he was the only one on the block who did his own yard work. From his deck, he could see out over the other homes in the development, the pines swaying above them. He could see the Welches' kids playing behind their fence at the near end of the yard, and at the far end he could hear Joy Halloran—the sunbather—laughing about something into her phone. She was thirty-eight and separated. She was one of the few people Max liked in the Oaks—she was comfortable with herself. She smiled a lot, but you got the feeling that she might be smiling even if you weren't there. Lilli despised her. The former trophy wife—that was what Lilli called her.

Joy noticed Max crossing the yard and waved to him.

"Morning, sunshine," she called down.

"Morning," he called back.

She put her phone away and leaned over the steel railing to talk. From her position on the deck she was ten feet higher than he was, her black hair wet from the shower, wearing her bathrobe loosely over a swimsuit; he could see the tan lines around her collarbones, the freckles on her nose. He wondered if she had heard about Harley, but of course she would have—the news had gone all over the neighborhood.

"How are you guys holding up?" she said.

241

"Fine, I guess."

"If you want a drink, I was thinking I'd make a batch of mojitos. Kill the day in proper style."

He wondered if he ought to make up some excuse about Lilli, but then Joy said, "I ran into Lilli this morning. She was with Tom Stockton—they said they were going to the river."

"I wondered where she'd gone," he said.

"Judy was with them, of course."

"Of course."

She pulled her bathrobe around her. "You're a good man, Maxwell. I'm sorry as hell about what happened."

"He'll be fine," Max told her. "It's just going to take a little while."

"He's a brave kid," she said.

Max had gone into Joy's house once, when Lilli wasn't home. They'd had a few drinks, and he'd admitted to her that Lilli was only the second person he'd ever slept with. He'd expected something to happen, and he guessed Joy had, too, but he hadn't been able to initiate it. She had seemed a little hurt, but then she had forgiven him, maybe even respected him for it.

"I've been thinking a lot," he told her. "I've been getting this feeling I ought to move away and just start my life over."

"Why not," she said. This was how they talked.

"That's the conclusion I've come to."

"I think you should."

He grinned and they looked at each other.

"Anyway," she said, after a minute, "come over anytime. You don't have to knock."

"I will," he said.

"I'll keep reminding you."

His throat got tight, and everything inside him began to feel warmer. "I better get mowing."

Joy smiled and cracked an imaginary whip at him before walking off the deck into her bedroom.

•

All around Max, the grass was lush and nearly shin-high, the sound of the Welches' kids drifting over the fence. He ought to be jumping the pickets to Joy's house right now. Instead, he made himself cross the lawn to his woodshop, where he kept the mower and gardening tools. He had not been in there since the Accident, and the order of it all, the way there was a space for everything—saws, clippers, trimmers, all outlined in marker on Peg-Board—almost made him cry. He was embarrassed—Joy knew, everyone knew, how badly Lilli treated him. Knew how long he had put up with it. It seemed like a miracle, or maybe a curse, that since the age of twenty he had only slept with one person. There had never seemed to be any hurry. He was not enough of a risk taker. That was what his brothers had always told him.

He pushed the mower out to inspect his lawn. It was a sunny day with a few big white clouds, the skyline of Houston visible ten miles away. With the grass so tall, the mowing would not be easy, but it was a fine time to be out. He was about to start the machine when something caught his eye. There were bees everywhere and flowers, thousands of them. Some sort of purple-and-white wildflower. He knelt down to examine them and was again filled with emotion—this was just what he'd been thinking, there was life everywhere. The universe in a handful of dirt. These flowers had lived here forever, but he'd never known it. He'd been cutting them down since the day he moved in.

He was certain that Lilli had not noticed the flowers either, just the overgrown lawn. Things had been bad for a year, he figured. But that was not even true. Things had gone bad the minute they moved there. She had become embarrassed by him. If you do wear a T-shirt in public, she said, you definitely shouldn't tuck it in. And you shouldn't wear those jeans. Or your running shoes. He had allowed her to buy him new clothes, but it did not seem to matter how many times he gave in. There had never been real equality; he had never been the decision-maker. He looked at the lawn and all the color—their yard was a sea of flowers. Forget-me-nots? Spiderwort? The fact that he didn't know, that he could not identify this tiny flower, felt like a crime against himself. Against everything that was good. He would never cut them down.

Of course, there were practicalities. Any day now, they'd be reported to the community association. Lilli would be furious, yet she should have been here to see these flowers, which had come from nowhere. He pushed the mower back into the wood-shop, then unscrewed the sparkplug, and hid it in a jar of screws. Max Callahan: protector of flowers.

Meanwhile, his wife was out with Tom and Judy Stockton—his least favorite people in the development, a serious accomplishment given the competition. Tom Stockton had a pair of nineteen-sixties Corvettes that he told everyone he'd restored himself, but one look around his garage and you knew—there was not a single toolbox. That was the problem with most of the men who lived here—despite their pride at being Texans, they'd grown up in cities, worked in office buildings, and, truth be told, they had more in common with people from New York than they did with their own parents.

Max remembered again where he was, standing in his yard. Joy Halloran was back on her deck, talking into her phone, the sun directly behind her. She had taken off her robe, and for a moment it looked like she was wearing nothing at all; she looked like something nature itself was offering him. He lost awareness of everything but her—if she would just make a gesture he would go to her, but she was distracted by her phone call, and she stepped back suddenly from the railing and disappeared from sight.

He knew that he was in a fragile state, but, at the loss of her, he had the brief feeling that he had left his body, a sense of such overwhelming despair that he wanted to obliterate himself from the earth. If he could only summon the energy, he would walk out of the yard, past the gates and into the traffic on the highway.

Instead, he sat down in the flowers, which came nearly to his chest now. He was aware of his own heart, wearing itself down to extinction. The End—he had always known what it would look like. Things would simply get dark, a ring of blackness closing around you; he had seen it happen to his father. He eased himself down onto his back. From the ground, he could see only the pine trees bordering the yard, the very blue sky with the fat clouds of a nearly pure whiteness. He wondered if he was dying, if his heart was about to stop, but after some period of time he began to feel settled again, returned to his body. Of course he was not dying. It was the opposite: he was alive. Lying in a bed of flowers. And, Christ, the sky and those clouds: he ought to be up there among them, an actual pilot. He ought to have been a pilot in Alaska, flying a small plane just big enough for one, a vast wilderness beneath him.

His mind was moving quickly now. Their old neighbors in Huntsville were selling their house—five acres in the Piney Woods, close to Max's brothers, a small house but well kept. If he and Lilli sold their place here, even in this market, they could buy the Huntsville one for cash; they'd have no payments except taxes. He could sell the shop—business was steady, but he'd been bored with it for years, bored with being in charge. He had not laid hands on a car in months, there was so much to do in the office. He could sell the shop and this house and have breathing room to figure out exactly how they would adjust to their new situation. When Harley was better—anywhere from six months to several years from now, according to the doctor—Max would turn the house over to him and begin his journey.

Lilli stayed out with the Stocktons all day, and Max turned in early. He was barely aware of her coming to bed. Later that night a noise woke him, and he thought, It's just Harley coming in, and then he heard another noise and woke up all the way.

Lilli was lying on her side with her back to him, and he reached and touched her hip lightly. She was small and delicate; she looked like a pixie, like something from the movies. Even now, at forty-two, she seemed to glow in the dim light. She didn't pull away from him, and he stayed there with his hand like that, looking at the curve from her shoulder to her small waist and up to her hip, aware of the feeling of her not pulling away. Put all your weight on me. That was what she used to say to him, but she hadn't said it in more than a year, not even during those few days of intense lovemaking after the Accident. They had both been sore, but they had not been able to help themselves; it had felt like having a new partner.

"No," she said now.

"I didn't know you were awake."

"Well, I am."

"Did you hear that noise? I think a window might be open."

It was quiet. Lilli said, "You know there isn't even a word for what we are, leaving him in there like that."

"You shouldn't think that way."

"We should have had more children," she said.

"You should have told me he was doing cocaine."

He wondered if he'd gone too far, but then he didn't care. He got out of bed and went into the bathroom. He heard Lilli begin to cry, softly at first, and then she was sobbing. He wanted to go back to her, but he stood with his hands on the sink, looking at himself in the mirror. In the soft moonlight that came through the window, he really didn't look much different from the way he'd looked at twenty, and at forty-one he was not even old—he had plenty of time and life left. He had recently told Lilli this, and she had laughed at him. But he was certain he was right. They were not the same person. When he first met Lilli, his love for her had been so intense that he had wondered if he would survive it. He had dropped out of college for her, changed his path on earth. Whereas Lilli was the opposite. She would survive anything. He had always thought of this as an admirable quality, but now he was not sure.

Of course, he himself was not perfect. It had occurred to him that maybe this love he felt, this intensity of feeling, maybe that had not really been about Lilli after all. Maybe it was simply the way he preferred to feel. He had begun to feel the same thing for Joy Halloran that afternoon at her house, which was why he had not slept with her, because compared with that feeling the sex would have been nothing.

He could hear his wife crying in the other room. He could feel his feet trying to move on their own, but he forced himself to stay put. It was a large bathroom, all polished cement, two sinks, two showers—they shared nothing. Lilli's guilts were not the same as his, either. At some point after they moved here, she had become more of a friend to Harley than a parent; Harley had been miserable at his new school, and Lilli had stopped setting boundaries. A sort of club had formed, a family within the family that did not include Max.

And yet this question—the question of who was responsible—would not change anything. Max passed back through the bedroom, where Lilli was now silent. Naked, he went down the stairs and out onto the deck, to look out at the skyline of Houston, all the buildings lit, even on a Sunday night. He touched his toes and felt the muscles of his back stretch, then reached forward and kicked up into a handstand, holding himself with his feet straight up in the air, naked on his own deck. Then the feeling left him. He eased back onto his feet. The light in Joy Halloran's bedroom was on, but Max was thinking about his son. He was thinking, You are the one who did that to him.

Which was true but not the entire truth. The truth being that he, Max, needed to get away from this place. Needed to walk out, turn his back on all of it, leave Texas and never return. He had good hands; he could support himself indefinitely. Porsche, tractor, chain saw—he could fix it. Remake himself as his ancestors had done: they had left Kentucky with just the clothes on their backs. Meanwhile, he'd lived his entire life within sixty miles of his home town.

Yes, he would leave. It was that simple. It felt good to have a plan, even a vague one. It felt good to stand out there, a slight breeze in his hair, only the sound of the crickets. Lilli could have the house, his car, his business, everything; she could sell it all. He would start again from nothing. She would not have trouble finding a husband, and wherever Max's legs gave out, that's where he would settle. He would not make any of the same mistakes. He would not surround himself with people who wanted to be anything but what they were.

He wondered if Lilli would do that to him, if she were able. Part of him was sure of it. He wondered if that was why he had made the decision to leave Harley in jail that second night; he wondered if he had done that to punish his wife. But he did not think so. It was simply the sort of choice you made, a hard decision for which there would be consequences, the sort of decision that showed you your life was different from what you'd always thought it was.

Harley had been pulled over for speeding, and the police had found a vial of cocaine in the car. Texas was not a good place to get caught with drugs, even if you were white, even if you lived in the Oaks, but Harley was not the sort of kid to think about those things. He had just turned eighteen, he was just like his mother, and in that sense maybe it had been his destiny for this to happen.

Neither Max nor Lilli had come from anyplace important. Max had grown up sharing a room with two brothers, but he'd been taught to be proud. When he was sixteen, a tornado had touched down in Huntsville, torn the roof off his house, and knocked down plenty of others. Most of the neighbors had spent months living with blue tarps, but Max's father had pulled all three boys out of school and in a week they'd had the roof reframed, sheathed, and shingled, all the fallen trees limbed and bucked, as if no storm had ever occurred. Max's father was a machinist, a man who came from cedar choppers, from laborers; a man who had plenty of excuses to be hard on his children. Except that he was the opposite. When their church's steeple was infested with pigeons, when even the minister had resigned himself to shooting them, Max and his father had climbed up there in the dark, while the pigeons were night-blind and reluctant to fly, and caught them by hand, a hundred pigeons. They'd stuffed them into burlap sacks, then released them thirty miles away.

Whereas Lilli came from a different sort of family, had grown up in a double-wide trailer, the kind that looks like the owner is a collector of things. She had left home, moved in with a boyfriend at age fourteen, but maybe you never escaped your family. She'd met Max at nineteen, finished her associate's while Max supported her, and then she got pregnant just after their wedding. Max dropped out of A. & M. the same year. He hadn't wanted to keep the baby—they were barely into their twenties and broke—but Lilli was suddenly desperate to be a mother; it was as if Max's love was no longer enough.

The light went out in Joy Halloran's bedroom, and Max went back inside, down the steps to Harley's room. There were clothes all over the floor, posters, and he didn't know what, cocaine probably, hidden somewhere. The only drug Max had ever tried was alcohol, and this saddened him now—he should have had those experiences. He looked around as if someone might be watching. It was strange being naked in your son's bedroom. He picked up a T-shirt from the floor and smelled it: it smelled like his son, and also like his son's sweat, and also like cigarette smoke. He draped the shirt around his neck. The Cure, it said. He picked up another shirt from the floor. This one smelled like his son and something else, something sweet. A girl's perfume. He wondered who the girl was and realized he had no idea so he put that shirt down, the one that smelled like the girl, and sat on his son's bed.

He didn't remember falling asleep, but when he woke up he felt more rested than he'd been for weeks; he'd had the kind of sleep you get from good dreams. It was the best he'd slept since Harley had left the house that night.

At two in the morning, they'd got the call. Max would have expected Harley to sound different, humbled maybe, but he was the same.

"I'm in jail," he told Max. "I'm going to be here at least till morning, when the judge comes through."

"What happened?" Max said.

"I dunno. They're saying I had drugs in the car."

"Did you?"

There was a long silence, and then Max realized that Harley must be standing in a room surrounded by police officers and was probably more scared than he'd ever been in his life. "Don't answer that question," he said. "I'll call a lawyer."

There was another pause and Harley said, "Tell Mom to come and bail me out tomorrow."

It was an order. Max felt all the sympathy go out of him.

"Dad, did you hear me?"

Max still didn't answer—he was thinking about the time he'd been arrested in College Station for driving drunk. He was twenty, two years older than Harley, but he'd been too scared to even consider calling his father, not scared of punishment but scared of disappointing him. And so he had stayed in jail until his brothers collected the money to bail him out.

"Dad?"

"I heard you," Max told his son.

"They said I can call again when the judge sets the bail."

One extra day. It had not seemed like a long time, and Lilli, to Max's surprise, had agreed. She was ashamed; it was as if she herself had been arrested. It was clear to both of them that a bit of scared straight would be healthy for their son, that an immediate rescue would do more harm than good.

When Harley called the next morning, Max told him it would take another day to get the bail money. Harley asked to speak with his mother. I'm sorry, honey, she told him. Well, Harley told her, I guess that's the way it is. Max had felt simultaneously proud and awful. They retained a lawyer in the Skyline District, but Max spent all day worrying that they had made a mistake.

The guards found Harley the next morning. They claimed he'd fallen down the stairs. Of course it was a lie. Harley had mouthed off to the wrong person, guard or inmate, or maybe he had not done anything wrong at all. Maybe he had just been in a place he was not meant to be.

The day after Max slept in Harley's bed, he stayed late at the shop to finish some paperwork, and when he got home there was no sign of Lilli. He walked around looking for her, room to room, but there was no note. Her car was still there, and there were any number of things she might be doing. Recently she'd been spending a lot of time with the Stocktons. People told stories about them, threesomes and foursomes. Max did not entirely believe those things, but the fact remained that whenever Lilli went over there she came back acting like she'd smoked pot.

Tom Stockton was hairy and barrel-chested, and Max imagined him penetrating Lilli from behind, his enormous body pressed against her small frame. It made Max sick to think about. He went to the kitchen and fixed a rum-and-Coke, then found himself standing by Harley's room again.

The door was open, and there was Lilli, asleep in Harley's bed. She had not gone to the Stocktons' after all. He stood for a long time and watched her breathe; she was in a deep sleep. It was a thing they had in common now, and he thought about getting in bed with her but decided against it.

The next morning he ran into her in the kitchen. He looked past her, out at the yard. The flowers were continuing to spread; you could see their color now from a distance, and he tried to recall what they had smelled like.

"I talked to the doctor yesterday," Lilli said. "I forgot to tell you."

"We didn't see each other," he replied, which was not entirely true.

"They're going to wake up Harley tomorrow. They said we'll be able to bring him home soon."

"What time?" he said.

"What time what?"

"What time are they going to wake him up? What time should we get there?"

"I didn't ask."

"I guess we'll have to call them back."

"I'm sorry," she said.

"Did they say anything else?"

"I don't think so."

"Are we going to need a nurse or someone like that to watch him?"

"I don't know."

"I'll call them back."

"Fine," she said.

"This is good news," he told her. "I don't understand what's wrong."

"I guess I'm worried they should keep him there longer, maybe. I'm worried something could happen if he comes home too soon, like maybe it's just the insurance company trying to push him out before he's ready."

"We have good insurance," he said, but he could tell she wasn't listening. She was looking at her reflection in the glass door.

"We got married so young, Max. Don't you ever feel that way?"

Max felt such disdain then that he could barely stand to look at her. His wife might have been a strange woman he'd seen on a street corner. He had the feeling that if he never saw her again he would not mind. It was quiet for a while before he said, "I'll take care of Harley."

"What are you talking about?"

"He can live with me. I'm not staying here anymore."

"Max," she said.

"You can come with me, or you can do whatever you want, but I'll take care of him."

He was surprised he'd said it, and so was Lilli. He could tell it knocked her right off her tracks, and he could see her mind working to catch up.

"Do you want me to come?"

He could see himself with Joy Halloran, in her bedroom and elsewhere—she was the sort of person Lilli would never be, and he could see himself making a life with her, only it was a more distinct, more real version of himself. They would be living in the hills beyond Austin—Joy's family had a ranch there, her father had a collection of airplanes; she had told him that afternoon. Max had always imagined himself in a place like that, dry air and forty-mile views. Harley would be off at college. Then things closed in again, and he could see Lilli alone, living with her family in Huntsville. Things would not be as easy as she thought. It would not be easy for him, but it would be even harder for her; she would not understand until it was too late.

"Yes," he told her. "I want you to come with me."

That night after work, he picked up Chinese food from a place Lilli liked. He had spent the entire day with a feeling of lightness, although there had been nothing but problem customers, the type who could not really afford their expensive cars. The type for whom owning a car like this meant they had accomplished something with their lives, the type who spent their weekends rubbing fenders with carnauba wax, taking their kids for long drives, not telling their wives that they were one big repair bill away from having to sell. Anyone else would have told them all to go to hell, but Max felt sorry for them. Gave away parts and labor. And today that hadn't bothered him.

The lights were out throughout the Oaks when he got home; some sort of power outage; the city was always having brownouts. He took a flashlight from the garage and carried the bag of food into the kitchen and saw Lilli sitting by herself in the enormous white dining room, eating by candlelight. She wasn't wearing any makeup. He couldn't remember the last time he'd seen her without makeup. She was a beautiful woman, better than Max had ever deserved. He'd known that since they first met—it was the end of summer, and he was about to return to A. & M., but he'd realized that he was making a mistake. So he had made his way back to her. It had been twenty-one years, but at this instant it seemed to him that this feeling had not faded; it had only grown richer, more complex.

But, when he looked at her again, something was wrong. She was eating cold leftovers. Eating without him.

"I brought the Chinese," he said. He set the bag on the long table that seated twelve people. Nothing in this room was his—the furniture, the pictures on the wall. It might have been his money, but it all belonged to his wife. "I said I'd get dinner."

"I don't know, Max. The power went out and I guess I just got hungry and I wasn't sure."

"I said I would bring Chinese."

"I know you did. I just wasn't sure."

He sat down across from her.

"I think I want to eat by myself."

He carried the bag of food into the kitchen, but it wasn't right—Harley's room was just there, on the other side of the wall. He got up and went outside, through the big glass door.

It was pitch black, a cool, clear night, and even the Houston skyscrapers were dark. He went to the far end of the yard and sat in the grass. A familiar feeling—he had thought he was doing the right thing, only to learn he wasn't.

He sat there in the darkness, listening to the crickets and night birds, a whip-poor-will; the lights of the city were out, and there was not a single human sound. It might have been the end of the world. The last instant. His father asking them to open the blinds and Max looking at his brothers; they all knew, and then his father was gone, just like that, his light winked out the same as any murderer's. Pure biology. A habit of breathing. Harley would be no different, and at the thought of that Max lay on his back. He could sense the dew settling on his face, above him were all the stars, uncountable—the black universe would swallow them up, he himself, everyone he had ever known.

Only . . . he did not really believe that. He could not explain why; he knew it was true, but he did not agree with it. There was Lilli sleeping on the couch at his shop while he pulled all-nighters.

There was Harley swimming at Lake Livingston. The last time they had gone, Max had got out because a storm was coming, a big norther, but Harley had paddled out to the middle so that he could float on his back and watch the storm blow in over top of him. To raise a son like that, who was not afraid—he was not sure how he'd done it. Men like that built empires, they crossed oceans, they became the stuff of history.

As for his own life, he was barely to the middle of it, and his son's was just beginning. He realized that he had been looking up at the sky, the stars visible as in his youth, and his dark house seemed strange to him now, a place from some half-forgotten dream, a place he had gone to pass his days. The next morning, or the morning after, he would go and pick up his son. He could see them both clearly, two figures on a remote highway, at the saddle of some unnamed pass. They were carrying their burdens easily. They were already fading from sight.

TWINS

C. E. MORGAN

The boy and his twin brother grew up on the streets of Northside, down in the little choke valley, befouled by industry, between the university hill to the southeast and the neighborhood to the north, College Hill, which had no college, despite its name, only modest white houses hinting at the white suburbs to come. College Hill breached the valley, a finger rising out of a soiled palm, pointing the way north, the way out of the city. The boys' mother, Marie, was the first in the family to make her way out of Over-the-Rhine with a high-school diploma and an associate's degree, and she was planning to be a teacher—to teach children just like her own—until she got sick. She wasn't sick when they were little. She was tall and straight, small-footed, big-breasted; she wore her hair in its natural twist behind a rolled white scarf. Lipstick the color of a plum with Vaseline smeared over it. The boys laid their heads upon her, one to each pillow breast, and looked at each other across the distance of her chest, each thinking himself dark or light, depending.

But again, the valley: They lived in the valley, four miles from the river, and whenever the waters rose, as they had in 1884 and again in 1937, the gray river coursed along the low arteries of the city and swamped the heart of Northside. The wealthy lived on Cincinnati's seven hills, and when the flooding came they gazed down from their hills, troubled.

Just east of their neighborhood, the Harrogate factory ran day and night, never ceasing its production of soap, churning kernelate, chloride, silicate, sulfate, and, once upon a time, pork fat, until the fumes rose and drew down the sky to a low lid the color of aluminum, so that even on the clearest day the Mill Creek ran gray beneath it. Cars tunnelled through the smog-drift in the fading afternoon, passing over the viaduct from downtown and through the graceless valley on their way to the suburbs. Some days the sun fractured the filth in the air and made a hundred thousand rainbows of it. Sherbet, roses, and cantaloupe orange, wedding pink, white. The first thing Allmon would think of his tiny purchase of sky: I want to eat it.

In the valley, asthma was rampant, and both boys suffered from it when they were young, their bodies twisted by little crowing fits as they took their evening walks down Hamilton Avenue. People on the street noticed the two boys, found them mismatched against the brownfields and storefronts, their faces rosy in the polluted light, copper-sulfite highlights in their hair. They gripped their mother's hands. No one had ever said she was beautiful, but she was young and that was a kind of beauty. People driving north sometimes thought momentarily, fondly, of their own mother, of her scent and the dry-handed grip that once secured them to her. Others would think, Black girls have kids way too young, as Marie and her sons walked south to Spring Street and Trace, the site of their first apartment, the first place the boys called home.

The boys lived in a three-story building with its entrance on Trace, so when they stood in the foyer gazing out through the glass they witnessed the riot of the neighborhood passing by. Dark shadows of migrating birds lost in the swallowing shadows of cars. The diffident faces of teen-age boys, old women with bawling strollers, the police who chatted with their mother as she swept the cigarette butts and leaves from the stoop every morning. She paid ten dollars less in rent in return for that chore. When she was done, she would sometimes lean on her broom handle, on the other side of the wavy glass, and make a game of speaking to the boys; they heard nothing, just saw the moving shape of her mouth. She made faces, they made faces, and only when one of them made a face of alarm, of soon-to-be crying— that was usually Allmon—would she open the door and come in.

Upstairs, in the hundred-year-old apartment, the ceilings were high, and bevelled French doors led to a tiny half-moon balcony overlooking the street, but their mother kept the doors duct-taped shut—the lock had been broken for years. No one ever came to fix it. Most nights they all slept on a mattress on the living-room floor, so that, when they woke to the astonishing crystal light of morning flooding through the huge windows, they woke as a family.

In that apartment, summer came like an Egyptian plague. Marie drew the blinds against the broiling heat. She took off her dress and walked through the apartment in her underpants and nothing else and when she breast-fed the boys she simply sat cross-legged on the floor like a worn, hapless Buddha, a child on each thigh. The plants drooped in the darkened air, the sun-rimmed blinds moved not an inch. She soothed the boys' heat rash with creams and kissed their sweating heads. Sometimes she cried over their pertussive crying. These were her babies—she crushed them to her despite the heat. And when they napped she sang a hush song, sang, "Hush-a-bye, don't you cry, go to sleepy, little baby. When you wake you shall have all the pretty little horses, blacks and bays, dapples and grays, coach and six little horses, hush."

Sometimes there was a man in the apartment. He was a white man, and he came and went.

The boys lived in that first apartment until 1984, when, just as they were shaping memories out of the clay of their lives, as they began to recognize themselves as Allmon and Mickey, they moved. They moved because the white man came around less and less, and when he came there were fights. He was not a tall man—he was shorter than their mother—but he was beautiful, despite a terrible thinness, with a red-brown mustache like a fish draped over his lip and a silver cigarette case in his back pocket that made white bands of the denim there. If they touched that rectangle of tobacco, he would slap their hands away, saying, "Watch yourself." He was like a dry bath; to lie against him was to feel empty and sure, clean. Their mother placed green glass ashtrays all over the apartment so that when he came he had only to reach over their heads to find an ashtray and tap the butt to the glass. They said, "Where you been?" And he said, "North and South Carolina, Georgia, Florida. I just spent two days on Lady's Island. You know what they got there?" They did not know. "Ladies!" He laughed, they laughed. "And I went to St. Augustine. You know what they got there? All the stuff you don't know shit about." They napped against him, but before their minds washed out to sleep the younger by three minutes, Allmon, studied his father, this man like a monument: pale marble chest, long dark hair, a brief nose, thin lips, green eyes. And the voice of somewhere else. His father said, "You are some strange kids."

His arrivals always came unannounced, and now the checks, too, became irregular, then boxes began to gather in the center of the living room. The handleless pots were packed away, then the aloe and oxalis planters and the many tiny shoes belonging to the boys, and their mother sat on the red plaid sofa with her head in her hands, her fingers dug deep into her hairline. Allmon clung to her thighs. "Momma, Momma, what's wrong?" "Nothing." "Momma, what's wrong?" "Nothing, I don't know." Then she looked up and her eyes pinned him to her with a ferocity he wasn't yet frightened of. "I can't lose nobody else. I can't do it by myself."

Out of their apartment on Trace, they moved down seven streets toward the southern end of the neighborhood, the cheaper end, where the viaduct crossed the sewage-strewn Mill Creek to Knowlton's Corner, an intersection of five streets, where the commerce had been so heavy a hundred and fifty years before that on any given Sunday the crowds spilled off the sidewalk and shoppers were forced to walk in the street as they milled past the butcher's and the stationer's, the grocer's, the coffin carpenter, the pharmacy, all souls touching shoulders. When the city grew, the crowds drifted north, up the hills, and the southern end of the neighborhood went to the poor working white, then to a checkered mix, then to mostly black, and the city considered Knowlton's Corner a place that once had been. The intersection now was as careworn and antique as a wagon wheel, its spires strewn with broken glass and cigarette butts and glimmering oil, its hub home to a decaying costume shop, a gas station, a White Castle, and Garvey's corner store. Their mother rented a two-room apartment above Garvey's, a tiny place, shrill with the sounds the boys would associate with life: the freakish wail of sirens, men's voices calling, Metro buses gusting by, dogs baying, children screeching in play. In July, the boys looked down from their bay window and howled with delight at the passing Independence Day parade. In the winter, the snow went as gray as tobacco ash as soon as it touched the street. And it was in this apartment that Allmon asked, "Daddy coming home?" And his mother still said, "Yes, baby." He learned to wait before he knew what waiting was, learned to want before he had the words to want with.

Then a day came, as if a result of his waiting and wanting rather than the happenstance it was, when his father appeared again and took them both—one boy under each arm—and tossed them into the back of a gold Valiant and drove them to someplace in the city that Allmon could never exactly locate again. Somewhere on the university hill around Fairview, with its expansive views of the river. Allmon would not later remember clinging to the chrome handle of the car, crying for his mother, his father pulling him away, saying, "God damn it, quit acting like I'm gonna kill you," while Mickey was not crying at all, already running toward the woods, the soles of his red shoes flashing. Their father carried Allmon past a chain-link fence, through a low tunnel of greenery and thorns, Allmon sniffling against his shoulder all the while, and his father saying, "Quiet! Don't you wanna see where I hung out when I was a kid? I had fun up here." Then, as they approached the fossil-strewn overlook, "Mickey, get the fuck away from the edge!" Mickey scrambled back from the precipitous drop, as Allmon clung to his father's neck like a baby bear to a tree.

"I was down here two years in high school, instead of Toledo," their father said. "We used to smoke up here and nobody fucked with us, you know why? 'Cause you hang out with niggers, nobody fucks with you. Word to the wise. We used to do some crazy shit up here. Look—a steamboat." He took Allmon's chin in his hand and forcibly turned his head around to gaze upon the expanse. "Look," his father said again, and he looked and all he would remember later was the river like a snake, and barely the city at all—but what a city! A queen rising on seven hills over her Tiber, forming the circlet of a crown. A jagged cityscape of steel and brick and glass, with its own bright nightless burn and, beyond it, the fretful, historied amplitude of Kentucky, that netherworld. This was Cincinnati—the capital of pork, the first truly American city—sprawled before the eyes of two little boys under the momentary aegis of one Mike Shaughnessy, truck driver, halfhearted Lothario, collector of children, poor Irish agnate, known in high school as that fucking Irish fuck. This one man their mother had the misfortune of loving—end and beginning and middle of story. The two children, one dark-skinned and one light, gazed down at the city and its brown river that seemed far too wide and far too deep to be swum but, oh, children, it was swum.

First inkling: She swings him in wide arcs and for a moment he is loose, weightless in the air, neither up nor down but fully stopped, not yet burdened by gravity's pull, and, just as he would fall, her arms are a cradle around his body and her voice says, "Who's my black baby."

Second: An old woman imparts a secret.

They were walking up Hamilton Avenue hand in hand, Marie in the middle with a boy on each side, skipping at her heels. It was their summer ritual to search out the neighborhood's meagre garage sales. Today they needed new pots to replace the ones that had long ago lost their black handles. But, as they walked, Marie dreamed up the men she imagined her children would be; she read them their fortunes.

"In the future ball," she said, "I see I'm gonna be a teacher. I'm gonna go back to school pretty soon here and get a degree. Mickey, I think you're gonna be a . . . TV star, 'cause Lord knows you love attention."

"And me?" Allmon asked, peering up at her.

"Hmm," she hedged.

"A trucker!"

"Like your daddy?"

"Yeah."

They passed the neighborhood bars where midmorning loungers leaned squinting in doorframes with amber bottles in hand. Here were the closed and locked churches, the apartment buildings with windows flung open to stave off the emergent heat, laundry hanging down like wrinkled flags. Women leaned on sills smoking above the laundry lines, waving absently at the boys, bored. Mickey waved back with mad enthusiasm.

Marie shook her head. "Always gotta flirt." Then: "That's where I work at now," and, still grasping their hands, she pointed toward the first floor of a building that had once housed a pharmacy owned by Germans.

"A teacher," Mickey said.

"A receptionist," she said, "for a dentist. A dentist drills big old holes in your teeth."

"You ain't a teacher?"

She hesitated, as if trying to decide how to respond. Then a smile broke across her face. "Look at that yard sale there!" They dodged passing cars to get to the opposite sidewalk, where a tiny rise of lawn was strewn with colorful clothing—shirts, coveralls, patterned rayon dresses. An old woman sat there in a plastic lawn chair, her face a ruin of living. Behind her leaned an enormous house, its grandeur blunted by time, and now, paint-peeling and black-molding in its senescence, it sagged visibly from the patched roof to the porch. As Marie approached with the boys, the woman stood up, or tried to stand, but her back was askew, and she stooped like an old crone as she gazed down on them from a small rise of spring grass, a considering expression on her face. Her hair was braided down one side, white untended sprigs on the other, as though she had, for some reason, ceased the effort halfway.

"Morning," their mother said. "Looks like it's gonna be hot."

"Mmm-hmm," the woman said.

"Makes me want some air-conditioning," Marie said, and she fanned her face once with her fingers pressed together.

"Always be hot up in here," the woman said and she made a half-hearted gesture over her shoulder at the spavined house, but she wasn't looking back toward the house; her gaze had drifted down first to Allmon, then inched its way over to Mickey.

"Yeah. You lived up here a long time?"

Instead of answering, the woman said, "That your baby?"

Marie didn't have to follow the single crooked finger pointed at Allmon. "Yeah."

"You sitting that other one?"

Marie paused a moment, then looked down at Mickey. A careful smile that didn't prick at her eyes. "No, this one here's my baby, too."

"Ha!" the woman laughed, but, when Marie did not join, the woman looked swiftly back and forth from Mickey to Allmon, as if trying to see them both at the same time, and then she said, "How you get a white baby and a black baby the same age?"

"Twins," Marie said quietly.

"Naw they ain't! For real?" The woman hooted with laughter, her unkempt eyebrows bopping up and down. "You kidding me? Come here, come here, come here." And she herself came forward down the sloped lawn, stepping right on top of the clothes she'd laid there, her head jutted slightly from her shoulders, and when she said, "I ain't never seen such a thing!" Allmon hauled back on Marie's hand with such force that she hissed, "Ow! Allmon, quit!" And he stilled.

"They don't know they own strength," the old woman said. Stooping toward them now: "Ain't nothing to be scared of. I ain't gonna hurt you."

"Now," Marie said quietly, gripping their hands, but not stepping backward, so that the boys were trapped before the judgment, which even they could feel was coming.

The woman's gimlet eyes turned them up and down and over as she did the math of them; first Allmon, who turned and ground his forehead into his mother's soft outer thigh, and then Mickey, who only stared up into the woman's face with a strange openness like entrancement.

The woman said, "This white one got good hair."

At this, Allmon lifted his face from his mother's leg and peered around her at his brother. He looked at that hair, which lay smooth and orderly against a cream forehead. It was black, but fell to his brow with barely a wave, as if a mother's hand had tended it just so. Then, with the smallest of movements, Allmon turned his face back to his mother's thigh, so he didn't see her when the woman said, "Oh, girl, you know I got to ask," but he felt her stiffen right down the length of her leg. "You do it with a white boy and a brother at the same time?"

At first, Marie neither moved nor spoke, and Allmon felt her momentary paralysis and was already seized with alarm by the time she found her direction, turned, and began hauling the boys down the sidewalk in the direction they had come. She yanked them with such force that Allmon began to whine.

"Naw! I ain't dissing your children!" the woman called behind them. "Them children is fascinating! Come back! Come back!" And she keened with laughter and watched the figure of the young woman as she retreated, her batik dress swaying, her sandals snapping smart and a boy dragging at each hand, tripping from foot to foot, the black one crying like a girl, and the white one glancing back with deep, black eyes.

Round the corner they went and down another half-block, then Marie stopped abruptly and released Mickey so that she could dab roughly at Allmon's tears with the hem of her dress, her own eyes glistering with frustration. She said, "Quit crying, Allmon. Be a man. Be a man."

Behind her, Mickey said, "Who that?"

His mother ignored him and he punched at her leg once.

"Who that?" he asked again.

"Nobody, Mickey! I don't know!" She wrenched about to look at him. "How'm I supposed to know?"

"Nobody," he said. "Her name Nobody."

Marie didn't comprehend for a moment. Then she laughed so suddenly and so hard that she let go of Allmon and stood up straight with her hands on her wide hips and her head thrown back. Mickey laughed at her laughing while Allmon, still crying, reached out for his mother, whispering "Up, up" to her turned back.

Down behind their building, through the dank shaft of the rear stairwell, was the spot Marie called the cement garden, their playground, the hollow heart of the turn-of-the-century tenements that formed the court of their block. The buildings towered forty feet high on every side and made a shady grove where the neighborhood children played in the summertime. A Rottweiler lay permanently chained in one corner, snoring with its caramel chin on its paws. Girls streamed from the buildings in the morning—one always climbing out through her kitchen window—and they argued and danced and screamed and double-Dutched until the noon sun blazed up the cement to a skillet. Then they huddled beneath a lintel and sucked orange Popsicles passed through a window until the two-o'clock shadows canted across their playground, and play resumed.

Mickey was the first of the twins to venture out, while Allmon maintained a blinkless vigil at their kitchen window, on the second floor. He watched how his other half ran onto the cracked cement, saw how the girls swarmed around him like honeybees, enfolding him in their crowd of bodies until he disappeared from sight. When Mickey returned ten minutes later, his cheeks were pink and his hair mussed upright and his eyes full of devil. The next time, Allmon went with him. But as they emerged from the shadows of their building he was seized with a reserve so sudden and so crippling that he simply stood on the stone step clutching the doorjamb, gazing at the girls through the veil of his lashes. They were oblivious, jumping and calling while a bandy-legged girl skipped through the lines, her hands perched on her lean hips, her beads up and down and clacking. As he watched, a tiny bunch of foil fell and two beads sailed off and spun away on the cement.

"Your hair! Your hair!" the girls screeched, and the jumper leaped from the eggbeater, her hands to her head, and then she spotted the boys. Her eyes sparked with excitement, and, with two fingers pinching the braid tight, she cried, "The Oreo babies!"

"The Oreo babies!" Seven girls, a gaggle, all sweat and brightness and exhilarated jostling, pressed in toward Mickey as Allmon hung back in a shy twist of limbs, but the girl who had lost her beads came to him and smiled down and petted him on the head as though he were a sweet dog.

"This one has a face like an old man," she said as she inspected the preternaturally heavy brow, the knife-jut cheekbones, the hollowed cheeks.

"Danelle, why you always talk so white?"

"I don't!" she cried, wounded, whipping around.

"Yes, you do!" in a chorus.

"Danelle wanna be white!"

"I don't!"

"You do!"

"I want some babies like you," another girl interrupted, stepping forward, ignoring the jeering. She was their tall, unspoken leader and her words stanched the argument. She still held the ends of the fallen ropes in her hands.

"I ain't no baby," Mickey said, indignant splashes of red on his cheeks.

"Baby!"

"Baby!"

"Baby!"

"How you get white if you got a black mama?" someone said.

"I ain't white!" Mickey cried, slewing about to find the speaker.

"You white!"

"Your daddy white?"

From the midst of all those arms and legs and cocked heads, Mickey's eyes found Allmon, and he said, loudly, like a dare, "My daddy black."

The girl petting Allmon narrowed her eyes. "Is your daddy really black?" she asked, but Allmon, under the impress of her hand, could only gaze up at her with an adoration like heartache.

"Jump, jump!" one girl cried, and they took up the chorus and then they were re-formed and slinging a single rope and Mickey jumped, his little knees pumping, his hands splayed, his pale face angry with concentration.

"Double, double!" The second rope sloped in and Mickey hopped from leg to leg and the girls clapped a duple rhythm and were about to sing when Mickey's toe tagged the rope and he went over in a bruising tangle. In a moment, the girls were on him, screeching and kissing his face and lying on top of him, so that he had to scratch and bite to emerge from the giggling heap, a little convict up on his toes and ready to run.

Allmon was watching, Allmon was ready, and when the girls again said, "Jump, jump!," it was he who stepped forward this time—a muscular little boy in a ragged white undershirt, his hair poufed slightly out of form, his brown eyes recessed beneath his brow. He bore the tiniest hint of a smile on his lips. The girl at his side gave him a soft shove between the shoulder blades. "This one wants to jump!" she said.

"Let him jump!" And then he was jumping simple on the single line, so that he could look up at the turner who bobbed her head open-mouthed with each swing, her pink tongue visible through her missing front teeth. He looked right into her eyes, and she looked into his as she swung the rope with dutiful focus.

"I like coffee, I like tea," they sang, "I like the Oreos to jump with me! Double-Dutch!" Both ropes rasped now. Allmon pattered and played and turned around twice for the whoops and hollers, and he was much better than Mickey, because he'd stood and watched from the window, watched the girls, memorized the patterns of their feet. A shadow of cloud swept the playground and the turner glanced up, and while her chin was uplifted, Allmon judged the descent of the rope and faked a hop and went down with a thud and a false "Ow!" and rolled on his back for the welcome, his arms wide.

They were on him. They laid their bodies over his and took his face in their hands and kissed on him. Their breath was hot and their mouths sticky. Their wings beat on him lightly and he laughed and the clouds went speeding along over the cement casting shadows as big as airplanes.

"What's your name?"

"Allmon."

"Almond, Almond, Almond!"

They kissed his mouth.

"Mickey!" It was their mother's voice calling. "Allmon!"

The girls sprang back from his supine body and there was Marie, leaning out their kitchen window, calling down, "Don't you molest my child!" The girls just studied the ground, and then one in their midst said, "Ain't nobody molested nobody," and Marie leaned even farther out the window so that she looked about to tumble out, saying, "Ain't been on top of my boy, then? That child is five years old! Don't be putting your hands on my boy's business." Someone tittered. Then Marie yelled, "Turkey vultures!," and the girls were gone just like that, scattered like jacks into their respective apartments, but, when Allmon looked up into the sunlit air where his mother was gazing down, she was smiling. "Get on up here," she said. "I got good news to tell you boys." By the time Allmon had risen, still feeling the weight of the girls on him, Mickey was halfway up the stairs.

"Guess what?" Marie was crouching down to their height when they tumbled breathless into the apartment.

"What!" they cried.

"It's a surprise! Guess what?" She was whipping them up, grinning madly at one, then the other. Her dimples were deep enough to fit a child's thumb. Allmon's blood was up; he was so excited, he hopped on one leg with a pained expression on his face, his hands about to flutter off his wrists.

"Daddy's coming to visit and y'all are going to the Northside carnival!"

"Aaah!" they screeched in tandem and went tearing through the apartment, careering from couch to chair to bed. A plant toppled, and Mickey became so overheated he pinned Allmon down on the bed, pummelling him with his fists. Marie followed at a run and separated them by throwing herself down on her stomach with an arm flung out over each panting boy, pinning them.

"Now for a serious talk," she said.

"Aw," Mickey said, trying to wriggle away.

"Get serious now," she said, and they stilled. "Now, you know how long it's been since your daddy was up here? Oh, my Lord," she said. "It's been forever. But he's coming back. He is coming back. So I'm begging you. Allmon, Mickey, your mother is begging you. Y'all need to go get some good behavior and be on it, 'cause—"

Allmon watched her face grow grave.

"—'cause I need this family," she said, barely above a whisper. "Ain't nothing really real without that man. So just be good is all I'm saying. If we're really good maybe we can get him to stay awhile." She laid her head down on the bed between them and placed one palm to each of their foreheads. "Be my best."

"Yeah!" Mickey cried and gassed off the bed, flinging himself around the doorjamb. "I'm the best!" they heard him calling.

Allmon and Marie lay there, listening to each other breathe. Then the child said, "I miss Daddy," and, when Marie turned on

her side to look at him, the openness of his face and the unin-
sured hope she saw there caused her heart to stop. "Me, too," she
said.

Sometimes he woke with a start to the shattering loop of sirens, blue and red spangled on the bedroom wall. Other
nights, it was the screaming that kept him awake: the couple
upstairs, or the family across the cement garden, up on the third
floor. Summertime was the worst. With the windows open, the
screaming was a physical thing, like a hot wind in the room—he
dreamed of witches—until he cried out, louder than all of them,
"Momma!"

She was there. "Allmon." Her voice grated by exhaustion.

"I wanna go."

"Sh-h-h. I know."

"They be steady screaming."

"You got to pretend they ain't there."

"They in the room?"

"Ain't nobody in this room but you and me and Mickey."

Mickey was awake, but saying nothing. They could feel his
presence.

Staccato shrieks, followed by the great bellow of a man's
voice.

"Up, up."

"You're too sensitive, Allmon. You're gonna be in school
soon. I'm too tired for this."

But she was his mother, she held him anyway. She squeezed
onto his part of the sagging mattress and lifted his curled form
onto her lap. He snuggled his head between her breasts, his hands
clasped at his throat.

"Away, please," he said.

"Where you wanna go away to?"

"To Daddy."

"He's coming home soon, baby."

A foul curse word shot across the cement garden and Allmon cried out.

"Sh-h-h!" Mickey hissed in the dark.

"Sh-h-h," Marie said gently. "Just go on back to sleep."

"They saying bad things."

"Baby," she said. "You just got to pretend they're singing."

He came on a Friday morning, bounding up the stairs with an enormous box in his hands, which turned out to contain a new, stainless-steel cook set. Their mother was getting ready for work, but she stopped rummaging in her purse when he walked in with the summer air around him, stepped to greet him, and pressed herself against the length of his body. The boys barely managed their joy. This man's face, so wondrous after a long absence, brought mystery, the mystery of themselves. Allmon wedged himself between his parents' bodies.

"I'll be back at five," Marie said and, with a finger against their father's chest, asked, "Want me to bring you some dinner?" Her eyes were chestnut warm.

"Yeah," he said, shrugging. "Bring me dinner. Bring me something from the Fifth Amendment."

"A pastrami sandwich. I know you like that."

He made a face and rolled his eyes. "Naw. Bring me a burger. I'm tired of that pastrami shit." He looked down at the boys, grinning crookedly and reaching for his cigarette case. "You tell somebody that you like pastrami, then—*bam!*—it's pastrami all the time till you can't stand the smell of it. God, woman." He laughed, the tiniest dart of a look in her direction. His long, dark hair was gathered back in a ponytail to reveal his freckled cheekbones, stark from underweight. Allmon stared up at him wide-eyed.

"Now, the boys get a snack at ten and then—"

"I know, Marie." His chin marking the period.

She smiled. "I know you know." She kissed him again, and he let her have his shadowy cheek.

"Have fun," she said.

"Fun!" Mickey yelped.

And then she was gone.

"Well," Mike said. He heaved his skinny shoulders up and down once, and glanced around the sunny room. Then he made his way to the couch and stretched out, not bothering to remove his shoes.

"When we be gonna—" Mickey said.

"Whoa." Mike laughed. "That's some serious black talk from a little white boy. We're not going nowhere till way after lunch, so shut it down."

Mickey started back. "Now," he said softly.

"Nope, not till after lunch."

Mickey quit his grin. Then he leaned back against the door as if standing guard, watching. Allmon crept around the side of the couch where his father lay, sought out a hand, gripped it with both of his, and tugged gently.

"What kind of animals is at the carnival?" he said.

Mike freed his hand from that clinging grasp and ran his fingers lazily over Allmon's Afro. "Bears," he said. "Snakes, and horses and like um . . . They had baby crocodiles in some aquariums once, I think."

"What's that?" Mickey asked—the sound small, almost unwilling—from where he stood at the door.

"Oh, fuck, I'm so tired. I got like three hours of sleep last night. I drove all the way from St. Louis. Um, a crocodile is like a fish with a fucked-up grill and legs."

"Ah!" Allmon made a frightened face.

Mike tucked his hands into his armpits and closed his eyes. "You boys wake me up in two hours," he said.

Allmon immediately snatched a pillow from the couch and lay down on the floor in miniature imitation of his father. "Tell me a story," he said.

"A story," Mike said, settling further into the cushions, his brow furrowed. "I don't know any stories. I'm no good at that. No, wait—wait, here's one. O.K., here's a good one. So one time there was this football game, except it was really, really cold. Not just any cold, like forty below and shit. But this is football, you know, so you gotta do what you gotta do. But that shit was a mess; the guys couldn't feel their fingers and toes and the field was pretty much ice, so every time there was a tackle it was cutting through their uniforms and shit. Guys were bleeding all over the place, they were fumbling punts, Green Bay's kicker was missing the God damn field goals 'cause he couldn't feel his feet. So fourth quarter, everybody's all hypothermic and fucked up and it's about to be over, and then—tada!—make way for Bart Starr."

"Bart Starr?" Allmon said.

"Yeah, man. Bart Starr was Jesus Christ, the great white hope. So it's the fourth quarter, Dallas is up three, Green Bay's third and goal, and this is it. Starr calls a time-out, and he's gotta make a decision. They're really close, but his team is falling apart. They all just wanna go home, 'cause it's cold as a witch's tit. But Bart Starr knows what every dude figures out eventually: when the shit hits the fan, there's nobody looking out for you, there's only you, and you're gonna have to bleed to get the thing done. So you know what he does? Quarterback fucking sneak. He fucking dives in head first and burns Dallas down to the ground." He yawned so his face stretched horribly. "Nobody expected it. They thought he was gonna pass to buy a little time. Nope. Best moment in football history right there."

He stopped. He wasn't sleeping, but his eyes were closed again. "Best moment of my fucking life right there. So, hey, Allmon," he said and he yawned another deep yawn that shook his entire body. "You know what . . . Someday I'm gonna take you and . . ." And then he was asleep.

When Allmon awoke, the sun was insistent; it pressed smothering heat into his face, causing itchy rivulets of sweat to travel into his hair. His brother was no longer in the room. He reached up and touched the white hand of his father, which had fallen listless into the air between them. He gripped a finger and the man woke, his eyebrows starting.

"Hey, kid," he said softly. "Your ma got any beer in the fridge?"

Allmon went to look. He brought back a can of ginger ale. His father smiled, then hauled himself up to a sitting position, twisting around to peer over the couch back, his face weary and worn like a much older man's. There were lines from the pillow on his right cheek.

"Go open the fridge," he said, and Allmon did as he was told, standing there like a tiny game-show hostess with the fridge contents on display. "That's the beer," his father said, pointing toward a gold box. "Bring me two."

He drank the first in two draughts. The second he drank lying down again, in slow sips and spilling some, while Allmon stared at the sliding motions of his Adam's apple.

"How's your ma been?" he asked.

"Good," Allmon said brightly.

"Where's your brother at?"

Allmon made a confused gesture and Mike said, "Oh, shit," but he didn't rise. "One more beer," he said, then, "Two." And then, after drinking one, he was asleep again.

Mickey reëntered the room, and looked down soundlessly at the body of their father in its berth, at his thin hands crossed on his chest. Then he trailed around the room like a phantom, picking at dust from the sills with a fingertip, gazing down at the busy continuance of Hamilton Avenue. When Mike awoke suddenly, saying again, "Allmon, grab me a beer," Allmon jumped to his feet and fetched it, but Mickey just remained where he was, with his brows drawn and his eyes trained on all the animated figures outside wandering in the direction of the carnival two blocks up. He leaned against the glass and made a face at no one.

Soon their father began to snore, a lumbering, unhealthy, grownup sound. Mickey turned from the window, and with an expression on his face like dawning suspicion, more rudimentary than anger, he went and placed his small hand on his father's shoulder. He shook him once, then again and with increasing force until the man was rolling on the couch like a log in heavy water. Finally, Mike brushed Mickey's hand away. "Let me sleep," he said thickly, without opening his eyes.

Allmon could not later recall how they found themselves on the street. But his hand was in his brother's and his brother was leading the charge and they were caught in the stream of humanity—they were soldiers, they were refugees, the two of them and their third brother, impulse. The crowd absorbed them as it flowed northward toward the intersection, where the trucks had driven in with their animal cargo, though once upon a time the animals had rolled in on boxcars from Pittsburgh, halting just west of Knowlton's Corner, so, as the evening sun was setting, children in their beds heard the grieved crying of leopards and the hooting of monkeys in their enclosures and couldn't sleep for the thrill.

At the roped-off intersection, there was too much to see: snakes in grimy glass cages, a panther in a boxcar on wheels weaving from side to side in menace, a bald red wildcat in a harness hissing at passersby, a baby giraffe in a cage half the height of a building. All around, the people of the neighborhood were half-drunk on a day off work, or simply drunk, kissing their girlfriends in broad daylight like men on leave, carrying their children on their strong shoulders—Allmon saw them, those children held aloft like trophies by their parents, squealing at the animals, licking vanilla cones, calling to one another over people's heads. He saw girls he knew from the building, in bright dresses, weaving giddily through the crowd, which stood body to body, everyone sewn together like a great and continuous garment.

"Look!" Mickey said. In the center of the intersection sat a reddish-brown bear on its haunches, its fat belly protruding. A massive, rusty choke leash encircled its neck, the other end held by an old man who was as fat as his bear, all sloped shoulders and paunch, with gray eyes below his glabrous, sunburned scalp.

"You wanna guess his weight and win a stuffed bear?" the man asked, rattling the gargantuan leash with some effort. Though the tug of the leash caused the bear to sway slightly to the left, its eyes were trained high on nothing. It seeped a scent like a basement. When it blinked, Allmon saw the ponderous black sweep of its eyelashes. He reached up and felt the whisper-touch of his own lashes against his fingertips. He thought, I got wings on my eyes, and the thought was so odd and yet so pleasing to him that he felt suddenly that he was immensely special, that there could be no one like him in the world. He shivered.

"Guess his weight," the man said again. Mickey craned his head back to look at the bear. He frowned.

"In pounds," the man said, as if there were another option. He looked side to side. "Where's your mom at?" he said.

"This bear got a name?" Allmon said.

"Ten pound," Mickey said.

The man snorted and the bear shifted its shaggy weight, right to left, still sunk on its haunches. Its knees were patchily bald, showing wrinkled tawny skin, as if it had plucked its own fur out. If the bear's face bore an expression, it was impossible to tell. The language of its body was useless here.

"Come on, guess again."

"Twenty pound."

The man laughed halfheartedly, but Allmon was suddenly at the outer limits of his brother's fingertips. In the ruction, beyond the bear and the tidal force of all those people, stood a horse. The horse wasn't much to look at, just a nag bought up by a carnie for forty dollars before the slaughterhouse in Peoria. She stood there with a ragged cob in her eyes and surbate hooves almost too tender to walk upon, but she was tall, and still awesome in her shabbiness. She was fifteen hands high, though her back swayed dangerously down at the middle and her rear knees pigeoned inward. Like the bear, she seemed to be missing hair at her sides, as if a saddle had worn some of her pinto coat away. Her eyes were very blue, eyes void of protest or argument, full of calm, momentful existence, perhaps without memory. Was she sad? They were the eyes of a dwindling life, of a horse accustomed to the rowel on her silver bit, to a man's grim hand on her headstall. She moved her mouth gently, as though she were chewing on something. She turned her head, and one blue eye settled on Allmon.

He pulled at his brother's hand.

"A hundred pound," Mickey was saying, and the man, grown tired of the game, handed him a blue stuffed bear anyway, which Mickey grasped greedily to his chest.

"Now, where's your mom at?" the man asked again. Mickey didn't answer; Allmon was dragging him away in the direction of the horse, but before he could stand under her docile eye, before he could ask, "She got a name?," and the man beside her could say, "Molly. You want to sit on her back?," a woman's risen voice said, "Who do those boys belong to?," and another woman halted Mickey with a hand on his shoulder, saying, "Honey, where's your mama at?" In an instant, his shoulder slipped her grasp and they were on the run, screaming with laughter and wicked, free delight, skidding around bodies and trash cans and animals until five victorious minutes later, their mission complete, they stood breathing raggedly over the snoring body of their father, and there, in the yeasty gloam of the shaded room, they quieted. They didn't look at each other. Allmon tallied thirteen gold cans on the floor by the couch, one only half drunk. Mickey walked away without a word, then sulky footsteps knocked down the stairs leading to the cement garden, and a door slammed. Allmon stooped and studied his father's face with care: the sharp, sure lines of his cheeks and chin, his brow creased even in sleep, his freckles like tiny smudges of dirt. White skin. White skin the color of flour, of paper, of snow, of stars, of pearls, of dresses at church, of his brother's face.

"Wake up," he whispered and, when there was no response, a funny sound escaped him. His vision bled. Then he balled his hand into a little fist and, with all the strength he possessed, he struck his father on the bone of his shoulder. The snoring ceased and Mike's bleary red eyes opened. They focussed slowly on Allmon's face. Then one hand reached forward and stopped a tear as it tracked down a cheek.

"Hey, Jude," he said, "don't be sad."

BLUE WATER DJINN

TÉA OBREHT

By the time the boy climbs out of bed and goes outside, they are already searching for the Frenchman, a guest of the hotel, whose clothing has been spotted adrift in the kelp-logged surf by one of the local fishermen. The morning is hot and bright, and Jack stands at the entrance to his mother's bungalow with his toes in the shade-cooled sand, watching the crowd of hotel workers grow bigger and bigger at the bottom of the beach. He can see Fawad, the Ethiopian fisherman, and Mr. Hafez, who helps run the hotel while Jack's mother is away; he can see the pool boys in their yellow uniforms, and the lifeguards with their sunglasses on. For the moment, there is no panic. It is still early. The sun breaks a white line down the water and dances on the orange buoys, strung like ornaments along the curve of the cove, and on the hull of the glass-bottomed boat, just now returning from its dawn tour at Ras Um Sid. As the boat comes closer, past the atoll where the shipwreck lies, the boy can smell it, the thick, bitter odor of petrol. He rubs his eyes, heavy with lack of sleep, and goes down the slope to join the men crowding around the Frenchman's clothes. They are all talking about the Frenchman. They are saying, Perhaps he's gone swimming, perhaps we'll find him sunbathing on the other side of the pier, he must have gone out on the glass-bottomed boat again, but their voices are hushed. At first, no one notices Jack, and his stomach feels tight, as though something had pushed its way under his ribs. Then Fawad puts a calloused hand on top of Jack's head, and he stands there, yellow hair in his eyes, feeling the weight of the fisherman's arm and his own weight in the sand.

The Arab lifeguards have taken some long poles from the recreation room and are ladling the Frenchman's large shirt and trousers carefully out of the seaweed that has tangled in the shallows. The clothes are limp, draped like skin over the poles. The shirt is bright red, the trousers blue. Jack watches the lifeguards spread the shirt out and hold it up to the light. They are thin, long-legged men, and it takes two of them to stretch it out while the others laugh. Mr. Hafez, dressed in white, tells them to get on with it. Water, slick and iridescent, drips from the points of the collar and gathers in the creases of the Frenchman's shirt. Everyone knows whose shirt it is, but one of the lifeguards checks the tag anyway. There is no name written anywhere. The Frenchman's empty trousers are unbuttoned.

As the glass-bottomed boat comes closer, some of the fishermen wade into the water and wait for the mooring lines. Fawad goes to help them. Jack wants to help, too, but, with his mother away at a conference in London, he is not permitted to swim. Instead, he watches gulls gathering on the shore, picking through the sand for crabs. He can see already that the Frenchman is not on the boat.

Up and down the beach, the morning's first tourists are arriving with their towels and beach balls, their sand pails and striped umbrellas. They are coming down from the hotel bungalows with their beach mats rolled up under their arms, their skin already reddening with heat. The venders are arriving, too, setting up their stands of pots and jewelry, polished turquoise, hawk charms, papyrus scrolls on which they will paint your name in hieroglyphs. Jack watches them line up their trinkets. He has known these venders since he was very young, and sometimes they give him honeycombs, or rocks that he cracks open to reveal purple crystals nestled inside like candy, but he does not plan to visit them today. He is thinking about the Frenchman's limp clothes as the men tie the boat to the little wooden jetty and help the tourists down—sleepy children and women in loose white shirts, an American girl with a large orange hat, and a man from Bulgaria whose skin is peeling off in strips.

"Do you have the Frenchman?" Mr. Hafez calls out.

The captain says, "You mean—?" and spreads his arms out around his middle, and then he says, "No. He did not come today." The captain is wearing a big white hat with a red anchor on it and a shirt with the hotel logo stitched in gold over the left breast pocket. He bends down and picks up his satchel and the blue bucket where he keeps the boiled eggs he uses to tempt the humphead wrasse up from the reef, now empty. "I thought he had gone home," he says, and climbs out of the boat. If he sees the shape of the Frenchman in the clothes now lying on the sand, he pretends not to notice it. Instead, he smiles down at Jack from the pier and says, "You must come out someday, habibi. There were mantas twice your size on the Ras."

"Well," Mr. Hafez says to himself. The men gather around him in silence, and the boy puts his hands behind his back and looks down to where his ankles taper off and disappear under the sand, the dusty gray circles that have caked around his legs. To Jack, Mr. Hafez looks very old, much older than his mother— older even than Fawad now, the bottom of his face heavy and lifeless. Jack remembers seeing him like this once before, last summer, when a young man tried to pose for a picture with his head halfway inside the mouth of what he thought was a dead tiger shark, and the shark closed its mouth on him, so that, even with six fishermen's hands prying at the animal's blood-stained nose, it took a saw to the jaw-hinge to release the young man, and still he lost an eye. Mr. Hafez checks his watch and looks up and down the beach. "Perhaps," he says to Fawad, "he came out here last night for a swim and left his clothes on the beach and the tide washed them out."

"I have never seen him swim," Fawad says. The fisherman is picking at a scar on his bony elbow, a white strip of raised skin that looks as if it had been smoothed down with sandpaper.

Mr. Hafez takes off his sunglasses and wipes the sweat from his eyes with the back of his hand. Then he touches Jack's shoulder and says, "Go in for breakfast," and, for a moment, the thought of eggs and bread and dates with syrup is comforting to the boy, but then there is shouting farther down the beach. One of the lifeguards has made another discovery. A little way along the beach, where yellow bluffs project over the shallow, flat part of the reef, the receding water has left the tide-pool shelf, and, in one of the spongy starfish ponds, the lifeguard has found the Frenchman's flipper. Just one. The boy watches the lifeguard climb down from the tide-pool ledge and cross the reef with the flipper in his hand. The flipper is bright green. To Jack, it looks like treasure, like something Fawad might find in his net on the skiff, as he drags it up heavy with grouper and parrot fish or butterfly fish, vibrant, unintended casualties of the reef.

The lifeguard puts the flipper down in the sand at the foot of the Frenchman's outstretched shirt and trousers. Jack is dizzy with sleeplessness. The day's first bathers are making their way into the water, with masks and buckets and pieces of bread smuggled from the breakfast buffet for the benefit of the reef dwellers. Thirty feet out, the bright tubes of their snorkels circle the rocks of the reef. For the first time in two weeks, Jack does not see the Frenchman among them, standing like a boulder in the shallows, bending to either side of his enormous belly to peer into the water, his blue goggles tight against his face.

"We must be absolutely certain before we call in," Mr. Hafez says. "Absolutely certain."

One of the lifeguards says, "Maybe he took the tour to St. Catherine's. They left very early this morning." Jack tries to picture the Frenchman—sitting, as he does, with his hands folded on his lap, his back straight, his small bald head like a melon on top of his sloping shoulders—on a bus in the desert. He has seen the Frenchman sitting like this every morning in the shade of a beach umbrella, waiting for the glass-bottomed boat. He has seen the upright bulk of the Frenchman drifting away on the sun-lit deck of the yacht that takes divers out to the Ras, the useless, tag-along, bowling-pin shape of the Frenchman, who, like the boy, is not permitted to swim. Jack finds it difficult to imagine him going to St. Catherine's, struggling up the cracked desert trail to the monastery. He almost says something, but then Mr. Hafez replies, "Part of that trip is on camelback," and everyone knows that it would be impossible, that this is not where the Frenchman has gone.

Mr. Hafez says that they must search the hotel grounds thoroughly—without overlooking a thing. He splits the men up to search the reading room, the massage parlor, the sauna, any-where that the Frenchman might have gone—even though no one can recall seeing him anywhere, in the fourteen days he has been at the hotel, except the beach or the buffet room. Mr. Hafez tells his assistant to radio the driver of the St. Catherine's tour.

He goes to the Frenchman's room himself. Jack follows him. At first, Mr. Hafez does not appear to notice the boy, walking there beside him. Then he turns to him and says, "You should go and see about breakfast now," but he seems to forget that the boy doesn't belong there as Jack stays with him on the wooden path that leads up from the beach, past the pool, where young women smelling of coconut oil are lying bare-backed under the thatched canopy of the courtyard.

Jack has never been to the Frenchman's room, the last bunga-low in the east garden of the hotel. One of the men who clean the rooms is standing at the Frenchman's door, smoking a cigarette. On the floor beside his white sandals, there is a large tray with an empty wineglass and a dirty knife and fork, a small stack of plates, a few slices of lemon. Some flies are sitting on the lemon slices. Without a word, the cleaning man holds the key out to Mr. Hafez, who unlocks the door. "Good morning?" Mr. Hafez says from the doorway. "Good morning, monsieur?" But there is no reply.

The Frenchman's curtains are drawn, and it is dark inside except for the glow of the television. On the screen, a woman is giving the weather forecast in Arabic. Jack stands by the door while Mr. Hafez opens the curtains and then the veranda door to let the breeze come in. There is still something hopeful in Mr. Hafez's face as he peers outside at the unclaimed chairs and then opens the door to the wardrobe, which has a neat row of white shirts hanging inside. The shirts look like robes to Jack.

The Frenchman's large black shoes stand together by his suitcase, which lies open on the floor. In it, Jack can see the Frenchman's straw hat, and hidden beneath the hat an enormous curved shell, which the Frenchman has obviously been planning to take away. On the table by the bed, a pile of books. Some of the spines are turned his way, and the boy can see that the books are about fish, food, the history of the Suez. Jack moves forward a little, away from the door. Mr. Hafez is in the bathroom now. He pulls aside the shower curtain, and then looks thoughtfully into the trash can under the sink. He comes back into the bedroom and stops by the bedside table to pick up a little plastic box from behind the books. The bottom of the box is transparent, and colored pills rattle inside.

The bed is unmade, and covered with papers. Mr. Hafez leans over them, and when Jack comes closer he realizes that they are from the Frenchman's sketchbook. He has seen them before: under the Frenchman's arm or umbrella or pinned down by a rock on the Frenchman's towel at lunchtime. In thick lines of color, the Frenchman has drawn the shapes of the fish that filled Fawad's nets the last few mornings. Anything that emerged from the night's catch—squirrelfish or parrot fish, milky-eyed goatfish dead in the ropes, sling-jawed lionfish with their wings twisted— now lies spread in smudged colors across the Frenchman's bed.

Jack recognizes the wide outline of last week's manta, the picture the Frenchman drew on the first day that the devil rays winged into the harbor from the warm Gulf, and Fawad caught one and split it open on the sandbar like an envelope. The Frenchman drew it from the top first, its horned mouth wide and dead, then added a smaller sketch to the side—the rows and rows of shining gills he drew after following Jack's example and putting his hand in the ray's mouth to feel the cave of its insides. Jack remembers the sensation he had that day, of wanting to punch the Frenchman, but also of feeling sorry for him, surprised at how hard he had to breathe as he stooped to reach for the ray. Among the pictures, Jack notices the one of the emperor angelfish, whose colors the Frenchman got all wrong until Jack asked Fawad to bring it back in a bucket so that the Frenchman could draw it properly.

"But where are the pencils?" Mr. Hafez is saying as he lifts up the pages one by one and looks under them. Jack does not tell him.

Among the papers scattered on the bed is the picture of the turtle from the day before, green, sturdy, fat-necked.

The previous morning, the Frenchman had stood on the beach with everyone else, watching the fishermen with the turtle. It had become tangled in Fawad's net during the night, and was so heavy that he had not been able to raise the net and had instead dragged it through the water, slowly, carefully, until he reached the beach and called for help.

Jack heard Fawad shouting and came out to watch as the men pulled the skiff into the shallows, then lugged the turtle out of the water, the net gathered around its neck and mouth, its eyes quiet and serious in its billed green head. They turned it onto its back, and the shell drew a thick rut in the sand as they dragged it up the slope, its yellow-green underbelly wet, so soft it was almost obscene, its flippers drooping like towels over the edges of the shell. The turtle had been all night in the net, gulping air when it could, and was too tired now to fight when they stopped; it lay still with its eyes shut while Fawad got his knife and began cutting around its legs where the net was squeezing the flesh.

Jack touched the turtle's belly and the rough skin of its flippers, pitted with scars. Once its legs were free, the men had to flip it back over to loosen the tangles around its neck. Right side up, the turtle seemed to realize where it was, and, suddenly revived, made a dash for the water, plowing through the sand, so that the men had to throw themselves on top of it to hold it down, and even with four of them pushing on it it still kept moving.

By now the early risers—the Frenchman, the honeymooners from Spain who were preparing for a day of golfing, an old Portuguese woman and her dog, the dervishes from the previous evening's show, coming back from a night of drinking at the neighboring hotel—had appeared, and stood in a small crowd by the water's edge, watching the turtle drag the men, inch by inch, toward the sea. One of the fishermen, a young man who had never caught a turtle before, was laughing. The Portuguese woman took a picture with a small yellow camera. Jack did not like the way the Frenchman watched the turtle. There was something cowed and lonely in the Frenchman's face when he looked at the things that came out of the water. He clearly wanted to touch the turtle, but the struggle on the beach made that impossible.

About five feet from the water, the turtle fell forward into the sand, and for a second the men stopped shouting. At this moment, Jack ran forward, all the while looking at the Frenchman, and put his hand on the turtle's head. Fawad pushed the boy, hard. "What are you doing?" he said. "What's the matter with you?" By the time the boy picked himself up, Fawad had cut through the last of the netting and stepped away from the turtle.

Jack could see its shell now. It was enormous and brown, like a map, and there was a little yellow sticker on it, which he had seen on turtles before. The turtle wasn't moving. It lay in the sand, watching the people around it with its old, old eyes.

"Is it going to die?" the Portuguese woman asked.

"No, no, madam," Fawad told her in English. "Very tired. Resting." Then he made a motion with his hands, showing her how the turtle would escape. The Portuguese woman asked the Frenchman to take a picture of her with the dog and the turtle. Fawad stepped out of the frame.

"What's that on its back?" the Frenchman asked, after he had given the woman her camera back.

Fawad searched for the right word for a few moments, and when he did not find it he said, "It is to find the turtle." He made a globe with his hands. "Travel many miles, then come back each year to make eggs. See?" he said.

"I didn't mean the tag," the Frenchman said. He had got out his sketchbook and taken off his hat, which had left a red ring around the wisps of hair on his head. "I meant that thing on the shell, that split."

That was when the boy saw it, and he wondered how he had missed it. The top of the shell, just below the neck, was jagged and cracked, open like a ravine. The edges were sharp and uneven, white-rimmed. Fawad leaned in to take a closer look, and when he stood back again he said, "Shark." He said this without conviction.

"I told you there were sharks," the young Spanish woman said, slapping her husband with her hat. "I told you they were lying when they said, 'Oh, no sharks, madam, no sharks here.' "

But Jack knew, from the way Fawad smiled at him, that sharks had nothing to do with it, nothing at all. He knew from the way Fawad dusted off his hands and looked out to sea and then back at him, as the Frenchman began to sketch the turtle, and the Portuguese woman asked about turtle eggs, and the turtle started moving again and dropped down into the water, activating itself like a giant engine, and swam away.

Past the breakwater, out where the sea is as clear and bright as ice, is the ship that the atoll broke years ago, the waves dashing it against the rocks in a ragged bend on the eastern side of the lighthouse. It is an old ship, rusted gray and green, a Navy gunboat, and it lies on its flank like the eviscerated body of an enormous fish, its smooth glass-window eyes smashed in and crowded with darkness.

For Jack, the ship is the edge of the world, and it has sat there, on the lip of his knowledge, for as long as he can remember. He knows that other boats go beyond it, that far away there is the open sea. But, to Jack, there is the ship, and then nothing, and he knows that people do not swim to the ship or dive near it. They are not permitted; there are signs that tell them this, and the lifeguards will shout to swimmers who get too close. The swimmers come back without knowing why. But Jack knows. Fawad has told him all about the ship, which is the home of the water djinn.

Fawad has told him about late nights on the water, the eerie music of the ship when the moon is high. The strangeness of the dead fish smashed on the rocks, the split turtle shells, the strings of teeth and skin that arrive in the tide. "It is easy to say 'shark,' habibi," Fawad has said. "It is easy to say many things that are not true when we are afraid."

Fawad has told Jack about long spindly fingers, and voices that sound like rain when they strike the water, thunderclap voices in the dark, pulling ships in from the deep water. Jack knows about moist eyes and singing mouths, about webbed hands and coral combs pulling through hair as tangled and coarse as kelp.

He knows about sailors who have fallen in love and swum out never to return again, about capsized boats, about the skull cups the djinn keep in their underwater caverns as reminders of the men who have loved them.

It holds the boy, the corpse of that ship, because of its murky secrets, its rusted grottoes and metal lagoons. He thinks about it when the moon comes out of the water behind the atoll, thinks about seawater filling the cold cavity of the hull, the swelling walls of silver batfish up against the ceiling where the crusted barnacles live. He thinks about the water djinn: their teeth, their hands, what they see down there in the darkness. He has seen their lights around the ship at night, the green glow of their underwater torches, and he imagines them hovering in the waterworn doorways, their mouths red with the flesh of men, their wrists braceleted in seaweed, singing, weaving moonbeams into their hair.

It is lunchtime when Jack follows Mr. Hafez back to the beach. Mr. Hafez is carrying the Frenchman's drawings. The afternoon is hotter than the woman on the television in the Frenchman's room predicted, and there is an unexpected calm on the water. The wind from last night is not coming back, and a dead glaze of light stuns the cove.

Still no one has seen the Frenchman, so Mr. Hafez calls the police. The men of the search party wait on the beach for the police, and the chef from the restaurant, who knows what is happening, sends them lunch in boxes, carried by the young women who work at the hotel. The men sit on deck chairs out of the sun and talk about the tides, and about the police captain, whom they do not like, because he is always fining them, and then they talk about next week's soccer match against the neighboring hotel, and how this time they are going to win, because they have the new lifeguard, who is a wizard. Jack stands with his lunch box and listens to them talking until he sees Fawad turning over the skiff on the sandbar near the breakwater, and then he walks over and sits down with Fawad in the shade of the boat. Fawad eats fresh fish for his lunch, and today he does not volunteer to tell a story. Jack sits with his lunch box on his knees, until Fawad opens it for him and takes a French fry, and asks him why he is not eating. Jack says that he does not know, and Fawad puts a hand on his shoulder and leaves it there for a little while.

Jack sits in the heat, hungry and tired, his stomach tight against his ribs. The smell of the fries makes him ill, and he gives the box to Fawad and lies down in the sand. He can see all the way down the beach to where the Frenchman's clothes have been laid out. He must have fallen asleep, because suddenly there is new shouting down the beach, and, by the time he gets to his feet and remembers where he is, the lifeguards are all going into the water, and they have found something else. Fawad is with them. Jack does not want to go and look, but he runs across the hot part of the sand and onto the wet slope and stands there.

"What is it?" someone is saying. The lifeguards are gathered around something small that is floating in the water. Jack comes closer. He steps in up to his ankles, and then wades forward a little farther, just a few feet, until he is standing on the hard rock of the reef, and the water is resting against his thighs. He sees Fawad reach for what is floating in the water, and the shine of it strikes the boy's eyes. When he can see again, he sees that Fawad is holding the Frenchman's metal pencil case. He is holding it upside down and shaking it, and water is dripping out of it. The pencils rattle inside.

"Hey," one of the lifeguards says to Fawad, pointing at Jack. "He's coming in."

Fawad turns around and sees the boy standing in the water, and he says, "Get out immediately. Get back up there, do you understand? Wait for us."

Then Jack gets out and sits on the wet sand until the police captain, Abdul al-Basri, arrives; he is by himself, wearing a green uniform. The boy picks barnacles off the bottom of the beached skiff with the point of a jackknife, while the men show the police captain the Frenchman's clothes and flipper, the wet pencil box, the drawings from his room. Mr. Hafez talks for a long time, and then he becomes upset and sits down on a deck chair with his head in his hands until one of the lifeguards brings him a glass of lemonade.

The police captain looks up and down the beach, and then he comes to the skiff to talk to Fawad. He is shaking his head, and Fawad, who has begun readying the net for the evening, does not say anything.

"We will look," Abdul al-Basri says.

"Where?" Fawad says.

"At Pharaoh's Island, and also at Dahab," he says. "But with the currents—"

"You do not need to explain the currents to me," Fawad says.

The police captain flips through the Frenchman's drawings. He has a large mustache and thick hair that he sweeps out of his eyes with the back of his hand, and round, gold-rimmed sunglasses that are too big for his face. He is wearing a gold watch to go with the glasses.

"These are quite good," he says to Fawad.

"They are not so good that I would agree if I didn't think he was dead," the fisherman says, threading his line.

"They are good enough," Abdul al-Basri says, as he rolls the drawings up. "But there isn't much to hope for." He stares at the water, swaying a little on his toes, tilting his head upward so that he can look through the bottoms of his sunglasses, which are lighter than the tops. "By now there has been a shark," he says. "Or a propeller."

Fawad makes a little motion with his hands, and the police captain looks at the boy.

297

"My apologies," he says to Fawad, and Fawad shakes his head and continues untangling his net.

"He'll turn up," Abdul al-Basri says finally.

"It might be better if he didn't," Fawad says. The two shake hands and the police captain leaves.

Jack sits with his legs out in front of him, piling fistfuls of sand around his shins. Fawad smiles at him, his mouth full of clotted net. Then he looks down at the boy's legs and says, "What happened to your knee?"

The night before, Jack had been unable to sleep. In his cot by the window, he gazed up at the wedged plaster of the ceiling, listening to the soft breath of the wind outside, and the absence of his mother, which had a sound all its own—no quiet shuffling of papers or clink of coffee cups, no sliding of the liquor-cabinet door. A dotted pink lizard with large eyes was inching up the wall opposite his bed, its skin runny and transparent. Jack watched its slow ascent, then he coughed and the sound sent the lizard scuttling up to the rafters and the roof beyond. The beams of the house creaked like a ship. The blanket was stifling, and Jack struggled to kick it off. The dead ship on the atoll sat in the corner of his consciousness, as it always did when he was alone, ever since his mother had caught him sitting in the shallows of the mangrove swamp and had said to him, "Is that what you want—to die like this? To drown, to not be found? Eaten or mangled into shreds—is that what you want?" all without shouting, without once raising her voice, and then the next day Fawad had told him about the ship and the water djinn.

The boy lay with the blanket around his legs, and still he could not sleep.

Outside, the night was cold. Sharp, clear stars lay flat against the sky. When he stepped out of the bungalow, the sand under his feet was moist, still steaming with the heat of the day. He ran down the dunes, his toes stabbed by splinters of driftwood, and when he reached the wet edge of the sand he stopped to catch his breath.

It was high water, and the swells had cut the beach short. They opened out as they rose, white-capped rolls unwinding, smashing against rock and sand, tossing clots of seaweed up the beach. Jack felt the booming resonance of the surf all the way down to his bones, and he stood very still and watched the sand release its dwellers, tiny armies of crabs rising out of the ground. Out past the breakwater, he could see the atoll lighthouse dragging its yellow light in a circle over the curve of the reef, the shape of the ship chiselled out of the darkness.

The beach was empty and unfamiliar, the dunes white and shifting and snaked with shadows. The wind was leaning into the date palms. Jack looked out at the spinning light on the atoll, the blackness like a mouth around it.

The sea was making a sad, sad sound. It was a low sound, a sound he had never heard it make before, steady and unwavering. He went down to where the sea had run up among the rocks and the picked-over shells, and he sat down and put his feet in the foam. He was sitting like this when he saw it, a big green flipper that had washed up and got stuck under one of the boulders with the sand sucking down on it as the water rushed backward and forward. He got up and pulled the flipper out, and he looked at it, bright and wet in his hands. He had seen this flipper somewhere before, he thought. At that moment, the sound grew louder, a hollow, howling sound, and Jack held the flipper in his hands and looked into the darkness for the water djinn.

Out in the waves, in the black, pitching hillocks of water, something large and pale was bobbing in and out of view. At first he thought it was a buoy or a boat that had come unmoored, but then the pale thing crested on a large wave, and suddenly he saw them. He could see them now. It was them—they were making the sound, riding the waves, clustered heads in the water that called to him, laughed at him from the carcass of the ship—and he was so afraid that his limbs felt heavy and weak, and the rising waves in the distance seemed to put out hands to touch him, and still he couldn't move. He wanted to close his eyes so that he would not see them, so that he would not go blind, as Fawad had said he would, but the reality of the moment overwhelmed him.

A wave hissed over the beach and wreaths of foam sucked at his heels, pulling him down into the sand. He almost fell, waved his arms to regain his balance. When he looked up, the thing in the water seemed farther away, more abstract, round, bloated. Different. The voice on the wind formed a word.

And then Jack was running, sprinting for the sandbar and the breakwater. His chest felt swollen, his heart was too big for it, and the air was catching somewhere between his mouth and his lungs. He scrambled up the narrow ledge, which was slippery, wet with the tide, alive with tiny creatures scattered by his strides. He was still holding the flipper, and the rocks cut into his feet. He tripped, fell, split his knee, but he pushed himself up and ran again, the sea pulsing around his ankles. At the end, where the rocks plunged into darkness, he stopped.

It was the Frenchman—he could see that now. The Frenchman was naked, large and white and naked, and sitting on the waves as if he were being carried. Sitting perfectly still, his hands in his lap, bobbing up and down like a cork. The Frenchman's head was turning slowly from side to side as he sat there, looking down into the water, and Jack stood with the flipper against his chest. He could see that the Frenchman was holding some paper, his pencil box, holding them on his lap as if he were sitting in a class. Then he looked up and saw Jack, and he waved his great meaty arms.

Jack stared and stared, and then he found himself waving back. He raised the flipper high and waved with it, and the Frenchman waved again. He waved harder this time, and shouted something. Jack couldn't hear it, couldn't hear the word.

The water djinn were carrying the Frenchman away, Jack realized. But this was not how Fawad had told him it would happen. This was not a struggle; there were no webbed fingers pulling him down, holding him under. The Frenchman was sitting like a great fat pharaoh on the waves, letting them bear him away in their naked blue arms. He did not seem to care, as Jack did, where they were taking him. Jack wanted to know where. Jack wanted to know why.

The Frenchman shouted again. This time Jack heard it, a desolate word. *Help*.

Help, the Frenchman was shouting for help, and, suddenly, Jack realized that the Frenchman was thrashing and rolling over in the water. Jack stood stiff and still on the rock, but he could not move. He was not permitted to swim, and he could not run back to the hotel in time to get help.

He stood there for long moments, hearing the Frenchman howl and watching him fight the torrents of water that wrapped around him and rushed down his nose and throat. The current was strong, a glass line of suction that streamed past the atoll, past the ghost ship, past the horizon, and the fat man fought it, arm over arm, call by call, but he could not overcome it.

Then he went under, and Jack's throat caught. When he came up, he was far away, turning like an enormous white bottle, bobbing weightlessly down the channel.

Three days after the Frenchman goes missing, they find him. He floated, as Abdul al-Basri guessed, out to sea and into the Gulf of Aqaba—past Tiran Island and the blue hole of Dahab and the kelp beds where the whale sharks feed, past four cruise liners and an oil rig, until at last his swollen form came to rest against an orange buoy just off the coast of Nuweiba. There, the Frenchman's arm snagged on a rope, and as he lay face down in the water the gulls stood on him and ate his back.

Jack goes down to the beach to watch them bring him in. It is a hot morning, heavy with mist, the prow of the police boat caked with wads of rust as it cuts through the waves. Fawad swims out, shoulder-deep, to help the policemen lower the Frenchman onto a stretcher, very gently, and carry him ashore. Jack stands in the shallows, his shirt sticky with heat. As they pass him, he sees the Frenchman, wrapped from head to foot in yellowed linens, tied off at either end like a great parcel of sausage, and the stench of saltwater rot washes over him. He pictures the bloated blue corpse, punctured like a balloon by the teeth of dogfish, the claws of crabs, the mouths of lampreys, thousands of skittering things that have burrowed frantically into the flesh and deflated him inch by inch until he is as ragged as a web of tide pools.

Jack stands in the shallows, urinating, until Fawad pulls him out.

Mr. Hafez calls the boy's mother to tell her the news, and, from London, she suggests that they hold a wake while they wait for the Frenchman's family to collect him. The Frenchman has a brother, Jack hears at the hotel, a man who works in a garage, who is coming for the body. Mr. Hafez has offered him a free stay.

For the wake, they light candles and find a priest from St. Catherine's, a man who comes down to read verses from the Bible over a cross that they have buried in the sand near where the Frenchman's belongings were found. Night falls and the priest says things that Jack does not understand, and the soft honey smell of smoke and flowers fills the air above the courtyard until it is so thick that Jack cannot find room in his lungs to breathe. Some of the hotel guests come dressed in black. The old Portuguese woman is there, wearing a faded green sweater. There is a piece of fish in her hand, and during the service she feeds little bits of it to her dog, whom she is holding against her moist underarm. The Frenchman is not in attendance; he has been cleaned, perfumed, wrapped in new linens, and stored in the hotel's meat locker, between blocks of ice.

When the fire burns low, Fawad goes out to pull up his nets. Jack follows him and watches him put his bucket and rod into the bottom of the skiff, along with some bottles of water and a small pot of goat stew. Jack wishes that Fawad would ask him something, but the old man doesn't say a word. The boy tries to help push the skiff into the water, but Fawad waves him away, and then he sits on the beach, watching the fisherman alone in the boat, the even swing of his arms as he rows himself along the line of the breakwater, through the low waves and away into the darkness. When he is gone, Jack goes back to his room and gets the Frenchman's missing flipper out from under his bed. He will wait for Fawad on the beach, he tells himself, and in the morning he will tell the old man everything.

Jack makes a burrow for himself in the sand and lies on his back with the sky pressing in around him like an overturned bowl.

When he wakes up, there is silence. He thinks he has heard his mother calling his name, looking for him, but then he stands up and remembers that she is far away, that she is in London, and that the Frenchman is dead. The dead man's flipper is in his hand.

When he looks around, the water is gone. At first, he thinks that sleep is playing a trick on him, and he rubs his eyes but still the sea has vanished. He can hear it, somewhere in the distance, very far. The tide has pulled the water out like a net, and has left behind the pale, crooked body of the reef, white and empty and stark in the moonlight. Jack has lived his whole life on this beach, but he has never seen the tide so low. He can see the water now, when he looks very hard. It is buffeting the side of the atoll that faces the open sea, the roar of it singing in the metal belly of the ship.

His first step out, Jack realizes that the reef is slippery. Grass, silk-soft, has grown up out of the living rock. All around him stand small towers of coral, gray breathing things. The retreating water has dragged the starfish from their moorings, left them red-backed and raw in the sand, reaching for their hiding places. Sea urchins cluster together, spines shining. Twenty feet out on the crenellated alleys of the reef, the underwater forest begins. The grasses are longer here, thicker, and as he steps through them Jack's bare feet touch the still bodies of butterfly fish, emperor angels. A lionfish lifts its feathered barbs at him from a cradle of water in a rock. Under the boy is the porous face of the reef, its millions of crawl spaces, nets of tunnels swollen with tiny hidden monsters.

The atoll is different. Its rocks are sharp, and he cuts his feet on them as he climbs up and over, toward the ship, toward the water. Toward the water djinn. Salt stings the cuts in his heels. The ship clings to the edge of the atoll like a rusted clamp, its metal flank striped with light. Beyond it, the sea is breathing, coming slowly back over the rock.

When he reaches the hull of the ship, he puts the Frenchman's flipper between his teeth and hoists himself up until his head is wedged through a rusty porthole. At first, he sees nothing. The inside of the ship is black, swollen with dark water. But then his eyes adjust and the moon comes out from behind a bank of cloud. Shafts of light fall through the gnarled holes in the metal and slice the green water inside.

When he sees it, it is more than he expected. It wheels, weightless and slow, skimming the cracked husk of the ship, more graceful than any he has ever seen, even though he has sat on the beach for years watching them come and go. It swims, compressed, into the bottom of the ship, its beaked head darting at cracks that are too small to let it out, trapped in a metal tide pool on the edge of the abyss. The water sighs, sloshes around the iron trough, and Jack catches a brief glimpse of its black eye, the globe of its shell, as it turns and dives once again, trying to press its body out into the sea.

DAYWARD

ZZ PACKER

Early yet, the morning clouds the color of silver fox, and Lazarus was running. His sister, Mary Celeste, hadn't heard the dogs chasing after them—nor could hear them, being deaf—and, despite his signing to her what the plan was and for her to keep up as best she could, she'd nevertheless been treed, and soon so would he, if he was lucky and could make it to a likely pine in time. Earlier he'd thrown rocks, possibly wounding two of the dogs, which he'd heard nothing from in a while, but the third was still in full barking pursuit.

"Stay!" he yelled at his sister. But of course yelling without signing did no good, and all he could hope was that she'd made the rustle he'd sensed, ten or so pines away. Such an animal ranting he'd never heard before and hoped never to hear again. He couldn't help cursing his luck for getting split from Mary Celeste, then cursing her for being so stubborn and full of vinegar and so deaf.

From the sound of it, the dog that had been tailing him was neither gaining nor retreating; there was just an incessant yelping that was part snarls of threat and part screams of feeling threatened. Perhaps it had already found its quarry up a tree. If so, that left Lazarus with nothing to do but stop and push away the pounding blood in his head and struggle to divine where each round of sounds could be coming from. Perhaps, though, the quarry the dog had found was Mary Celeste. He cocked his ear, subtracting all the echoes bouncing off the pines until one spot seemed sure. With no time, he ran toward it until he got to the trees where wood sense told him she might be. No real knowing about it, but the dog leaping out at him from nowhere proved him right.

Two years free, Lazarus was hoisting himself up a pine like a runaway, digging his nails into the soft bark, aiming toward the clouds above, and praying that the next branch up wasn't nearly as far away as it looked nor the hound below as close as it sounded. Where its two companions had gone, who knew, but this one gnashed its teeth and ripped and ranted and barked so mightily Lazarus swore he felt the tree shake. It was one thing to be chased by hounds as a runaway slave, and another thing entirely to be a runaway once free, with a deaf sister who'd spent the first unchased part of their journey traipsing off in the woods as if she had time to examine every leaf that caught her fancy.

"Git!" he yelled, catching his breath on the second or third branch, hanging like a possum, but all the dog did was yell and curse back in its own language. It was now just a small picture below, but that terrified Lazarus even more—no scent, no trail. No trail on him, and the dog would go after Mary Celeste, who, being a girl and only nine, mightn't climb so high or so fast. He would simply have to do something—however foolish and foolhardy—as he could not leave a deaf sister, his charge, up in a tree, liable to fall at any moment.

"Mary Celeste!" he yelled. He knew it was useless, but he did it again. He got back nothing.

He had no way of telling her progress up her tree, but he scaled his own, wondering what was the use of it. It mattered not whether he was safe. She'd get killed by Kittredge's dog, or perhaps the other dogs would come from nowhere and claw her to death.

It was all his fault. Back at Four Daughters, when Lazarus had told Miss Thalia that he and Mary Celeste were striking out to reunite with their own people in New Orleans, their former mistress had called the African race an ungrateful lot of thieves for deserting once emancipation came round. "All I got to say," Miss Thalia said, curls agog as if she'd been caught in a freezing rain, "is that we always fed and clothed you slaves."

"Some might say," Lazarus ventured, " 'twere the slaves that's fed and clothed you."

Lo, the weather of her face.

Lazarus hadn't mentioned the deaf school for Mary Celeste—it was none of her business—but he had let loose a great deal else about what he thought of their mistress. He'd got into trouble before for back talk, acting first and thinking later. Egg, the blind man with whom they shared a cabin, used to tell him he was tempting fate when he talked out of his head so. That if he wasn't his father, and couldn't deliver the goods, he ought not to talk like his father. Sure enough, that same night, mere days after they'd buried Egg and told her they were leaving, Miss Thalia had knocked on their cabin door to announce that she'd decided to have them sicced by Kittredge's dogs and in all probability hanged, but that she was giving them a half day's head start. Kittredge—Miss Thalia's overseer in slavery, and her hired hand when freedom came—was surely happy to be enlisted once more.

If Lazarus had thought she was joking about the dogs, or about the head start, he was wrong on both counts. Of course, he and Mary Celeste were good and free by law and by poor dead Abe Lincoln himself, but Kittredge and his dogs came after them anyway, and no amount of pepper that Lazarus shook behind him would sneeze them off.

Now the hound below sent up a howling message, as if from Kittredge and Miss Thalia both. With nothing else to do, Lazarus growled back, which set the dog to cussing him out in hellhound once again.

"Lazarus!" It was Mary Celeste. She would not have called out unless she thought all danger was gone or thought she'd be in more danger if she didn't call for him.

It was all his fault that they were in it like this. Ever suspicious of a God who hadn't spoken to man, woman, or child in more than a thousand years, he nevertheless sent up a pinprick-brief prayer, even as he felt his throat try to puke up his heart. He knew what he'd have to do to keep her safe and alive: he'd have to kill himself.

His father, who'd run off not once, or twice, but three times, had heard tell of a man in Missouri who'd had no river or brook or stream water to plash through to cover his scent; instead, he wrapped some homespun from his shirt round his hand and rammed it down a dog's throat to choke it. The mutt had left the hand nothing but blood and gristle, healed over with a few blond whiskers poking through, but the man would hold up his stump with pride, testifying, "My hand's back in slavery, but the rest of me's free, by God. The rest a me's free."

Lazarus unbuttoned his shirt with one hand in order to keep his other in full grip of the tree. He wound the shirt round his fist. He shimmied midway down the pine and let himself drop to the ground. He knew not whether the dog leaped back or pounced forward, only that he felt the terrible bristle of stiff hound fur at his throat, across his neck, along his belly, the animal trying to twist him out of his soul inasmuch as a bear bones a fish. No matter which way he turned, there was nothing but dog—dog teeth, dog claws, dog hunger, nothing but dog forever—and he knew that the dog would either bury him here, under the cool of the pine needles, or leave his body out for days like one of Miss Thalia's half-carved Sunday roasts.

And still he fought, until, suddenly and without knowledge of how it had been done, he risked everything—his life, Mary Celeste's, the dog's, he hoped—and plunged his hand down the beast's throat.

The dog both choked and gasped as if half-drowned, mastering itself enough to sink teeth into flesh, and now Lazarus heard his own screams as teeth struck bone, then reared back without loosening their hold; he screamed for mercy, the teeth pulling his flesh as if yanking at taffy.

Still, with his free hand Lazarus punched the beast's throat, punched the tongue thick as pork loin, hollered all the while as the teeth stabbed him worse than the nails rammed through the poor Saviour. Lazarus pulled every which way to get his hand out, cursing his lying daddy, who'd probably never met the Missouri man at all, cursing Mary Celeste and her everlasting deafness, cursing as he howled worse than the dog, wrestling the dog's body from the anchor of its mouth until he felt the cool, chill silent scream of his own blood meeting air for the first time, pulsing out of him like gushes of water at the pump, some ripped artery or vein begging mercy, begging through Death, which spoke to him in his mother's voice, then his own voice, as if he had no choice but to agree.

But it had worked.

For the first time in a long while, he heard no growls, no snarls. Then he knew: he'd choked the dog with his own hand, and the dog was dead.

He climbed Mary Celeste's tree as best he could, but he must have passed out, for the next he remembered he was on the ground and she was looking into his eyes as if peering at fish in a gully. When he stood, the blood gushed more.

It hardly looked like a hand, or anything, really.

Nasty, she signed.

"Well, I can't help that, can I?"

I'm just commenting, she said.

"You ain't saying nothing, so just hush your hands."

You can't make me.

Mary Celeste was not one for blood, never was, but when the hand began spurting anew she quit signing anything, just led him like the blind until they found freshwater, and had him plunge the hand into a stream somewhere outside Lafayette County. His blood bloomed red, then pink, in the water, and little whip-tailed tadpoles and fish came to nibble at the meat of his hand. He felt an awful pride rise up in him, having done it, and though the hand looked like something a plow had tried tilling into the earth, he'd saved his sister, and kept his promise to his dead folks of never leaving her to harm.

Now, with that part over, he understood just how far they'd come. He didn't know if they'd made it out of Mississippi or even out of the county, but he knew they'd been two days walking, and one day with hounds on them, and that was enough to get them somewhere. He felt both a sadness and a relief at being the farthest from home he'd ever been.

You think we in Canada? she asked.

"There ain't no such place," Lazarus said. "Besides, it's New Orleans. Ain't that where you wanted to go? To the school and to our folks?"

She said nothing to that, just smoked a few puffs, the last of his tobacco.

The hand, now clean, looked all the worse: teeth holes, erupted muscle, and mangled tendon, and something bubbling and maroon at what seemed to be its core.

We got to go back and get a doctor, she signed.

"You more than anyone should know about a blamed doctor." He felt cruel, having said it, but didn't take it back: more words only made everything worse. When she was five, she'd woken from a fever hearing nothing save a buzz—a sound, she'd reported, remarkably like a trapped June bug, travelling the road from mouth to ear and back. Her hearing might have been saved had Miss Thalia and the late Master Thompson called in a white folks' doctor instead of Mr. Swope, the county veterinarian, who specialized in horse carbuncles. The horse doctor had advised both Master and Miss to refuse to tolerate the girl's melancholy and to end her bed rest. If they would merely tend to their property and cease abetting the girl's masquerade, he said, they would quickly find her hearing repaired. He then packed away his stethoscope, his silver thumping cone, his verruca salts, his jar of leeches. A month passed, her hearing going from a buzz to a muffle. She said the voices sounded as though people were being suffocated, desperately trying to speak but hampered by pillow down, or straw ticking, or pond water. He didn't want to know what it sounded like—listening to their mother moan about it was punishing enough—but Mary Celeste was ever the talker, and the more deaf she grew the less she talked to others and the more she talked to him. She told him how the sound became a strict calm of long corridors, unaccompanied by anything. She seemed not to grasp what it was until her deafness was final, and no amount of straining or interpretation would bring sound, much less words, to her ears. When she came to understand this, she screamed for days on end. But that, too, ended, and she wiped her tears with the brave resolve of a child seeing the family hog off to slaughter.

No doctor! Her hands tsked at him in disbelief. *You just ornery.*

"Nan bit of thanks from you. I'm the one with a busted hand, liable to be cut off."

Remember Daddy's story about the man with the stump?

"No."

Yes, you do.

"We got to go. Who knows where Kittredge is. Could be right behind."

He ain't behind. I ain't seen this place before.

"You ain't hardly been out of house and field since deaf, so what you know?"

"I know lots," she said, speeching it. When she wanted him to get her meaning, she'd do both. She was always going on about the lady from up North who'd held and warped her hands into signs, some relation of Miss Thalia's who'd wanted to take Mary Celeste off North to a school that no children could attend but those as deaf as Mary Celeste. She hadn't known if Colored were taken on or not, but even without knowing she seemed ready to wager everything that Mary Celeste should leave mother, father, and brother to go there. When Miss Thalia refused, this aunt or cousin or cousin-in-law outfitted Mary Celeste to sleep in the Thompson house, even if it was at the foot of the bed, where Mary Celeste said the woman's feet gave off a powerful stink.

And Mary Celeste was right. She did know more than she should. She could tell when it was going to rain, when a body would die. She knew how to make a garden grow twice as big in half the time. Cats always came her way. She was of such magic, people half expected she'd heal herself of her own lost hearing. But that didn't happen.

"Just shut it and hush," Lazarus told her.

He upped himself from the streambank and began walking. He wore his bloodstained shirt, soaked with the smell of dog, perforated to cheesecloth with innumerable bites and tears. He knew with a certainty that he was going to lose the hand. Mary Celeste whiskered her feet behind him to catch up.

He was fourteen years old. Perhaps fifteen.

For forty-two days after the dogs, he and Mary Celeste survived on blackberries, tiny fish, and questionable mushrooms. The hand went from bad to worse, a throbbing thing that some hours felt as though it would calm itself if he could only plunge it into some ointment, and other times as though chariot wheels were running over it with every bounce of his gait. At first it refused to scab over, and they suspected gangrene; Mary Celeste used her pinafore to wrap the thing. It smelled like unsalted hog in a summer sun, and each day they walked he couldn't help unwinding the pinafore from his hand, every fresh unveiling aching like skin unskeined from flesh, the new air like a razor to it. One night, he woke himself with his own howling. Still, he kept going, though it got so bad near the end that Mary Celeste brought out the knife and asked where to cut.

"Don't you know anything? That won't do it," he told her. "You'd need an axe, at least."

You need someone else then, too. I'm not chopping anything off anyone with an axe.

They'd started out on the high roads, then took the low ones. Later on, they'd outwitted old swamp-dwelling veterans and vagrant hunters alike, and barely escaped from a dirty old Confederate who'd made it his business to collect a passel of girl orphans from the war, selling their innocence in a thicket of mulberry bushes. The man had taken Mary Celeste away from Lazarus when he'd been dead asleep, and he'd had her for a full sun hour before Lazarus tracked and ambushed him, tackling him to the ground. The man finally bested him and pulled out an ancient pistol, pushing it against Lazarus's mackinaw cap to blow his head off.

He pulled the trigger.

After the smoke and cordite cleared and the clowder of little-girl voices quit their chiming screams, Lazarus touched his temple, his finger finding a dab of blood no bigger than a drop of claret. The man drew back, amazed, now convinced that the skulls of colored men were hard as iron. Back at Four Daughters, blind Egg had laid his hands on Lazarus and told him he had a gift of being hard to kill. Egg had many a time congratulated him on his name bringing him good luck, but Lazarus had reminded the old-head that he'd heard of nearabout two score slaves named Lazarus in Lafayette County alone, and still the name hadn't brought additional life or a trip back from the dead for a single one.

Now poor Egg himself was dead. He'd named the date, and had been late one day, but the hour was true: after eight, after sundown. Lazarus and Mary Celeste laid him in the ground and began to plot their way to New Orleans.

Lazarus thought on it all. How their father had come to be killed, not from his ear being nailed to the post but from scratching it day and night until it pussed over. How their mother had run off into the woods, witless and mad, after their father's death. She'd been gone nearly three days, then caught pneumonia and died before she could be properly whipped for attempting to escape—if churning around the same copse of trees less than four miles off could be called escaping.

Mary Celeste hugged his head, her grateful tears wetting his face; meanwhile, the old Confederate was running as far and as fast as his spindly legs and his rope-tied girls would allow. All the activity of wrestling Mary Celeste away had torn Lazarus's hand anew, and though he could see its throbbing, he couldn't at all feel its message.

Lazarus thought on the Missouri runaway and the blond-whiskered souvenir of his stump. *My hand's back in slavery, but the rest of me's free, by God. The rest a me's free.*

It had been his father's favorite bedtime story.

His father had liked to whip them sometimes before bed, and when they asked him "Why, Papa?" after they'd brought in the moss for the bed ticking and limed the eggs and poured ashes and hair clippings on the little collard garden and done all their tasks right and proper and in full obedience, their father wouldn't or couldn't say. But other times he peeled them pawpaws and told them stories that kept them up with the horribleness of their endings, which were not at all like the ones Miss Thalia told when she gathered the tykes around her at Christmas and Easter to read a page of "Ivanhoe" or "King Arthur" or "Robin Hood."

Lazarus's once-upon-a-time girl, Savannah, had told him that her father did the same—beat her—but that it was only to show

318

he could be a man, the same as Master Thompson or Kittredge; he was only trying to say he owned her more. That made sense enough to Lazarus, and after that his mind wasn't so sore to get whipped, despite being sore in body and spirit.

By the time they set foot in Louisiana, landing on the far banks of the Pearl River north of Bogalusa, the Gulf sun was tracking them without pause, and each day broiled with the smell of hot swamp water and the sound of mosquitoes. He could not walk for fainting; it was as if the gentle air were full of nails and the sun a hammer, striking his hand each moment it shone. It was the first time in a while that Mary Celeste had seen him cry, tears and tears without stop, and she looked disturbed and rabbity.

Lazarus might as well have been wearing a loincloth instead of trousers; the sleeves and apron of Mary Celeste's dress had also been stripped into rags long ago to stanch the bleeding soles of her feet. They kept on, limbs weighted with heat, shredded by thorns. No water left in their eyes, no feeling left in their joints. The last stretch toward New Orleans they did nearabout in their sleep. Starved, chigger-bitten, something flaking from their skin like rust.

And the hand got worse, but by then he couldn't feel it at all.

New Orleans itself seemed days in approach. Herons rose up and over them, a litter of wings, soundless flaps turning to white rags against a white-rag sky. Even with Lake Pontchar-train a mile behind, there were still herons aplenty, after them like beggars. In no mood to be shat upon, they turned off their road and down another, a twisty, long, and brambly path. Mary Celeste was given to dawdling, and he'd had to yank on her, on occasion, with the one good hand. Then the thrips and dragon-flies gave way to street Arabs, ornery Creoles, and armed whites spitting razor strops about the loss of the Sesesh. They knew by the gas lamps and wooden walkways that they'd made it to New Orleans.

The city was beautiful, even in its filth. On every corner, someone was selling berries or apples or hot corn pone; someone was offering to cobble your shoes right then and there, if you were lucky enough to be shod in the first place. Fishmongers in sandpapered gloves held up gleaming, still quivering fish, then plunged them back into water-filled haversacks. They passed by shops selling cigars, shoes, clarinets—a whole piano, even.

Runners—white boys—came up to any couple, well-dressed man, or broken-down carriage and yelled, pleaded, or sang the merits of the hotel or boarding house that had sent them to drum up business. Men paced the planked sidewalks like preachers, offering to sell you the very same flowers you'd see growing out the ground for free.

How, Mary Celeste signed, *are we going to find Aunt Minnie here?*

"We got to ask after her plantation," Lazarus told her.

You want me to do the talking? she signed.

"You hush."

Stop saying that. I'll talk. We'll get into less trouble that way.

He made a show of ignoring her. She'd been after him about the dogs, and, it seemed, about every little thing she felt he'd wobbled on or mucked up. The dogs were the least of it: no pallets to sleep on, no way to know how far to Louisiana, then no way to know how far to New Orleans. She probably blamed him for Egg's death. For Mama and Papa, too.

They walked the city as if without aim, and he bought Mary Celeste a peppermint, though she let him split it. The entire day he found no one he could trust, no colored people to help them like those they'd met on the road. The more they walked, the more soldiers he saw, Union officers everywhere.

It had been a day to behold when the Union soldiers first arrived in Oxford, Mississippi. All the whites in a conniption fit, running about, the whole town burned, all the slaves happy as Christmas about it, saying stuff about white folk and to white folk that Lazarus had never before heard in his natural-born life. Insults and oaths and threats about a fool master that one might have muttered in the safety of a cabin to a wife who'd heard it all before, but never in open air.

He thought back to Miss Thalia, fairly screaming over the Union's having used her place as a pigsty, only to file out carrying whatever wasn't bolted down. Hens, gone. Piano, ruined. They took all the chicory. They even took from the slave quarters, so there was no fun in that for them and Egg, but it was worth it to see someone like Miss Thalia brought low. If it weren't for her, Mary Celeste might very well have her hearing. If it weren't for Miss Thalia, his mother and father might still be alive. "Bottom rail's on top, top rail's on bottom!" Egg said. But that night, when Lazarus watched the far-off glow of Oxford burning, he felt that he could stand a good deal more top rail being brought low, and knew that, given half a chance, he would kill Miss Thalia and Kittredge, too. Even if he had to go back to do it.

Mary Celeste could always smell out thoughts like a water stick: *Stop thinking about Miss.*

"I ain't," he lied.

They had the name of the plantation and the directions to it, but didn't make it too far outside town the first day, as Lazarus had to wrap and rewrap his hand endlessly as it oozed. The second morning finally brought them to the place, and after inquiring about their Aunt Minnie they were told the road that led to where she lived. Indeed, a few miles from the plantation lay a metropolis of shantytowns, housing colored folk who'd lit out for New Orleans and Baton Rouge after emancipation and found that their freedom ended right here, in a township of mangroves and muskrats, stranded and muleless.

The road narrowed to a path so choked with low-swinging catalpa and mangrove they had to swat at dangling fronds and Spanish moss with every step; it seemed unlikely that anyone's house would be at this end of the world.

Nevertheless, Lazarus heard some noises through the trees: the cries of a colicky infant, yowling as unceasing and otherworldly as a tomcat at night. Then came more noises: rhythmic thrumming on what sounded like a drum, the sizzle of something frying. The closer they got, the more they heard: a passel of children spewed insults, their bitter argument punctuated by a crash of pewterware. A woman's voice climbed atop the children's fuss, yelling, "I got but two words for the lot a y'all! *Be*have!"

Her yelling had its effect: all was silent.

They'd never met their Aunt Minnie, but she was nonetheless their last living kin on earth. And yet when his mother had told stories about Minnie Lazarus had only half listened to the reminiscences, which seemed to have no real beginning or end and, unlike "Ivanhoe" and "Robin Hood," no hero in sight. It was always something about how Minnie could sew the best, or how she had a piece of mirrored silver that she wouldn't let anyone else use. How she had loved her sister more than anything, but had stolen away at the age of fifteen, wearing every dress their mistress owned—three, one on top of the other.

A morning rain started up, with drops of water as fat as pumpkin seeds. Another round of quarrelling came through the leaves. He cupped his ear and cocked his head toward it to let Mary Celeste know. *She's that way*, Lazarus signed to her with his one good hand, then tugged her toward where he'd heard the tangle of voices. Mary Celeste couldn't hear the racket, but she could always tell when something was amiss. She shook her head no.

322

But Lazarus pulled her along so that they both battled through the vines and bluebottle flies and brush. It was Mary Celeste who finally spotted the shack, engulfed in wilderness.

"You say you Clarissa's childrens?" the woman who opened the door said.

"Yes, Ma'am."

"Then where the hell Clarissa at?"

"She passed, Ma'am."

The woman's face had more yellow to it than their mother's had, and not a healthy yellow, either, but the wan, sickly color of cornmeal past its prime. "Clarissa," she said in the dark of the room, talking to no one save herself. "Clarissa, Clarissa . . ." She cantillated the name as if she either knew a Clarissa or were trying to remember if she did.

"You Minnie?"

The woman said nothing; instead, she drew up a cheroot and smoked it, her cheeks going hollow from the drag. With the same hand, she rubbed her eyebrows, then her frown lines. Lazarus searched the planes of her face and the carry of her lip for any likeness to their dead mother. Yes. There was a resemblance, somewhere around the eyes, but it flickered off and on like a firefly.

"What's that smell?" she asked. Lazarus held up his rotting hand, which looked like some species of toadstool.

"Hounds," he answered.

She nodded, once, like a white schoolmarm. As though everything he would ever tell her was something she already knew. So he didn't tell about Miss Thalia and Master Thompson, or what they'd done to Mary Celeste to make her deaf; or how both father and mother had come to their ends. He did not speak any further about what happened with the dogs treeing Mary Celeste or his nearly losing half his hand.

That night, when Mary Celeste began to sleepwalk, trembling and crying without sound, Lazarus had to prize her fingers from where she clawed at Minnie's door, trying to flee the sheets she mistook for dogs, confusing her own thrashing with being ripped apart by hounds.

He guided her back to their pallet, where she remembered not a thing she'd done. Minnie's seven children groaned and complained before they returned to their rest, and Lazarus lay in the dark unable to sleep, unwilling to rise from his first real bed in months. He watched Minnie, who'd got up to see what afflicted this deaf child and now sat at the cabin's lone table.

"Nine God damn children," she said to the dark. It was neither a curse nor a lament but a pledge.

Lazarus watched her. But nothing on Minnie moved; not her trumpet-flare nostrils or her lips, thin as an oak splint. Only the smoke from her cheroot danced up and through the air, like a spirit.

THE DREDGEMAN'S REVELATION

KAREN RUSSELL

The dredgeman had a name, Louis Thanksgiving Auschenbliss, but lately he preferred to think of himself as a profession. For the past six months, he'd spent each day and half the night pushing farther into the alien interior of the Florida swamp, elbow to elbow with twelve other crewmen, the "muck rat" employees of the Model Land Company. They were the human engine of a floating dredge, a forty-foot barge accompanied by four auxiliary boats—the wood barge, the water barge, the cookshack, and, for sleeping, the houseboat. The dredge had a giant crane riveted to its deck and a dipper bucket that looked like the tiny cranium of a serpent, poised high above the palm trees and the mangroves. The Model Land Company was digging a canal through the central mangle of the swamp, and the dredge clanged toward the Gulf amid blasts of smoke and whining cables, tearing up roots and rock and excavating hundreds of thousands of gallons of bubbling soil. In sunlight and in moonlight, everybody on the barge had to work under veils of mosquito netting—and the weave of that finely stitched protection was what the word "dredgeman" felt like to Louis. Like soft armor, a flexible screen. As a dredgeman, Louis was no different from anyone on deck. And on the dredge, in this strange and humid swamp, every yellow morning was like a new skin that he could slip into.

At seventeen, Louis was the youngest member of the crew. It was the height of the Depression, and sometimes the men turned to the past for distraction—talking about the girlfriends they'd left mooning after them in red diner booths in Decatur, their high-school teachers, somebody's family store in Rascal Mountain, Georgia, their Army stints, the dogs and the children still on terra firma, the debts they'd gleefully abandoned. Inside the suck of the other guys' nostalgia, Louis became almost unbearably nervous.

"What about you, Lou?" somebody eventually asked. "How did you get washed down here?"

"Oh, not much to tell . . ." he mumbled. Very little of his childhood felt real anymore. In fact, the vast and empty floodplain that spread for miles in every direction around the dredge's gunwales seemed to mock the notion that his childhood had ever happened. Two skies floated past them—one above and one below, on the water, whole clouds perfectly preserved. "One thing about me, though," Louis said, coughing, trying like the other guys to turn his past into good theatre. "One sort of interesting thing, I guess, is that I was born dead."

"Well, God damn it, Louis, you don't need to brag about it," Gideon Thomas, the engine man, said. He laughed. "Born dead—shit, son, everybody is!"

Of all the men on the dredge, Gid was probably Louis's best friend, although it wasn't exactly a symmetrical relationship, since Gid teased Louis without mercy and "borrowed" things from the kid that he really couldn't return, like food.

"I'm not bragging," Louis muttered, and he wasn't bullshitting, either. He was just repeating what he'd heard from his adoptive father—"born dead" was an epithet that he had used to needle Louis whenever he moved too quickly for the old man's fists. And although the old man had boiled his birth story down to two cruel words, they both happened to be true—Louis Thanksgiving had very nearly been a nobody.

At birth, his skull had looked like a little violin, cinched and silent. The doctor who had uncorked the baby from his dead mother in the chilly belly of the New York Foundling Hospital had begun shaking him to a despondent meter, thinking, *Ah, what a truly rude awakening!* Because this tiny baby—holding his breath, refusing to wiggle—was failing at the planet's etiquette. He did not blink. He was resolute and blue in the doc's blood-soaked arms.

"A stillborn," the doc told a nurse. "And the woman's dead, uterine rupture, terrible . . ." So this kid had missed it totally, then, his windy little interval between birth and death. His life. And the unwed mother, lying naked on a table in the Foundling Hospital, was now no one's mother or daughter.

The doctor lit a Turkish cigarette and let out a little cry, a sadness that registered in decibels somewhere between a gambler's sigh and the poor woman's grief-mad wailing at the end of her labor—and then another cry joined the doctor's. The stillborn's blue face opened like a flower and he cried even harder, unequivocally alive now, unabashedly breathing, making good progress toward becoming Louis. The baby's face was reddening by the second, and the doctor plucked the cigarette from his lips like a tar carnation. He would have liked to keep on smoking, and drinking, too, but babies—you couldn't just stand there and toast their voyage back to nothingness! Although. If the room had been emptied of witnesses—no nurses, no mother, just this baby's squalling eyes, and your own—could you maybe then . . . ? No, the better doctor inside the doctor insisted. We can't do that. So the doc put on his green eyeglasses and massaged air into the baby's chest with the flats of his hands; and when blood and air started to work in tandem and the midnight pigments in Louis's bunched-sock face had brightened to a yellowish pink he stared down at the baby and said, "Well, pal, I think you made the right choice." The mother's cracked heels were by this time cooling to putty on the table.

Exhausted, the doctor left the birth certificate blank. L-O-U-I-S read the alphabeads that two nuns strung on a little black bracelet for the baby, because the doctor remembered, or imagined he remembered, that the dead mother had at one point whispered this perfectly ordinary name to him. Louis's mother was an immigrant from a country that he could not have pronounced or found on a map—and if Louis ever did hear its name when he was growing up, well, it might as well have been Oz or the moon to him, an imaginary place.

One of the Children's Aid nuns came in to retrieve the newborn orphan, and Louis lost his true past in a few squeaks of her nun shoes on the linoleum. Carrying him away, leaving that widening blank of a woman behind him, this wimpled stranger wound the clock of Louis's life. The nun (who sometimes dreamed she was a man in advertising, writing copy for Hollywood movies) tucked a paper with a short description of his delivery into his blanket, thinking that this might help him to be adopted by a Christian family: MISLABELLED STILLBORN MIRACLE BABY ALIVE PRAISE GOD FOR LOUIS, THANKSGIVING!

Somewhere down the line, the nun's purple comma got smudged and then Louis had a surname.

When he was three days old, Louis Thanksgiving was added to a group of eleven orphans, accompanied by one nun, one priest, and one mustached Western agent who really did not care for children at all. He became one of those unfortunates who grew up in the Midwest, part of the human sediment deposited by the orphan train that ran from New York through Clarinda, Iowa. While plenty of boys and girls on the train found their way to loving adoptive families, such was not the case for Louis. The New York Foundling Hospital had placed a melodramatic advertisement in the newspapers of each of the towns along the railroad route, and dozens of farm families had gathered under a striped awning at the Clarinda station to size up the scabby knees from New York City. Louis was picked up by Mr. Frederick K. Auschenbliss, a German dairy farmer who treated him worse than he did his livestock. At least the cows got to stand still and swat flies; by the time he was ten, Louis was up to milk the cows at 2:30 a.m. and was spreading manure on the flat fields by sunrise. Mr. Auschenbliss was not an affectionate father. Picture instead a slave driver who grew into the hard hiss of his name—a hog-necked man with a high Sunday collar, his eyes a colorless sizzle, like grease in a pan, half his face erased by the shadow of the dark barn. Louis was zero when he arrived at the Auschenbliss farm, sixteen when he escaped it, and not even the nosiest guys on the dredge crew could get him to say one word about that time.

Louis, now grown into a bruised and illiterate young man, brother to no one in that house of twelve, escaped the farm and his adoptive parents and brothers as soon as flight seemed possible. He rode the rails southward on a voyage that had the fitful logic of interrupted sleep: suns set and suns rose. Forests dispersed into beaches and regrouped again in mountain passes. Lightning sent down its white spider legs outside the boxcar doors and crawled up the pine trunks, trailing fires. He hopped trains that crisscrossed the Midwest, touching golden millet fields and the black corners of the Atlantic, before finally pushing south, beyond the Florida Panhandle.

Florida, in those days, was a very odd place: a peninsula where the sky itself rode overland like a blue locomotive, clouds chuffing across marshes; where orange trees and orderly rows of vegetables gave way to deep woods and then, farther south, broke into an endless acreage of ten-foot grass. This, finally, was the vision that reached Louis through the boxcar door: a prairie that looked as vast as the African savanna. A strange weed or wild corn shifted restlessly in the afternoon wind—saw grass, a fellow-passenger said beneath the slouch of his hat. That was the name for the long stalks that swallowed men whole. Teams of government surveyors were working up and down the train routes, an eerie counterpoint to the dozens of herons and deer that Louis saw standing in the marshes. Then he noticed the dizzying height of the trees in the pinewoods, the thin millions of them extending as far as the eye could see. They were called slash pines, for the cat-face scars left by the gum tappers—already thousands of acres had been tapped for turpentine. The drained and solemn pines reminded Louis of a daguerreotype of Lee's emaciated Confederate forces that he had once seen as a child.

The woods were deep, but they were neither peaceful nor quiet—they were full of men. Axes swung and fell, a blue glinting at the edge of the woods, and Louis followed the axe handles to the stout arms and the square, heat-flattened faces of the Civilian Conservation Corps lumbermen. Nearly thirteen million job seekers were massing like locust clouds in the cities, but few of these money hunters had made it to the deep glade. From his train, Louis saw just a smattering of humans. When the train had a mechanical problem outside the Crooked Lake National Forest, the engine cut out and the metal moaned to a full stop in the middle of a wrinkled wood. Out here, Louis could hear the beginning of the wind, the hiss of the air plants and the crimson bromeliads. Oak toads chorused incessantly. If he could hear his own death in all that lively hubbub, he ignored it. *Home, home, home*, the rails sang, and the train lurched back to life.

Louis disembarked in Titusville, and signed a six-month contract with the C.C.C. He wrote his name down as LOUIS THANKS-GIVING, dropping the Auschenbliss, then looked up and down the dusty street as if he'd just got away with a crime. Why did anybody fool with guns, he wondered, when he had just dispatched Mr. Auschenbliss with one bloodless swipe?

"There's Indians, but they got their own camp," the recruiter told him in a patient voice, as if this were a concern he frequently allayed. "There's Coloreds here, though—we haven't segregated your camp yet." He glanced up from Louis's paperwork to see if this would be a problem. Louis stared incredulously back at him. He wanted to tell the man that he had spent the past sixteen years living with animals and a pack of brothers whose great entertainment on weekends was to devise "practical jokes" with bulls and farm machinery, one of which had nearly decapitated Louis. Louis had no problems with any man alive—black, white, or Indian—so long as his surname was not Auschenbliss.

On his first stint, he was deployed on a C.C.C. dredge barge with fifteen other men, who were introduced to him by their professions ("This here is the cook, the cap, the engineer, the fireman . . ."). He was now part of a government team surveying the woods around Ocala. Thirty dollars a month, and, try as you might, you couldn't spend more than five dollars of that unless you were a serious and self-hating gambler—what could you buy in the swamp besides cigarettes, penny stamps, and camp equipment? Louis bought a mess kit for fifteen cents.

Some of the veteran dredgemen grumbled that their outfit lacked a houseboat, which would have allowed the crew to sleep in dry bunks on the river; instead, they had to debark from the barge and make camp each night, after scouting for unflooded islands. Louis slept in a tent with five other men, the odor of sweat and cigarettes percolating inside the tent's bubble. Outside, rising from the ground like the earth's own exhalation, came the odor of peat, a great seawall of it, nothing so subtle or evanescent as a fragrance—no, this was stuff with a true stink. In open sunlight, the peat gave off an olfactory roar that recalled to Louis Thanksgiving the feculence that hung over Clarinda. *Cow patties*, Louis thought, wrinkling his nose; *farm perfume*. But out here the air was salted, the smell quadrupled. He complained about it affably, happy to have something to say to the other men at night. *Our legs are tangled*, he realized that first night, saying nothing and moving not one inch once he found his bedroll, the tent humid with the other men's careful closeness. Every man had to maintain a fixed position; you had to train your body so that even in sleep it remained a tethered boat that wouldn't rock. Louis had heard that a surveyor for the train company had been beaten to death south of Tallahassee after climbing into another man's bedroll stark naked—*a fairy*, *a funny one*, the men hissed.

Nights came and the moon was so bright that it penetrated the tent cloth. Louis was often awake until the filmy predawn, listening to the hum of the mosquitoes as if even this were something holy. He was in love with everybody, and also with the heat and the stink and the foul teakettle dredge that had cut a channel so far from his childhood. He was in love with the crushed oyster beds and the uprooted trees. He was smart enough, too, to keep these feelings to himself. Louis liked to hoard a kiwi all day and then wait until the other men were snoring to open it. He'd push a thumb through the furry skin and release the kiwi's perfume through the tent. The first time he did this, he'd watched as the men smiled in their sleep; after that he did it nightly, smiling himself as he imagined pleasant dreams wafting over them. His good mood spilled over into the mornings, and a few of the more taciturn crewmen grumbled that this farm kid must have a screw loose. Who woke up whistling in hundred-and-two-degree heat? What sort of special asshole kept right on beaming at you when his cheeks were flecked with dead mosquitoes and his own pink blood?

"Look who's grinning like an imbecile in the dead heat of noon," the lieutenant said, shaking his head. "You are the most good-natured boy I have ever met, Louis—honestly, it's a little worrisome. You better not snap and kill us in our sleep! I could tell you stories. Strange things happen to personalities this far out, you know."

Every so often, the captain passed around a flask of purple apple moonshine, joking that he hoped it wouldn't blind the men.

Louis thought the captain's hooch tasted like a mixture of Christian cider and gasoline—it didn't make his personality any stranger, but his smile shrank, and often he had to excuse himself politely to run and puke over the stern. Louis still had a kid's broad face, a farm face, but with a nascent sharp handsomeness lurking around his cheekbones—he had what people described as a "lantern jawline," with a Presidential thrust, a hint of bedroom avarice. It would have been irresistible to a woman, had there been any such creature in the general environs. The last one Louis had seen was the cook's wife, who had a tall and mannish figure, with a dishlike face, mean little eyes, and a dirty cloud of yellow hair. *That must be the cook's older brother*, Louis had thought as he watched them embrace at Fort Watson. *Why is the cook's older brother wearing a dress?*

"She's stately, you bastards," the cook had said.

The dredge barge clanked downstream with its dipper handle swinging. For the first time in his short life, Louis had real friends, all sorts travelling alongside him into the glade—calm men, family men, bachelors, ex-preachers, hellions, white men, black men, the children of Indians and freed slaves. There was Adams, who had kicked a coral snake away from Louis's naked big toe and thus saved his life with a casual grunt; ex-Army boys who followed the white-tailed deer into the briary midday darkness of the hardwood hammocks; drunks who took potshots at the queer golden cats that stalked the perimeter of their camp; gamblers who took all of Louis's money with a pair of jacks and then gave (some of) it back at day's end. Every man was Louis's friend. When there was light in the sky, they waded forward. They surveyed the old section lines of the National Forest during the workweek, and on weekends they "rambled," as LaVerl, the buck sergeant, said: shooting, fishing, sometimes even gator hunting along the nests that filled the unused railway bed. The cook told Louis to collect two dozen leathery eggs from these alligator nests, and made the whole crew a dinner of fishy-tasting omelettes.

When the light expired, they slept. White-tailed deer sprinted like loosed hallucinations among the tree islands. Sometimes Louis fell asleep watching them from the deck, and it worried him that he couldn't pinpoint when his sleep began: deer rent the mist with their tiny hooves, a spotted contagion of dreams galloping inside Louis's head. There were bad fires that blurred the world; in the summer months, you could see smoke rising almost daily, wherever lightning struck the peat beds.

Louis heard from the other surveyors that men all over the country were "hunting a week for one day's work." Sometimes when he thought about this he felt so lucky that he was almost sick to his stomach. Happiness could be felt as a pressure, too, Louis realized, more hard-edged and solid than longing, even. In Clarinda, he had yearned for better in a formless way, desire like a gray milk churn; in fact, he'd been so poor that he couldn't settle on one concrete noun to wish for: A real father? A girl in town? A thousand acres? A single friend? In contrast, this new happiness had angles; it had a jewel-cut shadow, and he could lose it. Well, Louis determined that he was not going to lose it, and that he was never going back. The Depression was the best thing that had ever happened to him. He had a crisp stack of dollars, a uniform with his name stitched in raspberry thread on the pocket, and pork and grits in his belly.

Elated, wanting never to leave, Louis Thanksgiving signed another contract, this time to dredge a canal clear across the swamp to the Gulf Coast, for the Model Land Company, a private firm that had bought up hundreds of thousands of acres of "virgin Florida farmland" that were still inconveniently covered in water. They were going to drain the swamp, and then develop and sell it, and they needed a team of skilled muck rats to do it.

But nobody had explained to Louis just how deep into the swamp he would have to go, or how *quickly* his bosses at the Model Land headquarters, in St. Augustine, Florida, would expect the crew to drain the floodplains with a single bucket arm—a herculean task for any machine, but especially for the ancient and fumy Model Land dredge, which made the government vessel look like some futuristic starship by comparison.

The dredge was there to spud down into the muck, and spud up with a bucket of oozing crust. And this in a swamp where you could sink a support platform through eighteen feet of peat before hitting stabilizing rock!

The crew had changed, too—none of the C.C.C. boys had signed on with him. LaVerl was going back to his family's horse farm in Savannah, and the lone Indian on the crew, Euphon Tigertail, who had survived subhuman conditions while working on the Panama Canal, decided that he couldn't work in the swamp any longer. He'd been undone by microscopic foes—the chizzywinks and the deerflies. "You sure *you* want to be a dredgeman for this outfit, Lou?" Euphon had whispered, both of them staring at the hulk of the dredge. Its digger arm was as tall as a house and sunk deep into a quagmire. A pair of enormous cast-steel feet gave the contraption a drunken, donkey-legged appearance. The stack slumped toward the saw-grass prairie, which looked like a drowned and shimmering field of wheat. For a second, Louis thought of the distant Auschenbliss pastures and shuddered.

"You'd be better off gum-tapping in the turpentine woods. It's all soup doodly in those prairies; it ain't like the pine rocklands. There's nothing piney about it. No elevation, Lou. No lakes or trees or breaks. It's just saw grass till you want to scream. You won't have a dry day again for months. You'll go in there and never come out."

How could you make a mistake when you had only one option? Louis felt that his hellish past exempted him from all regrets. But he was humbled by his friends' defection—and a little shocked, hearing their complaints about the last months. Ultimately, Louis felt an almost romantic embarrassment, listening to the grizzled guys talk. It turned out that the same nights and routes that he recalled as heavenly had been, to the other C.C.C. men, "god-awful months, a nightmare" and "the valley of the shadow—only full of mosquitoes!" When the dredge anchor hit at Chokoloskee, their whole C.C.C. fraternity came loose like a knot, and Louis and Euphon and LaVerl parted at the dock like strangers.

Louis's first job on the new dredge was described by the splinter-toothed captain as "involved": he had to dive overboard with a knife clenched between his teeth and cut the slimy ropes of cattails away from the dredge's wheel and shaft. "Removing detritus" was what the captain called this labor. *Dee-tree-tus*. A name from a book, Louis figured, as he removed the knife from his mouth and spat copper. He had split his lower lip; the water tasted like brine and sour blood. Five times his first day he had to jump overboard into that stinking gator marinade and hack at the weedy ropes.

"What do I do if there's a gator?" Louis asked at supper the first night.

"You put that knife between the blamed scalyback's eyes, he'll lay offa you. Or get the base of his neck, sever his spinal cord," Ferguson, one of the cranemen, said. He had gone gator hunting with some drunk white gladesmen near Flamingo Bay once, and now claimed to be a scalyback expert.

"Don'tcha go for the eyes themselves, though—the crocs can retract those." He held up two gnarled fingers and jerked them back into his fist.

"Thanks for the advice," Louis said. He imagined himself screaming underwater, and the tiny needles of salt against his gums and eyeballs. Curiously modest, he refused to strip before diving. He jumped in with his pants and cotton underwear on, and kicked beneath the dross of slimy marine plants. His legs floated like two planks behind him, every muscle tensed, ready to jerk away from an alligator's teeth.

Louis wasn't a particularly quick learner, but he was strong and docile, and within a month he was doing all sorts of jobs on the dredge: trimming greenish fat off the pork in the cookhouse, helping the sweating firemen to keep up steam. The men looked like beekeepers in their cotton gloves and mosquito veils, their lungs filling with black mangrove smoke from the smudge fires they burned constantly to keep the insects away.

"Line up, boys! Take your medicine," the cap said, pressing indigo flecks of charcoal and sulfur into Louis's cupped hands. Every time he asked what they were for he got a different answer: ear infections, hay fever, sties, skin lesions. Gideon Thomas said the pills were placebos, although Louis noticed that he still queued up to receive them, like a good Catholic boy in line for Communion.

"Ahhh," Gideon said, extending his chaw-stained tongue.

"Stick out your palm, you jackass. I'm not your damn mother!" the cap howled. If the pills were making a difference, it was hard to imagine how bad you could get without them. Men held their orangey scabs up to the sun and catalogued them like entomologists.

Week 1: They couldn't sleep for the bug bites; scratching at them, and fending off new ones, was an eight-hour endeavor. The insects had been a chronic irritation on the C.C.C. barge, but out here on the marshy open prairie they were pestilential, their sawing sound filling the air like a cruel ventriloquy of the men's own thirst. Their crawling bodies put a fur on the steel hull of the Model Land dredge. Theodore Glyde, the dredge's dour engineer, complained that he was working back-to-back shifts on the dredge, quitting the deck at sundown to work a second job as a bug killer.

Week 2: Everybody's legs acquired the cracked sheen of cockroach wings. Louis, who had hosted much more colorful bruises back in Auschenbliss country, poured a little vial of alcohol over his shins and returned to work. On the C.C.C. barge, the crew had never been more than twelve miles from a port with a doctor, but this dredge had entered an unmapped part of the swamp where wounds had the opportunity to fester. Headaches blinded half the crew.

Week 3: Sores began to ooze. Men told stories from their Army days about amputations, gangrenous infections. Of all the dredgemen, only Louis was still indefatigably happy. He volunteered to haul water off-shift and shared his larded fried eggs with everyone.

"Louis, are you on a diet, or what?" Gideon grumbled. He was leaning against the starboard railing next to Louis, gobbling down a plate of Louis's eggs with a guilt-racked expression. "You should eat, kid. It's not good to share the way you do out here. What the heck are you always staring at?"

"The landscape."

"The landscape!" Gid snorted. His broad nose wrinkled, as it often did when someone said something he didn't like, as if he were trying to sniff out what was wrong with it. "There's something . . . something *womanly* about watching that, Lou."

Louis grinned over at Gideon and shrugged; even the other men's ribbing made him happy. Daybreak, sunset: he liked to watch the red sun pour through the mesh veil of his mosquito screen until his blue eyes filled. Behind the screen, he had the face of a man in church.

"Hey, Gid?" he asked his friend later, when they were baling wastewater, the sun a pinhead of color behind the green trees. "Gid . . . are you anxious to get back?"

Warily, his friend turned to him. "Get back where?"

What Louis really meant was "anywhere." Back to land. Back to themselves, back to their names without jobs, back to any motionless, dirty place—or to either of the twin poles that the swamp road they'd been digging was meant to connect. He had heard of hydrophobes, and he wondered if there was a word like that for him. Or for what he was becoming. Terraphobia? It was a fear of the rooted, urban world, of cars and towns and years on calendars. He wouldn't be a dredgeman without the water churning under the machine, that was for sure. Sometimes, at night, Louis thought in a dreamy way about sabotaging the dredge—plucking parts like flowers from the engine room. It was only a thought, and a crazy one, but the closer they got to the Gulf the sicker he felt. His sweats grew worse when he pictured the dawn horizon solidifying—a sudden break in the mangroves that revealed the swallowing saltwater ocean, the big success for which the Model Land Company had hired the dredge and her crew.

"Jesus, Louis, you're just like what's his name? Greek guy. Narcissus! Making puppy eyes down at your face in that bucket."

"Sorry. I was getting a little . . . homesick, I guess. So you're excited for the end? For the Gulf side of things?"

"Fool, of course I am!" Gideon laughed, pouring the black water over the railing onto the head of a small and outraged alligator. "Am I excited for a paycheck and a woman and a bed? Am I excited to climb out of this soggy hell and get a pair of pants that's not infested with forty kinds of insects, and a pair of shoes where I can't count my toes? God damn, Lou, I'll be singing Ave Marias! I'll be diving for land!"

Louis spent the morning of May 12, 1934, beating himself at hand after hand of solitaire with Gideon's faded deck. He was off duty, and free to ruminate. He did not have any headaches that day, or dark presentiments. At noon, he felt a little hungry, so he ate some ibis jerky and considered rowing over to the houseboat to bathe. He lit sticks of dynamite and lobbed them into the marl, then watched as the white-tailed deer shot off through the swamp. For every ten hours of work, the canal grew a hundred and forty feet longer; they were still a month away from the Gulf and the end of their contract.

Louis was sitting on the starboard side of the dredge with his bare feet swinging, his calves hot against the metal rail, watching a pair of otters mock-duelling in the cattails. When next they appeared they were lovers, their bodies turning in a silly ballet, black volutes beneath the lily pads and the purple swamp hens. He was twenty-five feet from the engine room when a roar like a tidal wave nearly knocked him loose from the deck. He turned and watched flames engulf the roof of the engine room in one spectacular spasm; within seconds, a thick smoke had swallowed the entire port side of the deck and shrouded acres of the sunlit saw-grass prairie to the southeast.

What Louis saw next came filtered redly through one slit eye: a stencil of a man—Ira, Louis thought sleepily, or maybe Jackson—went flailing off the fantail. Louis heard him hit his head on the way down; another man jumped in after him. To save him, Louis thought, proud to have made the connection. Foggily, it occurred to him that he should perhaps do a thing, too. The fog seemed to have penetrated his brain from the outer world, because the whole deck of the dredge was lost in a roar of escaping steam. The boiler head has burst, Louis thought, and felt his pulse jump. He pushed himself up and started to make his way toward the smoking engine room, where the other men were already hauling water.

Louis held a hand to his face and found that it came away sticky. Blood was trickling out of one of his eyes, and the other didn't like to open. He felt tired, a terribly heavy tiredness. I could fall asleep right here, he thought. His own square face surprised him in the water below the boat; he had at some point pitched forward onto the railing. His reflection blinked up at him, as if it were trying to remember how they knew each other. The otters, he noticed, had vanished.

"Gideon needs a hospital!" Hector, one of the cranemen, screamed. "He's killed, he's killed!"

Apparently, Hector had forgotten the usual chronology of death and medicine as it worked on the mainland, Louis thought grimly—if Gid was killed, then it was late now for the hospital.

It was almost impossible to push through the wall of steam, and, when he finally stumbled into the engine room, Louis found the scalded body of Gideon Thomas. He was lying on the floor with his right hand wrapped around his throat. Dead, Louis thought—the steam from the boiler must have seared his eyes and lungs. But then, as Louis watched, the hand began to *move*, massaging Gid's black skin. His right eye opened like a blue crack of sky, and his other hand pushed flat against the metal wall— and then, impossibly, he was standing up, staring abstractedly at Louis, half his face a sputtering blank. His mouth was moving, but no words came. His jaw made convulsive chewing motions, and above this his right eye regarded the deck incuriously, with an ancient calm. *The mariner*, Louis thought—this line bubbled up to him from some long-forgotten event, a poetry recitation that the youngest Auschenbliss had given at a church assembly many winters before. *The bright-eyed mariner.*

Somehow Gid was now lurching toward him, trying to retch up smoke. *This is a bad miracle*, Louis thought as he watched Gid. *Go to him*, he thought, but he was frozen, staring. Gid took a step toward Louis and then said, with a grievous eloquence, "I believe my lungs are all burnt up, Louie. I do believe . . . ," before crumpling.

"A hos-pi-tal! A—"

"God damn you, Heck, shut up," Louis said with the first true viciousness of his life. "Hos-pee-tal" sounded like an imbecile's taunt. What place could they take Gid to? There were no

343

places here. That was the point of their continued presence, that's what they'd been hired by the Model Land Company to accomplish: to turn this morass into a real place.

Something was happening down below. The whole deck had begun to vibrate. Elsewhere, cranemen were racing around, hauling water to put out the small fires that had now spread to the houseboat. Flames licked at the bleached planks of the cookshack, too. The smell of burning metal stung Louis's lungs and throat. Lights rocketed up from the deep swamp like a July fireworks show, and then every bulb burned out at once—the governor belt on the steam engine must have broken, Louis thought. The cattails swayed inside the smoke, shushing one another and brushing close to the ship like alien observers.

Something or someone came crashing down onto the deck on the stern of the dredge and Louis didn't turn to look. The blood on his hands had become the blood in his hair, he noticed, the blood on his neck, on his dungaree jacket. Hector came to tell him that below them in the hold the backing drum, a crucial part of the hoisting engine, was reeling in its cable. But his scream dropped into his shoes and now he stared past Louis with a goggle-eyed, just-awakened look. He pointed at the engine room, where two coal lumps—two feet, Louis realized, Gideon's boots—were sticking out. The soles of his shoes flopped outward from the heel in a heart-shape. From the waist down he looked like a man relaxing on deck.

"Take his shoes off," Louis said. "Please, God damn it, just somebody take them off!" But the other men responded by moving away from the flailing Louis, as if afraid to be contaminated by his raving. Several of the crew had gathered now. Nobody knew what had caused the accident—corrosion, the captain speculated. He'd seen a two-inch rent in the boiler head.

As the men stood huddled on the starboard side of the barge, black shapes began to populate the sky: buzzards appeared and dotted the watery horizon in twos and threes, a half-dozen, dozens more behind them. They moved so swiftly that they looked like pure holes advancing through the air, a snowfall of inky holes. Talons began to hail down on Gid. The first batch dived and took Gid's hat, and tore at the buttoned collar of his shirt. Hector produced a rifle and shot wildly at them; a bullet grazed the captain. "Put the gun away!" the cap screamed. "You're liable to kill somebody."

Everyone was watching the buzzards. They were nothing like the red-headed turkey vultures the crew had been seeing since Long Glade; these were huge birds, black and wattled, and with their wings folded they made Louis think of funeral umbrellas dripping rain along the stone walls of St. Agnes Church in Clarinda. Several birds had formed a heaving circle around Gid now; within moments one had flown off with his cigarettes and another had torn his shirt sleeve loose from the elbow. Two buzzards worked industriously to tug a black shoe off his foot. Louis couldn't move or think; his mind was helium light. The taste of screws and pennies pumped into his mouth until he felt sick with it. Around him the cranemen were hollering "Fire!" at a pitch that became a single sheet of sound, draping like a canopy over the dredge.

What rolled through Louis's mind were like the shells of thoughts, a series of Os, round and empty, like the discarded rinds of screams. A fine tooth of purplish glass marked the spot on the deck where Gid's eyeglasses had been, and Louis got down on his knees to retrieve it; when he felt a prickling on his neck, he looked up.

In a scene that seemed as plausible and as horrifying as Louis's worst dreams, the birds descended on Gideon and hooked the prongs of their talons into his skin; perhaps a dozen of them lifted him into the sky. Gid's body shrank into the cloudless expanse. The sky that day was a bright sapphire, better weather than they'd had in weeks; for a long time, the men could see the shrinking pinpoint of Gid's black head, lolling below his shoulders, as if he were trying to work out a bad crick in his neck.

A strangled quiet came over the men. It felt like hours before anybody moved.

"You boys ever seen birds do anything like that?" Hector asked, close to sunset. His voice was a child's squeak, and it occurred to Louis that there was real bravery in the act of speech. Louis's own throat was a desert and he couldn't have got a word out for a million dollars. No, Louis thought, you saw a thing like that and you went deep inward; you didn't want to make a single ripple in the air.

"Never," the launchman said behind him. "Never seen a bird behave that way." His tone was mild and genial, as though he were discussing unseasonably cold weather, or food with a peculiar taste. Hector, in his panic, didn't seem to hear the answer. Some of the men were still staring at the spot in the sky where Gid had disappeared into a bone-white ridge of cloud. The moon was rising. The fires were nearly all snuffed. Louis, able at last to overcome his vast, black speechlessness, noticed something interesting that he pointed out to the other men: the buzzards were returning.

People began screaming, babbling obscurely; someone went splashing overboard. Louis heard the wet, frantic beat of arms on water. The birds had completely swallowed the dredge now. They were perched all along the trusses and gunwales and on the cabin roof, so that the whole structure looked as if it were upholstered in black velvet; it didn't seem possible to Louis that there could be so many birds in all the world. He saw a buzzard that looked as large as a man lift and stretch its wings; some possession or some part of Gid went winking from its beak and fell into the water. Finally, Louis felt a scream tear loose from his throat.

"Oh, shut up. They're just birds," Theodore, the tall, sallow engineer, kept repeating crossly, gesticulating at no one. "They're just filthy buzzards. They shouldn't hurt us at all—anyhow, men,

346

we're *alive* . . ." He went on and on like this as the buzzards grew in number. How could more be coming? Louis wondered. Hundreds more were coming. He stood there and waited with a pale, uplifted face. Theodore was still throwing his arms around, as if he could argue his death back into the hole of the moon.

"Here they come, fellas," Louis Thanksgiving said quietly, and beside him Theodore snorted with disgust and folded his arms across his chest as if he were impatient to prove a point.

Oh God, Louis thought. He didn't feel any more horror— just pure sadness, because he was seventeen that summer and he didn't want to go. His real life had begun less than a year ago. *I'm next.*

THE KID

SALVATORE SCIBONA

The boy wore a black parka, a matching ski cap, bluejeans, and sneakers; he appeared to be five years old; and he was weeping.

He stood at Gate C3, Hamburg-Fuhlsbüttel Airport, his padded arms limp at his sides. He was talking through his sobs—not shouting or pleading, just talking to one attendant after another—but no one could figure out what language he was using. It seemed, somehow, Polish. The hodgepodge dialect of a town that ten different empires had captured on their way to someplace else.

An AirBaltic flight had disgorged its passengers at a nearby gate less than an hour before. The flight having come from Riga, it may have been Latvian the boy was speaking. But by the time he materialized in front of the counter at C3 the plane from Riga had pulled away from the terminal and no AirBaltic employees remained at the gate or anywhere else in the concourse. He looked up at the agents behind the counter, stating his case incomprehensibly, while two hundred travellers watched, mesmerized, waiting for Lufthansa 531 to Amsterdam.

It might have been Lithuanian.

Soon the boy was barely forming words at all; he only pointed in the direction of Gates C1 and C2. But the custodian for whom half a dozen Lufthansa employees and passengers began to search the smoking cabins and bathrooms, and to whom the airport intercom called out in German, could not be found anywhere at the lower end of the concourse.

"*Je m'appelle Laurence. Comment t'appelles-tu?*"

"*Ich heiße Elisabeth. Wie heißt du?*"

But no one could get him to divulge anything that sounded like a name. And some of the adults around him began to think that their solicitousness only aggravated his distress. Each question elicited less of a response.

A nurse from Kazakhstan knelt at the boy's side, petting his hair, but he persisted in weeping. The boy's coat fit him poorly: the cuffs fell short of his wrists. Bits of batting poked out of several tears in its shell, which somebody had tried to mend with electrical tape. A Lufthansa clerk—whose age (about sixty) and whose vast, highlighted hairdo seemed to put her in charge— tried using English, Russian, and Dutch to extract a name. Yet to the Kazakh nurse it seemed that the boy *knew* they were asking for his name; and, in the nightmare of his present, his withholding the name was the only thing that tied him to the lip of the chasm into which he had slipped. He aimed a curving finger toward the labyrinth of the rest of the airport, as though in search of a misstep. He let the nurse hold his snotty hand. He led her and the clerk down the teeming corridor.

A young American who said he was an E.M.T. asked, "Would the boy like to breathe into this bag? *Quieres hablar conmigo, hermano?*"

The clerk said emphatically, "No, he is *Estländer*." But it was only a guess.

The intercom repeated in English, "Terminal 1, a child in lost-and-found," while the boy hustled along, incongruous: a body automatized with purpose, as though if you got close enough you would hear him ticking. And yet, under his crooked hat, his face was anarchic with spasmodic blinks and sniffles. The chest heaved in the little coat. The nurse tried to unzip it. She thought the boy must feel terribly hot. But he twisted away when she touched him. It was incredible that the head could hold so much liquid; he had been crying for so long now without a drink. The nurse and the clerk took him into the ladies' room to get him some paper towels.

After they came out, he wouldn't let either of the women hold his hand. He snatched it back when they tried to take it, and pointed this way, then that way, until they began to see that he was not retracing his steps after all. He was groping in a maze. For a parent. And he didn't want either of these strange women to help him. But he hoped they would stick around.

Soon after Elroy Heflin enlisted in the Army, he was assigned to an Office of Defense Cooperation attached to the U.S. Embassy in Riga, Latvia, as the country prepared to join NATO. Those were great days. All the boys billeted in a three-star hotel—an eighteenth-century palace, recently renovated with Swedish capital—that the Red Army had used for fifty years as a barracks.

His C.O. said, "I want to give you some perspective. Where do you come from, Heflin?"

"All over," Elroy said. "Las Cruces, Albuquerque, Radium Springs, Vado."

"Imagine a Russian base in downtown Albuquerque. Farm boys in Soviet uniforms are eating lunch at Lotaburger. You're one of them. Your side won the Cold War without firing a shot. How do you feel?"

"Cock of the walk, sir."

"And rightly so."

The local girls were going to dress slutty. The grunts shouldn't get the wrong idea. To the grunts, the outfits meant, Come take me for a spin. To the girls, they meant, This is how a real European dresses, right? So hands off. You're only here for eight months. The Latvian girls want to get married just like anybody.

That sounded all right to Elroy. He figured he was the marrying kind. And within a couple of months he had a steady girlfriend. It was so easy. Not like at home. He was drinking with some of the boys in the Old City, at a café on a cobblestoned street just wide enough for a fat horse. And the waitress was nice to him. She wanted to practice her English.

In bed she asked him, "How come you like my ear so much?"

It tasted funny. She didn't expend much effort in washing it. He had a little bit of the U.S.S.R. right here in his mouth. It tasted of sweat, sebum, and lemon-flower perfume.

"Twenty years ago," he said, "they would have sent me here to rape you and burn down your house."

"Silly," she said, turning the pages of a travel magazine. "We didn't have a house."

He awoke in her one-room apartment to find her polishing his shoes with her spit and an old sock. Several times she offered to wash his clothes, but he couldn't bear to take her up on it. He had done his own laundry and cooked his own meals, except in the service, since he was eleven years old.

Dank wind, then sleet. He bought two umbrellas for them. They walked through the Art Nouveau district, and she pointed to the tortured stone faces in the cornice of the law school. It was a Sunday. They happened upon Mass in a Catholic church, and for a nasty joke they both took Communion, in spite of the sport of the night before. He did not know what the priest was saying, except that, for the most part, he did know. Mass was common everywhere. He looked up at the bats hanging from the high timbers and spoke with the God of the place. He asked to meet her parents, but they were dead.

Her name was Evija.

He wanted to suggest that she go more conservative with the makeup; however, he respected other cultures. Before the deployment ended, he'd got her knocked up. He wanted to get married, but she didn't just yet. And somehow, through a chain of decisions—none of which seemed like decisions at the time but just like doing what events required—he found himself, while stationed in northern Afghanistan, sending a third of his pay to a bank in the former Soviet Union for the upkeep of a boy he got to see only about once a year. And, all the while, Evija was going out on dates with a Russian theatre fag, and writing Elroy e-mails about, Could she have his credit-card number? She wanted to take the kid on a cruise to visit Norway. He sought the advice of his new C.O. about, Was it wise, because what if somebody intercepted the message and got his credit-card number?

His C.O. said, "Private Heflin, a fucking cruise?"

He e-mailed her that he wouldn't pay for the cruise, and then he didn't hear from her for a few months. To force her hand, he stopped sending the money. Then, while home on leave, he got an e-mail about, Due to circumstances in her personal life, Evija was moving to Spain; she would not take the child; her family wouldn't take him, either; and that left Elroy; so when would he come get the boy, Janis; and apologies for such a rush, but within the month?

The Army had promoted Elroy to corporal. He had grown stouter, more savage. His skeleton had gained its final inch. He sat before the computer in his dad's retirement condo outside Los Alamos, eating a plum. The plum had detonated in Elroy's teeth and spattered his shirt with juice. He did not notice. He was leaking tears—of what? Of gratitude? He wanted them to be tears of gratitude, yes. And he laughed, free and loud. To the radiant screen he said, "I'll be damned."

Two days later—without a clear plan as to who would look after Janis once Elroy redeployed, and with the boy's immigration status uninvestigated, and lacking so much as an air mattress for him to sleep on—Elroy sat in his and Evija's old haunt, a café on Stabu iela, waiting. He had the blond, small-eyed looks of the local people, and the waitress threw the menus down and shot a stream of Latvian at him. He replied with a phrase that Evija had taught him to enunciate without slurring: "I'll need a moment to think things through, if you please."

Evija was going to come in with the boy. Then what? Elroy didn't know.

His post in the café wings gave him both a view of the plate-glass vestibule, where patrons entered, and cover from the prying eyes in the main dining room. If his feelings had to come out now, let them. But they didn't need to do it on a stage. He sat still, hands folded under the table, waiting. He had not slept on any of the planes or in any of the airports, from New Mexico eastward, and his complexion was splotched with little rashes. His eyes were parched from airplane air. His feelings need not happen on a stage. But, if they came rocketing out of his brain stem and began to ricochet across the roof of his brain, then did it make him such a child if he wanted a woman there with him, to not look away?

He checked his watch. He had thought to bribe Evija with flowers, but whatever it was he wanted from her he couldn't buy. Unless she offered it freely, it was worse than useless. Pointing at the menu, he ordered a glass of seltzer, and when it came he crouched behind a potted ficus, poured some of the water into his hand, and threw it on his eyes and the backs of his ears. He sat up, composed, hoping.

Every time he had gone to stay with Evija and the boy, Riga was cleaner, richer, with newer cars. The Russian stayed away when Elroy visited. Evija insisted that the Russian was a common homosexual who needed a girl to keep up the proper appearances, and that she had never kissed him on the mouth.

She cooked potato pancakes for Elroy and the kid, who abhorred sour cream, applesauce, anything presented to him as a condiment. These are the accidental kinks of habit that become our permanent selves. Elroy, as a child, had always preferred to sleep under sheets tight enough to cramp his toes. This preference had led him to take comfort in the austerities of basic training—

they break you down, they build you up again, faster, tighter—and he discovered that he had a talent for the breaking down, a talent for forgetting. And then a talent for acting on the impulse to kill.

The three of them used to eat on the balcony of her place. Evija called it "our place," including Elroy and Janis. She spoke English around the boy when his father was present, so the boy could practice. He was too timid with his English, both parents agreed. By some private rule, he spoke it only to the two of them, and always red in the face.

In the café, Elroy was ordering a plate of chicken livers when a crone came through the vestibule, speaking in harsh tones to what seemed a trailing dog, though it was hidden from view by the low clutter of tables.

The waitress went away. The crone looked down at a photograph and cased the room. And Elroy hit the deck.

His ass was in the chair, but his hands pressed the floor, his head bent below the table. The wood floor shone with varnish. He could not quite breathe. He seemed to have seen something without knowing it yet. The way you jerk back your hand from a hot skillet before you feel the scorch. He had shot between four and seven enemy insurgents without ever meeting the thoughtless fright of the present instant.

At last, he forced himself to stand. The woman adjusted her frayed shawl, looking around. The dog behind her was Janis, struggling to pull over the threshold a roller bag made for a child much larger than himself.

Elroy said in Latvian, "Madam?" and waved her over.

Evija hadn't come. She'd sent this emissary, this hag.

If it had been up to the woman and Janis, the transaction would have taken fifteen seconds. She looked at the photograph— of Janis and Elroy nearly naked at the beach in Jurmala the year before—and told the boy to go sit at the table. But he had already approached his father and was climbing into the seat next to him.

The boy told the woman in Latvian that she could leave now.

But Elroy wanted her to tell him what to do. "Don't you have anything to give me?" he asked.

The woman admonished the boy, and the boy said, "O.K., I know." And, when Elroy asked, the boy interpreted in a whisper that she was saying that he must not forget to take care of the papers stored in his bag.

Elroy watched the woman leave, and then felt a warm thing on the top of his leg. It was the boy's left hand. With the other hand, the boy was paging through the menu, as he looked at the pictures of the food. Elroy cancelled the livers and they left without eating.

They took a bus to the airport. He strapped Janis into his seat on the flight to Hamburg.

From New Mexico Elroy had brought a coloring book and a crayon. The boy wrapped his fingers around the crayon just so, while Elroy schooled him on how to press lightly so as to conserve wax. And yet, within moments, the crayon snapped in the boy's fist. And the boy glanced up with fear in his shaking mouth, as though he was about to be whipped.

In Hamburg, fresh off the plane, Elroy took the boy to a men's room stall and stuffed his coat pocket with money.

"I didn't mean to break the crayon," Janis said. "I'm sorry."

"Where do you keep my watch?" Elroy drilled, resealing the worn tape that patched the boy's coat. Elroy needed a moment to think things through. He needed ten minutes, fifteen. He would have to buy a book about how to parent. He would have to draw up a grocery list, like cereal, health insurance, allergy medication. The boy was allergic, and the condo was covered everywhere with the fur of Elroy's father's dog. Elroy needed a moment offstage, without the boy watching, so that later he could give the impression that he knew what the fuck he was doing. He needed a pad of paper and a pencil.

"I keep the watch in my pants pocket," the boy replied. "I'm sorry."

Elroy said, "Say you're sorry again and I'll give you something to be sorry about."

The boy looked up, his clothed haunches suspended in the toilet seat.

"Go ahead and cry," Elroy said. "What time do I come to get you?"

Janis showed a thumb and index finger. He said, "Two."

Elroy exited the stall. He told the boy to lock it, and then heard a scuffle, and the sliding of the latch. Elroy left the men's room, mindful to keep a moderate pace amid the mad clatter of Europeans racing toward him, overtaking him on either side. The corridor reeked of burned cooking grease. He paced away, trailing his bag and the boy's toward Terminal 2. The dented wheels of the smaller bag infuriated him by persistently tipping the bag on its side. He dragged the heavy thing wrong side up. Then he hoisted it by its sissy bar, which would not retract. He blew five minutes just looking for a clock, all while getting farther from the bathroom where the boy was waiting. In order to think, Elroy needed to buy a pencil. He blew another ten minutes in Terminal 2 looking for a stationery store. When he found it he realized he had, for reasons hidden from himself, left all of his money with the boy. Why had he left the boy with so much money? He didn't know. And now the cashier, who would have accepted dollars if Elroy had had any, would not let him make such a trifling purchase with a credit card. The airport intercom said something in German, like There was a kindergarten at one of the C gates. Elroy was executing a plan, evidently of his own devising, and yet he did not know its objective. His connection to London would begin boarding in three minutes. It was already well past two o'clock. He turned back toward the bathroom in Terminal 1, planning to get a little money from the boy, buy the pencil, buy some paper, sit a moment, think, go back again, fetch the boy, and make it to the gate in time for the final boarding call. He would need to draw up an agenda, like day care, catechism classes, haircut. What could he possibly have intended by leaving the boy with all of his cash? The intercom said something in English, like In Terminal 1 there was a lost-and-found. Something in the lost-and-found. He paused, listening.

With low inexorable thumps, an escalator drew arriving passengers down beneath the floor.

He turned. Back toward the London gate, the bags dragging. Like a boat that comes about though its anchor is dropped. The wind takes it. Water all around. You need a while before you come to see you're pointed the wrong way.

Janis sat in a little room, an office someplace in the airport. Three kindly Germans surrounded him, their voices soft. Hot chocolate on the desk. He knew that he was in Germany, so these must be Germans. And of Germans he knew exactly one thing, a saying he had heard from his mother's actor friend in Riga: *A German may appear to be a good fellow, but better to hang him.*

Do not be fooled by their chocolate.

Go ahead and cry, his father had said. And Janis had let himself cry.

Everything the Germans were telling him sounded like a question, the tone coming up sort of sweet and menacing at the end. Like, "Flik flik, bok bok, ACK ACK ACK?" He considered it best not to respond. Most of the grief he had met in life had come to him because he had talked.

Germany was in Europe. Latvia, his mother's country, was also in Europe. He had two homes: Riga with his mother and

America with his father, though Janis had never been there. Germany must be somewhere in between. His mother was on vacation and so was he, but "vacation" seemed the wrong word in his case because his father's house, where he was going, also counted as his own house.

Papa will come. By suppertime. Any minute now. So Janis should save room. He wouldn't eat any solid thing they gave him. Per Papa's instructions, he had stayed in the bathroom stall until the little hand of his father's watch had reached the two. Then he had waited a little while longer. Then he had stuffed the watch into his pants and gone back to the place where they had got off the plane. And waited. Papa was not there. So Janis had missed some aspect of their scheme. However, the coming of supper was an unchangeable law that neither he nor his father could get around even if they had wanted to. Papa would have to come by suppertime. Things were very bad, but supper would make them all right again.

Janis longed for the coloring book. His father had taken it back and put it in his bag. The book was the sort without captions and, in this respect, was excellent. He could not quite read yet, and disliked feeling that he was missing out on something. The book appeared to tell of a boy who feeds and tames a wild animal and is then rewarded with the animal's friendship. The book had no title, so Janis could come up with one of his own.

He took a sip of the hot chocolate while the Germans conferred. He didn't want to cry anymore, but he was allowed. It was one of his father's instructions that he was allowed to cry.

Two hours later, Elroy landed in London. He deplaned, walked to the perimeter of the airport, and boarded a bus that drove on the wrong side. He had met another of the world wonders—driving on the left. You kind of don't believe in it until you see it. Like the women he had watched float through the street in Kunduz, curtained in blue from cap to toes, a lace visor where the eyes should go. He had been warned: Keep your head down. You weren't supposed to look. But Kunduz had been like a "Star Wars" planet. Like, How do I process this, a kid like me?

Elroy got off the bus after a couple of stops, sneaked to the back of an apartment complex, and pitched the wicked little bag into a Dumpster. Then he figured out that he could go back to the correct side of the street—see, like everything was backward; maybe you do it wrong first so you can do it right later—and, yes, another bus came and returned him to the airport.

Heathrow, Terminal 5. A bright, oblong construction of glass and steel between asphalt runways. Ticketing. Bag check. A placard at security expressly forbade, among other items, crossbows, machetes, pliers, firearms, lighters shaped like firearms, harpoons, and catapults.

His mind was a seething hash.

He surrendered what he had to the conveyor belt and the screening cavern, and stepped through the metal detector, shoulders low, breathing deep. But the machine flunked him, cheeping, and a jowly attendant led him to secondary screening—asking, Did he have a pacemaker, a cobalt hip, a plate in his head?—and pointed him to the glass booth of a trace-detection portal.

Elroy breathed deep. Sometimes you went the wrong way to go the right way again. Like once, in the street of a vacant neighborhood in Kunduz, he saw a mound in the earth where the dirt lay neatly disarranged, and he got on his knees and blew on it, and he saw the pressure plate, and he stood up fast. And, before he knew it, he'd said, "Fuck it," and kicked the thing. Yet it didn't blow. Like God was saying, "I want you to live, little shit." And for a whole day Elroy feared nothing.

From all directions, jets in the portal walls spat air at him while the machine sniffed the chamber for cocaine, PCP, smack, methamphetamine; also for TNT, C-4, and Semtex.

THE KID

A green light flashed, and the portal opened in front. A new attendant led him to a backscatter X-ray. He stood before a wall, hands raised, palms out, while a raster of radiation scanned the length of him. At the controls, a cheerless Caribbean woman with gold crowning her incisors could not determine his fault and let him go.

In the afternoon autumn light, he sat in a file of Naugahyde chairs by the bank of windows. A color had gone out of the light this week: yellow, it seemed. All over Europe, the depleted light had been identical. And it had transported him back to an era of leaf piles, of cottonwood leaves stuck in the waistband of his underpants. Mountains heaped and demolished.

Jumbo jets faced the terminal windows like orcas nosing at the wall of an aquarium. The haze parted. The light squarely struck Elroy's shaved face. He bathed his neck in it, raising his chin and turning. A lattice of white steel overhead.

There was a sign about the name of the airport. Blocky letters in relief against a brass background. A hamlet had stood here once, called Hitherowe, Hetherow, Hetherowfeyld. A heath with a row of houses on it. Heathrow. Scrub oak and gorse in sandy soil, where the kids played amid the vegetation and rubbish until Mother called them in for tea.

He boarded, took his seat, and the plane tore through the atmosphere.

A while later, the Germans were trying to get Janis to do something, but he didn't know what. One of the men took off his own tie, and put it on the table, asking Janis a question and pointing to him. Then the man took off his jacket, too, and emptied the pockets: cigarettes, ATM receipts. Smiling, open eyes, like, See? Sort of a demonstration.

They wanted him to disrobe? He didn't know how to prevent them. A rule from his mother went: *No one gets to take your*

clothes off you, or take anything away from you that you have.
One of the Germans put her hand on Janis's hat, and he let her
take it off, exposing his ragged hair, but he could not keep from
crying. He was racked with hunger. They ought to feel awful
about what they were trying to do to him. They made him stand
up, and they took off his coat. Anything might happen now. She
laid his coat on the table and searched his pockets. They let him
watch. They found a Kit Kat wrapper. Gum. And two hundred
and sixty-three U.S. dollars folded in half.

T he great circle route westward over the Arctic.
        Gravity pressed on the plane. Yet the pressure beneath the
racing wings, together with the deflection against the flaps in the
plane's trailing edges, lifted it up, so that its passengers hovered
in the air, in a vessel weighing eight hundred and thirty thousand
pounds.

Elroy watched a glacier pour ice into the ocean. God crowded
the world with wonders so that you wouldn't forget what he told
you to do. Elroy didn't know if he'd forgotten or remembered.

He transferred at Boston Logan and landed in Albuquerque—
the fourth landing in the same day, although it had lasted thirty
hours so far. The chamisa pollen caught in his nose and broke his
heart. Mucus drained from his sinuses.

He had reserved a subcompact car online, but Avis had over-
booked his model, so he was given a Mustang convertible. He
drove it north, with the top down, on the straightaway interstate
through the valley of the Rio Grande, pointing his face straight
up at the stars, which had occupied the same places over the East.
He dared the car to veer out of its lane.

West of Santa Fe, he headed into the Jemez range, the thin air
insufficient for his breathing, so that he panted, the roads utterly
dark. At last he found a low adobe wall running the length of

three city blocks—he was navigating by feel, almost by remembered smell, like a hound—and met a gate, at one in the morning Mountain Standard Time. He hadn't eaten since the plane from London, and his longing for food registered as a physical panic. His breath moved shallow and quick. His spine went rigid.

A guard sat at the gate in a lighted cabin doing a Sudoku. He asked Elroy, in the rapid-fire English of native New Mexicans, whom he had come to see.

"But I find nothing here from Sergeant Slocum that he is expecting you," the guard said to his clipboard. The guard required a special note from the condo owner in order to ring after ten o'clock.

"Come on, man," Elroy said. "I was here three days ago." Finally he promised the guard twenty dollars tomorrow if he'd call his father's line.

Sergeant Slocum wasn't really Elroy's father. He was Elroy's stepfather. His ex-stepfather, properly speaking. He had let Elroy stay with him after the second divorce and sent him to St. Xavier's to finish high school. Then the old man had retired up here. Ma had run off. Who knew where.

The gate receded into the adobe wall, and Elroy eased the convertible into the compound. Hooded lights, rock gardens, low-slung stucco homes. He walked under the vigas of the porch and knocked.

When Sergeant Slocum came to the door, he was holding a fork, a half-hearted piece of weaponry.

"Hello, sir," Elroy said. "I hoped I would catch you awake."

"Elroy," the fat man said simply. He had been eating. The crumbs of a pastry littered his mustache. "*Am* I awake?" Sergeant Slocum said in the dim foyer. "I thought I was sleeping. These days, I feel asleep all hours. I can't read, I can't hear, I can't piss . . ."

"Ain't you glad to see me?" Elroy asked.

The Sergeant pointed his fork toward the dark behind Elroy's back. He asked, "And where is young Janis?"

A day later, Janis was awakened where he slept, on a cot in the airport office, by a man wearing a pilot's uniform. He introduced himself in Latvian as Kristaps, while the Germans looked on. *Latvian to strangers. American only to the ones you know.* A system that had stood Janis in good stead before. But he had to conclude that, in Germany, a stranger speaking to him in Latvian presented a special case. The pilot was trying to trick him in some way. Papa *will* come, eventually.

Janis went to the concourse with the pilot for some milk and an egg sandwich, and the pilot asked in Latvian, "Where is your mother or father?" Angry, as though Janis had done something wrong.

And Janis said, blushing, in American, "Can I have mustard?," intending to spoil the wondrous thing on his plate, lest he succumb and eat it.

"Where is the person who brought you here?" the pilot demanded.

Why did it feel *good* to cry? For ages, Janis had wondered what was the matter with him that when he cried, which was feeling bad, it felt good somehow.

Janis took the top off the sandwich, hoping that the white of the egg would be runny, but it had set perfectly; hoping the yolk would be green and hard, but it gave easily when he poked it. His entire being cried out for food.

He needed to eat. But he also needed Papa to come. And all this was a test of some kind. Papa *would* come, but only if Janis kept faith and did not eat.

The pilot cursed him.

Janis gnawed at the arm of his coat. The pilot got up for coffee. Janis felt his hunger as a throb beneath his sternum and a kind of wind inside his head. He decided on the title for the coloring book. The title would be "Joe Loves Foxie, and Foxie Loves Joe Very Much." He opened the little carton of German milk and poured it all over the food on his plate.

Around midday, they put him in a car.

They drove on an enormous road. There was a big city, with ships and cranes and railroad cars. It was so beautiful that Janis wondered whether he was in Heaven.

I was under the evident misperception you were coming with the lad," the Sergeant said.

"Yeah," Elroy said listlessly.

"I misapprehended?"

"Yeah, it didn't work out, you know?"

The Sergeant's cowardly dog, Mavis, appeared behind the glass door that opened onto the patio. She scratched at the pane and looked in at the old man with her ears back and her eyes gaping, like, I know I can't come in, but I'm a stupid bitch, and can I come in?

The Sergeant got up from the sofa and hobbled to the door, holding a magazine. He said, "*What* do I know, exactly?"

"Just, it didn't work out. He looks like me, though. A fucking miracle, right? You expect them to follow you in the face, but then you don't think they do, until they get to a certain age, and then you see it."

The Sergeant slid open the door, rolled the magazine, bent, and clubbed Mavis across her eyes. The dog shrieked and ran off. The Sergeant sat back down.

Elroy went to the fridge, which was stuffed with expired Tex-Mex condiments. "What happened to my baloney?" he said.

"I ate it," the old man said.

"No way," Elroy said, stricken. "You did, really?"

"It's my house. I eat the food here. I still outrank you, don't forget. Go to the store and get yourself something."

"Aw, man, I'd have to go all the way to White Rock." Elroy turned to address the old man's stocking feet, the left one wedged like a trowel: he had lost three toes in Vietnam. Elroy said, "You're supposed to be my dad."

At sunup, as the Sergeant was leaving to eat his breakfast at a diner in town, Elroy awoke on the sofa and asked, "Can't you get something down by the lab for me to eat?"

"Tenants don't eat free here," the Sergeant said, clicking the leash around the jubilant dog's neck. Wherever the Sergeant went, Mavis came along.

Elroy rummaged in his pants pockets—he had slept in his clothes—and discovered a crumpled mass of bills, which he handed drowsily to the old man.

The Sergeant picked out a piece of blue-green paper decorated with an oak tree. "What the hell is this?" he asked.

"That's a whatchamacall. A lat. Five lats—where'd all my real money go?" Elroy said, sitting up. He thought a moment.

"Hotshot killer, over here. Without a pot to piss in. Maybe you could pawn your Bronze Star, if you can remember where you left it."

"Would you bum me ten bucks?" Elroy asked. "Is that enough? For a pound of meat?"

Two years later, Sergeant Major Heflin was on his fourth deployment in Afghanistan, this time at Bagram Airfield, when he got an e-mail from Evija:

> My dear Ellie,
>   I arrived home to Riga this month, where I write you in the very café on Stabu iela where we used to go for party.

Of course I miss Janis very badly and you. I tremble thinking you may have another girlfriend now. What right have I even to call you "dear" after what I have done? Or to ask you forgive me? However it seems foolish and right to ask, like you wanted to run across the canal, and I told you, "Don't, the ice is not ready!" and you ran in any case, and you made it to the other side, still dry.

I have no right to ask you to come here and bring Janis. But this is where we belonged before. All three. I cannot stop from wishing that we could have another chance.

GARY SHTEYNGART

June 1, Rome.

Lucky diary! Undeserving diary! From this day forward, you will travel on the greatest adventure yet undertaken by a nervous, average man sixty-nine inches in height, a hundred and sixty pounds in heft, with a slightly dangerous body-mass index of 23.6. From this day forward, you will join me on the journey toward immortality. Why "from this day forward"? Because yesterday I met Eunice Park, and she will sustain me forever. Take a long look at me, diary. What do you see? A slight man with a gray, sunken battleship of a face, curious wet eyes, a giant gleaming forehead on which a dozen cavemen could have painted something nice, a sickle of a nose perched atop a tiny puckered mouth, and, from the back, a growing bald spot whose shape perfectly replicates that of the great state of Ohio, with its capital city, Columbus, marked by a deep-brown mole. On most days I look like a Crisis-Net stream of our befuddled Bipartisan Defense Secretary Rubenstein, trembling through his press conference after our troops got routed at Caracas. *Slight.* Slightness is my curse in every sense. A so-so body in a world where only an incredible one will do. A body at the chronological age of thirty-nine already racked by too much LDL cholesterol, too much ACTH hormone, too much of everything that dooms the heart, sunders the liver, explodes all hope.

A week ago, before Eunice gave me reason to live, you wouldn't have noticed me, diary. A week ago, I did not exist. A week ago, at a restaurant in Rome, I took out my dated äppärät, with its retro walnut finish and its dusty screen blinking with slow data, trying to get a read on whether there were any High Net Worth Individuals in the room—a last chance to find some new clients for my boss, Joshie, after having uncovered a grand total of one during the whole year I'd spent in Italy trying to foist our Product on unreceptive rich Eurotrash. I approached a potential client, a classically attractive High Net Worth Individual. He looked up from his wintry *bollito misto*, looked right past me, looked back down at the boiled lovemaking of his seven meats and seven vegetable sauces, looked back up, looked right past me *again*. It was clear that for a member of upper society to even remotely notice me I would have to first fire a flaming arrow into a dancing moose or be kicked in the testicles by a head of state.

And yet Lenny Abramov, your humble diarist, your small nonentity, will live forever. As the Life Lovers Outreach Coördinator (Grade G) of the Post-Human Services Division of the Staatling-Wapachung Corporation, I will be the first to partake of eternal life.

During my year in Rome, I kept a paperback next to my bed: "The Unbearable Lightness of Being," of course. Every morning I reread page 8 and the sentences I had underlined as a moody, un-laid teen-ager already anticipating his deathbed: "What happens but once . . . might as well not have happened at all. If we have only one life to live, we might as well not have lived at all." Next to this I had written in shaded teen-aged block letters: "EUROPEAN CYNICISM OR VERY SCARY TRUTH???" Perhaps it was this book that had first launched my search for immortality. Joshie himself once said to a very important client, "Eternal life is the only life that matters. All else is just a moth circling the light." He hadn't noticed me standing by the door to his office. I had returned to my desk in tears, feeling abandoned to nothingness, mothlike, yet stunned by Joshie's unusual lyricism. The part about the moth, I mean.

Here's how I look at it. Money equals life. By my estimate, even the preliminary beta-dechronification treatments—for example, the insertion of SmartBlood to regulate my ridiculous cardiovascular system—would run three million yuan per year. With each second I have spent in Rome, lustily minding the architecture, drinking and eating enough daily glucose to kill a Cuban sugarcane farmer, I have been paving the toll road to my own demise.

But don't bury me yet, judgmental diary. A new Lenny heart beats more convincingly than the old one. Eunice Park will save me. You just watch.

L ast night, the last night of my Euro sabbatical, I told myself, Remember this, Lenny. Develop a sense of nostalgia for something, or you'll never figure out what's important. Remember how you met Eunice at your last orgiastic Roman party, how you rescued her from what's-his-face, the diabetic American sculptor with the Beatlesque mop and stubby teeth, how you dragged that nano-sized woman into the night with you.

But by the end of said night I remembered very little. Let's just say that I drank. Drank out of fear (she was so cruel). Drank out of happiness (she was so beautiful). Drank until my teeth and my whole mouth had turned a dark ruby red and the pungency of my breath and perspiration betrayed my passing years. And she drank, too. One *mezzolitro* of the local swill became a full *litro*, and then two *litri* and then a bottle of something possibly Sardinian but in any case thicker than bull's blood.

Enormous plates of food were needed to mop up this overindulgence. We thoughtfully chewed on the pig jowls of the *bucatini all'amatriciana*, slurped up a plate of spaghetti with spicy eggplant, and picked apart a rabbit practically drowning in olive oil. I knew I would miss all this when I got back to New York,

even the horrible fluorescent lighting that brought out my age—
the wrinkles around my eyes, the single long highway and three
county roads that run across my forehead, testaments to many
sleepless nights spent worrying about unredeemed pleasures and
my carefully hoarded income, but mostly about death.

I told her I didn't want to leave Rome now that I had met her.

She told me I was a nerd, but a nerd who made her laugh.

I told her I wanted to do more than make her laugh.

She told me I should be thankful for what I had.

I told her she should move to New York with me.

She told me she was probably a lesbian.

I told her my work was my life, but I still had room for love.

She told me love was out of the question.

I told her my parents were Russian immigrants who lived in
New York.

She told me hers were Korean immigrants who lived in Fort
Lee, New Jersey.

I told her my father was a retired janitor who liked to go
fishing.

She told me her father was a podiatrist who liked to punch
his wife and two daughters in the face.

"Oh," I said. Eunice Park shrugged and excused herself. On
my plate, the rabbit's little dead heart hung from within his rib
cage. I put my head in my hands and wondered if I should just
throw some euros down on the table and walk out.

But soon enough I was heading down ivy-draped Via Giulia,
my arm around Eunice Park's fragrant, boyish frame. She was
seemingly in good spirits, promising me a kiss, then chastising
my poor Italian. She was shyness and giggles, freckles in the
moonlight and drunken, immature cries of "Shut up, Lenny!"
and "You're such an idiot!" I noticed she had released her hair
from the bun's captivity and that it was dark and endless and
thick as twine. She was twenty-four years old.

My apartment could accommodate no more than a cheap twin-size mattress and a fully opened suitcase, brimming with books. ("My Text-major friends at Elderbird used to call those things 'doorstops,'" she told me.) We kissed, lazily, like it was nothing, then roughly, like we meant it. There were some problems. Eunice Park wouldn't take off her bra ("I have absolutely no chest"), and I was too drunk and scared to develop an erection. But I didn't want intercourse anyway. The next morning, she was kind enough to help me repack my suitcase, which refused to close without her help. "That's not how you do it," she said, when she saw me brushing my teeth. She made me stick out my tongue and roughly scraped its purple surface with the toothbrush. "There," she said. "Better."

During the taxi ride to the airport I felt the triple pangs of being happy and lonely and needy all at once. She had made me wash my lips and chin thoroughly to obliterate every trace of her, but Eunice Park's alkaline tang remained on the tip of my nose. I made great sniffing motions in the air, trying to capture her essence, thinking already of how I would bait her to New York, make her my life, my life eternal. I touched my expertly brushed teeth and petted the flurry of gray hairs sticking out from beneath my shirt collar, which she had thoroughly examined in the morning's weak early light. "Cute," she had said. And then, with a child's sense of wonder, "You're old, Len."

June 1: From the GlobalTeens account of Eunice Park.
Euni-Tard Abroad to Grillbitch.
Hi, Precious Panda!

So, guess what? I met the cutest guy in Rome. He is exactly my type, tall, kind of German-looking, very preppie, but not an asshole. Giovanna set me up with him—he's in Rome working for LandO'LakesGMFordCredit! So I go to meet him in the Pi-

azza Navona (remember Image Class? Navona's the one with all
the Tritons) and he's sitting there having a cappuccino and streaming "Chronicles of Narnia"! Remember we streamed that in Catholic? So adorable. His name is Ben, which is pretty gay, but he
was *so nice* and so smart. He took me to look at some Caravag-
gios and then he kind of like touched my butt a little and then
we went to one of Giovanna's parties and made out. There were
all these Italian girls in Onionskin jeans staring at us, like I was
stealing one of their white guys or something. I fucking hate that.
If they mention my "almond eyes" one more time, I swear. Anyway, *I need your advice* because he called yesterday and asked if
I wanted to go up to Lucca with him next week and I was playing
hard to get and said no. But I'm going to call him and say yes
tomorrow! *What should I do? Help!!!*

P.S. I met this old, gross guy at a party yesterday and we got
really drunk and I sort of let him go down on me. There was
another even older guy, this sculptor, trying to get in my pants, so
I figured, you know, the lesser evil. Ugh, I'm turning into you!!!!!
The first old guy took me to dinner at this restaurant, da Tonino,
which was like O.K. He was nice, kind of dorky, although he
thinks he's so Media cause he works in biotech or something.
And he had the grossest feet, bunions and this gigantic heel spur
that sticks out like he's got a thumb glued to his foot. I know, I'm
thinking like my dad. Anyway, he brushes his teeth all wrong, so
I had to SHOW A GROWN MAN HOW TO USE A TOOTH-
BRUSH!!!!! What is wrong with my life, Precious Panda?

June 4: Leonardo Dabramovinci to Euni-Tard Abroad.
Oh, hi there. It's Lenny Abramov. You might remember me from
our little time in Rome. Thanks for brushing my teeth! Hee-hee.
So, anyway, just got back to the U.S. of A. I've been practicing my
abbreviations. I think you said "ROFLAARP" in Rome. Does that

mean "Rolling on Floor Looking at Addictive Rodent Pornography"? See, I'm not that old! Anyway, been thinking about you. Coming to N.Y.C. anytime soon? You've got a place to stay here. I've got a nice apartment all set up, seven hundred and forty square feet, balcony, view of downtown. Can't compete with da Tonino, but I make a pretty mean roasted eggplant. I can even sleep on the couch if you want me to. Call or write anytime. It was really, really, *really* great to meet you. I'm committing the constellation of your freckles to memory as I write this (hope that doesn't make you uncomfortable).

Love,
Leonard

June 6, New York.
Well, I'm back! New York, New York. The Motherland. The dense stretch of humanity where your scrappy diarist, Lenny Abramov, was birthed to an anxious immigrant woman and her unhappy husband. Less than a week off the plane, and already so much important work to be done. My new way of thinking is this—if I'm to live forever, I have to make people love me. First up, boss man Joshie. I've got to show Joshie that I still matter at the workplace, that I'm not just a teacher's pet but a Creative Thinker and Content Provider. I have to make excuses for my poor performance in Europe. I have to get a raise and lower spending. I have to save money for initial dechronification treatments. I have to double my life span in twenty years and then just keep going at it exponentially until I gain the momentum to achieve Indefinite Life Extension. Secondly, Eunice. Even if she's far away, I have to think of her as a potential partner. I have to meditate on her freckles and make myself feel loved by her so as to lower stress levels and feel less alone. Then I have to beg her to come to New York and let her become, as quickly as possible, reluctant lover, cautious companion, pretty young wife.

First order of business when I got back: to celebrate what I already have. I began with the seven hundred and forty square feet that form my share of Manhattan Island. I live in the last middle-class stronghold in the city, high atop a red-brick ziggurat that a Jewish garment workers' union erected on the banks of the East River back in the days when Jews sewed clothes for a living. Say what you will, these ugly co-ops are full of authentic old people who have real stories to tell (although these stories are often meandering and hard to follow; e.g., who on earth was this guy "Dillinger"?).

Then I celebrated my Wall of Books. I counted the volumes on my twenty-foot-long modernist bookshelf to make sure that none had been misplaced or used as kindling by my subtenant. "You're my sacred ones," I told the books. "No one but me still cares about you. But I'm going to keep you with me forever. And one day I'll make you important again." I thought about the terrible calumny of the new generation: that books smell. And yet, in preparation for the eventual arrival of Eunice Park, I decided to be safe and sprayed some Pine-Sol Wild Flower Blast in the vicinity of my tomes, fanning the atomized juices in the direction of their spines.

I celebrated the difficult-to-assemble outdoor table (one leg still too short) on my balcony and had a pretty awful non-Roman coffee al fresco while looking out at the busy skyline of the Borrower-Spender-Financial-Residential Complex in lower Manhattan, some twenty blocks away from me, military and civilian choppers streaming past the overblown spire of the Freedom Tower and all that other glittering downtown hoo-ha. I celebrated the low-rise housing projects crowding my immediate view, the so-called Vladeck Houses, which stand in red-brick solidarity with my own co-ops, not exactly proud of themselves, but resigned and necessary, their thousands of residents primed for summer warmth and, if I may speculate, summer love.

With love in mind, I decided to celebrate the season. I slapped on a pair of white linen pants, a speckled Penguin shirt, and some comfy Malaysian sneakers, so that I easily resembled many of the nonagenarians in my building. My co-op is part of a NORC, or Naturally Occurring Retirement Community—a kind of instant Florida for those too frail or too poor to relocate to Boca in time for their death. Surrounded by shrunken NORCers in motorized wheelchairs with their Jamaican caregivers, I counted the daily carnage on the Death Board by the elevators. Five residents of the NORC had passed in the last two days alone. I guess you could say that while admiring those authentic old people I also hated them. Hated them for giving up on life, for letting the waves come and recede, their withered bodies in tow.

In my trendy old man's getup I ambled with easy grace down Grand Street, stepping off each curb with the profound "oy" that is the call-and-response of my neighborhood. I celebrated the teen-aged mothers from the Vladeck Houses tending to their children's boo-boos ("A bee touched me, Mommy!"). I relished hearing language actually being spoken by children. Overblown verbs, explosive nouns, beautifully bungled prepositions. Language, not data. How long would it be before these kids retreated into the dense clickety-clack äppärät world of their absorbed mothers and missing fathers? Then I caught sight of the wooden telegraph poles that now lined the streets.

I'd heard about the Credit Poles going up when I was in Rome. Their old-fashioned appearance was obviously meant to evoke a sturdier time in our nation's history, except for the little L.E.D. counters at eye level that registered your Credit ranking as you walked by. Atop the poles, American Restoration Authority signs billowed in several languages. In the Chinatown sections of East Broadway, the signs read, in English and Chinese, "America Cel-

ebrates Its Spenders!,," and showed a cartoon of a miserly ant
happily running toward a mountain of wrapped Christmas presents. In the Latino stretch of Madison Street, they read, in English and Spanish, "Save It for a Rainy Day, Huevón," with a
frowning grasshopper in a zoot suit revealing his empty pockets.
Alternating signs read, in all three languages:

> The Boat Is Full.
> Avoid deportation.
> Latinos save.
> Chinese spend.
> ALWAYS keep your Credit ranking within limits.
> AMERICAN RESTORATION AUTHORITY: "Together We'll
>   Surprise the World!"

I felt the perfunctory liberal chill at seeing entire races of human beings so summarily reduced and stereotyped but was also
voyeuristically interested in seeing people's Credit rankings. The
young Latina mothers, and even a profligate teen-aged Hasid
puffing down the street, were showing red blinking scores below
900, and I worried for them.

An armored personnel carrier bearing the insignia of the
New York Army National Guard was parked astride a man-size
pothole at the intersection of Essex and Delancey, a roof-mounted
.50-calibre Browning machine gun rotating a hundred and eighty
degrees, back and forth, like a retarded metronome, along the
busy but peaceable Lower East Side streetscape. Traffic was frozen all across Delancey Street. Silent traffic, for no one dared to
use a horn against the military vehicle. The street corner emptied
around me until I stood alone staring down the barrel of the gun
like an idiot. I lifted up my hands in panic and directed my feet
to scram.

My celebrations were turning sour. In front of a recently
shuttered Bowery scones-and-libations establishment called Pov-

erTea I found a cab and took it to the Upper East Side lair of my second father.

The Post-Human Services Division of the Staatling-Wapachung Corporation is housed in a former Moorish-style synagogue near Fifth Avenue, a tired-looking building dripping with arabesques, kooky buttresses, and other crap that brings to mind a lesser Gaudi. Joshie got it at auction for a mere eighty thousand dollars when the congregation folded after being bamboozled by some kind of Jewish pyramid scheme years ago. I have worked for Joshie since graduating from N.Y.U., that indispensable local educator of bright enough women and men. Back then Post-Human Services used to be a so-called flat organization, without titles or hierarchies, its organic, odorous young workers obsessed with but one goal—the total annihilation of death. After the mighty Staatling-Wapachung Corporation bought Joshie out for a grotesque sum of money, everyone was given a rank, the least enthusiastic among us simply told to go home.

The first thing I noticed upon my return was the familiar smell. Heavy use of a special hypoallergenic organic air freshener is encouraged at Post-Human Services, because the scent of immortality is complex. The supplements, the diet, the constant shedding of blood and piercing of skin for various physical tests, the fear of the metallic components found in most deodorants make a curious array of post-mortal odors, of which "sardine breath" is the most benign.

With one or two exceptions, I haven't made any work-time buddies at Post-Human Services since I turned thirty. It's not easy being friends with some twenty-two-year-old who cries over his fasting blood-glucose level or sends out a group teen with his adrenal stress index and a smiley face. A graffito in the bathroom that reads "Lenny Abramov's insulin levels are whack" is evidence of a certain undeniable atmosphere of one-upmanship, which, in turn, raises the cortisol levels associated with stress and encourages cellular breakdown.

Still, when I walked through the door I expected to recognize *someone*. The synagogue's gilded main sanctuary was filled with young men and women dressed with angry post-college disregard but projecting from somewhere between their eyes the message that they were the personification of that old Whitney Houston number—they, the children, were de facto the future.

The ark where the Torahs were customarily stashed had been taken out, and in its place hung five gigantic Solari schedule boards that Joshie had rescued from various Italian train stations. Instead of the *arrivi* and *partenze* of trains pulling in and out of Florence or Milan, the flip board displayed the names of Post-Human Services employees, along with the results of our latest physicals, our methylation and homocysteine levels, our testosterone and estrogen, our fasting insulin and triglycerides, and, most important, our "mood + stress indicators," which were always supposed to read "positive/playful/ready to contribute" but which, with enough input from competitive co-workers, could be changed to "one moody betch today" or "not a team playa this month." On this particular day the black-and-white flaps were turning madly, the letters and numbers mutating—a droning *ticka-ticka-ticka-ticka*—to form new words and figures. Disturbingly enough, several of my colleagues, including my fellow-Russian the brilliantly manic-depressive Vasily Greenberg, were marked by the dreaded legend "Train Cancelled."

As for me, I wasn't even listed.

Finally I heard the words "Rhesus Monkey." Joshie's nickname for me! Someone had recognized my special relationship to Joshie, the fact that I used to be someone around here.

It was my darling Kelly Nardl. A supple, low-slung girl my age whom I would be terminally attracted to if I could stand to spend my life within three metres of her non-deodorized animal scent. She welcomed me with a kiss on both cheeks, as if she were the one just returned from Europe.

"Hey," I said. "Vasily Greenberg's train got cancelled? He played the guitar and spoke a little Arabic. He was so 'ready to contribute' when he wasn't totally depressed."

"He turned forty last month," Kelly said, with a sigh. "Didn't make quotas."

"I'm almost forty, too," I said. "And why isn't my name up on the Boards?"

Kelly didn't say anything. We had once shared an entire bottle of wine, or "resveratrol," as we Post-Humans like to call it, at a tapas bar in Brooklyn and after walking her to her violent Bush-wick tenement I'd wondered if I could one day fall in love with a woman so unobtrusively, compulsively decent. (Answer: no.)

"Maybe I'll go to my desk," I said to Kelly.

"Honey," she said. "You don't have a desk. I mean, someone's taken it. This new kid from Brown-Yonsei. *Darryl*, I think."

"What do I do?" I whispered.

"It would help," she said, "if you looked a little younger. Take care of yourself. Go to the Eternity Lounge. Put some Lexin DC concentrate under your eyes."

The lounge was crammed full of smelly young people check-ing their äppäräti or leaning back on couches with their faces to the ceiling, de-stressing, breathing right.

"Hi," I said to anyone who would listen.

I went to the mini-bar where unsweetened green tea was dis-pensed, along with alkalized water and two hundred and thirty-one daily nutritionals. "Just got back from a year in Roma," I said, trying to pump the bravado in my voice. "All carbs over there. Need to stock up on the essentials like a cuh-*razy* person. Good to be back, guys!"

Silence. But as I turned again to the supplements someone said, "What's shaking, Rhesus Monkey?"

It was a kid with a small outbreak of a mustache and a gray bodysuit with the words "SUK DIK" stencilled across the breast, some kind of red bandanna strung around his neck. He was probably Darryl from Brown, the one who had taken my desk. He couldn't have been more than twenty-five. I smiled at him, looked at my äppärät, sighed as if I had too much work ahead of me, and then casually headed for the door.

"Where you going, Rhesus?" he asked, blocking my exit with his scraggly, tight-butted body, shoving his äppärät in my face, the rich organic smell of him clouding my nostrils. "Don't you want to do some blood work for us, buddy? I'm seeing triglycerides clocking in at one thirty-five. That's *before* you ran away to Europe like a little bitch." There was hooting in the background, the spectators clearly enjoying this toxic banter.

I backed away, mumbling, "One thirty-five is still within the range." There was more laughter, the shine of hairless hands bearing sleek technological pendants full of right data. Two and a half heartbeats later, the hooting abruptly ceased. The boisterous crowd was parting, the "SUK DIK" warriors slinking away.

And there he was. Younger than before. The initial dechronification treatments, the beta treatments, as we called them, already coursing through him. His face unlined and harmoniously still, except for that thick nose, which twitched uncontrollably at times, some muscle group gone haywire. His ears stood on either side of his shorn head like two sentinels.

Joshie Goldmann never revealed his age, but I surmised that he was in his late sixties—a sixty-something man with a mustache as black as eternity. In restaurants, he was sometimes mistaken for my handsomer brother. We shared the same unappreciated jumble of meaty lips and thick eyebrows and chests that barrelled forward like a terrier's, but that's where the resemblance ended. Because when Joshie looked at you, when he lowered his gaze at you, the heat would rise in your cheeks and you'd find yourself oddly, irrevocably, present.

"Oh, Leonard," he said, sighing and shaking his head. "Those guys giving you a hard time? Poor Rhesus. Come on. Let's talk." I shyly followed him as he walked upstairs (no elevators, *never*) to his office. He ran his hand through the fullness of hair at my nape and turned my head around. "So much gray," he said.

What had Eunice told me in one of our last moments together? *You're old, Len.*

"It's the pasta carbs," I stammered. "And the stressors of Italian life. Believe it or not, it's not easy over there when you're living on an American's salary—"

"You need to detoxify, Len."

"I'm going to drink fifteen cups of alkalized water a day," I said.

"Your male-pattern baldness worries me."

I laughed. I actually said "Ha-ha." "It worries me, too, Grizzly Bear," I said.

"I'm not talking aesthetics here. All that Russian-Jewish testosterone is being turned right into dihydrotestosterone. That's killer stuff. Prostate cancer down the road. You'll need at least eight hundred milligrams of saw palmetto a day. What's wrong, Rhesus? You look like you're going to cry."

But I just wanted him to take care of me some more. Joshie has always told the Post-Human Services staff to keep a diary, to remember who we were, because at every moment our brains and synapses are being rebuilt and rewired with maddening disregard for our personalities, so that each year, each month, each day we transform into different people, utterly unfaithful iterations of our original selves, of the drooling kids in the sandbox. But not me. I am still a facsimile of my early childhood. I am still looking for a loving dad to lift me up and brush the sand off my ass, as English, calm and hurtless, falls from his lips. Why couldn't I be raised by Joshie? "I think I'm in love with this girl," I sputtered.

"Talk to me."

"She's super young. Super healthy. Asian. Life expectancy—very high."

"I *love* love," Joshie said. "It's great for pH, ACTH, LDL, whatever ails you. As long as it's a good, *positive* love, without suspicion or hostility. Now, what you've got to do is make this healthy Asian girl need *you* the way you need *me*."

"Don't let me die, Joshie," I said. "I need the dechronification treatments. Why isn't my name up on the Boards?"

Joshie was silent.

"I'm sorry if I let you down by going to Rome for so long," I near-whispered. "I thought maybe I could understand my parents better if I lived in Europe. Spent some time thinking about immortality in a really old place. Read some books. Got some thoughts down."

Joshie turned away from me. From this angle, I could see another side to him, the faint gray stubble protruding from his perfect egg of a chin, the slight intimations that not all of him could be reverse-engineered into immortality. Yet.

"Those thoughts, those books—they *are* the problem, Rhesus," he said. "You have to stop thinking and start selling. That's why all those young whizzes in the Eternity Lounge want to shove a carb-filled macaroon up your ass. And who can blame them, Lenny? You remind them of death. You remind them of a different, earlier version of our species. Don't get pissed at me now. Reading. Writing. The humanities. It's the Fallacy of Merely Existing. F.M.E. There'll be plenty of time to ponder and write and act out later. Right now you've got to *sell to live*."

June 11: Euni-Tard Abroad to Grillbitch.

Hi, Precious Panda,

I know you're in Tahoe so I don't want to bother you, but things have gotten really bad with my dad and I think I'm coming home. Going to Rome was *such* a mistake. It's like the further I am from him the more he thinks he can get away with. I don't know if I can handle Fort Lee, but I was thinking of crashing in New York and going over there on weekends. Remember that girl you were friends with, the one with the really old-school perm, Joy Lee or something? Does she have a place for me to crash? I don't really know anyone in N.Y.—everyone's in L.A. or abroad. I think I might have to stay over at that old guy Lenny's house. He keeps sending me these long teens about how much he loves my freckles and how he's going to cook me an eggplant.

I broke up with Ben. It was too much. He is so beautiful physically, so smart and such a rising star in Credit that I am completely intimidated by him. I can never reveal who I really am to him because he would just vomit. It's so sad. I've been crying for days now. Crying over my family and crying over Ben. God, I'm sorry, Precious Panda. I'm such a downer.

The weird thing is I've been thinking about Lenny, the old guy. I know he's gross physically, but there's something sweet about him and honestly I need to be taken care of, too. I feel safe with him because he is so not my ideal and I feel like I can be myself because I'm not in love with him. When we were walking down this pretty street in Rome I noticed Lenny's shirt was buttoned all wrong, and I just reached over and rebuttoned it. I just wanted to help him be less of a dork. Isn't that a form of love, too? And when he was talking to me at dinner, usually I listen to everything a guy says and try to prepare a response, but with him I just stopped listening after a while and looked at the way his lips moved, the foam on his lips and on his dorky stubble, because he was so *earnest* in the way he needed to tell me things. And I thought, Wow, you're like what Prof. Margaux in Assertiveness Class used to call "a real human being." I don't know. I keep going back and forth on him. Sometimes I'm like no way, it's never going to work, I'm just not attracted to him. But then I think of him going down on me until he could barely breathe, the poor thing, and the way I could just close my eyes and pretend we were both other people.

June 11, New York.
God, I miss her. No messages from my Euny yet, no reply to my entreaty to move here and let me take care of her with garlicky carcasses of eggplant, with my grown man's practiced affections, with what's left of my bank account after my Roman sojourn and my demotion at work. But I'm persevering until the dreaded "Dear Lenny" letter pops up on GlobalTeens and she runs off with some hot Credit or Media guy, some mindless jerk so taken with her looks he won't even recognize how much this miniature woman in front of him is in need of consolation and repair.

Speaking of money, I went to my H.S.B.C. on East Broadway, where a pretty Dominican girl with a set of dying teeth gave me a rundown on how my financial instruments were performing. In a word, shittily.

My AmericanMorning portfolio, even though it was pegged to the yuan, had lost ten per cent of its value, because, unbeknownst to me, the idiot asset managers had stuck the failing ColgatePalmoliveYum!BrandViacomCredit albatross into the mix, and my low-risk BRIC (Brazil, Russia, India, China)-A-BRAC High-Performing Nations Fund had registered only three-per-cent growth because of the April unrest near Putingrad and the impact of America's invasion of Venezuela on the Brazilian economy. "I feel like I'm going to shit a BRIC," I told Maria Abriella, my account representative.

I was *hemorrhaging* funds. I turned away from Ms. Abriella's beautiful seagull-shaped lips as if slapped, and let death wash over me, the corned-beef smell of my damp neck giving way to an old man's odor rising from my thighs and armpits like steam, and then to the final past-due stench of the Arizona hospice years, an orderly swabbing me down with detergent as if I were some sickly elephant.

In more positive news, I think I'm doing O.K. on the Joshie front. The first week back at Post-Human Services is over and nothing terrible happened. I haven't been asked to do any Intakes yet, but I've spent the week hanging out in the Eternity Lounge fiddling with my pebbly new äppärät 7.5, with RateMe Plus technology, which I now proudly wear, pendant style, around my neck, downloading all my fears and hopes in front of my young nemeses, talking about how my parents' love for me ran too hot and too cold, how I want and need Eunice Park even though she's so much prettier than I deserve—basically, trying to show these open-source young'uns just how much data an old "intro" geezer like me is willing to share. So far, I'm getting shouts of "Gross" and "Sick" and "TIMATOV," which I've learned means "Think I'm About to Openly Vomit," but I also found out that Darryl, the guy with the "SUK DIK" bodysuit and the red bandanna, has been posting nice things about me on his GlobalTeens stream called "101 People We Need to Feel Sorry For." Also, I've spent an entire week without reading any books or talking about them too loudly. I'm learning to worship my new äppärät's screen, the colorful pulsating mosaic of it, the fact that it knows every last stinking detail about the world, while my books know only the minds of their authors.

June 13: Leonardo Dabramovinci to Euni-Tard Abroad.
Oh, hi there. It's Lenny Abramov. Again. I'm sorry to be bothering you. I teened you a little while back and I didn't hear from you. So I guess you're busy and there must be all these annoying guys bothering you all the time and I don't want to be another dork who sends you glad tidings every minute. Anyway, I just wanted to warn you that I was on my friend's stream called "The Noah Weinberg Show!" and I was really really *wasted* and I said

all these things about your freckles and how we had *bucatini all'amatriciana* together at da Tonino and about how I pictured us reading books to each other one day.

Eunice, I am so sorry to drag your name through the mud like this. I just got carried away and was feeling pretty sad because I miss you and wish we could keep in touch more. I keep thinking about that night we spent in Rome, about every minute of it, and I guess it's become like this foundation myth for me. So I'm trying to think about other things, like my job/financial situation, which is very complicated right now, and my parents, who are not as difficult as yours, but let's just say we're not a happy family, either. God, I don't know why I just constantly want to open up to you. Again, I'm sorry if I embarrassed you with that ridiculous stream and with the stuff about you reading books.

(Still) Your Friend (hopefully),

Lenny

June 14: Euni-Tard Abroad to Leonardo Dabramovinci.

O.K., Leonard. Fire up that eggplant. I think I'm coming to New York. It's "Arrivederci, Roma" for this girl. Sorry I've been out of touch for so long. I've been sort of thinking about you, too, and I really look forward to staying with you for a little while. You're a very sweet and funny guy, Len. But I want you to know that my life blows major testes these days. I just broke up with this guy who was really my type, stuff with my parents, blah, blah, blah. So I may not always be the best company and I may not always treat you right. In other words, if you get sick of me, just throw me out on the curb. That's what people do. Ha-ha-ha!

I'll send you the flight info as soon as I can. You don't have to pick me up or anything. Just tell me where to go.

I hope this doesn't make you uncomfortable, Lenny Abramov, but my freckles really miss you.

Eunice

P.S. Have you been brushing like I showed you? It's good for you and cuts down on bad breath.

P.P.S. I thought you were pretty cute on your friend Noah's stream but you should really try to get off "101 People We Need to Feel Sorry For." That guy with the "SUK DIK" overalls is just being cruel to you. You are not a "greasy old schlub," whatever that means, Lenny. You should stand up for yourself.

June 18, New York.
Oh my God, oh my God, Oh My God! She's here. Eunice Park is in New York. Eunice Park is in my apartment! Eunice Park is sitting *next to me* on my couch while I'm writing this. Eunice Park: a tiny fragment of a human being in purple leggings, pouting at something terrible I may have done, anger in her wrinkled forehead, the rest of her absorbed by her äppärät, checking out expensive stuff on AssLuxury. I am close to her. I am surreptitiously smelling the garlic on her breath, diary. I'm smelling a lunch of Malaysian anchovies, and I think I'm about to have a heart attack. Oh, what's wrong with me? Everything, sweet diary. Everything is wrong with me, and I am the happiest man alive!

When she teened me that she was coming to N.Y.C., I rushed out to the corner bodega and asked for an eggplant. They said they had to order it on their äppärät, so I waited twelve hours by the door, and when it came my hands were shaking so badly I couldn't do anything with it. I just stuck it in the freezer (by accident) and then went out on the balcony and started to weep. From joy, of course!

On the morning of the first day of my real life, I threw out the frozen eggplant and put on my cleanest, most conservative cotton shirt, which became a monsoon of nervous sweat before I even got to the door. To dry off a little and gain perspective, I sat down, the way my parents always sat down before a long trip to pray for a safe journey in their primitive Russian way. "Lenny!" I

393

said aloud. "You are not going to screw this up. You've been given a chance to help the most beautiful woman in the world. You must be good, Lenny. You must not think of yourself at all. Only of this little creature before you. Then you will be helped in turn. If you don't pull this off, if you hurt this poor girl in any way, you will not be worthy of immortality. But if you harness her warm little body to yours and make her smile, if you show her that adult love can overcome childhood pain, then both of you will be shown the kingdom. Joshie may slam the door on you, may watch your heartbeat stutter to a stop in some public-hospital bed, but how could anyone deny Eunice Park? How could any god wish her less than eternal youth?"

I wanted to meet Eunice at J.F.K., but it turns out that you can't even get close to the airport without a plane ticket anymore. The cabbie left me at the third American Restoration Authority checkpoint on the Van Wyck, where the National Guard had set up a greeting area, a twenty-foot-high camouflaged tarp beneath which a crowd of poor middle-class folk huddled in anticipation of their relatives. I almost missed her flight because a part of the Williamsburg Bridge had collapsed, and we spent an hour trying to turn around on Delancey Street next to a hasty new A.R.A. sign that said "Together We'll Repare [sic] This Bridge."

I waited under the tarp for the UnitedContinentalDeltAmerican bus, pacing nervously until the men with guns began to look at me funny, then retreated into a makeshift Retail space by a Dumpster where I bought some wilting roses and a three-hundred-dollar bottle of champagne. My poor Eunice looked so tired when she huffed off the bus with her many bags that I nearly tackled her in a rejuvenating embrace, but I was careful not to make a scene, waving my roses and champagne at the armed men to prove that I had enough Credit to afford Retail and then kissed her passionately on one cheek (she smelled of flight and moisturizer), then on the straight, thin, oddly non-Asian nose, then the other cheek, then back to the nose, then once more the first cheek, following the curve of freckles backward and forward, marking her nose like a bridge to be crossed twice. The champagne bottle fell out of my hands, but, whatever futuristic garbage it was made of, it didn't break.

Confronted with this kind of crazy love, Eunice didn't withdraw, nor did she return my ardor. She smiled at me with those full purple lips of hers and those tired young eyes, abashed, and made a motion with her arms to indicate that the bags were heavy. They were, diary. They were the heaviest bags I've ever carried. The spiky heels of ladies' shoes kept stabbing my abdomen and a metal tin of unknown provenance, round and hard, bruised my hip.

The cab ride passed in near-silence, both of us a little ashamed of the situation, each probably feeling guilty about something (my relative power; her youth), and mindful of the fact that we had spent less than a day together in total and that our commonalities had yet to be determined.

She was disappointed by my apartment, by how far it was from the F line and how ugly the buildings were. "Looks like I'll get some exercise walking to the train," she said. "Ha-ha." This was what her generation liked to add to the end of sentences, a kind of nervous tic. "Ha-ha."

"I'm really glad you're here, Eunice," I said, trying to keep everything I said both clear and honest. "I really missed you. I mean, it's kind of weird . . ."

"I missed you, too, nerd face," she said.

That single sentence hung in the air between us, the insult wedded to the intimacy. She had clearly surprised herself, and she didn't know what to do, whether to add a "Ha!" or a "Ha-ha" or just shrug it off. I decided to take the initiative and sat down next to her on the couch. She looked at my Wall of Books with a neutral expression, although by now my volumes stank mostly of Wild Flower Blast and not their natural printed essence. "I'm sorry you broke up with that guy in Italy," I said. "You said on Global-Teens he was really your type."

"I don't want to talk about him right now," Eunice said.

Good, I didn't, either. I just wanted to hold her. She was wearing an oatmeal sweatshirt, beneath which I could espy the twin straps of a bra she did not need. Her rough-hewn miniskirt made out of some kind of sandpaper fibre sat atop a pair of bright-violet panty hose, which also seemed unnecessary, given the warm June weather. Was she trying to protect herself from my roving hands? Or was she just very cold at her center? "You must be tired from the long flight," I said, putting my hand on her violet knee.

"You're sweating like crazy," she said, laughing.

I wiped at my forehead, my hand coming away with the sheen of my age. "Sorry," I said.

"Do I really excite you that much, nerd face?" she asked.

I didn't say anything. I smiled.

"It's nice of you to let me stay here."

"Indefinitely!" I cried.

"We'll see," she said. As I squeezed her knee and made a slight movement upward, she caught my hairy wrist. "Let's take it easy," she said. "I just had my heart broken, remember?" She thought it over and added, "Ha-ha."

June 18: Euni-Tard to Grillbitch.
Dear Precious Panda,

Sup, my little Busy Bee-iotch? I'm baaaaaaack. America the beautiful. Wow, I still can't believe that everyone's speaking English and not Italiano around me. Well, in Lenny's ghetto neighborhood it's mostly Spanish and Jewish, I guess. But whatever. I'm home. Things are quiet on the Fort Lee front, at least for the time being. I'm seeing my parents next week, but I think my dad just quiets down when he knows I'm across the river.

I miss Ben a lot. There was something so compatible about me and him. Like we didn't have to say much to each other, we could just lie there in bed for hours, doing whatever on our äp-päräti, with the lights turned off. It's different with Lenny. I mean, cause there are so many things wrong with him, and I guess I just have to fix them all. The problem is he's not young, so he thinks he doesn't have to listen to me. His teeth are in so much better shape since I got him to brush correctly and his breath is fresh like a daisy. If only he would take care of his gross feet! I'm going to make him set up an appointment with a podiatrist. Maybe my dad. JBF! My dad would freak if I told him I had a very old white, um, "friend." Ha-ha. And then he dresses awful, in all these like old-school hipster outfits with the wide collars and these awful acrylic shirts from the seventies. I hope there's a smoke detector in our apartment cause he just might set himself on fire one day. Anyway, I told him from the start: Look, you're *thirty-nine* years old and I'm living with you, so now you've got to dress like a grownup. He feigned defiance, my little nerd, but next week we're going shopping for stuff actually made out of *animal products* like cotton and wool and ca$hmere and all that good stuff.

You know what's funny. Lenny keeps a journal of all the things he's "celebrating." It's dorky, but I wonder about all the things I should be celebrating. So far my favorite thing is just walking down the street with him. He'll tell me all these things I never even learned at Elderbird, like that New York used to be owned by the Dutch (what were they even doing in America?), and whenever we see something funny like a cute weenie dog we'll both just totally break out laughing, and he'll hold my hand and sweat and sweat and sweat.

We fight a lot. I guess it's mostly my fault because I don't appreciate his great personality and just keep focussing on how he looks. I told him I was leaving him and going back to Fort Lee and then my poor sweet nerd got down on his knees and started crying and saying how much I meant to him. He was so pathetic and so cute. I felt so sorry for him that I took off all my clothes, except for my TotalSurrenders, and just got in bed with him. He felt me up a little but we fell asleep pretty fast. Damn, Precious Panda. I'm just one chatty ass-hookah these days. I'm going to sign off, but here's an Image of me and Lenny at the zoo in Central Park. He's to the left of the bear. Don't gag!!!!

June 25, New York.
When I walked into our synagogue's main sanctuary one humid morning, Little Bobby Cohen, the youngest Post-Human staffer (I think he's nineteen years old at the most), approached me wearing a kind of saffron monk getup. "Come with me, Leonard," he said, his bar-mitzvah voice straining under the profundity of what he was about to do.

"Oh, what's all this?" I asked, my heart pumping blood so hard my toes hurt.

As he led me to a tiny back office where, judging by the sweet-briny smell, the gefilte-fish supply used to be stored, Little Bobby sang, "May you live forever, may you never know death, may you float like Joshie, on a newborn's breath."

My God! The Desking Ceremony.

And there it was—my new desk! As Kelly fed me a ceremonial garlic bulb, followed by some sugar-free niacin mints, I surveyed all the pretty young people who had doubted me, all those Darryls and friends of Darryls, and I felt the queasy, mercurial justice of the world. I was back! My Roman failures were near-erased. I could begin again. I ran out into the synagogue's sanctuary, where the Boards were noisily registering my existence, the letters "LENNY A." flipping into place at the very bottom of one of the Boards, along with my last blood work—not so hot—and the promising mood indicator "meek but coöperative."

My desk. All three square feet of it, shiny and sleek, full of text and streams and Images rising up from the digital surface. I spent the bulk of my working week behind it. Opening up several data streams at once, and affecting a godlike air, I scanned the files of our prospective Life Lovers. Their white, beatific, mostly male faces (our research shows that women are more concerned with taking care of their progeny than with living forever) flashed before me, telling me about their charitable activities, their plans for humanity, their concern for our chronically ill planet, their dreams of eternal transcendence with like-minded yuan billionaires. I guessed that the last time they had been so painfully dishonest was when they penned their applications to Swarthmore, forty years earlier.

One of my Intakes, let's call him Barry, ran a small Retail empire in the Southern states. When he came into the office he looked suitably anxious. We accept, on average, eighteen per cent of our High Net Worth applicants, our dreaded rejection letter still sent out by actual post. The Intake process lasted awhile. Barry, trying to subdue any remaining trace of his Alabama drawl, wanted to sound knowledgeable about our work. He asked about cellular inspection, repair, and reconstruction. I painted him a three-dimensional picture of millions of autonomous nanobots inside his well-preserved squash-toned body, extracting nutrients, supplementing, delivering, playing with the building blocks, copying, manipulating, reprogramming, replacing blood, destroying harmful bacteria and viruses, reversing soft-tissue destruction, preventing bacterial infection, repairing DNA.

I gave Barry the Willingness to Live Test. The H-Scan Test to measure the subject's biological age. The Willingness to Persevere in Difficult Conditions Test. The Infinite Sadness Endurance Test. The Response to Loss of Child Test. He must have sensed how much was at stake, his sharp Waspy beak aquiver as the images were projected against his pupils, the results streaming on my äppärät. He would do anything to persevere. He had three children and would cling to them forever, even if his present-day bank account would not be able to preserve more than two for eternity. I entered "Sophie's Choice" on my Intake äppärät, a major problem as far as Joshie was concerned.

"How soon?" Barry asked. "When will all this be possible?"

"We're almost there," I said, despairing. Signing up a new client would trigger an automatic bonus deposit into my BRIC-A-BRAC account; that, in turn, would help fund the first of my beta-dechronification treatments. But Barry was a dead end. Forget my name on the Boards. The train was pulling out of the station, and I was running behind it, my suitcase half open, white underwear spilling comically along the platform.

Barry was exhausted. The Patterson-Clay-Schwartz Language Cognition Test, the final barometer for selection, could wait for another session. I knew already that this perfectly reasonable, preternaturally kind fifty-two-year-old would not make the cut. He was doomed like me. And so I smiled at him, congratulated him on his candor and patience, his intellect and maturity, and, with a tap of my finger against my digital desk, threw him onto the blazing funeral pyre of history.

June 25: Euni-Tard to Grillbitch.
Hi, Precious Panda,

Sup, meathole? Oh, man. Or, "Oy, man," as my Jewish boyfriend would say.

Oh, Panda of mine. What am I doing with Lenny? What kind of freaked me out was that I saw Len read a book. (No, it didn't *smell.* He uses Pine-Sol on them.) He came home from work looking really down, and I guess he didn't even notice that I caught him reading. And I don't mean scanning a text like we did in EuroTrash Classics with that "Chatterhouse of Parma," I mean seriously *reading.* He had this ruler out and he was moving it down the page very slowly and just like whispering little things to himself, like trying to understand every little part of it. I was going to teen my sister but I was so embarrassed I just stood there and watched him read, which lasted for like *half an hour* and finally he put the book down and I pretended like nothing happened. And then I sneaked a peek and it was that Russian guy Tolesoy he was reading (I guess it figures, cause Lenny's parents are from Russia). I thought Ben was really brain-smart because I saw him streaming "Chronicles of Narnia" in that café in Rome, but this Tolesoy was a thousand-page-long *book*, not a stream, and Lenny was on page 930, almost finished. I was intimidated by Ben in Rome because of his looks and I never felt super-secure in bed because of that. With Lenny, I'm intimidated by his brain-smarts, but it's easier. I can be myself, because everything he does is so sweet and honest. I gave him a half-gag CIM blow job and he was so grateful he actually started to cry. Who does that? I guess sometimes I just want to want him as much as he wants me. And I want him to relax and maybe not always be so cute and caring and trying to please me, so that maybe I can pursue him a little myself.

June 28, New York.
I learned how to say "elephant" in Korean this week.

We went to the Bronx Zoo because my Media friend Noah Weinberg said on his stream that the American Restoration Authority was going to close the place down and ship all the animals to Saudi Arabia "to die of heatstroke." I never know which part of Noah's streams to believe; the way we live now you can't be too sure. We had fun with the monkeys and José the Beaver and all the smaller animals, but the highlight was this beautiful savanna elephant named Sammy. When we ambled up to his humble enclosure, Eunice grabbed my nose and said, *"Kokiri."*

"Ko," she explained, "means 'nose.' So *kokiri*. Long nose. 'Elephant' in Korean."

"I hab a long dose because I'm Jewish," I said, trying to pull her hand off my face. "Dere's duthing I can do aboud it."

"You're so sensitive, Lenny," she said, laughing. "I heart your nose so much. I wish I *had* a nose." And she started kissing my comma of a snout in full view of the pachyderm, going gently up and down the endless thing with her tough little lips. As she did so, I locked eyes with the elephant, and I watched myself being kissed in the prism of the elephant's eye, the giant hazel apparatus surrounded by flecks of coarse gray eyebrow. He was twenty-five, Sammy, at the middle of his life span, much like me. A lonely elephant, the only one the zoo had at the moment, removed from his compatriots and from the possibility of love. He slowly flicked back one huge ear, like a Galician shopkeeper of a century ago spreading his arms as if to say, "Yes, this is all there is." And then it occurred to me, lucky me mirrored in the beast's eye, lucky Lenny having his trunk kissed by Eunice Park: *The elephant knows.* The elephant knows there is nothing after this life and very little in it. The elephant is aware of his looming extinction, and he is hurt by it, reduced by it, made to feel his solitary nature, he who will eventually trample his way through bush and scrub to lie down and die where his mother once trembled her haunches to give him life. Mother, aloneness, entrapment, extinction. The elephant is essentially an Ashkenazi animal, but a wholly rational one—it, too, wants to live forever.

And here's another thing the elephant knew. He knew that I would never make it as a past-tense man in a world set to the future. He knew that I would never make it as a Life Lovers Outreach Coördinator (Grade G). He knew that my name would fall off the Boards soon enough and that Joshie would find a way to fire me. He knew that all the green tea in Japan would not regenerate my liver, that SmartBlood would never run through my veins.

Then I thought of what I knew. I thought of Eunice Park and her pH-balanced body, healthy and strong. I thought of the warm early-summer day gathering in force, the New York of early summers past, the city that used to hold so many promises, the city of a million I.O.U.s. I thought of Eunice's lips on my nose, the love mixed in with the pain, the foretaste of almonds and salt. I thought of how it was all just too beautiful to ever let go.

"Let's go home," I said to Eunice. "I don't want *kokiri* to see you kissing my nose like that. It'll only make him sadder."

THE LANDLORD

WELLS TOWER

At ten-thirty, Armando Colón comes to my office. It lifts my mood to see him. Armando lives in one of the worst properties I own, an apartment complex so rife with mold and vermin that, when I sent a man to clean a vacant unit there, he developed an eye infection that didn't clear up for a month. You would never know it to look at Armando. His shirt is crisp, his stomach is trim, and his hairline is freshly razored into aristocratic darts. He operates a squeezeball with his right hand. His cologne, applied with restraint, has a wholesome cedar scent, and his presence in the stale air of my office is a force of orderliness and industry.

Armando has been my tenant for two years. He has great ambitions in the business world. He always pays his rent in person, because it affords him an opportunity to sit in the red leather client's chair and palaver with me as though we were having a high-management powwow. Often, he brings one of his motivational books with him. He will say, "May I sow a seed into your life, Mr. Pruitt?" And then he'll read aloud an epigram or two: "Long-term results are mainly determined by short-term decisions"; "There is nothing more futile than trying to stop a corpse from stinking."

Today, Armando has left his literature at home. He is nervous and abashed. Armando owes me thirteen hundred and fifty dollars, three months' rent, and he has probably come here to determine whether I will evict him when the debt grows, as of the first, to eighteen hundred.

"I don't feel good about myself, Mr. Pruitt," he says. "I don't feel good messing you around. I don't mean to disrespect you. A man doesn't let his debts run up."

"Yet here we are."

"Check it out, though. I'm here with good news. I've been in dialogue with my pastor about my situation, and through the blessing and favor of my church, I can get you what I owe."

He passes me some paperwork on letterhead of the Family of the Infinite Redeemer. The church's rent-arrears team seems to know its business. The forms ask rigorous questions about Armando's rental history, his lease term, the amount of his deposit, the number of bedrooms in his apartment, whether there is pool access. I answer these questions, and in the space provided I write a brief note praising Armando's agreeableness as a tenant, and explaining what little he's shared with me about the extended family he supports in Cali, Colombia.

Armando reads the comments, and then looks at me. His mouth is a taut line, pursed with the pain of this humiliating errand. I can feel him building toward some grandiose pledge or apology that I lack the energy to hear. His pumping of the squeeze-ball quickens.

"You're really giving that thing hell, Armando."

"I don't idle well," he says, a country phrase that he picked up who knows where.

He lingers. Armando is a proud man, and he wants to restore our relationship to its old footing, equal businessfolk. His gaze lights on my shirt.

"A man like you should get his shirts tailored," he says.

The shirt *was* tailored, but that was two years ago, when I owned fifty-three properties. I own nineteen now. At first, the pain of financial exposure was an articulate anxiety. But, after a while, I'd called myself so many names that they ran out of bite. Now all that combusted equity registers only as numb heat. Every waking moment, my scalp throbs at the root of each hair. My ribs give off a queasy warmth that kills my appetite. I've lost thirty pounds without a stroke of exercise.

"Get me that eighteen hundred dollars and I'll get a new shirt."

"Got to," Armando says. "As a matter of fact, I'm putting together a clothing line, Mr. Pruitt. I notice you don't wear a tie. My suits will be uniquely designed so they don't need a tie. Very sharp, very clean." Armando spreads his hands in a horizontal flourish, as though displaying letters across a marquee: "Celebrate being a man. Every day. With Armando. Armando Colón. Signature Collection."

I thank Armando for coming in. He shakes with his left hand so as not to interrupt his program with the squeezeball. His palm is dry. My knuckles creak in his grasp.

As Armando is leaving, Todd Toole comes in with Jason Bell. Todd is a carpenter and rent collector, and the foreman of my maintenance team. He has worked for me for several years. I hired Jason only last month. He is young, though, as far as I can tell, he's a willing worker.

"That's the dude who stays at Kado Street?" Todd asks, jerking his head in the direction of Armando Colón's departure.

"Yep."

"He pay?"

"No, but it's all right. His church is going to cover the back rent."

Todd gives me a look of pure disgust. "You just let them fuck you, Coates. The only explanation is you must like it, you pogue. You just let them fuck you raw. They pick you clean and piss on your bones, and you go, 'Mmm, thank you, that feels nice,' you goof."

Todd is in his sixties, and he is a venomous human being. He is angry that I don't feel the same bile toward his co-workers or my tenants as he does. He is angry that, owing to the frailty of his liver and esophagus, he has only a couple of dozen good drunks left in him, and he must spend them wisely. He is angry that he once went to jail for shooting his ex-wife with toilet paper wadded into a .41 Magnum cartridge, which in his opinion did not constitute a deadly weapon. Yet, when Todd can be persuaded to work, he is an artful trim carpenter, and so unappealing to other employers that I'm able to hire him at about one-third the going wage.

In our conversations, Todd says "you dumb motherfucker" the way Jason says "sir." Our unspoken arrangement is that Todd abuses me freely and I brook it with good cheer. In fact, I'm grateful for his curses, because they are a symptom of his stupidity, and Todd's stupidity is one of my most precious assets. Toole is the only man I've ever hired who is literally too stupid to lie about his hours or cart my roofing tin off to the salvage man.

Todd has come by for money: advance pay and travel expenses for a trip to Idaho, where he and Jason will spend a month making cosmetic repairs to a cottage I inherited from my parents. The house has twelve hundred feet of water frontage on the granite-bottomed lake where I learned to swim. The mortgage was settled long ago. I'd planned to retire there, and it pains and perplexes me to have no option but to sell the place. One day you are so apprehensive about debt and monthly payments that you're reluctant to take out a credit card, and the next you're a man with hot bowels and twelve properties in greater Winston-Salem that are at risk of seizure by the bank. Suddenly, there is nothing to be done but send Todd Toole and Jason Bell to Idaho to paint and replace molding and re-Sheetrock the ceiling in the cottage's great room. With any luck, they'll conceal evidence of a roof leak that is too costly to fix.

I trust Todd to do a good job out West. I do not necessarily trust him to make it out of state without being arrested by the highway patrol.

"What'll fuck me, Todd, is if you're stuck in Winston with a bracelet on your ankle when the listing goes up next month. You got your license on you? Your registration up to date?"

Here, Todd leans across my desk and thrusts his face into mine. "Open your eyes," he says. "What do you see, Coates?"

I see blue eyes of startling clarity and nearly unlined skin that doesn't show a single dilated pore. Somehow, Todd has found the secret of eternal youth. The formula is fourteen gallons of Pepsi-Cola a week, heavy use of Black & Mild cigarillos, and hatred of all living creatures.

"I don't know, Todd, what?"

"You blind son of a bitch, you see a mustache on me, Coates? Do you see any beard? I put the cap on my truck, too. Ain't a cop in the world can't see me, man. I am rolling incognito. Now, I hope you have my cash."

I hand Todd a billing envelope containing four hundred and fifty dollars. He counts the money and pockets it. Then he blows his nose into the envelope. He checks the cellophane window and puts the envelope into his pocket along with the bills. Jason Bell watches this procedure.

"What are you looking at, you stupid motherfucker?" Todd asks him.

Jason has five inches and forty pounds of muscle on Todd and is less than half his age. His brow dips. "You want to repeat that, sir?"

Todd balks. It flashes in his black and cloudy mind that, whatever our agreement regarding his abuses, he has no such compact with the younger man, whom he hasn't known a week. It is a bad moment. Do I see panic in his eyes?

Fortunately for Toole, the caged bird beside my desk lets out a raucous shriek. The diversion lets Toole put aside the business with Bell and instead make an enemy of the parakeet. "Now, what the fuck is that bird, Coates?" Toole hisses at the cage. "Who the hell gets a bird? It's like having loud fish."

My daughter has come from Los Angeles to live with me. Rhoda is thirty-one, and she used to work in advertising, but now she's a painter and a maker of other art that I'm not sure how to describe. Her field is bummers. Rhoda's past exhibitions include leukemia-cluster art, floating-yuan art, water-rights art, and mental-health-funding-cuts art, which was piles of clothes painted bronze and rigged up with speakers that yelled. She has also made a lot of hand art and hair art. Eight years ago, shortly into her new career, while getting the hang of a radial-arm saw, Rhoda severed the index, middle, and ring fingers of her left hand. The surgeons reattached them, and Rhoda recovered nearly complete range of motion, but the shock of the injury caused some of her hair to fall out. She keeps her head shaved close now, a style that improves the plainness of face she inherited from me. Bald, she looks about fifteen years older than she is, but also terrifyingly smart and owlish, Lady Malcolm McDowell.

Rhoda claims that she came home because she ran out of money, yet she drove here in a C-Class Mercedes with only eighteen thousand three hundred miles on it. She hasn't asked me for a dime. I'm sure she has more in the bank than I do, and not a hundredth of my debts. She's come here for her work, to do a new body of paintings, relating to: "To some extent, your problems with the real-estate stuff, and my parallel humiliation at having to move in with you. But in a broader sense it's about our collective lack of integrity and total fucking childishness in the wake of the financial crisis, i.e., the national epidemic of petulance and bratty outrage over the fact that poor people don't get to buy castles on credit anymore, that execs don't get G.D.P.-size bonuses, that not just any housewife with a real-estate license gets to be a millionaire, and that you can't stick a chopstick in a dog turd and sell it at Gagosian for the price of a yacht. 'A Pestilence of Petulance' is what I'm tempted to call it but probably shouldn't."

Her first full day here, Rhoda took her camera on an exhaustive search of my house and grounds, looking for material. She likes the yard full of yellowed sod that failed to take. She likes the massive oak limb that lies on my back deck. It fell two months ago from its dead but stately parent. The limb crushed the grill, knocked out some balusters, and crimped the copper finials on the rail posts. Second Piedmont Savings & Loan won't let me rework the balloon loan that, six months ago, raised my mortgage payment to six thousand dollars. I haven't sent them a check since. They'll take the house pretty soon. To hell with it—it's their oak limb now. This is good petulance for Rhoda. She snapped a dozen pictures of the limb and of the scattered glass fragments from the window on the grill.

When my telephone makes the text-message sound, and then makes that sound again every five minutes for an hour, I know that something has gone wrong at the home of Connie Legg.

The first messages are complaints about cockroaches. The later messages are complaints about my character. The campaign won't stop until I go over, so I grab the insecticide pump rig, which Todd usually operates, and I drive to the house that Connie rents from me.

A potluck is happening on the porch when I get there. Connie is standing next to a thing of salad dressing, lecturing a young man with matted hair. "What this is, it's a kombucha vinaigrette," she tells him. "There's some active yeast in it, a little bit of cumin, flaxseed oil. What you're gonna want to do, you're gonna want to shake it up and put it on these greens, which are dandelion and mache."

She sees me. "There he is, my savior."

I follow her inside. Connie is a handsome woman in her late forties. She lives in a good part of town, in an Eisenhower ranch for which she pays six hundred dollars a month, a square deal. When she first moved in, I had plans for a romance with Connie Legg, because she means well, from time to time, and because the sight of her bottom touches my heart. But I've learned that it doesn't work when you're their landlord. With Connie and the other single-woman renters in their middle years, it's like we went through a bad divorce before I even got to hold their hands. I'm responsible for their comfort and security, and they're bitter that I don't do more to keep them comfortable and secure.

I took Connie to a movie once, and we had a good time. Not long after that, she removed a floor grate in her house and stepped into the air return, and tried to sue me for her scraped shin. Connie runs a Third World knickknack store, but she believes herself to be an expert on the law and on real-estate statutes. I think she intended the lawsuit not as a malicious act but as an expensive, high-level chat about the concept of liability and the Minimum Housing Code.

In the kitchen, while I peer under the sink, Connie fills me with more legal knowledge. "If I choose to, I can stop giving you rent for this place anytime I want to. Did you know that, Coates? I only pay you out of courtesy. By law I don't have to pay you a cent. Did you know that there is not a word in the U.S. Constitution that protects the right of a citizen to charge a fellow-citizen for a place to live?"

"I hadn't heard that, Connie."

"That's because it wouldn't suit you to hear it, Coates. It goes against your interests. See, look at that, there they go."

I've sprayed a jet of poison beneath the sink, and now a horde of about a hundred baby roaches are teeming up the backsplash, fleeing into the cupboards.

"Have you ever seen anything so disgusting?" Connie asks. "And when I'm not looking at them I'm smelling them. They have a smell."

"Well, it's just these little guys, at least. Not such a big deal. I can knock them right out." In fact, Connie's is a serious infestation. A large roach is not necessarily cause for worry. He may have come in from outside, seeking water. But when you see a lot of little babies like this you know you have a breeding ground. I notice that Connie stores her cheese and butter on the counter, Europe style. I'll have to put the house under contract with an exterminator. At least two months' rent taken care of there.

Connie goes back to the potluck, and I empty the sprayer in her kitchen. When I'm leaving, Connie hails me over to her salad station. "You look skinny, Coates. Why don't you take a plate?"

I don't really want any of Connie's leaves or brown grains, but to refuse the offer would give her cause for resentment. I heap some stuff into a Chinet bowl. She thrusts the salad dressing into my hand. "This is a kombucha vinaigrette," she tells me. "There's some active yeast in it, a little bit of cumin, and flaxseed oil. Shake it up and put it on these greens."

Connie Legg is a woman who believes in the quick dollar. So far, she has tried to get me into Quixtar (an Amway spinoff), a farm share, a meat subscription, and a license to sell a product called Xanthone Soda. Her salad dressing, I'm sure of it, is another scheme. I make for my car with my food, the tank and spray wand clanking on my back.

"Coates!" she calls after me.

"Yes?"

"How about we get a drink next week?"

"For sure!" I say, and pull the car door shut.

The picture that develops on Rhoda's canvas is not my oak limb but the Creature from the Black Lagoon.

"You remember when you took me to see this?" Rhoda asks. "I was maybe eight. You made us leave the theatre because I was crying. You were super pissed, because you'd deliberately sought out a boring, hokey movie that wouldn't freak me out, but every time the creature came on, it just scared the holy shit out of me. Some things I went through with Heinrich just reminded me of that."

"Aha," I say. This is the first I've heard of Heinrich.

"See, I just had this crazy revelation about why I was so freaked out. I don't know if you knew this or not, but back then I'd gotten into the habit of sneaking into your closet and checking out those old porns you kept in there."

This was a stash left over from college, a few passed-around copies of *Oui* and some others. Yellow, bright-lit, not-nice stuff. Women on the john. My ex-wife, Joanie, Rhoda's mother, was always after me to throw them out, but I held on to them to make some point that is lost to me now.

"I was totally obsessed with those magazines. Every time you left the house, I was curled up in your porn closet like a squirrel. But at the same time I had this massive, Old Testament–magnitude guilt about it, like I was doing something deeply, satanically wrong by looking at this stuff that you were presumably also getting off on. Incest trauma by proxy. So anyway, the reason I started losing my shit at "Creature from the Black Lagoon" is that the movie is so clearly about the gruesomeness of the sexual id. Not that I was thinking in terms of id at eight or whatever, but I still got it that the Creature is pretty obviously a walking compound genital."

"Is that when there's a bone poking out?"

"Just look at it. See how glans-ish the head is? The mouth is patently a vulva. And all these scrotely wrinkles here. There's no way it wasn't a deliberate resonance on the director's part. I was sure you picked that movie to fuck with me, because you'd found out what I was up to with the magazines and you knew what a disgusting little kid I was, which you pretty much confirmed when you yanked my arm out of the socket, dragging me to the exit because I wouldn't stop screaming."

"Rhoda."

"So anyway, more than you want to know, but it got to a point with Heinrich where it was clear that he'd rather take a hot cinder in the eye than have sex with me. I'd try with him, and he would literally push me away, and this cold wash of self-disgust would come over me, this crippling rinse of sex-shame that somehow was the exact same sensation I had sitting next to you and watching 'Creature from the Black Lagoon.'"

"For the record, I wasn't trying to show you a movie about a compound genital," I say.

"My shrink would be interested to hear you say that."

"Anyway, what's this painting got to do with the economy?"

"Maybe fifteen grand, give or take."

Rhoda is up at dawn, filling my house with the smell of oil paint and a confusing music that has no beat, language, or tune. She has been curt with me the past few days, and I wonder how long she intends to stay here. I rise, put on my sap-spangled work pants, and decide to get the oak tree off my deck. There is satisfaction in clearing away the limb, the hard wood's helplessness against the chainsaw teeth, the albino purity of the sawdust on my shoes. But it's a fraudulent satisfaction. My latent motive in at last dealing with the limb, it occurs to me, is to oppress Rhoda with the sound of real work.

When the job is finished, I do not go inside but instead take a stroll around the neighborhood. The full autumn inferno is still weeks away, but the maples advertise its approach hysterically, in glow-stick shades of ruby and chartreuse. I walk down Hawgood Street and cross Pepper Lane, the drop-off point of the neighborhood's invisible property-value butte. At the corner stands a modular house in lengthwise cross-section. My friend Tim Stroud used to live here with his wife, Beth. I passed many afternoons on their porch, drawn by the warm company and the fiery ginger beer that Beth used to brew. They divorced three years ago. Afterward, Tim took a trip to Bangkok. He came back with a twenty-year-old gap-toothed cherub he found dancing in a bar. In Bangkok the girl shared an apartment with ten relatives, yet in North Carolina a manufactured home with two gables and a sunroom was not sufficient to her needs. So Tim sold this lot, and they moved into a condominium with fixed-pane windows and electric air fresheners that whir from the wall plugs, putting out the aroma of new diapers.

Half of Tim's home went to the landfill two months ago, but, to the neighborhood's chagrin, the lot's new owner has lost interest in hauling away the remaining portion. The wind turns the ceiling fan in the halved living room and herds leaves along the kitchen counters. Looking at the flayed house, even in passing, you feel the sordid burden of unsolicited intimacy.

Last year, I had to have my prostate whittled, and, ever since, my bladder has stopped giving much advance notice. Suddenly, it feels close to rupture. I cross Tim's yard and, grabbing hold of a steel framing member, swing myself into the open corridor. The air in the bathroom is close with mildew but not unpleasant. Though it's unlikely anyone will ever set foot in here again, I nevertheless want to be a gracious guest. I don't use the decommissioned toilet but aim a neat stream into the sink drain, hardly splashing the basin. I shut the flimsy door behind me and hop down to the lawn.

The day's chill is solidifying. When I get home, I build a fire for Rhoda, to warm her while she works. The limb I cut up this morning makes a lively pyre, having died and seasoned for two years before it hit the ground.

The telephone rings at 5 a.m. It is Jason Bell. "I'm sorry, Mr. Pruitt," he says. "There wasn't any other way."

"Other way where?"

"He rode me and rode me. The first couple of days, he was all right. But then he started in."

"Todd?"

"I mean, I couldn't pick up a nail without 'Broke-dick this' or 'Cob-ass motherfucker that.' I thought maybe a little cabin-fever relief might settle him down. So last night we headed up to Pocatello. We went to a place and we were swapping rounds at the bar. Only every time I got him one he'd put it down somewhere and forget I'd bought one for him. The whole twenty miles back, it was 'You Jew motherfucker, you Jew bastard, can't even buy me one damn drink, you cheap son of a bitch.' I took a hundred dollars out of my pocket and threw it on his lap. That's how honked off I was, but it didn't make any difference. He kept right on. Then I said, 'O.K., Todd, I've had it. Do we need to settle this right now?'

"He was all, 'You God damn right we need to settle this thing.' So I pulled the truck off the road."

"You shouldn't have done that, Jason. You can't let Todd get to you. If you ignore him, he runs out of steam."

"I tried that. He just wasn't running out was the problem."

"So what did you do?"

"Well, sir, first I beat him with my right hand until I broke a knuckle. Then I beat him with my left hand until I broke another knuckle. Then I drove to Utah. I'm in Utah now."

"Where's Todd, Jason?"

"Well, he's still in Idaho."

"Where in Idaho?"

"On the side of the road, I guess. Maybe he walked somewhere by now."

"You didn't kill him, did you?"

"No, sir, he was still cussing me when I drove off."

"You've got his truck?"

"Yes, sir, I do."

"You need to go back there, Jason."

"Mr. Pruitt, there isn't money that would put me back in Idaho."

Colleagues, I miss them:
Harold Lane stabbed himself in the heart; no hesitation wounds. Dan White is doing time for tax evasion. David Butler, a partner at the firm where I used to practice law, took three million dollars from clients' escrow deposits and disappeared. A year later, the newspaper ran a report that he'd been seen in Buenos Aires with a young brown man on his arm. Reading that, I let out a cheer and pounded the counter in the doughnut shop. Six months later, the police found David in a public park in San Diego. He was standing barefoot in a line of people waiting to get a free peanut-butter sandwich from a teen-age Marxist group. David Butler is doing time now, too, though not in the same place as Dan White.

Rhoda is thirty-two today, which she seems not to care about at all. Her work is not going well. In two weeks, she has made three paintings, all of which depict the Creature from the Black Lagoon. She is in the darkest of moods, and I'm afraid to speak to her. She had terrible rages when she was younger. Once, as a child, she brandished a hatchet at her mother. Perhaps her first drawings would be worth some money now, but none of them survived her childhood. Every time Rhoda got angry, she would tear her pictures from the wall and shred them with her little hands.

Today, she makes me plead with her all morning and afternoon before finally consenting to let me take her out for dinner at a restaurant in the hills. As a special treat, I take the long way, out Route 116, an untrafficked rural byway connecting one-stoplight towns like Snead to no-stoplight towns like Bugleville. The beauty of the land out here is nearly absurd. Full-fed, ale-colored cattle watch us from fields of grass so vivid in the late light that each blade looks hand-tinted. Fall-blooming sneeze-weeds dot the ditches, woozy with the weight of their broad red heads.

What Rhoda notices is a roadside billboard showing a crucifix, some digits, and a glowing telephone. "After Abortion: Hope," the sign reads.

"For the Altoids account," Rhoda says. "After Abortion: Mints."

At a scenic lookout, I stop to take in the sunset, a wash of orange strewn with black storm clouds. "It's a shame you didn't bring your camera," I say. Ordinarily, I'm not a connoisseur of country vistas, but now Rhoda has turned me into a ninnyish Ruritan, desperate to get her into a rhapsody over the green dales of her native state.

"I mean," Rhoda says, "between inventing new viruses and making sure the tides and planets don't get out of whack, doesn't it sort of blow your mind that Jesus or whoever still has time for acts of cut-rate sentiment?"

"It seems to me, Rhoda, that Los Angeles, or something, is making you hostile to wonder. What would it take to thrill you? If this doesn't amaze you, tell me what I could possibly show you to put some wonder in your life."

Rhoda muses, thrusting out her lower lip in contemplation. "A Pegasus fucking a unicorn," my daughter finally says.

By the time we reach the restaurant, Rhoda has made me regret the whole dinner mission. She will ridicule the faux-Bavarian décor. There will be snide routines about the local wine. Our table isn't ready, and I walk ahead of my daughter and take a seat at the bar. To spite her, I order a scuppernong champagne.

"Two," Rhoda says.

"Need to see your I.D., sweetheart," the bartender, a square-built woman about my age, says. Rhoda digs for her wallet. "Not you, him," the woman says, coquetting with me, a surprise.

"Touché," Rhoda says.

"Don't you know a compliment when you hear one, honey?" the bartender says to her, as she passes my license back. "What I wouldn't give to get a man who hides his age so well."

I have seen Rhoda pull out her longest knives over fainter slights than this. I dread a scene. Instead, my daughter smiles and slips her arm around my neck. "Oh, he's not my man," she says, dragging a finger along the rim of my ear. "He has to pay me for it, but I let him have it cheap."

Todd Toole calls from Idaho. He speaks to me with such urgent penitence that his voice keeps breaking, like a boy's. He needs cash is the thing. His face took ten stitches and he had to spend his food money at the emergency room. Yet he doesn't say a word against Jason Bell, who did, as it turns out, make the trip back to Idaho. "You want to hate me over this, Coates, go ahead. But you won't hate me a hair as much as I hate myself. I know I put the pecker to you, man, but I ain't had a beer in three days, and I won't sleep until we're completely squared away. I intend to make this right."

This is Todd's Jekyll face, yet I know that he means everything he says. I'm maybe the last person in Todd's acquaintance who won't call the cops when I see him at the door. This means something to him, as it should. This call is not about money but about making sure that he hasn't irreparably damaged whatever mutant strain of friendship obtains between us. Though Todd is the most terrible person I've ever had more than one conversation with, and though I know he'll be back to vinegar and motherfuckers before his stitches come out, his heart isn't entirely rotten. I tell him not to worry, that if he keeps his act together I'll go halves on his hospital tab when he gets home. I sincerely wish a good life for Todd, the way you sincerely wish the ulcers on a growling stray would heal.

The first week of November comes and goes without a check or a phone call from Armando Colón. I try his number and get the watery tones of the "not in service" flute.

I pay a house call to Kado Street. If I were more generous with Rhoda, less dainty about her opinion of me, I would have invited her to come and prop her easel in the yard. This is Rhoda's kind of place, a bad motor lodge in miniature. Four one-story units of Baptist brick, benignly marred here and there by kids' graffiti in Easter hues of sidewalk chalk. The yard is a ramp of bald dirt, empty except for a child's drum set capsized in a tire. Before long, the bank will have this place. But if I get close to asking price for the Pruitt home in Idaho, I may buy these apartments back. Forty per cent of what I currently owe would be a fair offer. There is still promise in this neighborhood. It's just on hold for now.

Armando's door, No. 3, swings open when I knock, because the knob is gone. When the tenants in No. 4 departed, they left me with the by-products of a homespun brothel: three fragrant mattresses and a thirty-gallon garbage can filled with spent condoms. Armando, the tidy entrepreneur, hasn't left so much as a discarded matchstick on the floor. No cobwebs in the corners. Pine-Sol in the air. Second Piedmont Savings & Loan, however, will be dismayed to discover what he carried off: the louvred doors from the bedroom closet, the bathroom fixtures, the kitchen faucet, and the stainless-steel double basin. The stove and the refrigerator are missing, too, a pair of bright squares in the linoleum marking their absence. The only sign of Armando's years between these walls is a Post-it, stuck to the window above the hole in the counter where the sink used to be.

The note is not for me but for him, a bit of affirmation written in his native tongue: *"El dinero viene fácilmente y con frecuencia."* I have a little Spanish. "Money comes easily and frequently" is what this means. I put the note in my wallet and I leave it there.

ABOUT THE CONTRIBUTORS

CHIMAMANDA NGOZI ADICHIE was born in Nigeria. She grew up in the university town of Nsukka and moved to the United States to attend college. Among her degrees are a master's in creative writing from Johns Hopkins and a master's in African studies from Yale. She is also the recipient of a 2008 MacArthur Foundation Fellowship. She is the author of "Half of a Yellow Sun" (winner of the Orange Broadband Prize), "Purple Hibiscus" (winner of the Commonwealth Writers' Prize and the Hurston/Wright Legacy Award), and "The Thing Around Your Neck." Adichie contributes frequently to various publications, including *The New Yorker*, *Granta*, and *The Guardian*. She divides her time between the United States and Nigeria, where she leads a creative-writing workshop.

CHRIS ADRIAN is the author of two novels, "Gob's Grief" and "The Children's Hospital," and a collection of short stories, "A Better Angel." His third novel, "The Great Night," will be published in the summer of 2011. He lives in San Francisco, where he is a Fellow in Pediatric Hematology and Oncology at the UCSF Medical Center.

DANIEL ALARCÓN is the author of two books of stories and the novel "Lost City Radio," which won the 2009 International Literature Award. He lives in Oakland, California.

DAVID BEZMOZGIS is a writer and filmmaker. His first book, "Natasha and Other Stories," was published in 2004. His novel,

"The Free World," will be published in 2011. In 2009, Bezmozgis's feature film, "Victoria Day," premiered at the Sundance Film Festival. His work has appeared in numerous publications, including *The New Yorker*, *Harper's Magazine*, *Zoetrope: All-Story*, and *The Walrus*, and his stories have twice been included in "The Best American Short Stories" (in 2005 and 2006). He has been a Guggenheim Fellow, a MacDowell Fellow, a Sundance Institute Screenwriters Lab Fellow, and a Dorothy and Lewis B. Cullman Fellow at the New York Public Library. Born in Riga, Latvia, Bezmozgis immigrated to Toronto with his parents in 1980.

SARAH SHUN-LIEN BYNUM is the author of two novels, "Ms. Hempel Chronicles," a finalist for the 2009 PEN/Faulkner Award for Fiction, and "Madeleine Is Sleeping," a finalist for the 2004 National Book Award and winner of the Janet Heidinger Kafka Prize. Her fiction has appeared in several magazines and anthologies, including *The New Yorker*, *Tin House*, *The Georgia Review*, and "The Best American Short Stories" (in 2004 and 2009). The recipient of a Whiting Writers' Award and an NEA Fellowship, she teaches writing in the M.F.A. program at the University of California, San Diego. She lives in Los Angeles.

JOSHUA FERRIS is the author of the novels "Then We Came to the End" and "The Unnamed." He lives in New York.

JONATHAN SAFRAN FOER is the author of the novels "Everything Is Illuminated" and "Extremely Loud and Incredibly Close," and one work of non-fiction, "Eating Animals." He lives in Brooklyn, New York.

NELL FREUDENBERGER was born in New York City in 1975 and grew up in Los Angeles. She has taught English and creative writing in Bangkok, New Delhi, and New York. She is the author of a novel, "The Dissident," and a collection of stories, "Lucky Girls," which won the PEN/Faulkner Foundation's PEN/Malamud Award and the Sue Kaufman Prize from the American Academy of Arts and Letters. She has also been the recipient of a Whiting Writers' Award and fellowships from the John Simon Guggenheim Memorial Foundation and the Dorothy and Lewis B. Cullman Center at the New York Public Library. She lives in New York with her husband and daughter.

RIVKA GALCHEN is the author of the novel "Atmospheric Disturbances." Her stories and essays have been published in *The New Yorker*, *Harper's Magazine*, and *The New York Times*.

NICOLE KRAUSS is the author of the international bestseller "The History of Love," which was published in 2005. It won the William Saroyan International Prize for Writing and France's Prix du Meilleur Livre Étranger, was named the number-one book of the year by Amazon, and was short-listed for the Orange, Médicis, and Femina prizes. Her first novel, "Man Walks into a Room," was a finalist for the Los Angeles Times Art Seidenbaum Award for First Fiction. In 2007, she was selected as one of *Granta*'s Best Young American Novelists. Her fiction has been published in *The New Yorker*, *Harper's Magazine*, *Esquire*, and "The Best American Short Stories" (in 2003 and 2008), and her books have been translated into more than thirty-five languages. She recently completed a fellowship at the Dorothy and Lewis B. Cullman Center at the New York Public Library. Her third novel, "Great House," was published in October, 2010. She lives in Brooklyn, New York.

YIYUN LI grew up in Beijing, China, where between the ages of twelve and sixteen she was trained as a mathematics prodigy. In 1996 she came to the United States to pursue a Ph.D. in immunology but left the field in 2000 to become a writer. She is the recipient of a 2010 MacArthur Foundation Fellowship. Her books, "A Thousand Years of Good Prayers" and "The Vagrants," have won the Frank O'Connor International Short Story Award, the PEN/Hemingway Foundation Award, and the Guardian First Book Award, among others. Her second story collection, "Gold Boy, Emerald Girl," was published in September, 2010. She teaches at the University of California, Davis.

DINAW MENGESTU was born in Addis Ababa, Ethiopia, in 1978. He left the country two years later and settled in the great state of Illinois with his mother, father, and older sister. After graduating from Georgetown University, he moved to New York, where he did his M.F.A. at Columbia University. He published his first novel, "The Beautiful Things That Heaven Bears," in 2007. He moved to Paris shortly thereafter, got married, became a father, and in 2010 published his second novel, "How to Read the Air."

PHILIPP MEYER grew up in Hampden, a working-class neighborhood in Baltimore, the son of an artist and a college science instructor. He attended city public schools until dropping out at the age of sixteen and getting a G.E.D. He spent the next five years working as a bike mechanic, and at the age of twenty-two, on his third attempt at applying to various Ivy League colleges, he was admitted to Cornell University. He graduated with a degree in English and headed for Wall Street to pay off his student loans. Meyer joined an elite group of derivatives traders at the Swiss invesment bank UBS, where he stayed for several years before deciding to take a crack at becoming a writer. While waiting, he worked as an emergency medical technician and as a construction worker until receiving a fellowship from the University of Texas at Austin's Michener Center for Writers in 2005. There he wrote the novel "American Rust," which has been published in sixteen countries and in ten languages. Meyer lives with his wife in Austin, Texas, where he is an avid outdoorsman and hunter.

ABOUT THE CONTRIBUTORS

C. E. MORGAN studied English and voice at Berea College, a tuition-free labor college for economically disadvantaged students in the Appalachian Mountains. She received her master's in theological studies from Harvard Divinity School, where she studied religion and literature. Her first novel, "All the Living," was published in 2009. She lives in Kentucky and Virginia and is at work on her second novel.

TÉA OBREHT was born in Belgrade in the former Yugoslavia in 1985, and has lived in the United States since the age of twelve. Her writing has appeared in *The New Yorker* and *The Atlantic*, and is forthcoming in "The Best American Short Stories" and "The Best American Nonrequired Reading" (both in 2010). Her first novel, "The Tiger's Wife," will be published in March, 2011. She lives in Ithaca, New York.

ZZ PACKER is the author of the short-story collection "Drinking Coffee Elsewhere," a PEN/Faulkner Award for Fiction finalist and a *New York Times* Notable Book. Her stories have appeared in *The New Yorker*, *Harper's Magazine*, *Story*, *Ploughshares*, *Zoetrope: All-Story*, and "The Best American Short Stories" (in 2000 and 2004) and have been read on NPR's "Selected Shorts." Her nonfiction has been featured in *The New York Times Magazine*, *The New York Times Book Review*, *The Washington Post Magazine*, *The American Prospect*, *Essence*, *O, The Oprah Magazine*, *The Believer*, and *Salon*. She is a contributor to *The Huffington Post*, and has appeared as a commentator on NPR's "Talk of the Nation" and on MSNBC. She is the recipient of a Guggenheim Fellowship and was recently named one of America's Young Innovators by *Smithsonian Magazine*, as well as one of the Best Young American Novelists by *Granta*.

KAREN RUSSELL is the author of the story collection "St. Lucy's Home for Girls Raised by Wolves" and the forthcoming novel

"Swamplandia!" Her work has appeared in *The New Yorker*, *Conjunctions*, *Granta*, *Zoetrope: All-Story*, *Oxford American*, *Tin House*, *The New York Times*, and "The Best American Short Stories" (in 2007). She teaches writing at Columbia University and lives in Washington Heights.

SALVATORE SCIBONA's novel "The End," was a finalist for the National Book Award and won the 2009 Young Lions Fiction Award from the New York Public Library and the Norman Mailer Cape Cod Award for Exceptional Writing. He received a 2009 Whiting Writers' Award and a 2010 Guggenheim Fellowship. "The End" has been published or is forthcoming in France, Germany, Italy, and the U.K. Scibona's other work has appeared in "The Pushcart Book of Short Stories: The Best Stories from a Quarter-Century of the Pushcart Prize," *The Threepenny Review*, *A Public Space*, and *The New York Times*. He administers the writing fellowship at the Fine Arts Work Center in Provincetown, Massachusetts.

GARY SHTEYNGART was born in Leningrad in 1972 and came to the United States seven years later. He is the author of the novels "Super Sad True Love Story," "Absurdistan," and "The Russian Debutante's Handbook." "Absurdistan" was named one of the ten best books of the year by *The New York Times Book Review* and *Time* magazine, as well as a book of the year by *The Washington Post*, the *Chicago Tribune*, the *San Francisco Chronicle*, and other publications. "The Russian Debutante's Handbook" won the Stephen Crane First Fiction Award and the National Jewish Book Award for Fiction and was named a *New York Times* Notable Book and one of the best debuts of the year by *The Guardian*. Shteyngart has also been selected as one of the Best Young American Novelists by *Granta*. His work has been translated into more than twenty languages. He lives inside his own head.

ABOUT THE CONTRIBUTORS

WELLS TOWER is the author of "Everything Ravaged, Everything Burned," a collection of short fiction. A recipient of the Plimpton (Discovery) Prize from *The Paris Review*, the New York Public Library's Young Lions Fiction Award, and a National Magazine Award for fiction, Tower divides his time between Chapel Hill, North Carolina, and Brooklyn, New York.

For Q&As with each of the contributors, visit www.newyorker.com/go/20under40.